WITHDRAWN

Date Due

И Н С Т И Т У Т

Katherine Christian

BOOKS BY

HUGH WALPOLE

NOVELS

The London Novels

FORTITUDE · THE DUCHESS OF WREXE
THE GREEN MIRROR · THE CAPTIVES
THE YOUNG ENCHANTED · WINTERSMOON
HANS FROST · CAPTAIN NICHOLAS · THE JOYFUL DELANEYS

Scenes from Provincial Life

THE CATHEDRAL · THE OLD LADIES
HARMER JOHN · THE INQUISITOR

Herries

ROGUE HERRIES · JUDITH PARIS
THE FORTRESS · VANESSA · THE BRIGHT PAVILIONS
KATHERINE CHRISTIAN
THE BLIND MAN'S HOUSE
THE WOODEN HORSE · MR. PERRIN AND MR. TRAILL
THE DARK FOREST · THE SECRET CITY
*THE PRELUDE TO ADVENTURE · *MARADICK AT FORTY
*PORTRAIT OF A MAN WITH RED HAIR
*ABOVE THE DARK TUMULT · A PRAYER FOR MY SON
THE SEA TOWER · JOHN CORNELIUS
THE KILLER AND THE SLAIN
JEREMY · JEREMY AND HAMLET · JEREMY AT CRALE

Short Stories

THE GOLDEN SCARECROW · THE THIRTEEN TRAVELLERS
THE SILVER THORN · ALL SOULS' NIGHT
HEAD IN GREEN BRONZE

Omnibus volume

FOUR FANTASTIC TALES
(*including the stories marked with an asterisk*)

BELLES-LETTRES

JOSEPH CONRAD: A Critical Study · THE CRYSTAL BOX
ANTHONY TROLLOPE (*English Men of Letters*)
THE APPLE TREES (*Golden Cockerel Press*)
THE ENGLISH NOVEL (REDE LECTURE)
READING: *An Essay* · THE WAVERLY PAGEANT
THE CATHEDRAL: A Play
(With J. B. PRIESTLEY)
FARTHING HALL: A Novel in Letters

Miscellaneous

ROMAN FOUNTAIN

HUGH WALPOLE

Katherine Christian

A NOVEL

CARL A. RUDISILL
LIBRARY
LENOIR RHYNE COLLEGE

DOUBLEDAY, DORAN AND COMPANY, INC.

Garden City, New York

1943

823.7
W16K

19560
june 1943

THIS BOOK IS
COMPLETE AND UNABRIDGED,
MANUFACTURED UNDER WARTIME
CONDITIONS IN CONFORMITY WITH
ALL GOVERNMENT REGULATIONS
CONTROLLING THE USE OF PAPER
AND OTHER MATERIALS.

COPYRIGHT, 1943
BY DOUBLEDAY, DORAN & COMPANY, INC.
ALL RIGHTS RESERVED

PRINTED IN THE UNITED STATES
AT
THE COUNTRY LIFE PRESS, GARDEN CITY, N. Y.

Contents

Note

Sir Hugh Walpole did not live to bring to its conclusion the story of Katherine Christian and those members of the Herries family with whom her fate had been so strangely linked. The last page he wrote was dated May 24, 1941, and his sudden death on June 1st frustrated his ambition of completing his brilliant panorama of four centuries of English life and history with the panels that should connect the Elizabethan scene of *The Bright Pavilions* with the eighteenth-century setting of *Rogue Herries*. Thus tragically it happened that *Katherine Christian* was left unfinished and there were no notes among the author's papers to indicate the future development of the story after the crisis it had reached with the opening of the struggle between King and Parliament. The publishers nevertheless feel that they owe it to the author's memory to carry his great project as far as he was permitted to achieve it, and that they may offer this novel to the public as it stands, not as a mere fragment but as a work fully worthy of a place with its famous predecessors in the Herries Chronicle.

PART I

The King of Stutters

NICHOLAS HERRIES IN HIS HOME

ROBERT HERRIES LOOKED UP, staggered to his feet and, chuckling, started across the floor towards his father.

Nicholas Herries, his father, and Rosamund Herries, his mother, looked at him with love and pride. Nicholas, a vast man, was in this year 1603 fifty-nine years of age and his wife thirty-seven.

They were in their own house at Westminster and all was very well with them. Robert, their only child, was now three years of age. In build he was broad and well-formed but short, his sturdy legs strong on the ground, his round head well-set on his thick neck, his eyes steady and piercing.

He was still a baby but already he had self-confidence and independence. He was a grave baby now: he chuckled only when his father was at hand. Everything that was told to him, the rhymes that his mother sang to him, the cautions and admonitions that Mrs. Margit, his nurse, gave to him—all these he took in and remembered.

Already it was facts that he liked the best; his mind wandered at fairy-stories. Any tale that he was told must be well substantiated. That was perhaps the reason that his father meant more to him than any other in his world, for there was no doubt or question about his father, so large was he and solid, so strong in the arm, and when he held his son against his breast the thumping of his heart was like the reassurance of a great beating drum.

Already Robert felt safe against any sort of peril if his father were there. But he was not in any case a nervous baby and he had already a firm preponderance of the Herries matter-of-fact common sense. Facts indeed were facts and it was already his rule of life to go by what you could see, feel, hold, and even seize. And what he seized he held. At this present he was holding what was just then his favourite possession—a Fool with silver bells, a red cap, and a great hooked nose. As he crossed the shining parlour floor to his father he held the Fool tightly in his chubby fist and the bells carolled gaily.

Nicholas had been almost asleep, for he had had a hard day that had included a visit to the Queen. Then the fire was blazing finely in the open hearth, throwing its erratic lights on the colours of dark green, gold, and brilliant blue that Rosamund was working into her tapestry.

Nicholas had been almost dreaming—dreaming about his long life and the principal scenes in it, of the girl Catherine he had loved who had given her life for him, of his dear brother Robin who had been tortured to his death in the Tower, and after that of England that he loved so dearly. He had come to full awareness with a start, crying: 'England is a lovely place: I would have no other.' And then, realizing his son, he had stretched out his great arms: 'Come, Robin—come!'

At once Robin had started across the floor. They had given him his pet name after his beloved uncle but he did not hesitate, as his uncle would have done, seeing both sides of the argument. He saw only one—that he liked above all things his father's arms, their warmth and strength and perfect safety.

So he started at once across the floor, the red-capped Fool, with his proud nose, held captive in his fist.

Nicholas picked him up, carried him to his mother who kissed him, then he took him from the room high on his shoulder.

Later Nicholas returned and stood, his legs spread, warming his back before the fire. Rosamund asked him about the Queen.

'She can live but a little time. Indeed she is already dead. That old woman, seated on the floor rolling her head from side to side, is nothing. Her greatness has flown to the skies where it belongs for all time.'

'And so it will be James of Scotland.'

'Yes. They say strange things of him. He is a scholar, a great Latinist, but has superstitions like an old dame of the village. He is

resolute and unresolute. Avaricious and generous. And his moralities——'

'His moralities?' she asked, laughing up at him.

'Are not for ladies' ears.'

She gathered up her tapestry.

'I must go to Robin.' As she passed him she kissed his cheek—
'Ladies' ears have a wider compass than men can fancy. I have heard—
this and that.'

In the early morning of March 24th, he was lying in the big four-
poster with his wife and very fast asleep. He woke as though someone
had tapped him on the shoulder. Rosamund's hand was lightly on his
left breast and, very gently, he removed it. What had disturbed him?
Moving his big body with great care lest he should rouse her, he sat
up and listened.

There was no sound except the wind teasing outside the window.
He stayed there, bothered by the little worrying thoughts that come
to every wakeful man in the middle of the night—thoughts about
Mallory, a new gardener he had who was one of these Puritans, always
preaching to the other servants and rebuking them for pleasures that
seemed to Nicholas most natural and wholesome, thoughts about
moneys and whether he should buy those two new fields towards the
far paddock—but thoughts especially about the plague. There were
signs already that it would be returning this summer and, if a hot
summer, it would be a bad case. Had he better now, before April,
move with Rosamund and Robin to Mallory? There was nothing to
keep him in the town, and although he loved his Westminster house,
he loved Mallory yet more. He thought of a play that he had seen
three nights back by that bawdy fellow Ben Jonson, and then, with
that, the bore that a week ago at dinner Lord Henry Howard had
been with his long-drawn-out complaint against the fellow because
Jonson had struck one of his servants.

He stretched his arms and yawned. He scratched his chest. None of
these was the real matter. There was something further. He dropped
his naked feet on to the floor, stood up, and moved gingerly to where
was his furred gown. He turned and listened. Rosamund slept sweetly.
Moving with great gentleness for so vast a man, yawning again and
scratching his head, he unlatched the door and crossed into the little
room where he kept his large globe and his maps. Like every gentle-

man of his time he was deeply interested in the foreign adventures of his countrymen. There had been a time when, with Armstrong, he had thought to be one of those adventurers. He stood there, his fur gown caught closely about him, for it was chill, lit a candle on a silver candlestick, and stayed, twisting the globe with his finger. What was it that had brought him out of his bed? Then he was aware, or thought that he was aware, of a keener chill than the March air could provide. He put his hand inside the fur and closed it on his breast. He felt a quite frantic beating of his heart and the flesh within his hand was dank with a sweat.

It could not be that he was afraid, he who had never been afraid in his life save once when he had struck Armstrong in the face. And yet beneath his gown he felt that his knees were trembling. He stared beyond the globe that was golden in the wavering candle-light, out to the latticed window. The curtains were not drawn and he could see the clouds racing across the sky. Clouds swollen and black, and one of them that seemed to stay opposite the window had the face of an angry pig.

His heart hammered and stopped. His nails gritted on the wooden surface of the globe, for there was a shadow steadily gathering before the window, a shadow so thin that it was like a man's breath. His gown slipped behind his neck leaving the top part of his back bare, but he did not put his hand to it. He was held where he stood, for, in the uncertain light of the candle, it seemed to him that the vaporous air was forming a figure. Staring, his mind running ahead of belief, he saw the figure gather. Very, very thin it was, and the window and the night clouds could be clearly seen behind it, but all the body could be traced, the slim shoulders, the haunches, the thighs, and then the face—the face that he so dearly loved, that he thought of so many times, and about it he would say to Rosamund: 'Do you remember how his eyes were, how beautiful they were, and his mouth when he smiled . . . ?'

It seemed to him that that mouth smiled now. His gown fell off him and lay about his feet but he did not know it. He said one word: 'Robin!' He waited. Then he repeated: 'Robin! Oh, dear Robin!' He heard, very thinly but in the old beloved tone:

'Nick—the Queen is dead. The Queen is dead, Nick!'

'Stay—Robin . . . ' He moved forward, his legs catching in the tumbled gown. He was no longer afraid; love had killed fear.

But there was nothing to be seen—only the window and the black cold clouds.

He bent down and picked up the gown, wrapping it about him. He did not know whether it was Robin that he had seen, but he did know, beyond any kind of doubt, that the Queen was dead.

It was true enough, and on the next morning Nicholas, as did the whole country with him, relaxed.

Elizabeth had been a grand experience for her countrymen, who, however, had never known from one day to another what the next event might be. She had been always unexpected. The only two sure expectations concerning her—that she would be either assassinated or married—had both been disappointed. Through these expectations, however, the thought of her had always been interesting. Now there *were* no expectations any more!

Nicholas, walking through Whitehall that morning, felt quite suddenly that he himself had become a trifle dull. The vision of his brother, hallucination or no, had moved him extraordinarily, and it appeared to him now, in the cold March air, that with the withdrawal of Elizabeth part of himself had also been withdrawn and that Robin had wished to tell him that.

It was as though Robin had said to him: 'Nothing stays still. Your Queen is dead and your life as an active participant is over. You have now a duller rôle to play.'

He *felt* dull. He went to play tennis with Monteagle, who had curious, amusing, very bawdy tales to tell about the new King. He told him also some interesting things about the Gowrie Plot of three years earlier. Here Nicholas had a family excitement, for a cousin of his, Sir Hugh Herries, had been in the room—one of a crowd of Scottish gentlemen. It had been considered that young Ruthven had fathered the Queen's, Anne of Denmark's, children—or one of them at the least. And that James had rid himself of the brothers with his Pot of Gold imbroglio. At any rate, Monteagle avowed, James had never felt any passion for any woman.

'It's a pity, Herries,' Monteagle said, laughing and looking at Nicholas' superb figure in his playing-shirt and tight drawers, 'that you are not thirty years younger. There would be a fine place at Court for you.'

And Nicholas, like any other Elizabethan gentleman, thinking little of such matters, hit the ball lustily and swore a grotesque oath.

Nicholas was present with the crowd at Theobalds the night before King James entered London.

It was a superb sight. All the nobility of England and Scotland were there, riding into the First Great Court. Here all dismounted save the King. Then four nobles stepped to his horse, two before, two behind, and brought him forward into the Second Great Court. Then he himself (and very clumsily as Nicholas saw) dismounted. A young man presented a petition which the King graciously received. Then he came forward into the heart of the Court and there were the great men of England ready to receive him. Here was his real reception as King of England. Here were Chancellor Egerton, Treasurer Buck-hurst, and Nicholas' boring and malicious, spiteful friend Henry Howard, Privy Seal.

But the man who caught the eye was none of these but rather Secretary Robert Cecil, master of that house and indeed of all England.

Nicholas had often seen Cecil before and always marvelled at the power and presence there was in that deformed little body. There was something terrifying about Cecil. How men shouted and cheered at that meeting of Cecil and the King! It signified the reality of the bond between Scotland and England. Nicholas himself made a tremendous noise and there were tears in his eyes, for he was a sentimental man and easily moved.

They passed into the house and very odd they looked—the deformed Cecil and the loutish awkward King.

Nicholas had, with good fortune, been standing near to them and he saw the King look at him, for, with his great height and breadth of shoulder, he towered above the rest. Nicholas was a loyalist of the loyalists and would always be, but he could not deny that a strange stale odour came from the King as of manure and mice and straw. Nicholas did not give bodily odours an especial thought—many ladies he had loved had smelt strongly—but this odour of the King's was something peculiar and he was never to forget it. For the rest he got a good notion of the King's physical properties. Middle height and perhaps well-set, inclining to stoutness, but this was difficult to say because of the famous quilted doublet and stuffed breeches that he wore for fear of a dagger-thrust.

When he ambled in with Cecil he waddled like a duck and his stuffed behind stuck backwards like a separate entity. Nevertheless the face was not that of a fool nor was it unpleasant: he had large prominent blue eyes and they stared at the person with whom he talked as though he would read all the secrets. His cheeks were high-coloured and healthy, his hair brown, and his beard thin and scattered. Nicholas had the impression that he would see into men's hearts and minds more ably than they would see into his. Strangest of all, he reminded him, at the last, of his tragic and all-daring mother. While the trumpets blew and the nobles cheered, Nicholas remembered a moment when he had seen Mary on the steps of Chartley waiting for her horse to be brought. This King had both his mother and his weak father, Darnley, in his blood.

At the beginning of May, Nicholas went down to Mallory with his wife and child that they might avoid the plague.

Once again in his beloved place his energies returned. He was soon seeing to the cattle and the pigs and the garden and the fields and the labourers and the household servants as though he were yet twenty. And Gilbert Armstrong worked beside him as though he were his brother.

Now he gave himself heart and soul to the training of his young son. He was half a century older, there was no escaping from that. And it was of no comfort to tell himself that he had the powers to beget a million children more could he find women to bear them. It was of no use to talk of a million children; here was the matter of one, young Robert Herries. He had first all the surprise of discovering that his son promised in no way to resemble himself, a surprise very common to fathers. To begin with the physical side, young Robert was short and sturdy and would never be tall. His eyes were steady, unlighted by anger or astonishment. When his father held him naked in his arms the body was strong and well-shaped, but it was not an athlete's body, as his own had been from the beginning. Nor was it the body of a poet as his uncle Robin's had been. You could tell these things from the start.

When Nicholas held him thus young Robin did not start nor

wriggle. He lay quite still watching his father with his steady eyes. When Nicholas plunged him suddenly into cold water he neither screamed nor cried.

Mrs. Margit, an ugly old woman with bent shoulders and a double chin, but immaculately starched, wearing a high white ruff and a tall white cap, said that Robin was the steadiest child she had ever governed.

'He's no trouble and no blessing as you might say, Master. If I'm gone or come it makes no odds to him.'

But he loved his father and mother and Armstrong, and above all his father—and yet Nicholas could not but feel that he was something of a joke to him. As the months passed and then 1604 arrived, and then Michaelmas and Christmas, young Robin became ever more baffling. He learned quickly to talk but he did not speak unless he intended. Whether in London or at Mallory he amused himself.

He seemed not to know fear nor any passion violently save one— that of possession. And yet he was not cold-hearted. He loved to walk with his father, Nicholas bending his height, Robin's tiny hand in his father's vast one. He would hold on to his mother as though he were terrified that he would lose her.

Yet it seemed to Nicholas that his plans, those that he made privately in his mind, were apart from all of them.

Nicholas taught him all about nature—flowers, the farm, the reason for this and that.

'One day they will be mine,' Robin said, looking at fine and handsome cows and a bull that pawed angrily the ground but did not frighten him.

'First I must die,' Nicholas said, and he felt a strange tremor shake the little body although the child said nothing.

After a while Nicholas longed for the child to lose control as he, in his childhood, had so often done.

One day he took out of Robin's hand the old Fool with the red cap and the silver bells. It was battered now, the cap torn, the nose broken. Robin loved it above all his things.

'This is broken,' Nicholas said; 'you are weary of it. Christmas is coming and you shall have better things.'

He had taken it out of the chubby hand and made as though he would throw it into the fountain. Robin, his legs planted, made no movement, only he drew a deep breath and watched his father closely.

Nicholas was certain that the child knew that he would not destroy it. But he continued to tease him.

'See—I will throw it away. It is old and dirty and perhaps has the plague. His nose is broken and his cap torn.'

Robin said quite simply: 'It is mine'—as though he would say: 'You know that it is. You are a just man. You have never done me a wrong, nor will you do me one now.'

This argument was irresistible. Nicholas returned it to him and the fat fingers closed round it as though they were lock and key.

He could laugh and play like other children and hug his father and mother with kisses. He was indeed entirely normal.

On his fifth birthday he was in London and children were invited to a party. Like all children at all times they over-ate and were sick, wished for things that were not theirs and screamed to have them, struck their relations in temper and tore their clothes.

Robin was the quite perfect host. He had been given by his father's cousin, Alicia Turner, a box made like a cock's head to hold money. This was his best present, and when the other children took it to examine it he watched them with grave intensity until it was given back to him again. He wore a new very handsome suit of cerise and silver and carried a baby sword at his side, but he showed no silly pride in his clothes. They had for entertainment a conjurer dressed as a Turk. Robin watched him intently and on occasion nodded his head as though he had discovered the trick. When they were all gone and he was in bed he took with him his money-box, but when his great father knelt down by the bed, put his arms around him and asked him whether he were happy, he laid his cheek against his father's and sighed: 'When I am grown,' he said, 'I too will be a magician, for people are easy to deceive.' He said the word 'people' with so grown an air that Nicholas also sighed. His baby was no longer a baby.

Towards the end of that famous year 1605 Nicholas experienced an odd connection with the most famous event in it. The incident was to have a later influence on his own affairs and so on all the fortunes of his house.

Once in his life when he had been drinking at a party in his uncle Henry's London house he had seen a strange hallucination in a mirror, and out of that mirror had come the greatest servant and friend he was ever to have, Gilbert Armstrong. Now, in the dank shadows of a cellar he was to see another's face also like an hallucination and it would not be thus seen for the last time. . . .

The whole affair began when on Saturday evening, October 26th of this year 1605, he took dinner with his friend Lord Monteagle in his house at Hoxton. It was a pleasant house, the party was intimate and family. Nicholas was altogether at his ease, seven o'clock had just but echoed in silver tones from the clock picturing Venus rising from the ocean at the foot of the stairs. They were about to sit down to supper, when a footman approached Monteagle and presented a letter.

'What is this?' Monteagle asked. The ladies had already gone into the dining-room. Monteagle, Mr. Ward, a gentleman in his family, and Nicholas were still gathered in the hall.

Monteagle undid the letter but his eyes were not too strong.

'Where did you get this?' he asked the footman.

'A man, my lord, at the door: there is a great wind and his cloak was blown about his face. He said that this was for your lordship and that you must have it instantly. At once he was gone.'

'There! You read it,' Monteagle said, pushing it into Mr. Ward's hand. The three stood close together. Mr. Ward said: 'A secret business this. Even when opened it is still sealed.' He read the letter:

My Lord—Out of the love I bear to some of your friends, I have a care of your preservation; therefore I would advise you, as you tender your life, to devise some excuse to shift off your attendance at this Parliament; for God and man have concurred to punish the wickedness of this time. And think not slightly of this advertizement but retire yourself into your country, where you may expect the event in safety. For though there be no appearance of any stir, yet I say they shall receive a terrible blow this Parliament, and yet they shall not see who hurts them. This counsel is not to be contemned, because it may do you good, and can do you no harm: for the danger is past as soon as you have burnt the letter: and I hope God will give you the grace to make a good use of it, to Whose holy protection I commend you.

'And what make you of that, Nicholas, my friend?' Monteagle asked slowly.

Nicholas held the letter toward the lustred candelabra that he might read it the better.

He repeated slowly in his deep rich tones the sentence: 'For though there be no appearance of any stir, yet I say they shall receive a terrible blow this Parliament, and yet they shall not see who hurts them'—and—'for the danger is past as soon as you have burnt the letter.' He repeated this last—'Now what may that mean?'

For a moment they all drew closer together: the night was wild: shutters clamped and doors banged. The candles blew in the candelabra and the lustres swung.

Two ladies stood in the door laughing: 'Now—are we to wait for ever?'

By a curious chance he was concerned in the sequel, for he was passing into his house in Whitehall before midnight on November 4th when he, the wind bewildering him, ran slap into a small band of men and found at the head of them an acquaintance, the pompous and pursy Sir Thomas Knivett, a magistrate for Westminster. Knivett seemed quite delighted to encounter him and Nicholas soon found that the whole party was in a state of anxious nervousness.

Knivett took him aside and seemed to find the greatest comfort in his brawn and breadth, for he, as it were, sheltered under him and almost laid his head on his chest. It appeared that Monteagle had taken the letter to the King and the King had been assured that the meaning of it was gunpowder with which to blow up the Houses of Parliament. So a search had been made in a cellar belonging to one Whinyard who had let it to Thomas Percy with the adjoining house. Monteagle, who conducted this first investigation, seeing a man standing in the corner, asked who he was and was told that this was the man left in charge of the cellar by his master. Monteagle carelessly remarked to this man that his master was well provided by his large stocks of fuel against the blasts of winter. They made no further search but returned to the King. The King was not satisfied, having this gunpowder certainly in his head, and bade them return and search the faggots.

It was this that they were now about to do. Knivett caught Nicholas' arm as though he loved him—'Come with us, Mr. Herries—you are strong as any man in London and will see order enforced if need be. That there is gunpowder I cannot doubt, and a spark set to it——'

So Nicholas went with them.

Whinyard, the Keeper of the Wardrobe, was with them. It was he, in fact, who was the disguise, for he was to pretend that they were come in search of some hangings that he needed.

Outside the door of the cellar they all paused and even Nicholas discovered that he was not as brave as he had once been, for the thought of being blown to pieces and its discomfort came to him, whereas twenty years before he would never have considered it.

However, in they went, Knivett looking as important as he might. At once there was an event, for just inside the doorway they discovered the man whom they had interrogated on the other visit, but now booted, with his travelling cloak, as though about to set off on a journey.

Knivett for once showed presence of mind, for he instantly had the man apprehended and told the others to remove the wood and coals. This man at first made no resistance but stood very haughtily looking on. Nicholas did not look at him at this time, being eagerly interested in the men who were clearing away the logs and coal. With a shout they came on a barrel of gunpowder and soon no fewer than thirty-six barrels were discovered. Everyone realized that a kingdom-shaking event (that might have been a Parliament-shaking event) had occurred, and Knivett and Whinyard were amusing to watch, for they were all mixed up with this importance, the glory that would accrue to them, the danger that the King and Parliament had escaped, and still more the danger that *they* had escaped. Knivett indeed was in such a condition of excitement that he was literally dancing on his heels and he threw himself on the dark man, crying out in childish treble: 'Search him! Search him! . . . Have him searched! For God's sake and the King's search him!' He himself tore off the man's cloak and with his own fingers began to scrabble at his tunic and waistband, crying: 'Ah, you wicked fellow! You would destroy the King's Majesty, would you!' When their hands were all about his body this man, who was Fawkes, began to struggle. There were at least half a dozen upon him and he was bent back almost double, his black-haired chest bare and torn, his hose pulled about his heels so that he was shamefully naked. He fought like a devil, and it was now that Nicholas, feeling a kind of pity although he was a devil, moved forward to prevent their shaming him further. Fawkes swung round, throwing two men off as the bear throws the dogs. His furious gaze met Nicholas': his mouth was drawn with rage, blood poured down one cheek, but it was the eyes, dark, full, eloquent, that Nicholas was to remember. For they were the eyes of his old lifelong enemy, Philip Irvine, of the man who had tortured his brother, whom he himself had finally slain in the wilds of Eskdale in Cumberland.

It was as though Irvine looking through those eyes cried out to Nicholas: 'I am not dead, you see! You are not finished with me yet!' At last Fawkes, three-quarters naked, his arms trussed behind him, his hair wild about his forehead, was held on his knees a prisoner. All he said between his teeth was: 'Had I been within the cellar instead of by the door I would have fired the train and blown you all to hell.'

They found matches on him and in a corner a dark lantern. But what most excited their curiosity was a small pocket watch in his possession which he had had to know the exact moment for firing the train. Such pocket watches at that time were very rare.

It was not to be, however, for another two years that Nicholas Herries' new history properly began. These two years were in many ways the most unhappy of his life. There comes to many men, after they have reached fifty, a sense of disappointment. They realize that there is possibly no great portion of life remaining to them. They look back over what has been and feel an acute chagrin. Is this *all* that life has been intended for? Birth, marriage, and later, death. Nothing achieved that marks them out from other men. The moments of acute pleasure have faded: the body is beginning to weaken, and beside the body, what is there?

Unlike his brother, spiritual things had never mattered greatly to Nicholas. He had been a man of his hands. All his delights had been physical. No, not all. He had loved passionately two persons—his brother and Catherine, the witch's daughter. But he had not been able to save his brother from a shameful death, and the revenge that he had taken for that death seemed now to have something poor and pitiful in it. Catherine he had never possessed.

It was true that he loved his wife and that she was the best companion a man could desire—but passion had never been there, as she herself well knew.

During those years he felt a penetrating and incurable loneliness. It was not only in himself but in the state of his beloved England that he felt it. The *beat* of the country, the rhythm of its life was slackening. All men were aware of it.

This Scottish man was not truly their King as Elizabeth had been their Queen. His oddities, amusing at first, began very soon to have something humiliating about them. Nicholas had never worried his head overmuch about religious affairs but now he was forced to attend to them. At the very beginning of the new reign some leading clergymen of the Church of England had asked for certain mild laxities of ceremonial and observance inside their Church. This was to assist the new Puritanism. But James had been altogether intolerant. 'A Scottish Presbytery,' he had cried, 'agrees as well with a monarchy as God with the Devil. . . . Then Jack, Tom, and Dick shall meet and at their pleasure censure me and my Council.' After the failure of the Hampton Court Conference three hundred Puritan clergy were ejected from their livings. The clergyman at Mallory had been one of those. Nicholas had liked and admired him. He was an old man with flowing white hair and a fiery eye: he was a good man with much kindliness towards the sick and needy. On the day that he left Mallory all the people had been there weeping and asking for his blessing. The blacksmith, an old friend of Nicholas, had said in his ear: 'This is the way to raise the Devil. Mr. Symons goes and in his place worse will come.'

On the other side the Roman Catholics suffered a desperate moral blow from the discovery of the Gunpowder Plot. Every ordinary Englishman felt that all that had ever been said against Jesuit influence in England was now utterly justified. From that fatal November 5th the anti-Roman passion in England was a lively never-ceasing factor in English politics.

From the start of the reign the Navy began to decline and was soon woefully neglected. The many stories that came from the Court were anything but handsome. This stuttering, stammering, awkward man with his Scottish accent, his familiarities with his handsome young men, his sudden access of royalty and his equally sudden humiliating abandonment of it—these and many more became known to all men, and the almost mystical worship of the Crown that had been everywhere in Elizabeth's time was quickly falling into vapour.

Nicholas was a passionate Loyalist. It had always seemed to him that the Queen or King appointed was there by Divine Right. But could it be by Divine Right that this oddity was on the throne? So his spirit withered, he became lethargic. Only his wife and Armstrong could rouse him to his old energy and they too often failed. Then came a day, in the spring of 1607, when his life began again.

The post brought him a letter. He saw that it was from his cousin, Tobias Garland, who lived in Cumberland. Tobias was a stout jolly man, a few years his junior, whom he greatly liked. He had married Barbara, the daughter of his uncle Henry and sister of his cousins Edward and Sidney. By her Tobias had three children, Rashleigh, Lucy, and Peter. They lived in a house above Seascale, a little village on the Cumbrian coast. He had not seen any of them for many a day.

He did not at once open his letter. He was sitting, the warm sun on his face, in the pleached garden near the fountain. While he sat there, the letter on his lap, Rosamund his wife stole up behind him, put her fingers in front of his eyes, and whispered in his ear, 'Who is it?'

He kissed her hands and drew her on to the seat beside him. Rosamund was a plain woman but she adored her husband and lived only for him and her child, and had humour sufficient to know that she had been her husband's second choice and yet have a happy life in spite of that.

'Weeping, Nicholas?'

He turned on her indignantly, then drew her close to him and kissed her, then sighed a deep portentous sigh, then said:

'What ails me? Cure me—for only you in all the world can.'

She looked at him most lovingly. He seemed to her often more her child than young Robin.

'What ails you,' she said, 'is that you have had for too many years now too many blessings and no danger. Go. Make love to some woman in London who refuses you, fight with an enemy, sell Mallory . . .'

'Sell Mallory!' He was aghast. 'You would be happy again if you, I, and Robin begged our way on a broken-backed horse to the North —the North!'

She clapped her hands. 'You and Armstrong shall ride to Cumberland again. It is five years since you were there. The ghost of . . .' She hesitated. 'Do you mind if I speak of it? All ghosts are laid now. Go and prove it so.'

'The North!' he said. 'There is an omen in that. For here on my lap is a letter from Tobias.' But he did not open it. Instead he shook his head. 'Why should I go back? I am too old to begin again.'

'We begin nothing again,' Rosamund said. She knelt on the warm grass at his feet, holding her hands on his knee.

'Dear Nicholas. You don't know, for you are not made to think of such things, what fortune I feel it and have always felt it to be married to you. Since I was a very ugly little girl I loved you and no man else. But I never had any hope for you. And then the first time you asked me I refused although I was longing to have you—and you know why—and the second time I said yes because I knew you could never have her. I was second-best, but what did that matter to me when you were my first, the only desire of my life?

'We have been very happy until of late. I know that you love me but I know too that I am not one to create new life *in* you although I have created new life *out* of you.'

She knelt closer to him. He put his arm around her.

'You are still haunted by the past, Nicholas. You saw Robin the night the Queen died. You saw Philip's eyes in the man Fawkes. You will not go to the North because you are afraid of ghosts. Ride North! Ride North and challenge them. Make a new world for yourself.'

'It is easy to make a new world when you are young. That first day I challenged Irvine north of Keswick I was young in the world. But the world has lost its spring. At the Court the Queen is neglected for fancy boys. They lie drunk on the decks in Portsmouth harbour. The New Puritans fight the Old Catholics. You say that I am to make a new world—but I am an old man. An old man with a young son!'

He got up, standing away from her. His voice had a bitterness that she had never heard from him before.

'I tell you, wife,' he said, his voice muffled, 'Philip Irvine is even not now finished with me.'

For a moment she who was as brave as any woman in England was frightened. In the still spring air it was as though it were not his voice at all. 'Then,' she cried, 'go North and challenge him again as you did before. You are not a man, Nick, to be frightened with ghosts.' He swung round.

'No, by God, I am not!' he cried.

The letter had fallen onto the grass. He bent down to pick it up, broke the seal and read it.

'Gilbert and I ride North to-morrow,' he cried.

THE MAGICIAN AND HIS LITTLE DAUGHTER

NICHOLAS HERRIES drew up his horse and stopped. Directly in front of him on the road was a pool of rain-water mirroring a ragged cloud like a furred tongue. On his right the sea rolled in like unfolding oilcloth. Behind him was the heavy pile of Black Combe stretching out to the ocean.

It was at this moment that he met the ghost that had been haunting him for so many years. He was a man of common sense and of no great imagination. But he believed in ghosts. He had seen one in Fawkes' eyes. Had he not watched Fawkes fighting in that cellar that November night he would not be here, in all probability, now. He had come here to lay that ghost. In the quick passage through life one thing leads to another,—as doors close behind you as you pass swiftly through the rooms of a house. Was a door to close now?

There was no sound. This northern world often held itself still and steady—as it was doing now. The shining pool with the cloud was still in front of the horse's hooves. Gilbert Armstrong was still on *his* horse. Only the sea hissed and lisped beyond the low sand-dunes. Nicholas sat looking in front of him. They were on the sea road between Ravenglass and Seascale. Nicholas was staring but he saw more than could be seen with the physical eye. For he knew every detail of this country. It had been here, in the Eskdale wilds, not far from this spot, that in the one day he had lost the love of his whole life and killed his enemy.

This was the wildest piece of country in all England, all its wildness packed into a tiny compass, and yet within half an hour you could be lost in it, lost for days and nights. Within walking distance was the Kendal road, the Kendal road that was now a pack-horse route but had once been a Roman road, and following that you would come to Hard Knott Hause, where even now as Nicholas breathed he could hear the old proud Romans moving about him, the Romans, the only power that had subdued the savage North, setting up a fortress as here, so strong that the skeleton of it would last for ever, so deep that the stones sink into the centre of the earth, so beautiful

because all around it are the greatest mountains of Cumberland—
Great End and the Pikes and Scafell. Here, over this Roman land,
the clouds pile in great bastions, and the light travels in bands of gold,
in flaming red, from rock to rock, from flying cornice to deep-hewn
cleft. Under the clouds the Romans move and you hear the clang of
their harness and a bugle blows over Harter Fell.

But Nicholas' gaze pierced on beyond Hard Knott into the heart of
that glorious wilderness. Here, within a ten-mile circle, you pass out
of time and away from the life of man. There is no other piece of
wild country in all England like it. Over the Ure Gap to Langstrath,
or, turning left, into the heart of the great inner valley, the valley
walled in by the crags of Scafell, the Pikes, Great End. Yes, Nicholas
knew all this country. He had ridden and hunted over it many a day
when his centre had been his brother's house at Rosthwaite in Borrowdale. He would be gone a week, a fortnight maybe, with Armstrong his only companion. Best of all he loved the Sprinkling Tarn
and the Angle Tarn. These had always seemed to him the fairy waters
of the world, thinking of them in London streets or even, traitor that
he was, when his nose was stuck into the hearts of the dark roses
of Mallory. These tarns are perched on watershed ridges; Nicholas
and Gilbert had bathed in them naked on a sun-scorching day, but
best of all was it when the clouds swung up like waterspouts into
the sky and the light spread from behind the cloud edges, teasing with
its rays the soft vaporous snow-piles on the heads of the mountains,
and then turning those mountainsides into fire. On such a day the
water of Angle Tarn was still like glass, then leapt to the light and
seemed to turn on its side, blazing with fire as though it would inflame
the bog and peat and grass below it. The whole of Eskdale, proud
in its own untouched rough solitude, would flame as the mountains
grew dark. Then in a sky blue as an eggshell the evening stars would
shine and across it birds wing their way home.

Nicholas knew all this. He knew that this place was the desire of
his soul but that he had avoided it because of his lover and his enemy.
Would they come to meet him now? He challenged them. He sat
his horse, and his soul cried: 'Catherine! Catherine! . . . Irvine!
Irvine! . . .'

The burden fell off his back as it had once done from Christian's.
His horse splashed through the rain-pool. He turned round to Arm-

strong and his brown face under the feathered hat was merry again, as it used to be.

'Seascale is only a mile or two,' he cried. 'I'll race you for it.'

Their horses pounded down the road, Ned Laxham, the boy, following on the pack-horse with the luggage more slowly.

Seascale was little more than a hamlet, a cluster of cottages gathered above the broad shining sands, while the Isle of Man hung like a large burnished blackberry on the horizon. To the right above the sands was the Hall, the property of the Senhouse family. In a field near by was a marvellous circle of stones, earlier, people said, than the Druids.

Tobias Garland's place, Little Garston, was on a rise of ground about a mile from the sea. A dark drive of trees led to an open court and a neat Elizabethan house. There was a fountain of Neptune and some dolphins in the middle of the court, and as Nicholas and Armstrong rode out of the avenue, they saw the sea across the fields blood-red while a host of yellow clouds like ducklings played in the faint blue sky. Behind the house the shoulder of Black Combe was dark and straight, before them the range of Lakeland hills lay like giants resting their chins on their hands watching the sunset.

Before they had time to dismount the family was upon them. Someone must have seen them from a window. There they were, Tobias, stout and sturdy, fifty-seven years of age, Barbara, pinched face, bony, anxious-eyed, fifty-nine, and their lovely, lovely children, Rashleigh nineteen, Lucy seventeen, and Peter sixteen. Those were their ages in 1607, when Nicholas saw them on this sunset evening, the first time perhaps that he ever did really see them, for they had been too young on the last occasion to claim a real existence. He would never, for the rest of his life, forget them as he saw them from his horse's back with the blood-red sea behind them, standing on the stone steps in front of the house, the three of them, Rashleigh with his arm around Lucy, and Peter a little apart.

It was Lucy who at that instant began his second life for him, Lucy who taught him a new kind of love. With Catherine Hodstetter he had known the physical, with Rosamund his wife, the domestic, with his mother the love of the spirit, with Gilbert Armstrong the love of comrade. Now with Lucy he was to realize the all-consuming, all-sacrificing paternal.

He would never forget either how they were dressed. Rashleigh was in the new fashion. He wore a large lace-edged collar and cuffs on his maroon coat that fitted loosely to his slim figure. Round the waist were silken laces fastened to his full breeches, which were also maroon. His dark chestnut hair was long and flowing, framing his lovely oval-shaped face, the long eyelashes, the noble forehead, and aristocratic haughty mouth. He was perhaps the most handsome boy that Nicholas had ever seen. Peter, who was plump and fair, and clothed in black with white lace collar and cuffs, had his hair cropped. He was very fair, with bright blue eyes and a smiling mouth. But Lucy—his Lucy, who came at that moment, as it seemed, through intervening space straight into his arms—wore a dress of dark green and gold braid. She had the figure of a girl, beginning to be a woman, her round small breasts almost revealed above the green velvet. Her skirt was drawn back to show a pale embroidered petticoat. She wore a muslin and lace collar. Her dark hair was drawn off her laughing, eager, friendly face into a knot behind, and the side pieces fell in ringlets on to her bare shoulders.

No, he knew then, as he looked at them, that here was a picture painted at that instant on his brain, never to be erased. And Lucy told him later that he had seemed to her in that sunset light like a god, seated on his great horse, a giant in carriage and strength, motionless like someone descended from heaven. . . .

Blessed days followed. He knew that life was beginning for him freshly. This was a new world for himself and his country. His rôle, as Robin had tried to tell him on the night that the Queen died, would now be different. He was no longer the centre of his own stage. The lives of others would make his own life.

Another thing that he realized was that he was everywhere now recognized as the head of the Family. For the first time in its history the Family *was* a Family. Tobias and Barbara both considered the various branches of the Family with real seriousness. There were *three* main branches—the Garlands, the Turners, and the Roger Herries. The Garlands were the Garlands and through Toby's marriage to Barbara belonged to the centre, descended directly from old Geoffrey Herries who had founded the family (this branch of the Herries-Howard stock) by buying the manor of Hurdicotes, in Cumberland, near Cockermouth, in 1420. The Turners also came into the family through the female, Ralph Turner of Edgecumbe marrying

Alicia, daughter of Lucy, daughter of Gilbert, son of Gilbert who married Alice Walpole, the Walpoles themselves being distantly related to the Howards and the Scotch Herries.

The Roger Herries were always called the Roger Herries because Roger II, from whom they came, was such a character, a wild brigand in the wars of the barons, fighting always for his own hand and amassing wealth and a castle.

They had always been Bohemian, the Roger Herries, although they had married into decent families like the Camperdowns and the Pickets—Rosamund's father, Nicholas' father-in-law, was a jolly old Bohemian at this very moment, a painter and a wanderer in the sight of the Lord. In any case, as Nicholas discovered, they all, Garlands and Turners and Courthopes and Camperdown cousins, looked upon himself as the King of the Herries Castle. He had not realized it until he came to pay this visit, and that was another thing that made him feel apart and different.

The three children—Lucy, Rashleigh, and Peter—all loved him from the first glimpse of him. They had been too young when they had seen him before to realize him sufficiently, but now, worshipping his size and strength, his horse-riding, his brilliance with a rapier, the strength of his hands, he was like someone from another world. And the boys, bathing with him, watching him walk upside-down, naked, on his hands, gazing astounded at his neck and chest and arms and thighs, could scarcely speak for wonder. When, added to all this, they discovered the simplicity and natural kindliness of his nature, their conquest was completed.

He, on his side, gathered them all there into his heart with a longing, desiring love and a poignancy as though he would barricade them against the troubles that were to come.

In this he was in no way disloyal to his wife and child. Rosamund and Robin were part of himself—his heart, his lungs, his secret parts. He loved them as he loved himself—without consideration. Where he was they were.

But Lucy and Rashleigh and Peter were creative in him, they were what he had been needing ever since his brother and Catherine died. He very soon discovered their natures. They were very different. Rashleigh was like a knight of old days, his only thought was for serving King and country. He was shortly to have a place at Court, and when

Nicholas heard this he was anxious. 'For looks,' he said to Tobias, 'he is handsomer than any boy of his age I have ever seen. And this new Court is no place for handsome boys.'

Old fat Tobias with something solemn in his face said: 'Nought can touch Rashleigh. He has no sin.'

There was truth in that. Not that Rashleigh was a prig or a virtuous moralist. But he had a dedicated air. He was a man born for one purpose, and one only. Peter was very different. He was Puritan by taste, although he was merry and had a warm loving heart. But in spirit he was of a deep seriousness: had he and Rashleigh not loved one another, they would have been always at odds, for they thought differently about everything. Peter was all for government by the people: he did not believe in Divine Right nor in King's Prerogative. In religion he was Protestant, and if he hated anything in this world it was a Jesuit. But because he was by nature mild and kindly and would not hurt any man, he was as yet no fanatic. It might be that he would grow into one, Nicholas sometimes thought.

And Lucy? At the present she loved simply to be alive. She was too happy to think steadily, too full of adoration of life to be vexed or chagrined by anything or anybody. She was still a child, impetuous, violently impulsive, reckless, fearless. But when trouble would come, as trouble must, there would be deep strong character there.

Tobias Garland, although he was fat, jolly, and had his purse well filled, was no fool. He had always been the kind of man who believed no further than he could see. He had made a fortune in Manchester, building and furthering the fashion in those new coaches that were now everywhere becoming the rage. Henry Herries, his father-in-law, had been in trade. No Herries had, either now or later, any dislike to trade—they were English middle class and were, in fact, frightened of anything higher. The Garlands had been prepared to be frightened of Nicholas, with his visits to the Court and his fine place at Mallory. Barbara, Tobias' wife, was something of a social snob—she had learned that from her valetudinarian mother and had been proud that her half-sister Sylvia had married so grand a man as Philip Irvine—but Tobias had never taken any pride in connections with the Court and had pitied his poor little sister-in-law for her most unhappy marriage. He had joked his Babs out of her longing for the life of the Court. At first she had protested with all her power against coming to live in so remote a place as Seascale. Manchester had seemed to her a poor enough little town, but here, on the edge of such barbarous country, no town within thirty miles, on the border of a sullen and reluctant sea . . .

Her adoration of her family and her real devotion to Tobias had saved her. She worshipped her children and thought there were no three like them in England. Sylvia's tragedy had warned her against the ambitions of a Court life, and on the other hand her adored Rashleigh would shortly be beginning his Court life in the household of Lord Monteagle, so that she would have it happily at second hand. She foresaw, through Rashleigh, a fine Court marriage for Lucy later, and now there was this amazing Cousin Nicholas, of whom she had always been afraid because of his size and the scandal about his brother's religion and illicit passion for Sylvia.

But now Nicholas had taken them all to his heart and would further the boys' fortunes,—so that his visit was indeed for the best, and she was not in the very slightest afraid of him.

Besides all this she had come to appreciate her position as country lady. Later, when the boys had made their way and Lucy had brought off a successful marriage, would be time enough for her London living. Her boys were the only males in their immediate branch of the Herries, her brother Sidney being dead and her other older brother Edward having only two girls, Janet and Martha. Rashleigh, she often thought, was destined to be the head of the family when Nicholas was gone.

She was not indeed in error when she thought him the handsomest young man in all England. Even Robert Carr (who at that very moment was hurting himself at a tournament and so arousing the tender solicitude of his monarch) was not so handsome.

Last of all, Barbara Garland, although she was something of a silly woman—her brother and sister had always thought her so, and until she had married Tobias, she had mostly lived under a Welsh mountain with her great-aunt Clyde—yet she had poetry and imagination enough in her to find something in this country where her home now was that she must love and boast of.

She forgot that Cousin Nicholas had been often in these parts and spoke to him always as though he had never known them before.

'When you have lived here awhile, Cousin, and ridden on an expedition to the Wastwater lake under Gavel——' she would begin, and Toby would interrupt—'Stuff, stuff, madam—when will you learn sense? Nick has lived outside Keswick many a day and knows these parts like his hand——' and then he would stop too, for it was with his brother Robin that Nicholas had stayed in Borrowdale, and that was a tragedy never to be mentioned.

But with Tobias Nicholas soon became intimate. These spring days were warm and the house was sheltered by its trees. It was open only on the courtyard side looking out to the sea.

A day came of a soft gold hazy light when the sea had no motion and the stones of the courtyard were hot to the hand. Nicholas and Tobias sat under the wall of his house talking—no sound save the birds and the fall of the fountain.

Tobias was telling of a trouble there had been in Seascale a month or so earlier.

'Have you heard of the new Puritans, Nick?'

Nicholas at once thought of his old, long-dead enemy Phineas Thatcher.

'Yes—if you mean a hypocritical God-be-with-you scoundrel! I knew one . . .' He stayed—that world was dead.

'Well, then,' continued Toby Garland, 'if you know the animal you'll be grieved to hear 'tis on the increase. There is a pestilential fellow pitched his tent between Gosforth village and Seascale and goes about preaching in the fields, on the shore, wherever he can collect some silly girls or open-mouthed lads. His name is Isaiah Holden.'

Toby Garland's stout, good-natured face was puffing with indignation—'They haven't so many followers as yet, but I fear that 'tis on the increase. They are set to make trouble against King and country wherever they may. They are against any dancing, gaming, drinking, wenching—any human pleasure of the body.' His round eyes stared, angry and puzzled, at the sea. 'They have always the name of God in their mouths. Wherever they go they are pelted with dirt and vegetables and this gives them the air of martyrs. This Isaiah is as thin as a rake and can talk. Lord! how he can talk! . . . But 'tis always that everything to do with the body is sinful. He would stop the propagation of children if he could, in so far as there is pleasure in it —aye, and even our daily motions. In any case, it happened a month back that they had a Maypole dance in the centre of the Stone Ring by the Hall there. It was a most pleasant evening and they came from Gosforth, Drigg, Ravenglass even. This Holden and some men with him broke in upon the gathering and carried off the Maypole. Then Holden stood on one of the stones and preached those that remained a sermon. . . .' Toby sighed. 'This is a new thing and dangerous, Cousin Nick.'

But Nicholas laughed.

'It is neither new nor dangerous, my Cousin Toby. There have always been fanatics of religion in the English blood. And in all countries. And not on one side only. . . . What about Bartholomew? I remember well how your brother-in-law, young then, made my hot blood freeze telling of the things he had seen. And he, poor lad, was never the same again after it.'

But Toby still shook his head.

'This is another matter—or it is as I see it. We had a Queen who, whatever she did or thought or ordered, was our glory. While she lived the throne in England was secure. And now we have a King. He has reigned four years and the Crown is already in the mud. When it was arranged that Rashleigh should go into Monteagle's service I rejoiced. But now . . . I don't know . . . I am hesitant. Not for the boy himself, for he is beyond contamination, but because for him the King is divine—and he will see with his own eyes—what will he see?—a waddling stutterer with his fingers in young men's pockets.' A new kind of eloquence was shining in Toby's eyes. 'What did we feel, Cousin Nick, about England while the Queen lived? England was in mighty danger but she was safe . . . even in '88 we were not afraid for her. But now! what are they doing, or not doing, to our ships? Where is our trade? And the Court. . . . What does it do but drink and whore and worse . . . ?'

Toby's fingers were trembling. 'There is much truth in the things that our Peter says. See, Cousin Nick, the cleavage that there is even in our own family. Those two boys love one another, but concerning the country and its governance they are altogether divided. Peter says he owes no obeisance to such a king, and Rashleigh, if he were of another family, would fight him for that. Peter says that this Scotch king, because he is Scotch, thinks that our Parliament must be subservient to the Privy Council, and he says that the day is coming when the Parliament will be subservient to no Privy Council, but will

obey only the orders of the People who have put it there. And Rashleigh, when he hears this, goes from the room, but I will hear him
say afterwards to his mother that the King is there by God's will and
by God's will he shall rule, and calling the Parliament "dirty, sweating
numskulls" and "fat-tailed rumps" and the like. But yet the two boys
love one another—and so always shall, whatever politics may do. But
I tell you, Cousin Nick, I tell you, that with such a Court and such
a King there is sorrow coming to this country. . . .'

Sorrow! The word rang no response in Nicholas' brain. He had
scarcely heard what old Garland had been saying, for he had been
lost in the golden, hazy air. 'This,' he might have been thinking, 'is
my happiest hour for many a day past. I am beginning life anew.
I will make my life again with my own little son and these three dear
children, helping them in any way that I can. At last the past is
truly behind me and a new life comes marching forward.' Even as he
thought this a new life was approaching, for round the bend of the
avenue, out from the darkness of the trees, came a strange little
coloured procession. First came a tall man wearing a red cloak and
on his head a peaked hat in alternate red and white colours.

Behind him marched a girl, a mere child, beating a small drum with
one hand and leading a donkey with the other. Behind her marched
a boy with a hump, carrying a table that also was coloured in red
and white.

They marched grandly, the man bearing himself as though he were
King of Egypt. The beating of the drum was very thin and intermittent. Behind the three was a huddle of men, girls, boys, laughing,
chattering, and then, at sight of Nicholas and Garland on their
wooden seat, suddenly silent.

In the quiet that followed, the tall man in the peaked hat marched
across the court with great dignity, his red cloak swinging behind
him.

When he came close Nicholas saw that he was a very curious fellow. His head was broad under his hat and then ran to a sharp peak,
his chin being long and thin. His nose was outrageously large and
was coloured, as was all his face, a dead white. His left cheek was
pockmarked. His hair was black and fell over the dirty collar of his
cloak. His most remarkable features were his eyes, which were veiled
as though they were half closed, lidded, and sleepy. His doublet and

hose under his cloak were red and white like his hat. He wore a number of flashing rings on his rather dirty fingers. Nicholas judged him a young man of about twenty-six, and he seemed to have a fine and alert body. He moved with great ease and with a queer, springy step.

When he approached the two gentlemen he took off his hat and bowed. Then he said, in a soft, rich, and musical voice:

'Sirs, I am travelling with my daughter' (he made a gesture at the child, who stood, her tiny hand on the donkey's ragged coat) 'to Scotland, and we pay our way as we go. I am a magician.'

He said this so simply and with so boyish an air that both Nicholas and Toby laughed. 'There are many sorts of magicians,' Nicholas said. 'Moreover, magic is against the King's law.'

'My magic does no harm,' the man answered. 'For example, good sir, you will find in your sword-pocket an egg coloured blue and a twist of rosemary——'

Nicholas felt at the pouch by his small rapier and produced from it a stone egg coloured blue and a twist of rosemary. Now the man had been standing at a distance from him. Nicholas stood up, looking at these things in his hand with amused wonderment. Toby Garland loved any sort of a game or a show and he clapped his hands delightedly.

'Show us another!' he cried.

At that same moment Lucy, Rashleigh, and Peter came together round the corner of the house from the garden. Lucy went to her father and kissed him.

'What have you found, Father? Whose are those . . . ?' Then she saw the child. With a little cry she went across to her. For in fact, as they all now saw, the child was beautiful. In age she could not be more than six or seven, but she held her head high, and stood as though on guard, fiercely. She had great black eyes, a proud mouth, and a body that the tawdry dress of orange and tinsel could not disguise. Her black hair fell on either side of her haughty, baby face. When Lucy approached her she did not move back. Only she raised her head a little higher. 'Oh, you baby!' Lucy cried. 'Look, Peter— such a baby!'

'Do not touch my donkey!' she called out, as though she were challenging the world, and when some of the crowd, who had by this time come closer, laughed, she turned as though she would spit at them. Nicholas, laughing, called out: 'Lucy! Lucy! See what I have! An egg and some rosemary!'

Peter had joined Lucy, looking at the child, who now was staring at the man as though she expected an order.

'What is your name?' Lucy asked her.

'Katherine Teresa Sibylla Christian,' she answered.

'What a pocket of names!' Lucy said, laughing, and touched her. Her whole body shrank. But she turned to Peter.

'Please, sir, my father needs me.'

It seemed that he did, for preparations had been forwarding. The hunchback boy had brought the table to the front of the court near the wooden seat. He had produced from somewhere a box with silver bands, a horn cup, and a stiff white cone. The child, as though she had been executing these movements from birth, went to the table, bowed to the gentleman with the utmost solemnity, and then stood rigidly at attention. The young magician seemed to have complete confidence—indeed, beneath his half-closed eyes he was almost impertinent. He spread his arms and began a long rigmarole in his deep, beautiful voice. He repeated his words as though he had said them a great many times before: he appeared to Nicholas to be infinitely bored. The small child stood at attention looking straight in front of her: she and her father were nothing but automata.

The human member of the company was the boy with the hump. His thin face was pale and freckled: he had the anxious, half-deprecatory look of one who has been deformed from childhood but his eyes never left his master's face. And there was more in them than obedience—there was devotion.

The magician said that his name was Dom Ferdinand Christian, that he was directly descended from the Queen of Sheba and that five of his ancestors had been kings. He said, moreover, that he had been born in Egypt in the tomb of one of the Egyptian kings, that his mother had been an Egyptian princess and his uncle a great Egyptian seer. From him he had learned the three great secrets—the immortality of not only the soul but also of the body, the transmutation of metals into gold, and the elixir of enduring love. . . .

Why, thought Nicholas, does he attempt all this nonsense upon us? But he could not seriously answer such a question, for he was bathed in such perfect happiness. He floated in this honeyed air which had a thick roughness as though its light were pollened with gold dust. He said things as in a dream. Turning his head he could discern over the tree-tops the heavy shoulders of Black Combe, wine-darkened, and before him the sea sparkled with a sunlight so fresh that his body was invigorated as though he bathed in it. Behind was the house, and behind the house the line of mountains. The two young men stood scornfully near their father, and Lucy, her eyes staring and her mouth a little open, had her hand on Nicholas' shoulder.

He liked to feel the pressure of her hand: his heart rose to meet it. He had been denied until now a daughter, and this protective paternity, this love that had nothing in it but purity and lovingkindness, was a wonderful new emotion.

He sat there, looking like a king, with his brown face, grey hair, and attitude of command. He was, at this moment, supremely happy. He remembered afterwards that it was at this moment when he realized his own happiness that everything changed. The magician, with his white pockmarked face and huge nose, was busy above the table. He held high his hand, opened his palm, and from it there dropped some white powder. The powder fell into the stiff-shaped cone. The magician uttered a cry and from the cone flew two white doves. The remarkable thing was that they did not, as is customary with the doves of conjurers, settle down to be caught up and put away and used for the next performance—rather they flew, with steady beat of wings, against the white-blue sky into the dark secrecy of the trees of the avenue and disappeared. Nicholas thought to himself, 'This is no ordinary conjurer,' and perhaps the more because now the magician fixed him, Nicholas, with his sleepy half-lidded gaze.

It seemed to him that the magician travelled with him to some very different place—to rough and stony ground where snow was falling and a strong wind blowing. Nicholas had his sword out, and, defending himself, while he uttered short gasps of exhaustion, was that thin dark man, his enemy, Irvine.

Nicholas had him in his arms, he raised him, pressing him to his chest, and, with a great cry, he threw him over and down . . . he threw him over and down . . . 'How did you know this?' he asked the magician.

'I was there.'

'But you were not there. Only Irvine and myself.'

'I was there because I am here. It is happening now. It is for ever. It can never end because time can never end. . . .'

He heard Lucy's voice in his ear:

'Cousin Nicholas, wake up! See what he is doing now! He must have the aid of the Devil, I think.'

He awoke with a start, rubbing his eyes with the back of his hand.

For now the magician was not looking at him any longer, but was rather drawing from the cone a medley of flowers, marjoram and thyme and rose and carnation—flowers of all seasons. His hands were full of them, and then, as his fingers opened, they fell, colouring the air, but before they reached the table they were gone.

A long-drawn 'Oh!' of wonder came from the crowd who had now drawn close to the table. Nicholas then saw the magician do a very strange thing, for he turned his head aside a little, put up his hand, and executed a large voluptuous yawn! His mouth was so open, from where Nicholas was sitting, that he could see all the strong white teeth and the very red tongue. But the yawn was prodigious and expressed an infinite and tragic boredom.

Now the small child was to be used. She stood on the table, her beautiful large black eyes staring out to the mountains. It seemed that she was in a trance. The magician ordered her to stand tiptoe.

Nicholas stared at her and it may be that he was dazzled by the sun, for it was now low in the sky. It seemed to him that this sky darkened and that the sea was silver—wrinkled like a snake's skin. Against this background the child grew. Her body sprang up until it was mature and the eyes that looked into those of Nicholas were a woman's, scornful, arrogant, and mocking. Above her, like gigantic birds, hovered the hands of the magician. . . .

He came to himself at the sound of a voice, harsh and imperative.

'In the name of the Lord,' the voice cried. Nicholas saw now everything with clear reality, for the table was there, the child standing on it, the magician half-turned toward the crowd. The air and sea were golden as they had been all afternoon. In the front of the crowd was standing a long thin man, dressed entirely in black, his head bare and his hair cropped. This man had the nervous posture and the tight thin lips of a fanatic. That much Nicholas could see.

'In the Lord's name,' he cried again, 'let this mockery cease. What hath the Lord said? "Thou shalt not bow to Ammon nor set up altars to the golden calf." '

But it was Toby Garland who was angry. He had jumped from the seat and strode across the court. Nicholas followed him.

'I don't know what the Lord has said,' he cried to the thin man in black, 'but this I do know, that this is my house and these are the grounds thereof—and the privacy of the place is mine.'

The thin man was in no wise taken aback. 'You should know, Mr. Garland, that this earth is the Lord's and He has declared against all magic and necromancy and weaving of spells wherever they may be— and I tell you, Mr. Garland, I am here on the Lord's work.'

'And I tell you, Mr. Isaiah Holden, that the earth *is* the Lord's and that I have paid monies—plenty of monies—to keep this portion of it for my own retiring-place and the giving of hospitality.'

At that point someone threw a stone at the magician, who was sitting, with apparent indifference, on the balustrade of the steps, swinging his legs. Nicholas had noticed the stone-thrower—a thick-set country lad—before this, and with a stride he was into the crowd, had the yokel swinging by his breeches and screeching for mercy.

The crowd was laughing, but not Isaiah Holden. Quickly and in a voice that seemed to be intended for Toby Garland's ear, he said: 'The time is not yet ripe, but the day is coming when the Lord will cry to His soldiers "Fall on and spare not!" Then on that day the sound of their horses' hooves will be as the clashing of thunder and the swords of the righteous will flash in the brightness of the sun and little rivers shall run with the blood of God's enemies. . . . Mark me, Tobias Garland, and see that neither you nor your sons be among them. As to that mountebank'—his eyes flashed across the court— 'his time is not yet, but he shall watch with darkening eyes the pouring forth of his own bowels.' With this pretty prophecy he had ended, for he turned down the avenue. The crowd slowly followed, looking back some of them, but knowing that the entertainment was ended.

It was so.

Garland gave the magician some money. He jingled the coins in his pocket. He looked at Nicholas with admiration.

'I have a place here for so strong a man with his hands, if you care to travel with us.' His voice was half admiration, half impertinence.

Nicholas answered laughing: 'Your flowers are of air, your woman that you make from a child is a fancy, your sky is not truly dark. I travel in more absolute company.'

Dom Ferdinand Christian stroked his great nose.

'Who may tell what is absolute? I could convert that Puritan jack-in-the-pulpit into a squirrel—or you would say that I did.'

He turned round to find his daughter. She had found Peter Garland. She was standing, her little hand in his, while he asked her laughing questions. She was such a baby and such a woman too. Hard life had made her this last. He was teasing her. She pulled at one of the silver buttons on his sleeve, his only ornament.

'Give me one.'

'Yes, for a kiss.'

At once she held up her mouth. The boy caught her in his arms and lifted her in the air. She did not struggle but threw her arms around his neck and kissed him. He put her down and with his silver knife cut off a silver button.

'There!' She took it, looked at him shyly, and ran at once to the donkey.

The little party made a procession into the trees as they had come—the magician swinging his red cloak, the child with the donkey, the humpbacked boy with the table.

MUSTER OF HERRIES

JAMES COURTHOPE enjoyed his sixtieth birthday in the November of 1610, and Nicholas, who was now himself sixty-six years of age, gave a family party to celebrate it at his Westminster house. He gave it for two other reasons not publicly stated—to show off his young son, Robert, who was ten, and to honour his dear Lucy Garland, who had been twenty only a month earlier.

All the Garlands were there as well as the Courthopes, the Broughtons, the Turners, the Pickets, Janet and Martha, Edward's daughters, the Gorings—all the tributaries that had for a long time now been flowing into the broad Herries river.

Nicholas, when he looked back on the gathering, saw four things—Lucy's look of foreboding of a tragic destiny, the look that he had caught first at his own wedding, when she had been a guest at Mallory; two angry young men fighting; his wife's happiness; and the poor bewildered monkey in his bright-green jacket that affected Janet Herries had brought with her, climbing one of the decorated banisters of the staircase in a panic terror.

For he detected in himself, for the first time, a new irony. He had never in all his life been ironic—he had been too active for that. It came with his detachment, the detachment that had begun with him on the night of the late Queen's death.

A detachment and yet not a detachment, for this was the very time, three years before, when he had begun to take so active an interest in the lives of the three young Garlands.

Since then Rashleigh Garland had come to take up his place at Court in Lord Monteagle's household. The boy was here to-night. He was now a young man, the handsomest man at Court. Even the favourite, Robert Carr, acknowledged it. There was about him a strange aloofness: no one, not even Royalty, was intimate with him. With every day the Court was becoming looser and more ribald and more extravagant. Rashleigh took part in the extravagances but was never of them. He had, Nicholas thought, dear Robin's aloofness, but it was not religion that kept him apart. He did not offend: his courtesy was perfect. He had no close friends and no bitter enemies. Peter, on the other hand, had many friends but of the learned sort. He was, at present, secretary to one Marmaduke Fettle, who was writing a 'History of the World' in a gloomy wooded house in the village of Chelsea. Peter had more lively friends. He was privileged to be one of the company at the Mermaid Tavern, the company that Raleigh, still in the Tower, had founded. He was a very subordinate, unattended member, but he had the pleasure of listening to the voices of Inigo Jones and young Francis Beaumont, Ben Jonson and Shakespeare, Sir Richard Martin, lawyer Selden, and Cotton, Christopher Brooke and Camden, John Donne, Chapman, Michael Drayton.

Sometimes the evenings were of a mortal dullness, sometimes of a foul bawdy, sometimes drunken, noisy—but there *were* evenings when, through the smoke of the tobacco, the bellowings of Jonson, the gloomy prophesyings of Donne, there would come an argument between Shakespeare and Jonson maybe, or Chapman and Drayton, or many of them together, that would light heaven with stars.

Nevertheless young Peter was growing as he had begun—very serious-minded although sweet-hearted. But he was against the Court, and some of the company that he was said to keep distressed Nicholas.

They were watching now a game of Blind-man's-buff, Nicholas with his arm around Rosamund's waist. They sat close together on a cushioned settle placed on a slightly raised dais.

The games and dancing took place in the central hall of the house. The four pillars and the balustrades of the wide staircase were wreathed in flowers and gold tissue. In the small gallery at the hall end were the musicians. The black-and-white chequered floor was now covered with laughing Herries.

Janet Herries was blindfolded and her tall bony figure in its crimson dress (too gay for a thin gawky woman) tottered about stretching thin arms and giving cries like a startled hen when she touched bodies and missed them.

Lucy Garland danced around more madly than any. Her curly hair swung against her cheeks. She was mad with pleasure. Her dress was over-decorated with little rosettes of gilt and ribbons that swung about her hips. Yes, she was almost mad with pleasure. Peter was politely talking to old amiable Alicia Turner, who was dressed meanly because Ralph Turner, her husband, was a miser. Everyone knew it and not the least his three sons, Matthew, Paul, and Mark. Turner was a *business* Puritan, that is a City man who went to church three times of a Sunday to do business there. But it was because Alicia Turner looked faded and neglected that Peter Garland was talking with her. And she was pleased—she looked up into his round friendly face with pleasure.

Nicholas' eye was always on one of the three.

'There was a time when I would have played Blind-man as madly as any of them. *I'm* sixty-six. But I don't feel it, wife, I don't feel it. Happy?' he asked her.

She put her hand in his and looked up at him.

'Most happy. And now I will take my son to his bed.'

They both looked to where young Robert Herries, aged ten, was politely playing Blind-man as though he were sixty. It had been found to be impossible to continue calling him Robin. He was *not* Robin, but Robert.

'The Lord be thanked,' Nicholas said, looking down at his young son, 'that Robert has a warm heart. For nothing else is warm in him. And if only one thing is to be warm in a man it had best be his heart. At Westminster School they say his mathematics are a marvel.'

Rosamund laughed. She was standing up. 'Say what you will about him, husband, he is ours and our only one. As he undresses he will tell me a hundred things about our feast to-night that I had not noticed. But when he is in his naked bed he will put up his arms and draw my head to his cheek and quite forget his mathematics.'

Nicholas nodded. 'Aye, he loves you and me and Gilbert. He will make a fortune and will marry a plain maiden with another fortune and then he will beget children on her, not for love, but that he may have sons to make yet other fortunes.'

He pulled her down on to the settle again. 'Wait an instant, my lady. I have the spirit of prophecy strong upon me.'

He laughed—that deep, chuckling, boyish laugh that Rosamund had loved to hear almost since her birth. 'You know that I have come to love these three children of Toby's most dearly. It has been a new life for me and so continues. But do you feel, wife, as I do, that some sort of doom lies about them? Now about your father and you, Rosamund, there never was such a thing, but about Sylvia and Robin always. I know not what it is, but men, I think, are not masters of their fate but only of their character. And for the ripening of that character, with one the circumstances must be tragedy, with another comedy, and with another, as with oneself, ripeness, which is everything, comes late, almost at the last. Robin's tragedy was necessary, that he and Sylvia and I—all must ripen. . . . Yes, and Philip too. Who knows?

'Peter was telling us yesternight that he was at the Mermaid a week back and that Shakespeare, the writer of plays, was close by him. This Shakespeare is a plump, merry, kindly man who puts plays together for his manager, a man, it seems, handy and quick, but of no great talent, but always with a kindly word and a generous hand. Jonson, who is his friend, mocks him and he takes it in excellent part. But Peter says there are times when Shakespeare is grave and sees deeply into things, and then Jonson and Drayton and the others listen with open ears.

'So it was the other night, when a lad of the place had stolen silver pieces from Drayton's pocket. The lad, in his terror, fell at Shakespeare's feet and Shakespeare gave Drayton his silver pieces and went away with the lad, no one knew whither. And Peter said that no one stayed him, or thought to stay him, as they went out—and ten minutes before that Shakespeare had been bobbing for cherries in a bowl. A week later the lad stole again, and he hanged himself, for, as he said on a paper, he could not meet Mr. Shakespeare's eyes. . . . I feel something, Rosamund, about these three children. Rashleigh could be a king among men, but he will give his life, as Robin did, for a notion. My Lucy is so mad for life that she will destroy herself as a moth in the flame. Peter will serve the State to his own destruction. I love them so dearly that I might have begotten them.'

'Not on Barbara's body,' Rosamund said, laughing. She had never been one to believe in prophecies, fortune-tellings, or anyone's overhanging doom. But she thought, as she looked at him with loving eyes, that in his old age he was catching some of his brother Robin's spirit. Perhaps not. It had always been his way to love with all his heart, even though his love for her was something different from that.

She went to fetch her son. He watched her as she went down into the hall, moving with that assured sensible compactness that was so especially hers. The dignity, the wisdom that she had! He reflected on the different kinds of love there were in the world, and his heart warmed, his eyes filled with tears (was he not by years an old man?) as he considered that perhaps, in the end, it would be this love that would be the strongest of them all. With no other human being had he ever been such a comrade, for Catherine he had never attained and in Robin there had been always a world that he could not enter, and for Gilbert Armstrong he felt something more or less than comradeship.

But Rosamund was his comrade. She knew him as no one else had ever known him. When, even at the first, he had held her in his arms, he had not felt that he had heaven there, he had not lost himself in any ecstasy, but he had known that he was secure and comforted and reassured.

This was the best in marriage, and the most enduring. He watched her as she moved among their guests. Blind-man was now ended. The musicians played softly. Rosamund stayed here a little and there a little. Young Robert moved towards her and now they were returning together, Robert looking as though he guarded her.

Nicholas was proud of his son as he watched him, of his sturdy bearing, his good manners, his assurance that was never impertinence. His hand was on his little sword; the long hair that was the fashion, even for children, became him. His long plum-coloured coat fitted his body handsomely. Nicholas could wish that he were taller and that in his eyes there might be some fire instead of that considering shrewdness. But there! no man, or child either, could be everything!

The boy knelt down and received his father's blessing. Then he went upstairs to bed. Most children would have protested, for all the best of the evening was to come, but Robert knew that he would do nothing with protests. Already he had learned the lesson of never wasting words. Nicholas, alone now, considered his kind-ironic view of his guests, of his relations.

He considered the three Turner boys, Matthew, Paul, and Mark. Poor boys! He knew very well what they were feeling, that they were conscious of their shabby clothes and their dowdy mother. He knew that Paul, an intelligent young man, and ambitious, hated his father. But Paul would make his way. Already he had some small humble office in the business of Cecil's secretary. He would not stay there. Mark was a loose lubberly young man, something of a rake and a glutton, though there were signs that he might mend.

But Matthew was the interesting one. Matthew, who was little with a large head, was dressed from head to foot in a faded black. He wore no sword. His forehead was noble, his eyes bright as stars. He was a strange creature with a stutter, a sharp, ironic tongue, and a passion for letters. He lived in a small upstairs room near the Strand. He read all night, so it was said, had a mistress as shabby as himself, starved without grumbling, and had friends of the queerest kind, cut-throats, pickpockets, bear-minders—and they all loved him. Such was his reputation.

Why had he come to-night? Nicholas felt that perhaps he would go and speak to this strange creature when someone caught his eye. This was Carey Courthope, the son of the James for whom this fine party was given. Carey was near thirty and, in Nicholas' opinion, would be better out of the world than in it. He was exceedingly handsome and, in the view of many, a finer man than Rashleigh. His body had poise and litheness; his hair, which fell in thick curls to his collar, was of a radiant blackness. He dressed with extravagance and always in the latest fashion. To-night he was ahead of the fashion in a crimson

coat with a vest of patterned purple silk. His breeches were less bom-
basted than was current. He wore earrings and his face was delicately
painted, a habit only just beginning. His eyes and mouth were weak.
His vanity was apparent in every breath he drew. Nicholas knew that
he was causing his father, the worthy James, much distress.

Even as Nicholas watched him he moved across the floor, well
aware that eyes were upon him for his handsomeness, and stopped
beside Lucy who, for a moment, was alone, and very hot and rather
dishevelled, fanned herself with her handkerchief.

Nicholas was to realize afterwards, when he looked back, that at the
moment when Carey spoke to the girl he, as though to protect her,
slipped down from the dais and moved towards them.

His movement was instinctive, an impulse within himself telling
him that he must go, and when he discovered himself between them
he had nothing to say. What he wanted to say was—to the girl, 'Go
and find my wife. Tidy yourself. Wipe the sweat off your forehead.
Two of those ridiculous rosettes are half torn from your dress.'

But he could say nothing, because the pleasure in her eyes was so
great that he could not dream of quenching it. She caught his arm and
he put his thick strong hand over hers, which was damp with perspiration.

'You are heated. You will catch a rheum.' But he laughed even as
he was speaking because she was laughing. Nevertheless he tried to
draw her away with his hand. 'Now come, Rosamund is seeing the
child to his bed. There will be no games before supper, and after
supper I have a surprise.'

'A surprise? Oh, by Jesu, I love a surprise! What surprise? A hobby-
horse, a pig with two faces, a bucket that turns from leather into gold
as you look, a masque with Psyche watching Cupid by the light of a
candle . . .' She sprang a little on her heels and clapped her hands.
'What care I so long as there is dancing? Dancing! I could dance into
the middle of next week.'

'That is why I came.' Carey, who had not yet spoken, interrupted.
'The first of the dances after supper. . . .'

'I believe the boy's in love with her,' Nicholas thought, with extreme
distaste. He looked at Carey, at the earrings of tiny pearls, at the faint
colour on the cheek, and the redder colour on the lips, neither of them
natural, and at that clear, undoubted beauty—a beauty weak, selfish,

but to a certain kind of woman irresistible. Was it so to her? He looked at her and feared that it might be, or was this a general joy sprung from her eagerness for life?

She was lovely with the intensity of her appreciation of life rather than with any actual beauty. Her dark curls glistened with the heat. Her mouth, a little large, was parted and the lips glistened. Her breasts heaved as though they would burst the bonds of the over-decorated dress. He felt her eagerness, her helplessness, her defence-lessness. 'Why, why,' he cried, as so many before him, 'has time passed so remorselessly?' But his hand closed on the gold hilt of his rapier— a gesture, although she did not know it, of protection. Carey felt, perhaps, her appreciation of him, or at least he was accustomed to be admired. He was completely cool, at his ease and self-satisfied. But was there, Nicholas wondered, something also in him unprotected, defenceless? He was foolish rather than wicked, and Nicholas felt the more indignant that the girl should notice him. Someone else had joined them. A gentle, stuttering voice said:

'Once upon a time, at Greenwich, four mighty Earls, of Lennox, Montgomery, Pembroke, and Arundel, offered the world a challenge to deny these prop-propositions.

'That in service of Ladies no Knight hath free will. That it is B-Beauty maintaineth the world in valour—that no fair Lady was ever false. That none can be perfectly wise but Lovers.'

Nicholas, looking at this young man, in his black faded suit, wondered that he could be so unconcerned—but there was nobility in that brow, sadness, and much considering wisdom. He liked Matt Turner, liked him so much that he now put his hand on the sharp bony shoulder, and the boy looked at him with a smile so sweet that he was still further won.

'That no fair lady was ever false?' Nicholas cried. 'Why, Matt, that is the greatest falsity!'

But Lucy broke in. 'Matt—will you dance with me the first dance after supper?' His cheek flushed. As he stood there, his thin black legs close together, he looked like a gentle, kindly scarecrow.

'Cousin, I d-dance abominably.'

Carey said, his voice shaking a little, 'You promised *me* that.'

Nicholas thought: 'This beautiful young man with the earrings is not clever. He cannot hide chagrin.'

Lucy said: 'I am a lady. I wish to prove myself false. I had promised you, Carey, but now I shall dance it with Matthew.' She pulled at Nicholas' arm.

'I know what a sweat I am in. Let us go and find Rosamund.'

But they did not get so far. At the corner of the first flight of stairs there was an alcove, with a cushioned settle. Lucy pulled Nicholas down on it, threw her arms around him and kissed him. She began to put herself to rights, talking as she did so. 'You think I am ill dressed. As you always do. I think you are right and I would wish to know why things are so handsome before I touch them.'

'Because you are always in a hurry,' Nicholas told her.

'I am in a hurry because I grow like the phoenix. Or is it some other bird? I must question Matt Turner. But this week we return to Seascale and then I shall be reading Eutropius with Mr. Mangin, riding Dapple, and asking young Mr. Senhouse—"And pray, Mr. Senhouse, how is your new madrigal?"—and he will then sing it to me, in a voice half cracked, like a door in the wind. I shall be there many months and the boys will *not* be there and the best entertainment will be a bull-baiting or a cock-fighting—and I am twenty!'

'You are to come next year to London.'

'Oh, I would not be for ever in London. I would not be for ever in any place. But why is it, Cousin Nick, I must for ever be doing! "Now think first!" says my mother, and "Think first!" says my father, and "Think first!" says——'

'Cousin Nicholas. And for why? Because living is dangerous. There are perils at every turn.'

'I wish life to be dangerous!' she cried, her eyes flashing. 'I would have it all, all! Pressed down into my lap—here!'

'One mistake and the wrong road! So it was with your aunt Sylvia. She married a villain, but loved a saint.'

'If *I* married a villain that would be no tragedy, for as soon as I knew him for a villain I would take his hair and tear it from its roots, and I would defend my saint.'

' 'Tis none so easy!' He took her hand and held it very lightly. 'I will tell you something. I love you as though you were my daughter. I am at the end of my life. I have had, in it, most things I would wish— all save one. But now, recovering it, I cannot discern its meaning. My brother spoke, sometimes, of the bright pavilions in Heaven which he would one day reach. Maybe he is in them now. I never cared for anything I could not touch nor see. I am such a man. But I do at least know that life has a meaning, and if it has been hid from me I would wish you to have something of Robin's vision, for that, I fancy, is where reality lies.'

She shook her head. 'I am like you, Cousin Nicholas. I will love and ride and bear children—and then, in the inglenook, be a wise old woman at the last. But not yet, not yet!'

'How wise are you?' He looked intently into her merry eager face. 'Of those two, Carey and Matthew,—which do you prefer?'

'Why, there's a question! And the answer is neither, for Carey is only for play and poor Matthew has no laces to his breeches.'

'Carey is dangerous.'

'Not to me! Oh, I could worry a dozen such Careys! When I want a line of Eutropius I go to Matthew.'

They were silent a little while, then Nicholas said:

'There are the trumpets for supper. You know I would live to be a hundred and fifty to see you secure.' He sighed. 'I like not the times. We have lost our guide. Men are no longer as simple as they were. Now they are all men of opinions. Once they were all for the Queen and for England. Now one is for the Communion Table to be shifted t'other end of the church, another is for the King to have money only when Parliament allows it, one is for the Netherlands, another for Spain. But no man is for England only. . . .'

'And I am for you,' she cried, throwing her arms around him and kissing him. 'When I find such a man as you I will marry, but not before.'

He felt as though he could not let her go, as though as soon as he released her she would slip into a nest of dangers. He realized that when you are old and love the young, you are quite helpless, for they cannot go your way and would not if they could. But at the top of the stairs they were laughing again.

'After supper there will be my surprise.'

'Whisper it.'

'Do you remember three years back a conjurer came to your house—a conjurer with a little girl.'

She thought. Then she clapped her hands.

'Why, yes! He had a big nose and a red cloak.'

'I have found him again. He is coming to-night.'

'He made flowers fall through the air . . .'

'Hush! . . . It is to be a surprise.'

In his heart he was not at all sure about his grand 'surprise'—but he was not going to say so!

It had been all a matter of impulse. Three days before, walking not far from the boundaries of Alsatia, he had witnessed the chase of a man suspected of being a Jesuit priest. The crowd had been stopped by a man in a fine hat and a velvet cloak who had with considerable courage harangued the people while the fugitive escaped. He had waved his hand at the crowd and the crowd had stopped and listened, whether it wished or no.

Nicholas, who had stayed at the crowd edge amused by the affair, discovered that this was his old friend Dom Ferdinand Christian of three years before. He would have known him in any case because of the humpbacked boy who watched his master with the old almost fervent devotion.

'Good-day to you,' said Nicholas. Dom Christian took off his hat with a grand flourish. He looked very much more prosperous than he had been. No shabby red cloak but handsome velvet, and his silken laces at his breeches were the brightest orange. He also wore elaborate earrings, circles of jet with little gold centres.

He was stouter but his face was as white and pockmarked, his nose as monstrous, his eyes as lidded.

Nicholas asked him as to his affairs. Oh, they were merry! The King had commanded him to Court to show his fancies and had laughed most heartily at the trick of the Naked Negro Boy and the Serpent in the Apple.

Nicholas, slipping aside to avoid the mud-splash from one of the new fandangle coaches, put his hand on Dom Christian's arm. It was as hard and as indifferent as cold steel. Dom Christian swayed a little on his feet, as though he were not yet properly awake, twitched his gloved fingers, and produced between them a silver comfit-box. He offered Nicholas a sugared jelly, and on Nicholas refusing it popped it into his own large mouth. Nicholas thought how satisfactory it must be to have sugared jellies hanging in mid-air when you wanted them —that is, if you cared for sugared jellies!

On the spur of this incident he invited Dom Christian to perform at his party, enquired his fee, told him the position of his house in Westminster, and went his way.

But now that the Herries family, seated or standing in his hall, awaited the magician, he was not sure of his wisdom. Rosamund had been very doubtful—

'The King is set against witches.'

'My beloved, this man has himself entertained His Majesty with the trick of the Naked Negro Boy.'

'If he tries so indecent a trick here, Alicia and Constance (and after all our celebration is *given* for James), Janet and Martha, they will all summon their conveyances, whatever they may be, and hurry home. The mere thought of a naked man is too much for them.'

'This is not a man but a boy. Besides, that is but the name of the trick. There may be no nakedness.'

For that was the trouble. He was not sure of his magician. The affair had been, until this, a wonderful success. At supper they had all drunk so much that now the waiting hall was chattering like an aviary. Janet Herries' monkey climbed on to Alicia Turner's shoulder and she screamed with horror. Nicholas looked over them all. He saw all the young men—Rashleigh, Peter, Carey, Somerset—standing together surveying the scene with some of the proud confidence of youth. Paul and Mark Turner sat, not too comfortably, by their mother. Matthew stood apart, not far from the dais.

When Dom Christian appeared there was a little drawn 'Ah!' from the company. He was dressed in cloth of gold and was spangled with silver stars. He carried a wand that terminated in a star. But it was not he that had stirred the wonder. It was his daughter. A child of not more than nine or ten, she was in common black, her shoulders bare. She was beautiful then, as she was afterwards, not because of the perfect colour and shape of her face, the symmetry of her body, but because of the spirit that shone through these beauties—her scorn and contempt that even now as a child she showed for everyone, her courage and independence, her loneliness, a loneliness of which she was proud. She had even then, as afterwards she had so abundantly, the power to draw all eyes.

'By the passion of Christ,' Nicholas said to himself, 'how that child despises us!'

The murmuring had died. Dom Christian began his magic. The

humpbacked boy produced a wicker basket. The basket was empty.
Dom Christian waved his wand and there was a French poodle jumping out of it. That was nothing. Every magician did the same. He
threw out his arms. Doves flew from them. They rested on the
shoulders of the girl, who was staring into the crowd as though she
would destroy them with a thunderbolt. The doves flew back into the
basket. This was nothing. Every magician could do the same. Then
everyone perceived that Janet Herries' monkey was in great agitation.
He chattered, scratched his head, and, quite suddenly, swung himself
along from pediment and pillar until, before anyone could stop him,
he was on the dais and perched in the middle of the table. He picked
up the white cone and put it on his head, then with a leap he was on
the magician's shoulder.

Everyone laughed and waited to see what the magician would do.
But, alas, no one was ever able to tell afterwards what the magician
did do!

'Nothing!' Constance Courthope declared indignantly to James in
their big four-poster afterwards. 'Nothing at all! A celebration of your
birthday! I stared. I even repeated the Lord's Prayer, for I will confess
to some fear. But I need not . . . I need not, indeed. . . . Only Janet's
monkey pulled the girl's hair . . .'

'Indeed it did not!' James said sleepily. 'The necromantic thing . . .
the necromantic thing'—he could scarce keep his eyes open—'was that
the stars on the man's coat separated themselves, dancing . . .' But he
was asleep, snoring.

It was not, however, at all so fanciful a matter. It was simply that
these Herries looked imaginatively where their fancy led them.
Matthew, leaning against the wall, feeling its cold impress against the
worn stuff of his sleeve, dreamed of the great things to do.

> But with an armed and resolved hand
> I'll strip the ragged follies of the time
> Naked as at their birth.

The works, the works! He saw himself another Jonson, the crowd
surging round him after such a play as *The Poetaster,* and the anger
about Captain Tucca who, with his lewdness and crawling cowardice,
had insulted all the ragged half-pay captains of Alsatia. No matter the
insults, the flying cabbages, the cat-calls!

'Make way! Make way here! 'Tis Matthew Turner, the writer of plays. Matthew Turner, the writer of epics. Matthew Turner, the lovely cozener of beautiful words. . . .' And the sun shines out above St. Paul's while the current of dirty water runs iridescent through the twisting streets and the honest booksellers by the church nudge and whisper: 'That is he! There he goes! Matt Turner! The only and rare Matt Turner! . . .'

Near to him the beautiful face of Rashleigh lightens with its dream. He had all but retired when he heard the magician announced. It was not magic that he needed but rather to strike, from the dark and twisted Court, a weapon so bright that the Crown of England might glitter and shine again before the world. He would lift it up. Oh! he would lift it up! There should be a King in his own future time, who would challenge his city-mongering, prayer-caterwauling, coin-grabbing enemies, and ride, all his servants behind him, on to the Hill of Splendour. . . . The Divine Right! The Divine Right! To fight for it, to die for it if need be! And Rashleigh stared at the magician, whose ugly nose and pocked cheek were beautiful in the great world that they prophesied.

Ralph Turner, in his decent party suit of grey, saw the air shining with coins. As the magician caught the light with the diamond on his finger Ralph Turner drew in his breath, for his lean quivering fingers dived into the bag, and as they dived the coins came tumbling down, falling on to his dried skin, and then he plunged his hands deep down among all those golden pieces. He felt their chill, their multiplicity, and his palms were piled with them, his fingers curved about them.

Carey also saw the body of the magician bend courteously towards him, and there were wonderful promises whispered to him—the naked bodies of beautiful girls and the wine in the flagon sparkling ruby-red before the leaping flame of the fire—clothes, clothes, wonderful clothes with colours most subtly blended and the jewelled buttons hard to the touch, and he walking, the well-beloved, the admired of all observers, across the shining floor of Whitehall, and the shambling King turning, catching sight of him with his little bright eyes, shuffling towards him . . .

And Martha Herries, whom nobody considered, having at last her little house—her little house with the decent man and the submissive maid, the rich settle and the handsome chest, the wood shining in the firelight, the parrot from the Indies of green and red in its cage, and the ladies entering, the envious, covetous ladies, taking their places while she, in her rich velvet, listened to their requests and felt her power, her power that she had never had, beating through the room.

Peter also had his vision—vision of justice and equity. An England where every man had his rights, where in a glorious Parliament the meanest voice might be heard and the humblest prayer answered. The magician seemed to promise him that. The magician and the child beside him, growing before his eyes, as she had done before, into a woman so lovely that he sighed and leaned forward.

For the spell was broken. The humpbacked boy was collecting the things from the table. They were moving, talking, saying their farewells.

Only one thing more. As Peter neared the dais the child, of her own will, came to him. She smiled; the scorn was gone from her eyes. 'I remember you. You lifted me in your arms and kissed me.'

He laughed. 'You have grown, Katherine.'

'You remember my name?'

She *was* now only a child, bending to ease the pressure of her shoe, with a little sigh such as a child makes, then straightening herself again.

'And what is *your* name?' she asked.

'Peter Garland.'

'Oh, I am so tired!' She rubbed her eyes with the back of her hand.

'Are you hungry? I could find you something——'

'No, I am not. My father is waiting for me.'

She gave him her hand very ceremoniously and he kissed it.

Later, when all the Herries were on their backs or their sides, asleep, in the dark hall, on the dais, a white cone of stiff paper lay like a little ghost.

KATHERINE: BIRTHDAY REMINISCENCE

KATHERINE CHRISTIAN, on an early spring day in 1616, this being the morning of her sixteenth birthday, sat in the Bird-cage house in the Strand thinking back, with considerable humour, malice, and good temper, over her past life.

For some years now she and her father had been in good state, living in a little house with a pretty garden on the river above Westminster. No Alsatia, or even threat of Alsatia, for him during the last five years! This had been largely because of their Court connections, her father having become a very firm friend of Lady Frances Howard who had married Robert Carr, the Earl of Somerset, in the year 1613.

This very grand connection had meant that there was no more of the old travelling about up and down England with the old tricks of the paper cone, the falling flowers, and the rest.

They were by far too grand for that now. Grand and not so grand. Frances Howard, the lovely, the exquisite, mixed in strange company. She was often to be seen in the Christians' riverside house, shut up in a room with Dom Christian, Dr. Pengelly, and Anne Turner, the procuress. It was Anne Turner who had two rooms at the top of this house of the Bird-cages in the Strand. She had also other resorts.

Katherine had never asked what Anne Turner, her father, Frances Howard, and Dr. Pengelly did together in the dark shuttered room by the river. Only, when she entered it after their departure, she sniffed the scent of incense, cat's fur, burnt wax, and heartily disliked it.

She had her opinions of Frances Howard and Anne Turner; she cordially detested both the exquisite saint-like beauty and the evil silent beauty of the procuress, but long, long ago she had learned to allow neither likes nor dislikes to affect her personal balance. She was armoured in scornful indifference.

Life had made her so. Now on this her sixteenth birthday, as she sat at the window of the Bird-cage house while her father was upstairs with Anne Turner, the beauty that would one day be so famous was already fully apparent.

It is interesting and peculiar that the few allusions to her in contemporary journals, histories, or biographies give us little detail in support of that generally acknowledged loveliness. There is a letter of Elizabeth Claypole's, Cromwell's daughter, that speaks of her (*Thurloe State Papers*) as 'dark and burning.' In *The Merchants' Remonstrance,* 'the beautiful lady' can be no other than she. In *The Calendar of State Papers* (*Venetian*) she is spoken of by name and called 'exquisite.' And there is an account of her arrival in Oxford in Lady Campden's *Oxford Treasure.*

But nothing of either present or future fame mattered to her as she sat on this April morning looking through the open window at the business in the Strand below. All about her was an almost deafening chorus of bird-twittering, for the sun was shining and the birds were greeting it. All down the wall of the lower half of the house were many gilded bird-cages. Inside these and many other cages in the open shop below were every sort of variety of bird from huge hooded falcons, enormous black crows, to the tiniest purple and gold-winged miniatures. Colours flashed and flamed—orange, gold, crimson, sapphire—as the tiny birds swung on their little perches or preened their necks, or quarrelled or flew from gilded bar to gilded bar.

In the soft spring breeze the cages swung ever so slightly and the whole loud chorus was an overtone to the rumbling and rattling of wagon wheels and coach-wheels as they trundled over the cobbles of the crowded street below.

Katherine, who knew that her father's interviews with Anne Turner were ever lengthy, thought this an excellent occasion for reminiscence. This was her sixteenth birthday. Her father was at the moment unaware of it, but before they left that house he would be made conscious of it, for she had something to say to him.

She had been preparing what she had to say for a long time now and had always intended her sixteenth birthday to be the occasion of it.

The elements of her beauty were as evident now as they would ever be, although she was wearing a plain dress of dark gold colour and no ornaments whatever. Her hair, that fell in ringlets to her shoulders, was of a peculiar darkness. Those black depths had in them a softness and intensity of colour for which richness was a poor word. Her face now was thin and sharp, her complexion pale, her eyes dark and lambent. Her body was also thin, her small breasts firm and strong, her limbs perfectly formed. The expression of her eyes was bold, challenging, her mouth scornful. It was clear that she feared nobody. But when, for an instant, she turned to glance at the birds in their cages, all her features softened into good-humour and even tenderness. She was almost a woman, but as she swung her long legs behind her dark gold gown, humming a little broken tune, there was still something of a child in her.

She looked back over her life as it had so far gone.

She was born, within Alsatia, on April 10, 1600, her mother dying in childbirth.

Her first conscious memory was of a man grimly murdered, and of this she would retain the details, both of sight and sound, so long as she lived.

She was an infant of four years and it was evening. In the room where she was there was an old black bed where she and her father slept, pitched in the room's far corner. The room had a crucifix, a high, grimy stone fireplace, a table, and a stool. She remembered the colours in that room, for over one corner of it was a torn red curtain with fragments of gold stuff, and piled against the wall a green box with brass nails, a gilt wand, and a white cone. She was alone in the room and asleep.

She woke to the sound of men's voices outside the door. These did not disturb her at all, for she was well accustomed to any kind of noise. She thought it was her father. Often he would come with friends and they would sit at the table, drinking and singing. She had already trained herself to sleep during any noise that they would make. She knew that when her father was there she could come to no harm. In any case, from her very earliest hour she had an utterly fearless spirit.

So when she heard these voices, she turned with a little sigh and settled herself to sleep again. A moon was shining in through the window and there was a moth-green light in the room.

When the men roughly entered she turned to see whether her father was among them. But he was not. There were two men who were pulling a third by the collar, his legs dragging on the floor. One of the men was laughing, and she thought that they were playing a game. One man was tall and thin, with a black beard, the other small and pockmarked. The man whom they were dragging was very fat.

The two threw the other on the floor and stood away, looking at him. The man with the beard laughed no longer and there was no sound save the snuffled breathing of the fat man on the floor, who lay in a thin pool of moonlight.

The man with the black beard began to talk, angrily, contemptuously. Katherine held herself tight against the wall without moving lest they should see her. She was in shadow.

Then the fat man pulled himself on to his knees and began with little gasps to utter broken words. He was in terrible distress and tears began to trickle down his cheek.

Then the bearded man ordered him to get up, which he did, and he stood there swaying on his fat trembling legs. The bearded man looked at him intently, quite suddenly caught him by the collar, swung him round, and made a plunge with his arm at his quilted back. The fat man wore a dress of light green. The man then turned towards the bed where Katherine was. She saw his eyes, very wide-open, puzzled and frightened. Then they closed as though he were going to pray.

Quite suddenly there came a gurgle from his throat and a great rush of dark blood poured from his mouth. It seemed as though it never would be done. Then he pitched with a soft thud to the floor and lay there on his face, his legs twitching and one arm spread out in the pool of blood.

The small pock-faced man bent down and felt in his clothes; without another word said, the two men picked him up and carried him out between them; they carefully closed the door behind them.

There was nothing unusual in the room then but the pool of blood which moved a little in the moonlight and afterwards lay still.

When her father came in and saw the pool of blood he was very angry. She was not, she remembered, at all frightened. She had the sense then, as she had always, that no one could harm her if she did not wish. When her father beat her, she told herself that the pain had nothing to do with herself and it had not.

She did not love her father—she loved no one—but from her very earliest years she had a sort of comradeship with him.

From the beginning of their life together he made her share in his magic, which always seemed quite natural to her. She realized, when she was only a baby, that he could make people see things that were not there, but oddly enough he had never that power over herself. She thought people great fools because they thought they saw flowers or birds or boxes. At the same time he taught her every kind of sleight of hand so that she became most adept, but she always despised these accomplishments. They had no attraction for her. He was in some ways very tender for her, allowing her no contact with the women who were his mistresses; no man might ever put a hand on her nor address rude words to her.

She liked his indifference to everything and everybody and shared in it. The two things he liked best were drink and sleep, but sometimes he would talk and talk to her and, although she did not for some years understand what he said, she appreciated that he should treat her seriously.

II

Although they were companions, she studied him quite dispassionately. She had seen him in every possible form, action, and gesture —naked, clothed, half clothed, furious with drink, with rage, with pride, bored—bored so that he could do nothing but yawn and yawn and yawn, hungry so that he ate like an animal, kind so that in bed he would gather her to his stone-cold breast and murmur to her baby endearments, arrogant and conceited so that he would strut before a smoked cracked mirror patting his bare arms and clapping his hams in a kind of ecstasy of self-indulgence, talking most learnedly to some old stinking worthy in a peaked black hat, playing jokes, like a boy, with his magic, thinking out new tricks and hypnotizing the humpbacked adoring boy, John Pickering, who worshipped him, making him strip and crawl on the floor thinking he was a bear, and asking him whether it were a crow he saw on the ceiling or a dish-clout or a lady's garter. Then he would laugh and laugh until the tears hopped on his big white nose.

And sometimes he was sinister. That would be when he would sit over a table with Anne Turner and another or two and they would mix powders, little quivering stamens of blue smoke would rise, thin glass bottles would gurgle as blue, red, green, or colourless liquids filled their throats.

Nevertheless her father was not much of a preoccupation. From the very first she had a life of her own. In her earliest days they lived very shabbily—in such a room, for example, as the one in Alsatia where the man was stabbed. But that was all the same to Katherine. She could always suit herself exactly to her circumstances. Poor or rich, bare or furnished, hungry or fed, cold or warm, there was nothing she could not endure, nothing she could not enjoy. From babyhood she was made free of the London streets and now, her whole life long, she was to enjoy them!

Now, as no more than a baby, she shared in all the sights, sounds, smells, accidents, crimes, triumphs, and sculdudderies. She would toddle out into the mud to watch with open mouth some remnant of the train-bands marching along with a drum and a tattered flag, the men drinking out of their cans as they passed, some lathered with mud, some with ragged gold lace and a feather in the hat; some clipt to prancing horses riding as though horse and man were one, some laughing and some drunk and some making obscene motions, some singing and some cursing—she stood, finger in mouth, watching them go by. Or a riot of the apprentices, men rushing from the shops belabouring one another with anything that was to hand, shouting and crying their cries, and twenty of them marching down the street at once to meet another twenty, and, when they met, what a smashing of heads and a running of blood and women hiding behind doorways and masters cursing and the happy adventurer stealing a thing or two while nobody was looking!

Or it might be a hobby-horse procession with a tawdry Queen in a bent and battered crown riding on a mud-bespattered horse, and the Fools with their prancing hobby-horses and the ass with his ears silvered and the mountebank turning somersaults in the mud.

Or it might be, and perhaps best of all, a procession to Tyburn, with the condemned tied on the drawn trestles and the crowd throwing stones and women crying. . . .

Whatever it might be, there was always movement and stench and bustle, with the smells malodorous, stomach-tickling, damp-ridden, rat-poisoned, flower-fragrant (as with roses, carnations, sweet-williams), and the voices crying and shouting, cursing and kissing, singing and bewailing, and all the bodies, fat, thin, tall, short, covered with this excess of linen and cotton and wool, sweating and panting and pushing and straining and loving and kicking—Katherine was accustomed to it all, loving it, holding herself apart from it but belonging to it, tumbling about it like a little kitten, nobody caring whether she lived or died, unless it were her father.

Until she was in her sixth or seventh year she had never been in the country. Then the three of them, her father, herself, and John Pickering, set out upon that wonderful journey to Scotland that was to change their fortunes. She had never been in the country before and for a long while she could not accustom herself to the silence. They found many means of conveyance, for everywhere they went they had a wonderful welcome. The English people had a great liking for the simple and more decent kinds of magic, and when Dom Christian discovered a gold egg in a leathern pocket or a sprig of rosemary in an old maid's ear there was no end to the shouts and cries of jubilation.

Katherine herself was the centre of admiration, for she was a beautiful baby.

She had wonderful poise and self-possession for so small a child. The inns at which they stopped for the night were noisy places. Her father had never any anxiety for her. He used to call her the Queen. Her mother had been 'whom he knew not.' He had been legally wed to her—she was serving at an inn in Eastcheap when he first saw her, a slight, delicate, shy creature who would not submit to him unless he married her. So marry her he did. He loved her in his own fashion, but she never belonged to him any more than his child did. He believed her to be of fine birth. She came, she said, from Devon and was related to the Raleighs—her mother had died when she was an infant and her father had sailed with Drake and never returned. She had been ruined at the age of eighteen by one of Essex's men returning from Ireland. She was but twenty when he married her. He used to wonder why she would not tell him the name of her family—she was ashamed, perhaps. He did not care.

She died in giving Katherine birth, but rather of languor and indifference than birth-pangs. When she discovered the sort of ruffian and villain he was and how ill-judged her love had been (which she did in the first week of their marriage), she just let herself die.

Dom Christian knew nothing of his own ancestry. He had been found in a barn and bred to every sort of perversity and wickedness by an old doctor who lived in Islington. This old doctor, Ephraim Christian, was as wicked a man as ever breathed but learned and gay. He had a perverse love for Christian and taught him many a trick, also some useful knowledge.

He discovered that the boy had hypnotic powers and hoped to make great use of him, but he died breathing by mistake one of his own poisons.

For a while young Christian was the kept boy of a shopkeeper in the Strand, who beat him and kissed him all at once and together. Then Christian broke away and lived on his wits, magical wits.

Such was the history of Katherine's father and mother. Christian told people that she was the daughter of a great Court lady who had married him secretly and died. You could believe it when you saw Katherine moving. She walked like a baby duchess. She was so fearless that no rough soldier or country man attempted any rudeness with her.

There came the day when she saw for the first time the sea. It was the same day when they acted in Tobias Garland's courtyard and she was kissed by Peter Garland.

Her first glimpse of that wonder was when they came out on the road from Kendal to the sea-road by Black Combe. It was splendid weather of blue and gold, and the sea lazily moved on the bright stretch of sand as though it slept. She was mounted on the donkey and she stared out over the sand-dunes as though she could never have enough. The combination of the smooth dark shoulder of Black Combe, the yellow sand, and this green-purple lazy sea caught her heart as it had never been caught before. She was wedded to this country from that instant. Over and over again in her later life she would describe it.

'I had never heard of the sea. My father had never spoken of it. I knew that men went across the sea to fight the Spaniards, but it was the Spaniards, not the sea, that I figured. The silence! The whole world has never been silent like that again. The only sound was the sea whispering. I loved it. I knew love for the first time. I could have run over the banks of sand and bended down and kissed it. I held the donkey's ears and would have stayed there for ever. Behind me the mountains, in front of me the sea. Cleansing! It washed me clean, for I had been always in dirty rooms and filthy inns and foul beds. I wished not to move. I could have stayed there for evermore.'

But of course she had to move, and she moved into Toby Garland's ground and was kissed by Peter Garland. This, as it turned out, was the second event of her life. She did not know it then, but she remembered it. That boy's was the pleasantest face her baby heart had ever known. She remembered the round cheeks and the kindly eyes and the soft touch of his lips. She thought of him afterwards and wondered whether she would ever see him again. She looked for him sometimes in the streets of London. Then she saw him again at Nicholas' feast. She was older now, but once again she thought his was the pleasantest, most honest, most kindly face she had yet seen. He became for her the type of uprightness and honesty, although she made no attempt to see him anywhere and did not perhaps wish that she should. He was a symbol for her.

At length, on this journey, they reached Edinburgh, and it was there that Dom Christian's fortunes changed. He met in that beautiful and very smelly city a certain Sir Alexander Canslie. This gentleman, whom later in London Katherine was to see with frequency, was thin to ludicrousness, with a fine red Roman nose and bushy pepper-and-salt eyebrows.

He had been long a dabbler in magic and spent much of his wealth over necromantic absurdities. For Dom Christian he became an easy victim. When he travelled down to London he took the Christians with him, and an absurd journey it was with Christian and Sir Alexander locked into inn chambers and producing smells, blue lights, and black poppies, so that, had it not been for Sir Alexander's wealth, they might have found considerable trouble.

Sir Alexander had a certain power at Court, being an old acquaintance of the King's, who, although he pursued witches with fanatical hatred, had, as that hatred showed, enough superstition to be interested in an experiment or two.

So the Christian fortunes expanded, and after a year or so the little house in Chelsea village was their home. A queer little place it was, embedded in dark trees and the rooms hung with dark-green hangings. An excellent rendezvous it was for any two or three who wished for secret visitings.

Early in the year 1613 Katherine, coming in with a basket of provisions and passing quickly through the green-lit parlour, saw, sitting in the shadow, a veiled lady. The veiled lady stopped her and, raising her veil, revealed herself as the most lovely human being Katherine had ever seen. She was lovely in everything, hair, features, and delicacy of body. She had a most sweet voice and she took the child of thirteen by the hand and made her sit beside her and paid her compliments on her beauty, and sighed and talked wildly of her unhappy life, and at last kissed Katherine on the eyes and on the mouth.

But Katherine, who was always sharp to detect any falsity, did not like her and thought her eyes had a sly look and the lines of her mouth a cruel tightness.

Her father came in and seemed anything but pleased that the lady should have discovered his daughter. When Katherine asked as to her identity, Christian told her. She was the beautiful and famous Countess of Essex.

After this there were many visitors at the Chelsea house. There was a sorcerer who could make the dead walk and women turn into bats. There was constantly present the only one of them Katherine had any liking for, Mr. Richard Weston. A man, Franklin. Most unpleasant of all, Anne Turner, the procuress.

Anne Turner was the most famous procuress in London. Everyone knew her. She could procure for young men at the Court or old misers in the Strand or hearty country gentlemen up in London for a fortnight's holiday, anything or anybody.

Katherine loathed her. Here for once the child departed out of her cynical indifference and allowed her feelings to be engaged. She felt always that Anne Turner looked on her with a speculative eye. She hated to be touched by her. The woman knew that the child hated her, but never relaxed her soft, smiling, sinewy ways towards her.

Katherine knew well that in this Chelsea house she was surrounded by the powers of darkness. It did not seem at all strange to her that the sorcerer should talk with the Devil. The Devil was always just round the corner in that green-shadowed little house.

She was afraid neither of the Devil nor of his accomplices, but she was during these years often lonely. She thought at times of that kindly fresh-cheeked boy who had kissed her in Cumberland. Her only friend during these years was poor hunchbacked John, who still persisted in his adoration of her father until, one night, he saw something that frightened him so badly that he ran away and was no more seen.

Then she herself saw something that frightened even her stalwart nerves. She slept in a small attic-room and always saw that the door was bolted, and lay with a little dagger beneath her pillow.

One early morning, between two and three, she was awakened by the horrible screaming of some animal, and curiosity having the better of her, she crept out and down the stairs and looked through an unglassed window into her father's room. Of all that she saw there she would never tell, but there was a big wax image of a naked woman with 'spread hair,' another doll magnificently dressed in silk and satin;

there was an animal being tortured. There were present her father, the Countess of Essex, a man called Sir Gervase Helwys, and the sorcerer.

She watched for a little and returned to her room. That night, on her bed, she swore that she would be armed for ever against the world. The world was evil and all men and women in it. She grew, during those hours, young in years though she was, from a child into a woman.

III

Towards the end of her fifteenth year there was the small affair of the little black dog. She found herself one day in Smithfield. She had always a liking for Smithfield, which at this particular time was moving away from the foul and ruinous state of Elizabethan days into the noisy, bawdy, paved conditions of Jonson's *Bartholomew Fair*. The ground was now raised in the middle and was a clean and spacious walk; channels were made to drain the water away; a thick railing was put up about the market-place for the safety of foot-passengers against the danger of the coaches that were becoming so common— carts, cattle, horses, too, made a terrifying battle of the ordinary ground.

The famous horse-pool was now quite decayed, the springs being dried up. What surface water there was fell into a small bottom, enclosed with brick and known as the Smithfield Pond.

Cow Lane, in which was the old house of the Prior of Sempringham, was a lane of houses, not all of them new, built over the site of the old gallows. The last of the old elms had been cut down. Hosier Lane and Chick Lane were newly become permanent resorts of trade and Long Lane was being lined with tenements for brokers, tipplers. There were brew-houses, inns, fine buildings, on the western side of Smithfield, as far as the Bars.

Smithfield was important in Katherine's life just at this time, for it was here that she received the deep conviction that she was moving with, and into, a new world, a conviction that through all the adventures and dangers of her later life was to help her in her aloofness from her own failures and successes. It was in Smithfield that she received deeply for the first time the certainty that great world movements were independent of human lives. The citizens of Smithfield were laying down paving-stones for the better convenience of their immediate customers, little knowing and thinking that in so doing they were serving history.

Katherine learned here, what she would never forget, that there were two concurrent histories—individual man, his soul-making, and the great movements in which a thousand years are but a day upward towards universal progress. She was never to be very greatly interested in her own soul-making, but she was to detect in the signing of a parchment, the sacrifice of a loyal servant, the prayers of a fanatic, the abandonment of a city, the retreat of an army, the execution of a king, the signs and tokens of the other history.

In any case, it was in Smithfield that she saw the little black dog. In her stern resolve to yield to no submission that would weaken her strong independence, she found that animals were the devil! She could not help herself. Her heart, that she was ever training for denial, refused to temper its beat at the sight or sound of a dog, horse, cat, parrot, or any small bird.

She could not be stern at the vision of this little black dog who, after sniffing at some garbage and the corpse of a donkey, swollen in death, discovered her as she watched workmen timbering a house and incontinently claimed her for his own.

It was perhaps the bright crimson dress that she was wearing or something very self-confident or independent that attracted him.

'This girl must be able to look after herself. She will look after me.'

In any case, he attached himself and refused to leave her. There were many dogs grubbing about and this was as clear a mongrel as any of them. He was black and tousled, with bandy legs. He had, however, eyes of a passionate burning brown. She astonished herself finally by picking him up and carrying him home to Chelsea.

She travelled by the river and attracted much attention by her beauty, her bright dress, and the mongrel dog. One fellow, with gold rings in his ears and an impertinent nose, in pretence of chucking the dog's chin, chucked hers also. She was only fifteen, but looked at him so fiercely that he shabbily apologized.

She enjoyed the pale gold of the afternoon sky, the swishing rhythm of the river, the breeze on her cheeks, but far more than these did she enjoy the defeat of the earringed man.

It was part of the unpleasantness of the Chelsea house that so little comment was made on the events that occurred in it. No one for many weeks said anything about the little black dog, although he followed her everywhere and even slept on the end of her bed.

She wished not to become attached to the animal, but attached she became. She was after all a very lonely child. For some months she was happy in its company.

Then one evening by candle-light she saw the beautiful young Anne Turner, who was frequently at supper with them, staring at it. Anne Turner had the nastiest stare in the world; when she stared at someone or something she seemed out of her body to spin some sort of glaucous web.

She had stared at Katherine many a time, but *that* stare had failed. Now she stood in the door of the room with green hangings, and while the candle-light flared up and down she stared at the little black dog. After she was gone Katherine felt the dog tremble against her breast.

She remembered the cry of the animal in the night.

So next morning she went down to the river, the dog following at her heels. There by the riverside she saw one of the new Puritans standing. He was a round, plump man dressed in plain black. He was saying his morning prayers, but so round and homely and kindly was his face that Katherine stood waiting beside him until he should finish.

'I will lay me down at night as a stone,' he said, 'and in the morning the Lord shall make me as a loaf of fresh bread.'

He smiled at her, and the moment was very pleasant, a cool air in the trees, the river rushing swiftly by, a new bright day beginning, and this round, cheerful countenance.

She offered him the little black dog. He accepted it.

'I do not know what my wife may say, but my little Benjamin will be joyful in the Lord.'

He laid his hand on her head, blessed her, and walked away, leading the dog by a string. To her own deep indignation her eyes were misted with tears as she watched him go.

IV

So she sat, on the day of her sixteenth birthday, by the open window waiting to speak to her father. She had something to say to him. The sun was now beating warmly on the walls of the houses, and all the birds in the glittering cages were singing and twittering and chattering so that there seemed to be two worlds, one airy and of an infinite lightness and mobility, the other human and earthly, rumbling, rattling, echoing with men's cries and all the daily traffic of the city.

She stood up and, turning, surveyed the room, which had in it a portrait of some Elizabethan in a ruff and a purple suit, a large rat-trap in a corner by the fireplace, and a table with a flagon that had fallen on its side. The room, in spite of the warm fresh air from the open window, smelt stuffy with the heaviness of a rat-liquor staleness.

She closed the window. At the same moment the door opened and her father came in.

He went to the table and set up the overturned flagon. He yawned and stared at her. She saw that he was disturbed, and then that he was frightened. His heavy white nose held drops of perspiration.

So unexpected was the fear in his eyes that she called out: 'What is it?'

He sat heavily down on a stool near the rat-trap. Then, hearing a cheeping, he saw that there was a mouse in it. He opened the trap, took out the mouse, killed it, and threw it into the fireplace.

His terror filled all the room. She did not speak. She had intended to tell him that to-day she was sixteen and from now was a woman and would lead her independent life. She would be his daughter but not his servitor. She would find for herself some position. He must recognize and acknowledge her freedom. She had been planning what she would say for weeks. She could hear dimly through the wall the singing of the birds. A strange mingling of some sort of anxiety for him, contempt and fear for him (none for herself), kept her silent.

He stood up and she saw that he was trembling. He took out a dagger, sheathed, from his pocket-bag, released it, and bent forward, chipping the table-edge.

The door opened again and Anne Turner came in.

She, too, said nothing, only stared straight through Katherine out to the window.

Their motionless silence was horrible.

Katherine said again: 'What is it?—What has happened?' As

neither of them answered, as the room seemed hot with a deep pene-trating smell, she walked past them, out of the room, then ran down the stairs.

Below in the street she looked up and saw all the gilded cages flashing and winking in the sun.

TWO HALVES OF THE POISONED APPLE

NICHOLAS HERRIES, on the very same day that Katherine was in the Bird-cage house, went to Whitehall in the company of Peter and Lucy to visit their brother Rashleigh. The history that was for ever to connect her with the Herries family received new links that fine spring day although none of them was in the least aware of it, and while the birds sang in their cages, the Strand rattled and roared, and Dom Christian bent forward cutting notches in the table, beads of sweat on his white nose, Nicholas saw double in a royal mirror. Peter and Rashleigh swore vows that would last them for the rest of their lives, Lucy, after being safe for so many years, stepped again into danger, King James feared a necromancer, Villiers was given some diamond buttons, Anne of Denmark looked into the room and went out again, three Scottish clergymen were unable to deliver the argument that they had so elaborately prepared, and a page-boy broke a window with a shuttlecock.

But something must first be said about Nicholas.

He was now seventy-two years of age, his wife, Rosamund, fifty, and his sensible son, Robert, sixteen.

His hair was now snow-white, he was as strong and vigorous as ever, and did not know an ache or a pain. Yet there were changes in him. He had reckoned by now quite resolutely on certain disappoint-ments. He would never create a child again; he would not any more have supreme charge over the affairs of Mallory; his son Robert would never be the romantic, idealist, adventurous son that he had once hoped for. There was nothing, no, nothing at all of his beloved brother Robin in his beloved son Robert.

For he did love his son and admired him greatly. For it seemed to him that Robert was very typically representative of the new England that was growing up around him, just as in London new buildings were growing up everywhere.

These new buildings were very different from the beautiful houses of his own youth—grave, serious, well-founded buildings intended for work and industry. It is true that Inigo Jones was a fantastic and a genius, and the houses that he was planning for the King would be lovely indeed, but Inigo Jones was a Renaissance figure and the Renaissance was almost gone.

The men of England seemed also to Nicholas quite different from the men of his youth. A figure like his old enemy, Philip Irvine, seemed altogether impossible and melodramatic in this new, more measured world, someone out of the dramatists—Webster, Marlowe, Ford. Men were as evil now and as determined on their own revenges, but in another fashion—there was no pose and strutting of evil any more. It was true that King's favourites like the doomed Somerset or the rising Villiers had that same glitter and display, but their motives were not naked, selfish, vain revenge, but every move, every gesture, and every grace was planned for self-advancement—deliberate and cool and calculated.

But such men as Carr and Villiers and Irvine were not the men of England—thank God they were not.

The men he had in mind were the men (and women too) who worked for him in the house and farm at Mallory, the men he saw in the villages, in the streets of London, on the country roads.

Those men were changed by one thing—the Bible. The publication of the Authorized Version in 1611 was only five years old and yet already there were copies of the Bible everywhere. Men and women could be seen reading it or having it read out to them at most unexpected places.

Nicholas noticed that whereas in earlier times they would be dancing round the Maypole or singing catches or drinking at the ale-house, they would now be gathered together seriously discussing or arguing or listening to a grave elderly sober-sides haranguing them.

Nicholas did not object to all this, but he had never been in any way a religious man and he was too old to begin it now. On the night of the Queen's death, when he had thought that he had seen his dear Robin, his world had died. Well, every man's world must die some time. It is of no use to repine. Many men before him and after him had wished and would wish that time stood still and that it might stay packed with the sweets of all its most delicious moments. But that could not be, and indeed must not.

He noticed that the gentlemen of his own class, and especially the younger of them, moved, many of them, actively against all this soberness and were the more wild and fantastic because of it; that he did not approve of either. Let a man serve as well as he might his King and his country, let him be reverent to his parents, courteous to everyone, and found a family—that was all that could be asked of him.

He found that he thought often of his old father. Had he had the good fortune to create another son he would have called him Michael, and would have planned that he should be just such another noble, kindly gentleman as his father had been. But there would be no son now but Robert, for Rosamund was past all child-bearing.

But—it has been said—he loved Robert and admired him. Had his love been allowed more expression he would have been pleased, but Robert was never one for demonstrations. He was a short, thick-set boy with steady grey eyes that had an ironical look in them, sturdy limbs that never doubted where they must go but went nowhere precipitately, and a round hard head like a bullet. He wore his hair long, but in such a fashion that the roundness and hardness of that head could never be doubted. He had a warm heart, but never allowed the warmth of it to get out of control. The three persons whom he loved best in the world were still the same three of his babyhood, his father, his mother, and old Armstrong, but they had all learned never to show him any demonstrations. He was sparing of words, and always before he answered a question waited and fixed his steady grey eyes on his interlocutor. He was of a sterling integrity, but that did not mean that he thought others were. He was already a cynic about human nature.

He had a great sense of possession and of property. He was not a miser, but what he had he held.

He cared nothing for London and never went there unless he must. He adored Mallory and especially the farm part of it. Although he was but sixteen he had already a wonderful knowledge of all cattle—their value, their food, their possibilities—and so Nicholas found himself, in spite of himself, already surrendering much of that side of the

Mallory life to his son. Robert knew exactly what he wanted and always quietly obtained it. He put no value at all on poetry, music, painting, or on grand clothes or on dancing or any festivities that wasted time.

Yet he was not dull company. He had a slow humour and something good in his heart made him pleasant and sometimes absurd. This last was what he could not *bear* to be. He was extremely sensitive about his short stature and round red face. He believed that everything should be quiet, steady, and decorous. Indeed, had it not been for his odd ironical humour he *might* have been dull. This did not truly belong to the solidity and common sense of his nature; neither his mother nor his father was in the least ironical.

He cared nothing at all about politics and was never heard to express an opinion upon them. Nicholas, watching him at Mallory, often felt that Robert was older than himself—'A woman later,' he thought, 'may do something to him.'

On this fine sunny morning, then, Nicholas, attended by Peter and Lucy, walked to Whitehall.

Lucy was now twenty-six and Peter twenty-five. Lucy was very much what she had been as a child, impulsive, excitable, loving, sometimes foolish, often not wise. She had grown tall and dark and more full in figure than she had once promised to be. She still dressed badly, appearing in something that she thought was a new fashion that was no fashion at all. When she was excited and happy, when her eyes shone and all her body moved in pleasure, she was beautiful. Many men had thought her so. She had had flirtations with a number and had once been engaged to a young man who was handsome and voluble but, as she soon found, a fool. None of these had any effect on her, and Nicholas sometimes feared that she still cared for her cousin Carey. He was abroad at the present in the Low Countries and very little good was said of him by anybody.

Peter had grown tall and plump and in spite of his age he still looked a boy. His hair was untidy and his dress often neglected, but he was as pleasant a young man as there was in London. He was a man of most serious ideas, learned and intelligent, and already was being watched by members of the anti-Court party who invited him to their meetings. His religion was at the root of his being, but this did not prevent him from gaiety, high spirits, and the full enjoyment of life. His eyesight was weak, and when he was walking, intent on some idea, he would stumble and trip and sometimes fall into a hole and spatter himself with mud. His great friend was Matt Turner, but he adored his sister and loved his brother Rashleigh, although now the two brothers were absolutely separated in all their beliefs and ways of life.

Rashleigh's position at Court was a serious one, but there was something about his great beauty, single-mindedness, purity of soul that kept him apart. It was said that the King did not like him.

Nicholas' house was at the time closed and they were staying in Southwark. As they crossed the river the sunlight was as fresh and brilliant as though it had been but just created; gulls swooped and rose and steadily beat the air, their hoarse cry coloured with the long swell of golden sea on marble shores and the wild beat of the wind against jagged rock. The river surface was covered with traffic, but here, too, Nicholas noticed how far more serious it seemed than in his young days, when boatmen sang as they rowed and flags waved and trumpets blew. Now there were no flags nor trumpets, but men rowing swiftly that they might carry their charges to business with reputable speed.

He remembered as he sat there, his long white hair blowing, his purple coat fastened about his neck with a gold hasp, how once he and Robin had crossed the river under the stars to a dance in his uncle Henry's house, and it had been on that very night that Robin had first met Sylvia. The pity of it! The pity of it! He sighed. Lucy pressed his hand. She was looking very fantastic. Because she was going to the Court she was wearing a crimson and seed-pearl dress with a high feathered hat. She looked like an actress, Nicholas thought, and then gave an eye to Peter, who was staring into the sun as though he saw a vision. He was by no means as tidy as he should be! How deeply can those whom you love irritate you by their inattention to little things, the more because you love them. He knew, too, that Lucy would take him aside and complain that Peter's white lace was not as clean as it should be, and that Peter would whisper something to him about Lucy's extravagant colours.

Nevertheless he pressed Lucy's fingers in response for most deeply did he love her.

'Why did you sigh?' she asked.

'Because, my dear, I was thinking of the past. I was remembering a night when Robin and I were both young men and we crossed this river in starlight. A fatal night for Robin it was!'

'Well, this is not a fatal morning for us!' she cried. 'This sunlight and the kiss of the water against the boat. Oh, I am happy this morning!' and she began to half sing, half recite:

> *'Cupid and my Campaspe played*
> *At cards for kisses; Cupid paid:*
> *He stakes his quiver, bow, and arrows,*
> *His mother's doves, and team of sparrows;*
> *Loses them too; then down he throws*
> *The coral of his lip, the rose*
> *Growing on's cheek (but none knows how);*
> *With these, the crystal of his brow,*
> *And then the dimple on his chin;*
> *All these did my Campaspe win.'*

Her voice was sweet and, as always when she did anything, she was lost entirely in it, her whole body and the soul within it surrendered to her happiness.

But Nicholas, looking at her, felt as he had done before, as he had done so many years ago at his own wedding, a shiver of foreboding. She needed to be protected as much now, when she was a grown woman, as she had done when she was a baby. Her feelings—of love and passion—might carry her into any disaster.

They landed and came up into Covent Garden, which was yet a garden with a fountain playing above daffodils that blew in the breeze and seemed to be obeying some ceremonial service to the sun. But here buildings now were rising and they could catch, through the still, bright air, the ring of hammers.

Indeed houses were rising in all directions, but it was when they came to Whitehall that there was complete confusion. Here, most truly, was there 'an age between two ages.' The King, who had a taste in such things, and the brilliant genius of Inigo Jones inspiring him, had been enjoying a wonderful game in pulling down and destroying the old ruinous buildings of Henry VIII and Elizabeth.

Here was a scene of chaos as though one of those terrible air fleets to come, of which Nicholas, Lucy, and Peter so happily knew nothing, had been wreaking their pleasure. Half-demolished roofs, gaping windows with the sunny sky blazing through them, rubble piled ruin high, gazed miserably to heaven while around and amongst them the new buildings haughtily began to lift their shoulders.

There were workmen everywhere, and again Nicholas noticed that they were not the workmen of the old days who would suddenly cease their labours and sing a madrigal or admire a passing beautiful woman, but grave young men intent on their work. And one elderly fellow was leaning up against a post reading his Bible.

There were holes and pits in the road everywhere, and Peter nearly fell into two of them. The King kept his rooms at Whitehall in the middle of this confusion, and Nicholas hesitated, not knowing where to enter.

A young gentleman, very elegantly dressed, came out of a postern door.

'Could you most kindly tell us where we should enter—at what door? I have an appointment with Mr. Rashleigh Garland.'

The elegant young man nodded his head towards a dark archway. 'You should enquire there, sir,' he said curtly and went quickly on his way.

'Manners are not at all what they used to be,' Nicholas thought regretfully.

This was in fact Nicholas' first visit to the Court of his Majesty James 1, and he was paying even this first visit with a sort of shame-facedness. As, holding himself very erect, his velvet hat tilted rather defiantly on his white hair, he stood there looking about him at the dust from the dying buildings, he thought: 'I shall like none of this. I should not have come. This is not my place'—but he had always promised Rashleigh that he would pay him a visit one day and Rashleigh had taken trouble about him, so on he must go. He was aware that many eyes were upon him and he fancied that some mocked him. In the corner of one of the alleyways, two boys in shirt and hose were playing battledore. They had paused and were staring at him, grinning. They were probably pages. A window above him was crowded with three laughing girls.

He looked up at them. Not so long ago he would have chaffed them and maybe kissed his hand to them. Now he felt that they were laughing at him for an old fool. With the shriek from some alley, the criss-cross sunlight, the thin recurrent tingle of the battledore game, the falling of bricks, men shouting, the dust in his nostrils, there came to him a sudden realization of the brevity of life, its meaninglessness, the mockery always when you came to the end.—'How many years I have lived, how many things done—and it comes to this—I stand here to be mocked. . . . This new world does not need old men.'

Nevertheless it had been for but a moment; bitterness could not stay with him long. He turned to Lucy and Peter.

'You've been here often enough—which way in is it?'

'This door will do as well as another,' Lucy said, laughing.

They went forward under an archway, up some steps, and were faced by a heavy black door. This was opened by a sentinel, to whom Peter showed their pass. They moved through a gallery and found themselves in an ante-room hung with a tapestry portraying in dark amber and crimson the Siege of Troy.

Nicholas knew this room; he had been here on many occasions in the time of Elizabeth. It led, as he knew, to the large ante-room that preceded the Court Room. Many a time he had sat in front of the armoured Achilles sulking in his tent and kicked his long legs in boredom before an audience with Cecil or another. Always, in the great Queen's day, there had been the greatest order and discipline everywhere within Whitehall or Richmond or wherever it might be that she was—a kind of golden hush that no one dared to break. How different here and now! Near to the door was a plate with the remains of a dog's meal—bones and broken meat. Against a superb gold-and-ebony escritoire with little ivory panels picturing different scenes of sport, rested a torn kite with blue ribbons streaming across the floor.

At a table near by two men were playing at chess, and Nicholas saw, to his horror, that they were both untrussed and unbuttoned. A piece of cambric shirt protruded at the waist of one of them. On a gilt-and-green damasked sofa a boy of some seventeen years was curled up, fast asleep and gently snoring.

All this, too, in the morning!

Beyond the room, from the larger ante-room, he could hear laughter and loudly raised voices. Through the open window came the odour, the whisper of the battledore and shuttlecock, the clang of the hammer.

No one stirred at their entrance, so they stood there wondering what they should do. At last Peter, a look of disgust on his child-like features, said:

'We had best move forward, I fancy——'

But when they moved, one of the men at the chess looked up. 'I take that pawn,' he said. Then he stood, a stout, dishevelled figure, yawning.

Something in Nicholas' splendid bearing affected him. He pulled himself into some sort of order and asked: 'Yes, sir, and what can I do for you?'

Nicholas showed him the order from Rashleigh. He was a long time reading it, scratching his head as he did so.

'Ah, yes—Mr. Garland. At your service. It is a fine day.'

'It is indeed,' Nicholas answered, smiling.

'I will send the boy over to find him.' He went to the green-and-gilt sofa, shook the sleeping boy by the arm—'Put your clothes on, and find Mr. Garland for this gentleman.'

The boy, with one amazed glance at the strength and sinews of Nicholas, vanished.

The stout dishevelled gentleman continued talking: 'You must pardon some disorder, Mr. Herries—we have been here all through the night and are waiting to be relieved.'

The stout dishevelled man yawned again and seemed sadly conscious of the disorder, for he picked up the kite and tumbled it behind the escritoire, picked up the plate and turned its contents out of window.

'You are from Sussex, Mr. Herries?'

'Yes.'

'From Mallory Court. I have heard of you. You have a fine herd of cattle. . . . Now in Wiltshire, I have a herd . . .'

He began to talk with some eagerness, his face resembling nothing so much as that of a fish hauled on to dry land and gasping for breath. But in a moment the page had returned and they were led through into the larger ante-room.

This was a wide, lofty room, its dark-blue ceiling stuck about with golden stars. On the long wall was the tapestry of Henry V and Agincourt, at that time very famous, and afterwards, alas, destroyed by fire.

The room was crowded with people and the noise deafening. Men, women, and children were here and they were all talking at once. A little girl with long flaxen ringlets was kneeling on the floor teasing a spaniel that snapped sharply at her. Two little boys in crimson suits ran chasing one another round the legs of a table. An old lady in a high white head-dress, her face a mass of wrinkles, stood quite motionless, her old eyes fixed with passionate intensity on the door from which the King would proceed. You could see her gnarled hand with its lace ruff tremble against the stuff of her dress. One young man, most elegantly dressed, pearl earrings swinging from his ears, his cheeks highly painted, passed eagerly from one group to another, whispering, giggling, plainly occupied with news that he thought of the very greatest importance. A parrot with crimson-and-orange wings was perched on a golden pole and was being fed by a fat courtier with sweetmeats. The face of the fat courtier was so oddly like the parrot's that Lucy, who was watching them, laughed.

At intervals the parrot gave a squeak of satisfaction. The sweetmeats being done, the fat courtier approached very near to the parrot and tickled its neck. The self-satisfaction on the face both of the parrot and the courtier made them melt into the same person.

There were beautiful women here, Lucy thought, but the faces of most of them were hard and staring.

Then she saw a girl, little more than a child, who reminded her of herself as she had been—shy, her eyes darting everywhere with amazed excitement, her breath eager between her lips. Such, ten years ago, she, Lucy, had been. Had that frantic anticipation of life been as yet justified? Indeed it had not.

Then she saw, with a thrust that seemed to turn her heart over in her breast, that a man had come up and was talking to the child, and the man was Carey! He had returned from the Low Countries! He was here. No one had told her. He had not tried to see her. Perhaps he had but now returned?

He looked a great deal older. Calculating swiftly she realized that he must be now thirty-four or thirty-five. She realized also that she loved him as truly as she had ever done—and also that he was worthless. Love did not blind her at all; she only wished to be taken in his arms and let the consequences be what they might. Now she had forgotten all else—the King, the Court, everything, everybody.

Even though everyone in the room might see, she stared at him as though she would draw him to her. And so in a moment she did.

He was paying the child compliments. He was older, his face harder, his eyebrows were darkened, the paint on his cheeks more brazenly applied, but his tricks were just the same. He bent forward to the child just as in the old days he had done to Lucy, fixing his eyes with grave and earnest seriousness, and the child looked up at him just as Lucy had once done. He must have been aware that eyes were fixed upon him, for he swung round and caught Lucy's gaze.

A look of astonishment and pleasure came into his face. He bowed to the child and then came across the floor.

In his soft easy voice that seemed to Lucy to belong to her whole life he said:

'You here! . . . I had not expected it.'

She looked at him coldly, although she was loving him with all her heart.

'Nor had I expected you. I had thought you were in the Low Countries.'

'And so I was—until this very week.' (He was lying—she knew it.)

'I hope you did good service there.'

'So-so. . . . So-so.'

He was looking at her with full admiration. It was obvious that she surprised him—her maturity, her full-bosomed beauty, and yet the child eternal in her.

'I have thought of you so very often.'

'We had all quite forgot you.'

He grinned. 'Oh no . . . my brother wrote that you enquired of me.'

'Oh, well—politeness.'

'Now that I am returned—I am at your service.'

'What will you do now?'

He lowered his voice a little.

'Somerset's in the Tower—and his good lady.' She knew that he had been one of Carr's adherents. He always followed the rising star. He was quite frank as to that.

'Now it must be Villiers,' he said, smiling at her.

'Why? . . . Why?' She could not prevent herself. Her eyes showed him how seriously concerned she was. He knew, from that moment, that his absence had made no difference. Because he knew, he raised a jewelled finger and a thumb and held a little bone in her wrist between them quite tightly.

'Why? . . . What do you mean, "why"?'

'This following of Court favourites . . . always the one who is at the top. . . . It is not worthy——'

'Worthy? My dear! I am not so high and mighty. I am no saint and in this Court it is as well not to be. I climb by any branch. . . .'

She moved her wrist from his fingers.

'Of course,' she said haughtily, 'I was not trying to teach you.' Then she laughed. She could not help herself. She was always laughing when she should not. Whatever might be wrong or right it was joy to her to have Carey Courthope physically close to her again.

She laughed, Nicholas heard her, turned around and saw Carey. He had not noticed him before because he had been talking to an old gentleman called Sir Humphrey Tryon, an ancient acquaintance. Sir Humphrey was a short, thick-set, red-faced man with fierce blue eyes. He was always snorting and snuffling. He was always indignant. He was indignant now. Nicholas was surprised to find that no one in this Court minded in the very least saying exactly what there was in their minds. In Elizabeth's time there were spies everywhere. He supposed there were spies here, too, but if there were, no one heeded them.

'Base . . . base. That's what it all is here!' Sir Humphrey snorted. 'An apothecary boy confesses on his death-bed and it's like taking the lid off a cauldron—all poisons bubbling in the stew! The Somersets in the Tower and soon they will have that lovely Mistress Anne Turner who has given so many pretty boys the pox with what she has provided them, and that flat-nosed necromantic humbug Dom Christian——'

Peter interrupted: 'Forgive me, sir—Dom Christian? Is he in this Overbury business?'

'Indeed he is. And it was lucky for Dr. Forman that he died in 'Eleven or he would have been in it as well.'

Nicholas asked some questions. Down at Mallory you did not hear all the scandals.

'Why, 'tis simple enough. Frances Howard marries young Essex and after three dreary years with him in the country wearies of him and charges him with impotency. Some worthy bishops grant it her and she is all for Robert Carr, Somerset as is. And he for her. But Overbury, Carr's friend, hates her and tries to dissuade Carr of the marriage, so she has him clapped away in the Tower and then poisons him or sees to it that poisoned he is. Shortly they are to be tried, the pair of them, and many a bawd and warlock with them. Why, surely, man, you have heard of it! The Court talks of nothing else.'

Nicholas' brow was frowning. 'Poisoning and wizardry!' he said. 'This is worse than anything in the late Queen's reign.'

'Indeed and it is!' Sir Humphrey snorted. 'And the way things are going there will be civil war in this country ere long. Out there in the street men are reverently reading their Bible, but inside these rooms there are perversions and necromancies——'

But it was now that Lucy laughed and Nicholas turning around saw Carey Courthope. He was displeased and, of course, Carey knew it. He looked teasingly at the old man.

'I am pleased to see you so well, Cousin Nicholas.'

'Since when have you returned?'

'This very week.'

'And when go back again?'

'Ah, that is as may be. First I must discover what there may be profitable in this place.'

'It should suit you most aptly,' Nicholas said angrily. He was furious with himself for being angry. At his age too! But he had a good capacity for hatred in him and he hated Carey now as he looked at him. Once again, as in the eyes of Fawkes, so in these mocking ones, he seemed to see the gaze of his old never-to-be-slain enemy, Irvine. He would have liked to have drawn Lucy close to him to protect her.

She had moved away to Peter's side.

'Did you hear, Lucy?' Peter asked her. 'Do you remember the man who came to our party—and his daughter? It seems that he is involved in this. And the girl. She will be a woman now. In such a horror. Do you remember her eyes? Her colour?'

But Lucy scarcely listened. Her heart was beating so that she could scarcely see.

But there was time for no more; the doors opened and the King, followed by a little group, entered.

Nicholas' eyes went first, not to the King, but to Sir George Villiers, of whom, even at Mallory, he had been hearing so much. Somerset was in the Tower—George Villiers was knighted—like the weather-figures in the toy, as the one comes in the other goes out! Nicholas even had heard from his wife the story how on St. George's Day of the former year young Villiers, for whose favour the Queen had been asked, waited outside the door of the Bedchamber while Robert Carr, Earl of Somerset, feeling perhaps his coming doom cold in his vitals, waited with his followers opposite him.

Inside the Bedchamber the Queen, Anne of Denmark, asked that the lovely young Villiers might be made a Gentleman of the Chamber. James knew well by this time how lovely he was and was weary altogether of Somerset's imperious peevishness, knew also quite well which way he was going; but he always liked the Queen to suggest first his young men to him so that, if she complained of them later, he could say to her: 'But you suggested him, my dear!'

Somerset meanwhile was sending into the Bedchamber, not over-tactfully, messages begging that the young man should be made nothing more than a Groom.

Inside the Bedchamber the King must have enjoyed himself greatly, feeling his power and also visualizing, through the boards of the door, the excellent fresh beauties of the young man on the other side of it, and the whole picture is made all the more enchanting and ethical when one watches Anne of Denmark thus imploring her husband—all for the young man's good!

And of course, in James' own good time, the young man modestly entered the Bedchamber, hanging his head a little. He was possibly reflecting on the musty smell the King had, but in all probability was summing up the stiff and withdrawn young Prince Charles as sharply as any. He foresaw, no doubt, that that grave-faced, solemn, sacred-looking young man must be won over if anything lasting were to be achieved.

Charles did not like him that day and it would need Villiers' cunning and charm . . . But oh, Villiers—glorious England-ruining Buckingham to be—had both cunning and charm and he was to win that stiff, solemn, rather sad young man into the very hollow of his beautiful hand. . . .

So Anne of Denmark, asking Prince Charles to lend her his sword, knelt to James and begged him 'to do her this special favour as to knight this noble gentleman whose name was George for the honour of St. George, whose feast he now kept.'

So 'this noble gentleman' knelt down and was knighted, and they say that when, in his young manly beauty, he stood up and looked at King James (turning his nose perhaps ever so slightly to right or left that he might not engross the full strength of the kingly savour) the King nearly fainted with joy and looked at his Queen with affection for the first time for many a week.

Nicholas knew the story as everyone knew it, and now, in so short a time, Somerset was in the Tower and Sir George Villiers was standing there, 'the sun of joy and the light of all our by-ways.' He certainly stood there radiant with a kind of boyish happiness.

Nicholas did not on that morning take in many marked details. He was soon turned to a consideration of the King and of his own dear Rashleigh who was part of the royal group.

But before he turned he gained an impression of Villiers in lustful, ambitious, challenging life that he was never afterwards to lose. Here was an evil man, that undoubtedly. An evil man whose character and action would affect the whole future of England, and, to speak of smaller things, settle the fate of several Herries then alive—but it was not an evil of the Elizabethan Philip Irvine kind. Here was a man of no conscience, no morals, of a selfish, arrogant egotism, overtopping conceit, no loyalties, no great abilities outside his own advancement, a poor general, no diplomatist, but there would always be with him a gaiety, an impudence, a buoyant lust for living and for getting everything, everything that was to be got from that life —here was a ruffian and a blackguard who might be saved before Heaven because he had loved life so ardently.

Within a year that shy, doomed, self-willed Prince had felt the charm and was to love him as in all his life he loved none other save the friend whom he betrayed to his enemies, his wife, and his children.

As they stood now close behind the King, the Felton stab in the back, the shame of the executioner's axe as it fell on that snowy morning—these things they did not expect, for already, young as they were, they held themselves to be above God.

But Nicholas would never forget that dark face with the thick ringleted hair, the mocking eyes and laughing mouth, the vitality that beat in the red blood and glittered in the eyes and curled the corners of the mouth, the dark wine-crimson suit, the gold-hilted sword, the sparkling buckles on the shoes—but always at the last the laughing, triumphant, exultant eyes! That was George Villiers on this morning at Whitehall in 1616 as the sunlight poured over the long high room and James, King of England, picked his nose with an almost eager curiosity.

Nicholas had not much time to study the King, for already Rashleigh had made a signal to him and would be, in a minute or two, standing at his side.

Nevertheless the picture of the King that he had then he was never again to lose: as will be found later, all the pictures that his mind received at this time were to be fixed on his brain as in fiery letters for ever.

He had seen him last on that day thirteen years ago when he was approaching London in triumph. He was not now very greatly changed. It was difficult to say whether he were more corpulent or no. His quilted doublet of not overclean dark-green velvet—the diamond buttons were fastened awry—made it impossible to guess at the size of his actual body. His breeches—plated with some sort of thin steel on the inside—gave him an absurd and wobbling posterior like an old duck's. His horror of steel was equalled by his horror of water, so that he seldom washed, hence the stale stable-straw smell that came from his body. His legs were weak—when seven years old he was still unable to stand—and Nicholas watched him now with amazement as he walked, wobbling in circular fashion, and his rather dirty bejewelled fingers engaged where the earlier Renaissance codpiece would once have been. He looked, Nicholas thought, extremely nervous, his body giving jumps and starts and his eyes restlessly wandering from place to place. While he spoke to anyone his eyes would be on the move, searching here, there, and everywhere, and if he saw a face or body he liked, the eyes would suddenly be fixed and he would stare and stare, greatly disconcerting the person who addressed him.

He had a funny perpetual little tee-hee cough, and when he spoke his words were thickened because his tongue was too large for his mouth. His beard was thinner than when Nicholas had last seen him. He had his hand now on his son Charles' shoulder.

Rashleigh had by now joined Nicholas, his handsome dark face lit with pleasure, for he loved these three. He was dressed in a suit of heliotrope and silver; his long curls were so carefully arranged that in another it might be dandified. But not with Rashleigh. He was apart from everyone in the room. All around his slim upright body there played a kind of spiritual separateness. He was not arrogant and yet it *was* a kind of unconscious pride. You could not imagine any man or woman—no, not the King himself—making love to him. You might touch his hand or kiss his lips, but you would get no farther into him.

Once only life shone in his eyes. He said something to Nicholas and looked at Prince Charles, who stood a little apart from the group about his father, grave with the large melancholy eyes of a pessimist and the tight-set lips of an obstinate formalist. Yes, the melancholy and the obstinacy, Nicholas saw them both. And then, at that moment, a lady with blue eyes and flaxen curls spoke to him and his smile was most winning, tender, and even humorous. Rashleigh whispered to Nicholas: 'Within ten years he will be my master—and I his servant to the death.'

The King, Villiers, and some others were now approaching near and James' wandering eyes very quickly lighted on Nicholas' snow-white hair, honest countenance, and vast body.

The King stared and Nicholas, nothing daunted, stared him back. James asked Villiers something. Villiers summoned Rashleigh, and Rashleigh, coming back to Nicholas, said: 'The King wishes you to be introduced.'

Nicholas stepped forward and everyone in the room watched. Most of them had never seen such a man. Even in Elizabeth's Court he had been but rarely in the later years, and in James' Court, as has been said, he had never been at all. There had been some tradition about him in Elizabeth's time, but already the Elizabethan figures were forgotten.

Moreover, Nicholas had never in all his life looked as well as now. Rosamund said that he was more handsome at this time than he had ever been, and she ought to know, for she had loved him since she had been a little girl. His white hair, the brown, healthy, good-tempered wisdom of his friendly face, his carriage of his immense body so that there seemed to be no old age about it, the dignity and breeding that all Herries men, even when they were at their wildest, had, all these made him, as he towered above them all, a god-like old man.

And what a shambling, waddling, awkward, stammering, stuttering, spitting, smelling oddity the King seemed in front of him. But neither Nicholas nor the King was a stupid man. The King saw that here was a man, and Nicholas, looking straight into the King's eyes, saw that, for all his oddities (and he threw his mind back to Darnley and Kirk o' Field and the terrible murderous babyhood, and the ruffian Scottish noblemen—yes, from Kirk o' Field to Gowrie), there was wisdom in those little questing eyes and wisdom in the lines of the mouth behind the thin beard.

We are as God started us and we ourselves finished the work—God have mercy on our souls!

Their conversation was not a lengthy one. The King, who spoke with a broad Scottish accent, said:

'Mr. Herries, I have seen you before.'

'I was present at your first entrance into London, your Majesty.'

The King was delighted. He gave some fat and pursy gentleman close to him a dig with his elbow in the stomach.

"That's gude for a royal memory. But a man of your proportions is not readily forgotten. You come seldom to visit us, Mr. Herries.'

Nicholas, smiling, said: 'I am a country man, your Majesty, and my legs never fitted neatly under a Court bench.'

The King chuckled. He fingered his nose and pulled his beard and his sharp little eyes never left Nicholas' body, wandering here, there, and everywhere.

'And how would you like it now, man—to come and visit us for a week or two? Hunting? We can give you a fine hard hunting party. . . .'

'I am seventy-two years of age, your Majesty.'

'Na, na. . . . Never think of your years with a body the like of yours.'

Their eyes met and stayed. It was a frank recognition the one of the other. The King seemed suddenly a wise, grave estimator of men. There was nothing foolish then.

Then Nicholas said: 'One of my family represents us. My young cousin, Rashleigh Garland, is in your service.'

'Ah, Rashleigh. Rashleigh.' The King looked about him, saw Rashleigh standing there, and Nicholas fancied there was a strange, wistful, almost lonely gust of feeling as though he said: 'There is someone has eluded me.' Then he turned half his body, and coughing his little 'tee-hee' said to Villiers:

'Mr. Herries will not be besought by us.'

Villiers, speaking softly, as though it were in confidence, answered: 'Mr. Herries has a fine breed of cattle at Mallory.'

'Aye, aye—we have heard of it.' He swerved round abruptly and was so close to Nicholas that his puffed doublet stayed against Nicholas' arm. 'And you have the right of it, Mr. Herries, for this court of ours is poisoned with warlocks. There are many griefs that I must bear and I wish to God, nay I pray for it and hope for it, that He will see both my best and my worst parts and will deliver us all from the Evil. I have carried a man so high that he has sold his presumption to the Devil . . . sold himself . . .'

He broke off and Nicholas saw that his eyes were full of horror. He looked about him as though the whole great room were filled with warlocks and witches, walked some paces, stumbled as though he could not see, and caught Villiers' arm. It seemed to Nicholas as though the King himself saw the Devil in person. And immediately after an odd thing happened to himself.

There was a high mirror with gilded edges hanging on the wall by the door and Nicholas saw himself in it blurred and double. His own body stood straight and foursquare, but shadowy, proceeding from it, was himself like a spirit, and around him the figures of men and women were also blurred and doubled. He shook his head impatiently and all was straight again. He walked forward a step and found that he was uncertain.

He said to Lucy: 'My eyes . . . am I going to be blind?'

She took his arm: 'The lights have bewildered you.'

'In that mirror—I saw double. I was frightened.'

But her mind was on Carey. She could not see him anywhere. She saw Peter. He stood rigid.

'Let us leave here, Lucy. Listen. I swear an oath. I swear to my Maker that this way of life here shall be destroyed and utterly rooted out. I—I——'

He was stammering with his earnestness, and Rashleigh, who had heard him, laughed.

'Dear Peter—I also will swear an oath—to serve the Divine Right and die for it.'

'And I, too, will swear an oath,' Lucy said, putting her hand on Rashleigh's arm, 'that from you both I will procure a cup of chocolate or disgrace you by swooning.'

The King had gone and Rashleigh must go too. He kissed his sister. She followed Nicholas, who was observed by everyone. He liked this perhaps, for he walked through the room as though he commanded England.

But to Peter it was all a bestial witchcraft; he slipped away and out into the street. The page-boys were still playing battledore. He thought of Dom Christian with the white nose and his daughter. He sighed heavily, for he was very young in mind and purpose and had kissed as yet only one woman outside his family in all his days, and she was the daughter of a warlock.

The warlock's daughter meanwhile had taken her place in the wherry that would carry her to Chelsea village.

It was a public wherry but not crowded: near to her sat six Puritan gentlemen, and one of them, short, thick-set, and apple-faced, was standing in the middle of them, one broad hand on his friend's shoulder, and was reading to them from the Scriptures. He was not at all of the fanatical type that Katherine so greatly disliked, but homely and pleasant, and he read in a soft, gentle voice. They were none of them fanatics and one of them, a thin slip of a boy, soon saw how beautiful Katherine was and his mind wandered from the reading of the Scriptures and he smiled.

She returned his smile. She could not help herself. She could not remember any time in her life when she had needed comfort and friendship as badly as now. She did not know what there had been in her father's face or in the dreadful eyes of Anne Turner. A kind of doom.

She knew, as though she had been told, that a crisis in her life had arrived on this lovely sunny morning of her sixteenth birthday. She would need all her independence and bravery. She caught some of the words that the apple-faced man was reading:

'And the Lord sent Nathan unto David. And he came unto him, and said unto him, There were two men in one city; the one rich, and the other poor.
'The rich man had exceeding many flocks and herds:
'But the poor man had nothing, save one little ewe lamb, which he had

bought and nourished up: and it grew up together with him, and with his children; it did eat of his own meat, and drank of his own cup, and lay in his bosom, and was unto him as a daughter.

'And there came a traveller unto the rich man, and he spared to take of his own flock and of his own herd, to dress for the wayfaring man that was come unto him; but took the poor man's lamb, and dressed it for the man that was come to him.

'And David's anger was greatly kindled against the man; and he said to Nathan, As the Lord liveth, the man that hath done this thing shall surely die:

'And he shall restore the lamb fourfold, because he did this thing, and because he had no pity. . . .'

The apple-faced rosy man had a sweet and clear voice. The words of the little story came separately to Katherine where she sat. She could not resist altogether the influence of the words, the serious, grave voices of the men, the smile of the young boy, the sun dancing on the water in whorls and streaks of light, the rhythmic sound of the strokes of the wherrymen, the friendly call of voices across the river, the distant ringing of a church bell, the silver-grey majesty of the splendid buildings on the bank-side—all these affected her so that if she had not been sixteen that same day and very proud, she would have burst into tears like a baby. She was so terribly alone in the world. In fact she could not think of any friend she had in the world unless it were that Mr. Peter Garland who had twice kissed her. But he must have forgotten her long ago!

She did not believe in God, of course, nor for that matter in the Devil either. Her father and Mrs. Turner and the others had claimed that they had dealings with the Devil, but she, Katherine, knew what nonsense all that was. They might compound poisons together—she knew that they did—but those orgies, and the cutting of the cock's throat and the mock prayers, they were but the excuse for other things, physical orgies of which Katherine, although she was only sixteen that day, knew horribly much.

She had, from all this, a terror of sexual intercourse and prided herself on nothing more than keeping her body free of all contact with other persons. She loved to wash herself in pure water and to sleep in a bed that no one had touched but herself and that her linen should be utterly white. She knew nothing about the soul, but she

did know about the body, for, as a small child, she had seen how base
it could be. As she sat there in the boat, the breeze blowing her dark
hair, she felt as though she were kept by a guard of steel from all
hateful men.

But was she? For now a terrible thought had invaded her mind.
Her father and Anne Turner were frightened by something terrible
that they had done. They were hunted. If the authorities caught them
and held them, would they not catch and hold her also? She was his
daughter and had often been concerned in his silly magic with him.
She had been innocent of any evil, but what would the authorities
care? That she had only sixteen years would not save her. They tortured children often enough. At the thought of torture her body was
turned to water, for, like all boys and girls of her world, she knew
what the torture-chamber was.

Worse than the hurt to her was the imagination of being stripped
before the naked torturers and their hot, sweaty hands laid upon
her body.

She stared over the sparkling, swirling water in a panic. She looked
at the quiet little body of men listening to the Scriptures and it
seemed to her that they were in some unreal world: the world of her
own imagination was so vivid. There was a strong driving impulse
in her to escape the moment that she landed in Chelsea. She must go
to the house, though, for money and clothes.

Also a queer unexpected sense of pity for her father came to her.
He had not been a bad father to her and he seemed to her altogether
more foolish than wicked. Women like the Countess of Somerset and
Anne Turner were wicked with their beautiful chill faces—her father
was a vain, lazy fool.

She must at least talk to him before she went away.

She walked up from the river through the little wood and the
crooked lane that led to the village. All was still with the summer
midday stillness.

The sun was shining on the house and her father's horse was
tethered to the horse-stone by the door. He looked at her and flapped
his long, rather melancholy ears. He had been ridden hard. She
paused before she opened the door because the silence, broken by
a wood-pigeon in the wood, was peacefully sunlit and cheering.

She was happier; he had ridden home and they would have dinner together and talk with the quiet sense that he could use if he were awake enough and normal enough.

Inside the house the sun was everywhere, but there was no one moving. She went upstairs and heard the cooing of the pigeon through the open window. The door of the parlour was open and she saw her father hanging from the beam. His tongue stuck out from between his teeth as though he mocked her. His heavy, clumsy body was bathed in sunlight, and the sun was full on his white eyeballs, his large nose, and his naked, dirty feet. He was in his shirt only.

His body swayed a little. On the shelf near him were a pack of cards, a white paper cone, and a bowl of goldfish.

She stared at his feet, then, because the cooing of the pigeon was terrible, closed the window.

THE LAKE

THE LAKE HAS NO KNOWLEDGE of time nor of man's history. Its own entity has its own history; it is the history of a soul; but of a soul as we may one day recognize the soul—a life without time, but always with purpose, and a purpose obedient within itself to a charge, all-seeing, wise, beneficent.

It sees indeed all that it needs to see. St. Herbert and St. Cuthbert prayed that they might die on the same day, and the Lake saw them pass and then the little chapel built and the mould made for making crucifixes to sell to pilgrims; the boats with their singing pilgrims crossed from Nichol End landing—but the Lake, as the crucifixes were sold at the little booth on the island's edge, still saw St. Herbert talking in the cool of the evening to St. Cuthbert, for the Lake is timeless.

At the same instant—but later for those who deal in time—the Lake heard the calls and the laughter of the men from the Norse and Danish settlements as they moved under the flower-opening symmetry of 'Skedhow' to settlements above the water, clearing the woods and watering their horses. Then King Ethelred and his soldiers came shouting and storming, throwing their craft on the Lake's surface, burning the settlements so that the flame and smoke burnt and clouded the water, but it was a noisy moment, breaking perhaps the

Lake's concentration but never troubling its heart. Norman barons built their little fortresses, and made tenants of the dalesmen, who also, like the Lake, are timeless, for they hold their real freedom now as they held it then and will always hold it. For a while they were told, these free men, that they held their land as fee for service against Border Scotsmen, and the stuttering, stammering King who for the first time united the two countries tried to force the money from the free men saying that they owned only because they must pay. But the free men fought in the courts for their rights and for once won them, and so are the statesmen of all time—even unto the end, glory be to God.

Not that the Lake minded—or only this far, that it thinks well perhaps to have on its borders men who are masters of their own land and slaves to no man. For the Lake is free in its very soul and spirit. Without taking any part, it would hear that they were no fools, these men, for it has a hatred of silliness, vanity, and folly, and of how in one place the men drove the plough in Latin, and in another some boys from school asked for their bill at a homestead in Latin and got it given to them in Greek.

The Lake knows very well, of course, the hills that bound it—Great Dodd and Causey Pike, Walla Crag and High Seat, Glaramara and Esk Pike, Scawdell Fell and Hindscarth, Cat Bells and Robinson—and many more. Some with their feet in its waters, some a little further distant, but they share its own preoccupation, beyond time and humanity, in secret purpose and wider values.

The Lake, indeed, has smiled on many childish customs that mark time for the ever-recurrent figure of the fork-shaped animal—the New Year stanging, the Collop Monday and Pancake Tuesday, the rush-bearing on the Saints' Days, the pace-eggs at Easter, the ploughings and clay-daubings and hunts and wrestlings, the lighted need-fire through which the cattle are driven, the kern supper at the Harvest Home.

All these things are cries and calls and tunes to fill in the colour of the outward life, as are also the lowing of the cattle, the flight of the eagle above Eagle Crag, the soft smother of the falling snow, the wind screaming down the fissure of Lodore, the rain with its friendly chatter, the moonshine, the sunrise, and the fierce sparkling of the star-sprayed sky.

But its true life is not touched. It tells nobody of its purpose, but grandly pursues it.

One of its purposes is beauty, but nothing in this that is self-conscious or even aware of what it is about. When, on a calm night, the brightest of all stars throws a single reflected spear of light across the waters, that is the star's business. When the reflection of a snow-scattered hill creates two more snow-hills deep into the Lake as though there is no end to it, that is not the beauty towards which the Lake is working. Amber-rose is no mean colour and for a brief moment will fire the whole Lake with its burning, but the Lake never wonders nor exclaims nor thinks of adjectives.

Deep in its heart there is for man a mystery, but that is only because, as yet, man is held for any revelation that may lead him to doubt his senses. He must believe in those senses, for only in those conditions can he be content to stay where he is.

The Lake does not care whether he stays or goes, for it is well aware that his eyes are still unopened like a baby's. In any case it is not the Lake's business to be conscious of man, although man, of course, thinks that it is.

The Lake has many depths of experience. None of the Past is lost, for there is no Past, but the Lake knows that instead of memory there is a constant recurrence of recorded moments—the wild man in his skins shouting to the eagle, the fire of the burning homestead giving wings of gold to the flying birds, the long ripple on the water's surface as the wild swan sweeps by, the lovers yielding as the oars drop and the boat is set free, the red moon like a scoured pan lighting the dark tree-bound bay—all these and millions, millions more are in memory, never to be lost again. But the Lake has found the attainable, and because of that no mere event can perturb her. She knows that the laws that she obeys, ordering her to live according to direction, to exist for a purpose that is not her own, to exist selflessly, bring her knowledge that answers all questions.

So she surrenders her will and fulfils her purpose.

The meadow that ran down to the Lake, between the town and the Lake, was on this late September morning gay with flags, Maypoles, and booths painted red and green and orange. This was Barley Bridge on Children's Day. No one knew how ancient was its origin. Barley Bridge itself was a children's game—Oranges and Lemons—and no doubt it had been played for hundreds of years by children all Europe over. But in the Keswick district it had an especial significance. It was said that once, inside Borrowdale (where so many strange stories were created), wolves had come down from the mountains and carried off a number of children while they were playing Barley Bridge. On the anniversary of this terrible event, the priest of the parish had led a procession to the top of Castle Rock and held a service there. Soon this had become a children's anniversary and then a festival. It had spread to Keswick. First there was held a service in the chapel at Rosthwaite, then the people and children of Borrowdale had, if the weather was fair enough, come, in boats and on horseback, down the road and across the Lake to Keswick. Meanwhile the children of Keswick had held *their* service in the Crosthwaite church, and then, carrying banners and the russet branches of the early autumn trees, dressed in white, had advanced to meet the children of Borrowdale. After the singing of psalms in the Town Square, they all marched down to the meadow by the Lake where there was a feast, games were played, and all ended with a great game of Barley Bridge and a mighty tug-of-war between the strongest men of Keswick and the strongest men of Borrowdale. After that, their boats lighted with torches and lanterns, the people and children of Borrowdale rowed back to Grange Bridge in their boats.

The Barley Bridge was always held in the last week of September, and that is one of the best months of the year in this district for weather.

In this year 1620 September was as fine a month as it could be, and this particular Barley Bridge day was gloriously brilliant.

Many of the townspeople were in the meadow and down at the Lake side waiting for the procession to come from the town.

In a corner of the meadow under some trees there was a group of ladies and gentlemen rather apart from the moving, wandering crowd. This group held Nicholas Herries, Rosamund his wife, Peter and Lucy Garland and Matt Turner. Nicholas and Peter were still on their horses.

This was the reason why they were there. The house at Rosthwaite that had belonged to Robin, Nicholas' brother, was now owned by strangers from Northumberland, but Nicholas, who had not seen it for many years, had a great longing to behold it again. The father and mother of Peter, Lucy, and Rashleigh were now dead, but Peter and Lucy, remembering their Seascale days, wished also to see their old home. Gilbert Armstrong, Nicholas' friend and servant, was now an old man, but his passion for the North was as strong as ever it had been and he too had wanted to see his home once more before he died. So he had come in July ahead of the others and he had found a little manor-house, recently built, beyond Threlkeld and had hired it for the summer. Nicholas and Rosamund had ridden North leaving son Robert, now a very able, practical young man of twenty, to supervise Mallory. They knew well that, although he loved them, he liked very well to have the running of Mallory to himself.

Nicholas had fallen in love at first sight with Barstack, with its rough-cast and threshwood and the mullioned windows and the open firespot and the cobble-paved hearth and the round massive chimneys.

He and Rosamund and Gilbert had settled in here most handsomely. Later in August Peter and Lucy had joined them, and afterwards that wild poetic Matt Turner, being Peter's great friend, had joined them too.

Over every part of that country they rode. Old Nicholas said to old Armstrong one day: 'Can you remember how once, many years ago, riding up Borrowdale I said that . . . But no. It was not you. It was to Robin I said it—that this was our true place and the place for our sons and our sons' sons.'

Armstrong, whose broad shoulders were bent a little, and his round brown face covered with wrinkles like a pippin apple, said in his deep voice that had something of a drum's shake in it:

'I can feel this earth in my boots—yes, when I'm three hundred miles away.'

Nicholas looked out on the sun-soaked meadow and the Lake, whose sheen was dazzling, and a deep sigh came from his breast: 'When you are old, my friend, the past is the present. At least I find it so.' He put up his brown thick-veined hand to shade his eyes. Ever since that day four years before at Whitehall, when he had seen double in the mirror, his eyesight had been strange. He must expect, as an old man of seventy-six, to see less well, but it was not that he saw badly—rather that he saw now a world that was not always real—people were not always people, places had strange lights and shadows. Sometimes where firm ground should be there was no ground.

The result of this was that his whole heart and soul now went out to the people who were beyond question real. His beloved wife first, Armstrong, Lucy, and Peter. Of Robert, his son, he must confess to himself in the silent hours of the night, he was a little afraid. Robert knew so many things accurately, domestic, agricultural things. Robert never said that his father was a fool; his behaviour was always most courteous and kind; but Nicholas sometimes found himself stammering before his son, even apologizing. And he had never been a man who cared for apologizing!

Another result of his uncertain sight was that the memory of the past things in his life was far more real and active than his consciousness of the present.

As he sat now on his horse, shading his eyes, his great head with its snow-white hair, his gigantic frame like that of some inhabitant of another world, so that eyes constantly moved to him, and little boys stood biting their thumbs and staring, and some broad strong Dalesman nipped his wife's arm to draw her attention, he was himself challenging Philip Irvine while the flames of the burning house snickered and yawned, and he cried joyfully to Gilbert in the little tower as the five ruffians advanced to the attack, and he stood beside Catherine Hodstetter as her mother walked alone down the Keswick street, he saw the doomed Queen stand in the firelit great Hall while the Dean mumbled prayers at her, he heard Armstrong tell him that he had married Catherine Hodstetter and he struck his cheek, he walked with his dear Rosamund down the flowery path at Mallory, he held Irvine high in his arms and flung him back into space while the wind raged, he heard the old Queen, rolling her head, squatting on her cushions, murmur that she was tired, he caught through the door the thin lamenting wail of his new-born child. . . .

Catherine Hodstetter! Catherine Hodstetter! The emotion was over. If she appeared now, walking across the meadow with her golden head held high, his heart would not beat a motion faster. And he remembered that agonizing night at Mallory when she had first slept there, and he had fought the Devil and conquered him. Everything passes! Everything passes!

What meaning has it then? Life? Can you call it Life when its moments are so quickly over, over before they can be savoured, and leading to nothing at all? Only in the memory of things past is there any reality when you are old—a reality, melancholy, regretful, ironical, because when they were there, those moments, you could not seize and hold them.

But it was not quite so. He looked to the left where Rosamund was standing, a mature, stout, full-breasted matron, in her wide-brimmed hat with its foolish little cord and tassels, a lace tippet over her shoulders, her hands, warm though it was, folded in a muff. No beauty—nor had she ever been. Lucy was a child no longer, having thirty years at least, but what a beauty, with her exquisite colouring, her little quivering, laughing mouth, her lovely hands (he knew how lovely they were although they were now concealed by long gloves). What a beauty she was beside Rosamund!

And yet Rosamund, although he loved Lucy, had his heart. He had never loved her so dearly as now—the absence of nonsense in her, her integrity, fidelity, and generosity of spirit. Especially this last. He knew now, gazing at this stout, dumpy, plain-faced lady, that this love created in the human heart the answer to all the irony, all the pessimism.

Such love as his for Rosamund and Rosamund's for himself resolved all the questions, for if poor men could create out of the muddle of this helter-skelter life such a relationship, then this poor life was lovely indeed.

Nicholas was no great thinker nor (to do him justice) had ever pretended to be. He knew, though, that he was as wise as any clever man in this, and, as though to prove to all the line of skrimshanked philosophers and lantern-jawed pessimists and curling-eyed ironists that he in this, at least, was as clever as they, he jumped off his horse, walked across to Rosamund, took gently her hand from her muff and, bending, kissed it.

'Why, Nicholas!' she said.

He answered low, so that the others could not hear:

'I wished you to know that I adore you—and never so greatly as now.'

'And why now?'

'I cannot say. I was sitting on my horse, and it came over me.'

There was a tear on her cheek. When she thought that no one was looking she wiped it with her muff.

One who would not notice was Lucy, for she had her own most

exciting thoughts. She had seen Carey Courthope only once since that morning at Whitehall. He had gone to Rome on a mission.

Then on the morning before this a note had been brought to her at Barstack. It said that Carey was in Keswick, and would see her on the next afternoon at the Children's Festival.

She stared out at the dazzling Lake but saw nothing save a sheet of light and Carey shining in the midst of it. She was thirty years of age although she looked twenty. She had preserved her figure wonderfully and there was something of the child still about her. Any kind of fun, pleasure—yes, and danger too—delighted her twice as warmly as it did an ordinary placid girl. There was to be one day, long after, a member of her family, a little lively woman with red hair who, if you took Rosamund and Lucy and mingled them, would make just such another. That woman, Judith Paris, though, would have, finally, in spite of her follies, wisdom—the sort of wisdom that Rosamund Herries had.

But Lucy had no wisdom, none at all. But she did have fidelity. Her life was almost over. She was thirty. The life that had promised her so much. She thought of the Herries Ball that Nicholas and Rosamund had given for old Courthope. All those years ago, but how well she remembered it! The conjurer, the monkey, the little girl who seemed to grow taller and taller. How she had danced that night, how terribly excited she had been, how sweet old Nicholas had been when he had sat with her in the alcove! And how much of life she had anticipated that night! What a wonderful glorious thing it was going to be! All the beautiful young men were in love with her!

And now she was thirty, still unmarried, still a virgin! Still a virgin and she thirty! Oh, it was a shame, a shame! She clenched her little hands beneath her gloves.

But whose fault had it been save her own? Again and again she might have married. She might have married the Prince de Guermantes: she might be at this very moment the Duchesse de Fonselles. The young Duke of Wrexe had been on the point of proposing to her and she had stopped him. These were members of the great world and she had refused them. It had not been difficult, for that could never be the world for her—too stiff and formal and restricted altogether.

There had been others in her own Herries world far more attractive. Young Matthew Tallboys with his handsome face and kind ingenuous heart, young William Lacey with his grave wisdom and integrity. Wild Humphrey Barber, hero of a hundred mad escapades, had sworn that he would remain virtuous for ever if she would have him.

Not to a single one of them did she give a thought. Only, always and for ever, it had been Carey.

Why? She could not conceive. It was a madness, a sort of necromancy. She knew that no one thought well of Carey. He was weak, faithless, not even very clever. She never cheated herself that he cared much about her. Seduce her he would like to, and then forsake her. She saw it all quite clearly.

Well, the seduction was worth it. If he would marry her, all the better, but if not—she was thirty and this madness in her blood for him would never rest until it was satisfied.

She had no shame left, especially after the death of her dear father. Lucy Garland, a disgraceful abandoned woman of thirty, who longed after a worthless man who did not love her. She thought of her two dear brothers, Peter and Rashleigh. They were both to her, in their different ways, like young knights in some Crusade. Peter was nearer to her and more familiar than Rashleigh, but Rashleigh she worshipped. What would those two young men say if they were to see the wicked lecherous thoughts in her heart? The first thing that they would do would be to kill Carey.

At that point she could bear her thoughts no longer, and turned to Matt Turner, who was standing beside her. Matt was an eccentric and looked like a clown out of a play, with his long, shambling body, his little canary-coloured beard, his sparkling, mocking, kindly eyes, his stutter and general incoherent speech. To-day as always he carried a book under his arm. Lucy asked what it was.

He showed it her. She read the title: *A Posie of Gilloflowers, eche differing from other in colour and odour, yet all sweete.*

'How pretty!' she said.

'Insipid translations from the Italian,' he answered scornfully. 'I bought it this morning off a chapman in Keswick. I were a bet-better translator myself.'

'Why don't you, then?' she asked, her eyes straining to the hill above the meadow.

Before he could answer her there was a cry that the procession was approaching.

Over the brow of the hill came the procession; heading it were fiddlers and a drummer. Behind these came the officials of Keswick, all in their grandest clothes. Then in their black robes and white bands the clergy of all denominations. Then the children all in white and singing very lustily a hymn to the accompaniment of the fiddlers. Of all the company in that meadow it was no doubt Matt Turner with his wide cynical eyes and tawny beard who saw best the fantastic beauty of that moment. For his soul was a fantastic one. He was one of those Herries who see everything 'just off the straight.' Their spiritual, mental, physical vision is a little askew. Nor are they the worse for that, containing in their honest but humorous souls all the sexes, the colours of the rainbow, and a vast saint-like tolerance.

Matt Turner was a poet and he had in his head 'The Epic of Charlemagne: In Ten Books.' And what an Epic that would be, with all the mirrors frosted, the knights in gold armour, and princesses like mermaids. Quite other than Mr. Spenser's Epic—with none of the saintly perfection of Philip Sidney's Sonnets. A queer crisscross Epic of genius—or so Matt Turner hoped.

Meanwhile his really simple soul was transfixed by what he saw— for behind the moving procession was Skiddaw, and on either side of the procession the woods and behind the woods again the hills. And above all this the blue sky soaked in light.

He was not accustomed, it must be remembered, to the fashion this place had of changing its beauties from minute to minute, and so he gaped, staring upwards with his mouth wide open. Ten minutes ago Skiddaw had struck the sky bare and scornful. Now on one of its twin peaks a holm-cloud was resting, soft and shining like a white rose with the sun on it. It was as though Skiddaw had put on a decoration to please the children. But most wonderful, to Matt, seemed the contrast between this soft and brilliant cloud and the shadow of deepest purple that darkened the mountain flanks. Ten minutes ago, when Matt had last considered her, Skiddaw was in full sunlight: now the shadows had caught her and the purple that had been scattered, of one depth only, was now suddenly gathered into a web of purple upon purple with shadows in that again of ebony, violet, and dark crimson.

Running up to the mountain were the woods, amber-gold, russet-dark, and wine-grape darkened. He knew very little about woods as yet, for he was of the city, but he saw how the tree-boles were clean from many rains, how the Scotch firs had a sheen on them above their dark thickness, and the birches were enfolded in purple haze. But had he known more—and very much more—he could not have told how at this especial moment the gold was both bright, so that it hurt the eyes, and dark like molten fire, or why the degrees of light hung in layers like veils, from thin feathered gold to feathers of orange, as though giant birds had dropped their jewelled wings.

'Such a moment cannot come again. . . . Such a moment will not come again.' His lips formed the words while his eyes stared. The singing voices came thinly across the clear crystal air. Children's voices with sharp edges and a sudden high catch of joyfulness.

He turned and saw the Lake sparkling with content. You could pick up the dark-golden islands in your hand and lay them on your table. The sun was of such a brightness on the Lake that the Borrow-dale Jaws and Glaramara and the others beyond it were hazy clouds of sun-threaded darkness. A magical land beyond the water, out of human touch.

Under the trees to the right of the meadow were the trestle-tables laden for the feast.

The music and fiddling ceased. Old Dr. Porter, the clergyman, now more than eighty years of age, came forward, his hands stretched towards the Lake to bless.

Now for Matt Turner the divine moment had come. Never, never would he forget it. For all the world stood still. Not a sound, not the rustle of a breeze nor the voice of the smallest bird, nor the cry of the youngest child was to be heard. The old man's voice, weak, trembling, but clear, asked God's blessing. The holm-cloud waited: the colour of the trees resolved itself into a settled harmony of glory. The figures, like fragments of nature, had no human aspect, neither aspirations nor fears, and were translated into the pattern of beauty that had been designed from the beginning of time for that moment.

'Lord God, Who seest all things and knowest all things, we pray Thee of Thy love and care for us to give us this day . . .'

'This moment will not come again . . .'

Matt Turner would remember it. The happy pause before the tempest.

Lucy, alas, had at that moment no eye for nature and perhaps at no time had a great deal. Her passion was for human contacts and most especially for one.

To the left of the procession and parallel with it, a small party of ladies and gentlemen rode their horses. Carey Courthope was one of them. The other three Lucy also knew. They were Sir Francis and Lady Alice Darling and their long, gawky, stupid daughter, Priscilla.

Nicholas and Lucy had on several occasions visited the Darlings at their heavy dank house off the Cockermouth road. Lucy had seen two beetles cross the parlour fireplace on her last visit there. It must be with the Darlings, then, that Carey must be staying. What an unendurable visit for him!

Dr. Porter had finished his prayer and the children sang another hymn. Then like a flight of starlings they flew in their white dresses across the meadow, passed so to the tables where the feast was spread.

The Darlings left their horses to the care of a stout country-looking servant and marched magnificently forward, having seen at a distance Nicholas' great figure—as indeed who could help it?

Sir Francis was a pompous fat man, and Lady Alice Darling was the silliest woman in the North of England. The girl Priscilla was silent and awkward, poor thing, because her mother was so loquacious.

'I wish my mother were dead!' she had burst out once to the startled Lucy. 'Indeed I do! If I say a word she is sure to come out with her "Fie, Priscilla! For shame, Priscilla!"—and if a young man should be by she will say in a whisper that all can hear, "Go with Priscilla! Take her into the wood, pray!"—for she would have me married at any cost. And so indeed I would be, but who will marry me when I am pushed so shamefully forward?'

Carey was with them. He was now a stout heavy man, and must be thirty-nine, Lucy thought, if he were a day. But he was still an elegant creature. He was dressed, in spite of his stoutness, in the extreme of fashion with the busked corset-like body, the pointed waist-line, the sloping skirt of overlapping tabs, and deep shoulder-wings. The outer thighs were decorated lavishly with ribbon loops and round his hat curled a magnificent ostrich feather. His colours were mulberry and gold, and two delicate emerald earrings swung from his small ears.

But his face was weary, she thought; there was something in his eyes that had not been there before. As their eyes met her hands trembled. He looked at her with eagerness as though he would say: 'Release me from my prison. I have found you again and this time I will not let you go!'

The two menservants of Nicholas and the Darlings had laid the food out on the grass and brought cushions for everyone's comfort. Sir Francis began at once, for he was never a moment late in stating his opinions, on the subject of the Palatinate. That summer a Spanish force had marched up the Rhine and seized the Palatinate. King James for once bestirred himself to defend the inheritance of his daughter and his grandchildren. He had summoned Parliament to see what could be done, but before Parliament had time to meet, his daughter and her husband were flying from Bohemia after a crushing defeat outside Prague.

This news was not yet known to Sir Francis, but he had nevertheless plenty to say—namely, that the English were worth all the foreigners in the world anywhere, and that if Parliament did not do exactly as the King wished, he, Sir Francis, would want to know the reason why.

This stirred Peter, who remarked indignantly: 'It is time that England had a free Parliament. The King must give the country freedom before Parliament can give him the money he wants.'

This rebellious statement stirred Sir Francis to apoplexy, and the more so that he was eating a piece of pigeon-pie at the moment. So he choked and spluttered while his round bulbous eyes started from his head. Now Lady Alice broke in with: 'Fie, Sir Francis. I will have no politics. You know well that I will not. But he is choking himself to death. William, clap your master on the back. And take some Canary, Sir Francis. If there is a thing I cordially detest, it is those politics. Made by men for men. Women are too wise to meddle their fingers in such matters! No, William—Sir Francis has had enough.' She bent a stern eye upon Peter. 'I am sure, Mr. Garland, you do not mean half that you say. Deny the King money, poor man? Why, who is to have money if the King is not? But there—I detest all such talk about money. It is vulgar and should never be mentioned between ladies and gentlemen. There, Sir Francis, that is better. Wipe your doublet, my love. I am sure Mr. Garland intended no such foolishness.'

Under cover of all this Carey was able to say to Lucy what she had had in her own mind:

'Now that I have found you again I will not let you go.'

She answered sadly:

'We are both older, Carey.'

He nodded. 'But not too old. You know how I have loved you for twenty years.'

'You use words lightly. In the last ten years you have seen me three times.'

He answered eagerly, leaning towards her, his hand touching her dress: 'What could I do? After the last time, that morning at Whitehall, I was sent to Rome. If you knew in Rome how I thought of you——'

'You never wrote.'

'No. Because I was uncertain of you. I felt too deeply to write anything but that I loved you. Trivialities were impossible between us.'

She knew that he was ardent now chiefly because he had spent a dreary fortnight, and he felt perhaps his growing age and his stoutness, and young ladies were not quite so ardent as once they had been. But she cared nothing for reasons. All heaven was before her eyes.

When the feast was over, the children dancing about the meadow before the games began, and the shadows lengthening over the hills, Peter Garland got up from the grass and wandered away towards the woods.

He had behaved badly. He was always behaving badly. Here he was, twenty-nine years of age, and he hadn't learned good manners yet. What was worse, he was not sure that he wished to learn!

He stumbled over tufts of grass as he walked, and his round good-natured face was frowning.

It was the old, old conflict for him that looked now as though it would never be resolved! The struggle between his temperament and his ideas. His temperament was all for the full enjoyment of life. He loved to dance, to go to the play, to kiss a girl. He hated fornication and lies and cruelty, but innocent fun he had still a small boy's love for. He could not say any longer that the strange Katherine Christian was the only girl he had kissed. He was strong and lusty, and wanted to be married. A man must have a woman or what sort of man was he?

So much for his temperament. But his ideas led him altogether into the other camp. For five years now he had belonged, in heart and soul, to the Presbyter, Puritan movement. He consorted daily with grave solemn men in black who thought only of the gravest affairs, who, if they had children, seemed to have them only by accident, who were altogether against dancing, play-books, and any kissing of girls, who could quote the Bible chapter after chapter and never be wrong in a word.

Peter detested the hypocrites and poseurs and self-advantage-seekers in this world as much as he detested the rakes and profligates at the Court. It seemed that there was no perfect world anywhere. His love of England was as much the basis of his faith as it was of Rashleigh's.

He would fight for England, die for England, and undergo any suffering to make her free. And she *was* not free! Abroad and at home she was a mockery. The thought of the Palatinate or the Spanish Marriage or Buckingham made poor Peter's heart hammer at his throat and he would clench his fists and stutter if someone spoke to him, and his round cheeks would grow crimson.

A man like this Francis Darling angered him so deeply that he was almost on the point of challenging him to a duel, and would probably have done so had he not been afraid of making a fool of himself before Nicholas, if he had not disapproved of duelling, if the choleric knight had not been so very much older than himself.

But now he strode when he didn't stumble into the woods that fringed the meadow and encountered, like the blessèd knight in the *Faerie Queene,* the most beautiful lady he had ever seen in his life.

She was standing at the wood edge looking, her lips parted in a smile, at the children who, from here, seemed like butterflies hovering in the light against the Lake that was now a brazen cup of red-gold. She was a very tall lady and very dark. He would never forget the dress that she wore—never so long as he lived.

She wore a dress of dark rose, two pairs of gauntlet gloves one upon another, beautifully embroidered, and a hat with rosy feathers. She carried a whip. Her eyes were the largest, blackest, deepest that he had ever even dreamed of. She was too tall for a woman perhaps, but her figure was most lovely. So he could go on in his catalogue which meant nothing at all. But he stared at her black ringleted hair, her pale cheeks, her parted lips. He stared like a yokel.

Then, miracle of all miracles, she turned and looked at him and said at once, laughing:

'Why, I know you!'

As he said nothing, she went on:

'I have forgot your name but you have twice kissed me. I knew your name once and—wait—wait . . . yes, I have it, the Christian name at least. Peter—Peter . . .'

He stared and then with a cry realized it. She was the magician's daughter! She was a woman now, but the voice was the same, although deeper in volume. There was the same separateness, humour, even malice. He could hear the child cry indignantly, 'Put me down! My father needs me . . . ,' and watch the lighted crinkling sea, and the man with the long nose, and the falling flowers . . .

'Oh, you . . . !' he said with a deep sigh. 'I have wondered so very often . . .'

'And now we meet in a magic wood . . .'

'Are you staying here?'

'Staying here? Working rather. I help to manage the affairs of Mr. Tofthouse of Keswick.'

'You . . . !'

'Ah, you do not know all that has happened to me—some of it not to be told to a fine gentleman like yourself. In the first case, my father hanged himself.'

Peter nodded. 'Yes. The Overbury affair.'

She looked at him grimly. 'The Overbury affair. Then I was in Geneva, afterwards Rome, then London again. But I had had always a passionate longing for this North Country. Ever since the day—do you remember?—when we visited your father's house and went on to Scotland—to our ruin, as it happened.

'So, a year ago, I rode up leisurely to York on horseback, and then to Carlisle. Six months back I discovered that no ground pleased me like this ground. In Keswick one night at the inn Mr. Tofthouse, drunk, wished to insult me, but discovered instead that I had a knowledge of figures. So, rather than lie with him, I added his sums for him. I live in a little house with an old lady and an old man in a village called Portinskill. There is a river under my window, Crosthwaite Church beyond it, so the Devil, whom I knew once, fears to visit me any longer. I am safe, you see, Mr. Peter . . . ?'

'Garland,' he said.

'Yes—Garland. To confess the truth I recognized you at the time you were crossing the meadow. First I saw that very tall old gentleman who once engaged my father.'

'Yes. My cousin, Nicholas Herries.'

At last she held out her hand, taking off her gauntlet gloves. Her hand closed over his with the strong, firm-boned grasp of a man.

'I am pleased to see you again, Mr. Garland, for you were good to me when I was a child, when I needed it.'

'I can still be good . . .' he said, stammering.

'Oh, but now I do not need it. Mr. Tofthouse is very kind and his son Christopher. Mrs. Tofthouse not perhaps *quite* so kind.'

He moved towards her.

She smiled: he thought scornfully.

'My horse is at the other side of the trees. I am riding to Portinskill. Farewell, farewell, Mr. Garland . . .'

Her beauty made him stupid.

'I shall see you—I shall see you.'

'Mr. Tofthouse is easily found in Keswick.' She paused again. Her voice was softer, gentler than it had been.

'You had a sister.'

'Yes, Lucy. She is there—over there—with the others. Come with me and see her. She would be greatly pleased.'

'Oh, no.' She shook her head vehemently. 'Did you not know? I—I am not allowed into the full daylight! Mr. Tofthouse and I—we work by a candle.'

Departure makes beauty to be twice so beautiful. Poor Peter was blinded and felt as though there had been witchcraft. She had risen from the ground more lovely than Helen of Troy and now he was blinder than Homer. He was naïf and simple for his years. Peter, Lucy, even Rashleigh, all had this in common. A vision had assaulted him. He felt ravished, weakened at the knees, his heart leaping in a bowl of water. Boys and old men see visions best. But he knew one true thing—that his life was, from that moment, changed.

Now the afternoon was advancing, the shadows were lengthening, and because it was late in September the evening would be chill.

So now the principal event of the day had arrived. The children had gathered into the middle of the meadow. The boy and girl considered most deserving for their work and character during the past year stood alone. On this occasion it was a girl with a grave face and gentle eyes, and a small stubby boy called John Bastable of whom more would afterwards be heard. John was short and stocky, with a round face, a snub, impertinent nose, and a most determined mouth.

These two faced one another and arched hands; then the children one by one came up and chose on which side they would be. They whispered either to the girl or to John and then took their place beside the one or the other. When the two strings of boys and girls were complete, they proceeded, first the one line and then the other, under the arched hands, and all sang together:

> *'How many miles to Barley Bridge?*
> *Three score and ten.*
> *Can I get there by candle-light?*
> *Yes, if your legs be long.*
> *A curtsey to you, and a curtsey to you,*
> *If you please, will you let the King's horses through?*
> *Through and through shall they go for the King's sake,*
> *But the one that is hindmost shall meet with a great mistake.'*

As they ran through, the girl and John had to catch the last one by lowering their arms. But when all were through and formed again, the long, thin schoolmaster with a villainous cast in one eye came forward and laid a handkerchief down. This was for the tug-of-war. The children pulled as though their lives and futures were at stake: then with a great cry John Bastable, although he had set his face like a rock and pulled to burst his heart, was drawn over the handkerchief, and the other side had won.

Immediately there followed the real tug-of-war, between the men of Borrowdale and Keswick. For this the reward was an old silver tankard said to be of the greatest antiquity, and held for one year by the victors.

The men were stripped to their shirts and drawers. Every man had his friends in the audience and shouts rose on all sides. The two leaders were famous tug-of-war men and of homeric strength. But in each team of twelve there was not a weakling. At the dropping of the handkerchief every man bent down and the strain began. You felt as though Glaramara were pulling against Skiddaw or the Gavel against Scawfell. For what seemed to the watching world an eternity there was no movement. Then quite suddenly the Borrowdale man's foot slipped and he was drawn over the handkerchief. But it was to be the best of three. At the second tug the Borrowdale men were victorious. At the third tug, after a fearful swaying first this way, then that, the Borrowdale men won the second time and a great roar of cheering went up.

Now the dusk was falling. The Lake was a silver veil. On all the boats the lanterns were lit. The lights bobbed and danced, throwing trails of colour on to the water. As the boats started off to the sound of the dipping oars, everyone began to sing.

The world was magical with happiness. Any who had cares or doubts or perturbations lost them in that moment. Lovers kissed in the gathering dusk, husbands and wives held hands, the children watched the lights and heard the singing voices and thought that they had never known such a day.

On a little promontory that looked over the Lake in the thick wood Carey and Lucy lay in one another's arms.

'Carey, Carey, I have loved you so long.'

'My adored Lucy . . . Oh, Lucy dearest.'

'Ah, Carey. . . .'

'Lucy, Lucy—my own—for ever.'

'Carey . . .'

The lights were a distant sparkle on the Lake, the voices very faint: the stars with a rush came out as though they too were singing.

'THE PEACOCK HAS FLOWN'

'THE PEACOCK HAS FLOWN' was the pretentious name of an inn situated two miles from Keswick on the lower flanks of Skiddaw looking over towards Bassenthwaite Lake.

CARL A. RUDISILL
LIBRARY
LENOIR RHYNE COLLEGE

A rough road outside the inn led ultimately to Carlisle. The inn was a rude and ready rendezvous for every order of men and women. It was hidden from the road by trees and had about it a certain air of secrecy and mystery.

The man who owned it built it some thirty years before this. Nick Bowater arrived in Keswick in the later years of Elizabeth with plenty of money to burn. He had made it, gossip said, in the Indies. He said himself that he had sailed with Drake. Less kindly chatterers said that he had never left England's shores and had made his money by blackmailing the Duchess of X——. He was handsome enough at that time to be guilty of anything—black-eyed, broad-shouldered, thin-flanked, with a deep, melodious voice. Some said he was an illegitimate son of Leicester's. He hinted at it himself.

In any case he had money, and he built the inn. A mad painter was in Keswick at the time and Nick asked him to paint a sign. He said that he would—but on one condition. He must paint what he pleased and name the inn. His own name was Sam Kittigrew and Nick had a very special partiality for him. He painted a peacock, a grand one with tail full spread, in the foreground, and then, in the right-hand corner, a small purple-greenish bird flying. He said the inn must be named 'The Peacock Has Flown.' Nick thought that a ridiculous name, but he stuck to his word and the inn was known as 'The Peacock' through all Cumberland and Westmorland. The Peacock sign still hung there and had but recently received a fresh coating of paint.

The inn was large and commodious, but, alas, Nick had degenerated with the years. Drink, women, gambling—the usual old stale vices—had been too much for him. Also he was involved in deep affairs and these had not gone too well with him. Some said he was a Catholic or at least in conspiracy with the Catholics, and since Guy Fawkes Catholics had not been very popular. Especially just now when Prince Charles and Buckingham were at Madrid over the Spanish Marriage, the notion of which was hated by the whole of the country, did the people of Keswick look upon Nick with hesitation.

Not that the trade at his inn seemed to suffer. There were always people about and of an evening the chief public room would be crowded. There were soldiers, sailors with wonderful stories of the Spanish Main, ladies and gentlemen on their way to and from Scotland, farmers, county gentlemen. Nick, who was now fat, thick-voiced, and purple-veined in the face, was astute at the business. And a sharp-visaged bony woman who was said to be his wife (nobody believed it. Nick had a better taste than that) managed the girls under her with a virago-like shrillness. Drink and food were good and the beds soft.

Nevertheless there was something unpleasant about the place. Although it was built just above the road it had always an isolated air. It may have been that Skiddaw towering above its chimneys made it appear remote. Odd silences fell upon it. You might lie in bed on a night of rain and hear the streams running fiercely, the rain beating on the windows, and the wind howling along some gully. There were stories too. There had been a violent death or two, and cries heard in the night, and the girls, having quarrelled with the virago or resisted Nick's amorous proposals, would return to their homes and spread tales.

Spies, on one purpose or another, were said to be constantly passing through, and however drunken Nick might be he was said always to keep his head and his secrets too.

The place, however, was, by this, winning a bad name for the many quarrelsome scenes that took place in it, and had not the food and drink been so excellent, would have fallen altogether into disrepute.

On a certain stormy winter night, Carey Courthope and Lucy Garland were having supper in the best parlour. From the public room came a great deal of noise, mostly of the rough, discordant singing kind. This was not a private parlour, for two other tables were occupied—one by two countrymen of a better sort and the other by a tall lady and a little cock-sparrow gentleman.

There was a roaring fire in the stone fireplace, the candles burnt brightly on the tables, and the rain beat on the windows, giving a warm cosy feeling to the room.

Carey was only too cosy, for he had drunk too much and his stout, pasty, handsome face was in an ill temper.

Lucy was pale-cheeked, and when she moved forward to correct a candle it was clear that she was far advanced in pregnancy. A pretty but sluttish girl brought in the food, and Carey pinched her arm. She gave a little cry and looked at him with resentful fury, but she said no word.

The two countrymen, who had also been drinking, were arguing. The larger and more domineering was talking loudly against an Act passed apparently years before in 1616 (he was always alluding to the date and Sir Wilfred Lawson and Sir Richard Musgrave who had enforced it locally) of rules concerning Church observance. It was a rule apparently that no one must eat or drink or remain in his house during Divine Service and that any person found walking or standing idly in the churchyard or market-place in time of Divine Service should pay twelve pence as fine, and that there should be no piping, dancing, bowling, bear- or bull-baiting, or any other profanation on the Lord's day. It was this last evidently that had dragged our friend into trouble, for it seemed that he had been training a sheep-dog puppy, using chickens for sheep, on a Sunday and had been fined for it. His indignation was extreme and his voice ever louder and louder.

'I shall be constrained,' Carey said, 'to rebuke this fellow.'

'Let us go to our room,' Lucy said. 'I am infinitely weary.'

He stared at her speculatively.

'You are mighty good company.'

'You know why I am weary.'

'Yes,' he answered, with the level quiet carefulness of a drunken man, 'and I am weary of hearing of it. One would think'—he paused and repeated it—'one would think—that no woman had ever borne child before . . .'

Lucy had an excellent spirit and the events of the last year had not cowed it.

'I shall not quarrel. It takes two for that. Besides that, Carey, I know you now so well that it would be myself I'd be quarrelling with. Nor,' she said, now in her turn looking at him speculatively, 'have I anything to reproach you with. I accepted the adventure on any terms. . . . Only I beg you to come to our room with me . . . now . . . I am not well. . . .'

She slowly stroked her forehead with her hand.

'You have a great contempt for me,' he said slowly, still staring at her. 'No one has ever despised me so deeply. And for why? I have given you a child and I could not marry you. And for why? Because of the French Madame——'

She answered:

'No, dear Carey, not for that—my contempt, I mean. Only because you are what you are. And have always been. And how could you help that? Or any man. We must all feel some contempt for one another after living together. Contempt, pity, tenderness—they are from the same source, I think.'

He closed his eyes and swayed a little as though he would fall asleep where he was.

'I understand nothing that you say,' he murmured. 'I have never understood you. That has been our mistake.'

But at that moment the big countryman banged the table with his fist and swore that he would go this moment to Sir Wilfred Lawson and drag his fine out of him even though he had to knock the town down first.

This was too much for Carey, who jumped to his feet and cried out: ' 'Fore God, sir, there are ladies here who would eat and drink in quiet comfort. What do you mean by it, sir? I demand an apology, sir.'

The big countryman rose slowly to *his* feet and stared at Carey, gathering his wits together, as the countryman will, until they shall all be marshalled in good order and ready for anything. He was a really vast man with a thick jaw and wide-open childish blue eyes.

'I was speaking to my friend,' at last he said.

Carey was very fine in his mulberry-coloured coat, jewelled buttons, painted cheeks, and earrings. He felt like Jupiter chiding the meanest of his earth-bound subjects. He was in a towering passion and it seemed to him that the room swayed with his words.

'I said, sir, that I was with a lady, and the loud noises that you have been making have greatly discomposed her, and that therefore I must have an apology, and at once, sir. Without a moment's delay, sir, or I must take steps, sir . . .'

All the room now was listening. The girl, holding a dish in her hand, was standing at the door watching. So the door behind her was open, and it appeared that in the big room there was plenty of quarrelling too. Voices were raised: someone was drunkenly singing. A plate dropped with a crash to the floor.

Beyond this the storm was getting up, blowing as it does on a Cumberland mountain in sudden half-enraged, half-playful gusts. So, at last, the countryman (His name was Matthew Swinburne. It deserves a place in the Herries family history because of what came of this) had to raise his voice, and he spoke to some purpose.

'I don't know your name, sir, and I intended no offence. This is a place where I have paid for my food and conversation with a friend.

You may not be accustomed to the way we speak in these parts. Quiet on the whole but making our points if the need arises. If I have disturbed the ladies I make my apologies. You are a gentleman from London by your appearance, and I would be glad of your opinion, sir, on these Church matters. I was explaining to my friend here——'

'I don't give a pox for what you were explaining to your friend!' Carey shouted, seeing himself more than ever as Jupiter and wondering why the room bowed and swayed to him as it did. 'If you cannot behave as a gentleman behaves, sir, you should leave this room to your betters, and if you make your beastly county of Cumberland an apology for your manners, then I say, sir, it is a mighty poor apology.'

That indeed was too much for the Cumbrian. He broke in his astounded indignation into the very broadest dialect, so that Carey did not understand a word that he was saying. He *was* understood, however, perfectly by a number of gentlemen who, hearing Carey's voice, had crowded the door. They were laughing, applauding, and calling out. Mr. Matthew Swinburne meanwhile explained that a personal rebuke he could take as well as any man, and he had made his apology for talking too loudly, but when it came to a gentleman from London making insulting remarks about Cumberland—why, then he was not one to sit quietly under it, and if the London gentleman did not apologize . . .

'I apologize! Apologize! Apologize! And I shall say, sir, exactly what I please about Cumberland, and from what I have seen of it, sir, you can have your Cumberland for the wettest, dirtiest, most muddy . . .' He was pleased with his adjectives, for, at the top of his voice, he repeated them again, adding some very obscure words to increase their general glory.

This was, of course, very much more than Mr. Swinburne could endure, and he would at once have thrown himself upon Carey had there not been an unexpected interruption.

The little gentleman who had been quietly eating his supper at the corner table with a lady surprisingly came forward. He was, in appearance, a ridiculous little gentleman, for he had a short snub nose, a squat body with a large stomach, and was gaudily dressed. However, with his hand on his small-sword and a very fierce look on his round face, he confronted Carey. He spoke quietly and with authority.

'It is not my place, sir,' he said, 'to interfere in a private quarrel, but you, sir, have made this dispute public before the whole room. I am sure if you had requested this gentleman to speak more quietly to his friend, he would have done so. He has made you a handsome apology. I was myself born not twenty miles from here, and you have, before the whole world, insulted my birthplace. On behalf of my birthplace I demand a public apology.'

Carey stared at the little gentleman as though he could not believe his ears.

'Why, you—you—you cock-sparrow! What business is it of yours? And if I do remark on your birthplace, sir, I do remark if that is my will. And if you wish to hear it again, I repeat that of all the rain-shotten, mud-grubbing, abandoned wildernesses, this Cumberland of yours is the worst in all the country of England.'

The little gentleman's countenance was mottled with anger. He did not, however, raise his voice but drew his rapier and said:

'For that, whoever you are, you shall fight me here and now. I take that from no man alive.'

At this there was great cheering from the doorway, the servant-girl cried out, and the landlord could be heard calling from the other room.

A sad thing, however, occurred, for at the sight of the rapier Carey's colour changed and his fury abated. He stared at the little man, mumbled something unintelligible, pushed past them all, and left the room.

A moment's silence followed, there was a roar of scornful laughter from the doorway, the little man, as though he could not believe his eyes, slowly sheathed his rapier, looking as deeply ashamed as though he himself had been a coward.

The lady who had been dining with the little gentleman had sat without moving throughout this scene. Now, as Mr. Swinburne sat down with his friend again and the crowd moved back from the door into the other room, she rose and, disregarding her little gentleman, went to where Lucy was sitting.

'You are ill,' she said in a deep resonant voice. She was very dark and tall, and Lucy, looking up and seeing how handsome and friendly she was, smiled and said quietly:

'Yes. The room is very hot.'

'Let me help you,' the lady said.

'Yes. If you would.'

She rose and put her hand through the lady's arm.

'If you could help me to my room . . .'

Indeed she could scarcely stand. Slowly they went together through the two rooms, up the broad staircase, along the passage, at whose windows the storm was driving fiercely, and into a dark chamber in which a fire was dimly burning. Lucy lit two candles and then, unable to resist her weakness, found her way to the bed, and lay down on it.

'Would you lock the door?' she asked.

The lady complied.

'I would prefer that he should not come in—not for the moment. I should speak my mind, which is always foolish if you cannot improve the situation.'

The lady stood, very tall and commanding, over her.

'And now I will fetch you something—some brandy?'

'No. . . . You are very kind. Some water.'

The lady went across to the ewer and basin, and poured some water into a glass and gave it to her. Then, kneeling, she stirred the fire until it leapt into bright flame.

'How very kind you are!' Lucy said. 'And how beautiful!' The lady looked back from her knees, smiling.

'Your husband——'

'He is not my husband. Oh, this child I am going to have is his,—but he is not my husband.'

The lady rose, and Lucy thought she looked glorious in her dark purple dress standing before the fire.

'Now you must not talk,' she said. 'I will come back later.'

'No. Please stay with me a little. I do not know you or why you are so kind. And your husband who so very gallantly——'

'He is not my husband either,' the lady answered, laughing. 'When I have a husband, if I ever do, he will be quite a different kind of man.'

'Nevertheless he was gallant. While my—gentleman——' She sighed. 'Poor Carey! I am so greatly ashamed of him. He has no character at all. None. I am weary to death of him, his face, his voice, all that he is —but I have a compassion for him, and I loved him so long—before I knew him.'

'I wish to know nothing,' the lady said rather sharply. 'In the morning you may be sorry that you spoke to a stranger.'

Lucy said: 'You do not seem to me like a stranger. And yet I have never seen you before.'

The lady smiled, a beautiful smile that had no weakness but was gentle, that gave no intimacy but was warming to the heart.

'But I have seen *you* before. And I have spoken to you. Once you held me in your arms.'

Lucy raised herself on her elbow and stared.

'Oh, no—it is not possible. I could never forget anyone as beautiful as you are.'

The lady came nearer to the bed. 'Look at me more closely. Do you not remember?'

Lucy looked. Their eyes met in a long encounter.

'No. . . . No. I have never seen you.'

'Ah, but you have! Three years ago, almost in this same place. Your brother also did not recognize me—until I told him.'

'My brother! Peter? Rashleigh?'

'Yes . . . Peter. It was a children's festival by the Lake. I saw you but you did not see me. Your brother asked me to speak to you.'

Lucy sat up, staring. 'That day! As though I should not remember it! Everything began that day. That lovely day in that lovely place. How often I have remembered it, and should be ashamed of it, no doubt, if I had any shame at all. But I think I have never had any shame. Nor have I now—very much. Except just now when he ran from the room. But his son may be born at any moment—and I would wish, if I could, not to feel shame of the father.'

'Well, then,' the lady said, 'I would ask you another question. Do you remember once in your father's house by the sea a magician and a little girl and some men who cried out against us——?'

'Yes. Yes!' Lucy clapped her hands. 'You are the little girl.'

'I am the little girl. My name is Katherine Christian.' She stood close to the bed, and Lucy stretched out her hand and drew her down and kissed her cheek.

'Oh, how wonderful! That you should be here when I need so

desperately someone. Not that I will put anything upon you, and perhaps you are leaving this place to-morrow . . .'

'I cannot say.' She was standing with straight stiffness again. Her lovely dark face was grave, reserved, apart.

'You should not have kissed me.'

'Why?'

'Because I did not mean, by reminding you of that old child story, that we had any bond. I have no bond with anyone. No one can touch me or harm or love me—and if they hate me I do not care.'

'I should like to say that,' Lucy said, 'but my nature will never allow me. I have had three years of disgrace, and it has not changed me. I must always be loved by someone or something. What weakness when I see so clearly that everyone and everything must always disappoint. At least now there will be my child who for a year or two will be what I have it to be.'

'You poor child!' Katherine sat down on the edge of the bed. 'How did you ever come to be in such a position—for such a man, I mean?— But there! I have been no very wise woman myself.'

Lucy, lying back on the pillow now and looking at Katherine, thought that she had never seen anything so lovely as the jet-black hair against the softness of the perfectly shaped neck and edge of the half-turned cheek. A man, she thought, must indeed go mad with the desire to hold those long curls in his hand and stroke the gentle colour of that cheek.

But the cheek was not gentle, nor the mouth. How exquisite her face when she smiled—but when she was grave it was almost a man's face. The dark round of her head had depths of colour in its blackness upon which the candle-light played. The whole form of her body, the breasts small, the waist slim, but the thighs long and perfectly shaped beneath the heavy skirt, delighted Lucy who impetuously loved beauty anywhere. She had never in all her years seen any woman so lovely as this one—so she asked, smiling:

'You wonder at my being with Carey. Then I may wonder at you— at your little gentleman.'

'Poor Granby—Lord Meresby. He has a place towards Penrith. But I was with him first in London before I knew he was North Country. I have been his mistress in London these two years on condition that he knew that I did not love him, that he supported me adequately, and that we parted when I wished it. We are parting to-morrow.'

'You have no liking for him, then?'

'Oh—liking—yes. He is brave like a little fierce dog. He is kind. He adores me but knows that he must lose me.'

'Have you been lonely?' Lucy asked. 'Your friends, relatives . . .'

Katherine laughed. 'My father, whom you may remember with the large nose, hanged himself about the Overbury affair. Then I kept honest for a long while. I came North and did sums for a lawyer in Keswick. Then soon after my meeting with your brother I travelled to London with a pretty young man who loved horses and called on his mare in his sleep. After that in London—there was this and there was that. Then at last Granby. He lives with a crazy wife in his place near Penrith. We have come up here to part. He goes to his lady, who has a passion, I understand, for thinking herself the Queen of Sheba, to-morrow. Poor Granby! He has his virtues . . .'

'And yourself?' Lucy asked.

'Myself? What matter? I belong to nobody and nobody belongs to me. I love nobody, I trust nobody. I fear nobody. I have a kind of impulse for living, but why I cannot say, for life would hurt you if it could, stick its claws into you if you let it. But I shall not let it, for I keep my heart to myself. There . . .' She took Lucy's hand in hers. 'You and your brother were once kind to me and if I allowed it that would make a sort of bond. But I will not allow it. I am no good to anyone as a friend. I have a fierce temper, no morality—and would hurt anyone, if I loved them, just to hurt myself. I am the daughter of a bad man and I never knew my mother. I have seen such things that God, if He existed, would hide His face for His own shame. So now—you must sleep—and I will look in at you again. . . .' She saw that Lucy was suffering. 'If labour comes—have you a physician here? Is there any wise woman in the place?'

But before Lucy could answer the lock of the door was violently tried, and then a fierce banging.

'That is Carey. He had better come in or he will rouse the place.'

Katherine went to the door and unbolted it. Carey, dishevelled but, it seemed, sober, stood there. He stared at Katherine, his weak mouth wide open.

Katherine said: 'She is tired and in pain. You had better fetch a physician. She is, I think, near her time.'

Carey had the look of a sulky abashed boy.

'Who are you? But it does not matter. She has been telling you that I am a sot and a coward.'

'I was in the room and saw it for myself.'

Carey was a gentleman although a sorry one, and he had never in all his life seen anyone so beautiful as Katherine.

'I was drunk. I did not know what I was about.'

Katherine moved impatiently.

'Have you found a physician?'

'No—I——'

'Then I will.' She moved to the door, looked back for a moment at Lucy, and went out.

He looked sheepishly at the bed, then approached it.

'Do you suffer?' he asked.

'No. It is better now.'

'You hate me. You think I ran away.'

She smiled up at him, then turned wearily her head on the pillow.

'Most certainly you ran away, Carey. But not for the first time nor the last.'

'You despise me. You have always despised me.'

'Always? Oh, no! I loved you for many years. You appeared to me the most gallant and most beautiful of men. Now—you are the father of my child.'

His lips moved. She thought that he was going to cry.

Because she hated it when he did that, she rose up and said gently: 'Come, Carey. Nothing is changed. Help me to undress.'

She stood up and he began to loose her laces.

'Who was that woman?'

'Nobody. She saw that I was unwell. She was kind to me—— Nobody.'

'She was most handsome.'

They did not speak. She threw her night-rail over her head, hastily pulling it over her body. Directly after doing so she looked into the round silver mirror above the table and she saw his face. He was not looking at her but staring at the wall, and, by his expression, she knew that he was going to leave her for ever.

He had made up his mind. He was a coward and a sot, but he could be obstinate. She knew his resolve as clearly as though he had spoken.

'Oh, God,' she thought, 'what shall I do? Alone here with the child and perhaps no money.'

Also looking at his weak, sulky, frightened face, she knew that she still loved him—as though he were her disobedient, disappointing, un-lovable son.

Her legs quivered under the burden and she feared that she was going to faint, but with a mighty effort she beat back all the attacking forces.

She laid her hand very gently on his arm.

'Now help me to the bed.' She lay down. She caught his head be-tween her hands, leant a little towards him and kissed him on the lips.

His mouth moved. She knew that he wished to say something. But he did not. He looked like a frightened, bewildered, shame-faced boy.

Then, on tiptoe, as though she were already asleep, he crept from the room.

BIRTH OF AN IMPORTANT MEMBER OF THE HERRIES FAMILY

THE DAY FOLLOWING these events was Christmas Eve and the storm of rain that lashed the windows on the preceding night had changed now to snow. 'Very seasonable indeed,' Katherine thought, as she washed herself in the small pewter basin, drying herself with the rough towel, standing in front of the crinkled mirror seeing that there was no superfluous fat on her, but especially rejoicing in the freedom of having no clothes, of being by herself, independent, free as from this day she would be.

Beyond the window she saw the grey smoking snow and in the fire-place the dead ashes, and shivered. The room was bitter cold. So she put on her crimson dress with the fur lining, and the Russian boots and the hat with the fur top.

She ran her hands through the long ringlets that lay in dark splen-dour on the stiff gold collar of her jacket. Within one lappet of the long coat was a thin sharp small-sword with a gold sheath, and within the other a small pistol.

She was wearing everything that might signify a glorious departure from her little lord. While she dressed she thought of Lucy and knew that, when this first thing had been done first, there would be another second question to settle.

Little Granby lay in bed in the next room, the fur rug that he travelled with pulled close up to his ears that protruded as with a conscious life of their own.

She went in, stood by the bed, and looked at him. She could see now his mouth, like that of a fish, open, and from it both bad breath and a whistling sound proceeding.

She knew well that no human being of any sex, age, splendour, or beauty should be seen or heard in the morning before rising; nevertheless it did seem to her amazing that she could have been for so long this little animal's mistress, known him with such intimacy, physical and social if never spiritual and mental.

It was true that she had never surrendered herself to him in any real sense: she blamed herself not at all, it being her present creed that she was to use all men and women to her advantage, that there being no honesty, loyalty, or charity in this world of savages, self-defence and self-help were the only doctrines.

But she could not altogether refuse the maternal. It was that that had made these last two years possible. She remembered what Lucy had said about *her* wretched cowardly man and she wished passionately as she stood there that she was not a woman. A man would yield to no such weakness.

Nevertheless, poor little Granby! He had been good to her after his kind, worthy and generous. That he had adored her body and given her what he had because of that, could not be counted to him for unrighteousness. And he was brave and he was honest and he was generous.

Gently she shook his shoulder. He stirred, snorted, wiped his face with his hand, and sat up, his yellow silk night-cap nodding at her as he raised his head. Poor little man—and this very day he must return to his hideous Queen of Sheba!

He stared at her, for she was a glorious vision. She was like an angel come down from heaven—and she was dressed to go out. He stared and then he smiled, rubbing his bristly chin in a shame-faced way.

'Granby—I have come to bid you farewell.'

He gurgled like a baby, then realizing the significance of the word 'farewell,' said huskily:

'Oh, no, Katherine—pray you—give me time to wash and dress before——'

'It is better as it is. It has all been arranged between us. You must have your breakfast here and when you come down I shall have ridden away.'

'But let us discuss——'

'There is nothing to discuss. All that is done.' She bent down and kissed his forehead. 'You have been very good to me, Granby. Always brave and generous and kind. But it could not continue. You have agreed to that.

'I must be alone, not only now but always. Forgive me when I have been hasty or angry. Think of me sometimes as I shall think of you. . . .'

She kissed him again, this time on his hot little mouth—and went quickly from the room.

Downstairs, she found the inn not yet alive to its daily enterprise. A blowzy girl was on her knees with a scrubbing-brush—another, half dressed, rubbed pewter mugs and glasses: a drunken farmer lay straddled across a settle, snoring. The snow drove against the windows.

Katherine pulled over her head and body a dark hooded cloak made of a waterproof that was then known as 'Holland cloth,' a material, in fact, more efficacious against wind and weather than anything invented afterwards. Her splendid hat she carried inside the 'Holland.' Why had she dressed in all her grandeur to go out into the storm?

As she began to climb the slope of the hill she smiled grimly to herself, for she knew that she had wished to provide Granby with one last magnificent sight of her before she left him. She resented impatiently her own weakness and vanity. And yet so it was. Her childishness and weakness were for ever breaking in upon her mature resolution. She was twenty-three years of age but she loved beautiful clothes and gifts and compliments and courtesies. She despised herself quite as thoroughly as she despised anyone else.

But she had come out to settle her determination on quite another question. It seemed to her that she was pursued by these Garlands or Herries or whatever they called themselves. It was not only that at certain intervals throughout her life they had appeared and held her attention, but members of that family—whether it was the gigantic old man with the white hair or this brother and sister—appeared to have an especial importance for her. To make a mark upon her. She remembered them as she remembered no one else. She recalled all details concerning them, what they did, what they said, even what they wore, as she did with no other human beings alive. Well, she wanted no traffic with them. She would be tied to nobody. This woman about to be delivered of a child in the inn, what concern of Katherine's was she? Why had Katherine gone to her and taken her to her room? Was it only a sentimental sigh for her own childhood? She knew that there was something in Lucy that drew her heart. Something in her voice, her smile, even as there had been in her brother's.

But she *would* not be drawn. She was, on this snowy Christmas Eve morning, free as she had for so long wished to be free. She was tied to no man, to no woman. She had no relation in the whole wide world. There were ghosts but she knew how to deal with the dead.

She stood on the slope and drew a deep breath. The air was sharp and sweet and odorous. The soft snow in her mouth had a fragrance as it melted.

The snow was falling more gently: it was thinning. Although no break in the sky was visible, the snow-flakes shone like silver.

Above her, the great white shoulder of the hill ran up to the grey sky, thrusting at it. There was a smell of pines in the air, and quite suddenly, blanketed by the snow, the melody of very distant church bells. On a snow-laden branch of a tree close to her a large black bird alighted and the snow fell from the branch in a cluster but with scarcely a sound.

She climbed higher and now was alone in spirit as she longed to be in body. The snow caressed her face and fell in little drifts from the peak of her hood. She was Katherine Christian! She was Katherine Christian! She stretched out her arms under the hood as though triumphing in her independence. No one could touch her or claim her or command. No weak woman with sparkling eyes in a bed, no little mousy man, snuffling, with protruding ears, no ghost of a dead man hanging from the beam, his red tongue between his teeth, no man with a young boy's face gazing at her with adoration.

She did not know what she would do when to-day she rode south from Keswick, but so long as she lived, from this day forth, she would owe no man anything or woman either, she would give her heart to no other until death—nor after that. She was free—free—and she would never be a captive again.

So, as she stood on that white-shining brow, the snow ceased to fall and above the cleft between the hills the shrouded sky broke and a dazzling silver light thrust like a spear. The sun, cold, remote, in itself a dull yellow, swung above the silver shining like a faded shabby orange, but the light drove on. The great slope to the Skiddaw height caught the brilliant silver as though it had thrown off its cloak. Far away below her the Derwentwater Lake, which until now had not been visible, rolled in a silver bowl into the space under the hills. The little wood of trees across the cleft seemed to spring into ecstasy, all the branches transmuted with white and dazzling glory.

A little breeze blew from the hollow and the snow rose in silver smoke. The Lake grew larger in its brilliance and then a glow of rose so pale that it was only a breath shadowed the white waiting tops of Glaramara, Cat Bells, and the rest. It was a kiss of reassuring benediction.

Katherine smiled in happiness, for this glorious beauty she could trust. It was not there because she was there. It did not care if she were struck dead in the centre of all its glory. That slow-winging bird would continue its flight, the breeze would rise again so that the silver smoke blew above her dead body. It wanted nothing of her. Like the Lake below her this world had its own rules and purposes. She could hail it and pay it her tribute without any obligation.

So she saluted it and started down the hill again.

She slipped up to her bedroom that Granby might not see her. She stuck her splendid hat on the pole of the bed and bowed to it. This should be a symbol of her life now—gorgeous raiment, a heart as hard as a stone, and a cynical spirit. The hat, with its audacious shape, and its furry crown and crimson colour and mocking tilt, set on the edge of the bed-pole, was truly the image of her future life.

She stayed there all the morning, but at two in the afternoon hunger drove her down to the parlour. Yes, Granby had departed. A great fire roared in the principal room. Snow like steel with its sun-edge of silver lit the world beyond the windows. There was a family party eating in the smaller parlour, all crazy with excitement at the thought of Christmas. The children, who were like bright-eyed birds, in hats of bright blue with white feathers, screamed with joy.

At a table by himself sat one of the new Puritans, short and fat but very pale-countenanced. On his way out he stopped at the family's table.

'The Lord,' he said gravely, 'did not intend the day of His birth to be celebrated with revelry and dancing—especially for these little ones, His angels. I trust, my brother, that you will be at the psalm-singing this evening. You are Mr. John Harner of Strangaith, are you not?'

'That's who I am,' said the broad, red-faced statesman. 'This is my wife and these are my children. We are all happy because we are together. That's no crime against God.'

'Nay, but a sober mind and a grave heart is needed to approach these mysteries.' He spoke with something of that twang that was afterwards to be a famous convention. Nevertheless he could not resist bending his fat neck and kissing both the children. 'May the Lord bless thee and have thee in His tender keeping,' he murmured to them, and then, like a little pious pony, trotted out of the room.

Katherine watched this scene with pleasure. However hard, independent, and cynical she was going to be from this day forward, she could not but be pleased with children. She even sighed a moment for poor Granby—what had he been but a child?

Now the little girl was sitting on the farmer's broad knee and pulling his hair.

Katherine knew that she must be going. It would soon be dark. She would sleep that night at a Keswick inn. Her clothes would be sent in a cart that was going from the inn that afternoon to Keswick. She herself would ride her own fine mare Juno that Granby had given her.

But when her meal was ended she stood in the room hesitating. Better, far better, to pay what she owed, bid farewell to the landlord, and ride off on Juno. Had she not, that very morning, vowed that she would have nothing further to do with this tiresome family that pursued her?

In her heart, as she stood there, was an odd foreboding—that this step taken now would affect one way or another all her later life. She was not her father's daughter for nothing and, although she despised superstition and everything that went with it, nevertheless she knew well, by now, that we are masters of our own fate and that our rewards and punishments are of our own dealing. She hesitated. That poor thing with that miserable man of hers, and she giving birth to her first child, and that illegitimate, and with no one to help her.

There could at least be nothing harmful in bidding her farewell, making sure that a physician was at hand, seeing, as a last office, that the little things that she needed were there. But one step—and you were bound! It was almost like a voice in her ears that warned her. 'One slip and you are caught—and may not escape.' The little parlour was deserted and already shadows were darkening. Snow was beginning to fall again. She fancied, as she had often fancied before, that the shape of her father stood there in the far corner, gazing at her. She thought that he was yawning, but his eyes, so deep and penetrating, stared right through her.

That was enough for her. Ghosts should neither frighten nor direct her!

So she went out and up the stairs, and knocked on the bedroom door. A faint voice called her in.

The room was bitterly cold, and before she even looked at Lucy she pulled the bell-rope violently. There must be a fire and that immediately.

She went across to the bed. Lucy, very white, her hands plucking a little at the bed-clothes, her hair, dank and disorderly, spread on the pillow, greeted her with a wan smile.

'Oh, but I was hoping that you would come! I did not like to send for you. . . . He has left me.' Beside her was a letter. She asked Katherine to read it.

DEAR LUCY—I have gone away and a worse deed I have never done. I have left money with the landlord. Your contempt for me is deserved and if I am to see our child it shall be later when, it may be, you will not despise me. You will hear from me but I am not worthy that you should see me. The child shall be cared for.

CAREY.

Katherine could scarcely speak for indignation. 'He leaves you now in childbed. It is the basest thing I have ever known.'
Lucy smiled.

'Oh, no—you must not wonder. He has left me many times. I have marvelled at my own weakness, but I shall, I think, love him until I die. I knew once a woman who saw a man but one evening. After that he wrote letters to her for a week or two and then, I fancy, grew weary. But she, although she never saw him again, treasured him in her heart, refusing all others until she died.'

'Yes,' Katherine said grimly. 'Had she been with him a month it is likely she would have never given him another thought.'

'All women must love someone, and that is the reason that many women, having no one human, turn to Jesus Christ, and there they are fortunate, for they can never be disappointed.'

Her voice was low and she was in pain, but Katherine was saying to herself: 'I will not be caught by this. I will see that she has what she needs and then be off. This is no affair of mine.'

She asked Lucy whether the physician had come.

'They could not find one.'

'Could not find one? But that is craziness. A man must ride to Keswick.'

'It is Christmas Eve and difficult.'

'I will see that they find one.'

There was a knock on the door, and a small rosy-faced country girl stood there.

'There must be a fire here and at once.'

'Yes, madam.'

'What is your name?'

'Mary.'

'Then, Mary, listen to me. This lady is in your care. When I am gone she is your duty. Do you understand?'

The girl looked at Lucy, then knelt at the fireplace.

'Oh!' Lucy said. 'You are going?'

'Yes. Within the hour I must be in Keswick. All is ready. I came only to say farewell.'

'Oh . . .' Lucy said, and turned her head on the pillow and began to cry like a child.

'No, no. You must not. I must go. I have business that must not be delayed.'

('The Lord forgive me for a liar!' she thought.)

'Very well——' Lucy began. Then suddenly she cried out. It was a
fierce, shrill cry that cut the room.

Katherine turned quickly to the little girl. 'The lady is in childbirth.
Where is a physician?'

The girl looked terrified.

'Madam, there is no one . . .'

Katherine stamped her foot.

'There must be one. And other things. . . . Heated water . . . clothes.'
She shook the girl's shoulder.

'Have you ever helped at a childbirth?'

'Oh, no. . . .' The girl was shaking with terror.

Lucy cried out again.

Katherine went over to her and stroked her forehead.

'Be brave. I will not leave you. I promise I will not. They must find
a physician.'

She turned to the girl again. 'Is there no one in this place—no
woman—who knows about these things?'

'There is Mrs. Mattison——'

'Well, fetch her, do you see? Fetch her. Hurry. Hurry.'

The child ran out.

Katherine sat on the bed edge.

'Is it very bad? I have never had a child nor seen one born. But they
say it is quickly over. There. Hold my hand. . . .'

Lucy clutched it. She said so weakly that Katherine could scarcely
hear: 'It is better. . . . I am glad that it has come. . . . I can endure it.'

'Think to the end. Soon you will be lying very quietly with your
child in your arms.'

The fire was burning now and she went to the jug and ewer, poured
some water out and took it to the fire to warm it. She was aware
that there was some deep intimacy between herself and Lucy:
only, maybe, of their common femininity and the grievous burden
placed on all women. 'Has she no friends anywhere?' she thought.
'What of her brother? He would not desert her, I am certain.'

She went back to the bed. Lucy was now lying with her eyes closed.

'Tell me—if the pains are not too bad—have you no relations, no
friend? Your brothers . . .'

'Peter and Rashleigh are in London. I would not allow them. . . .

They wished to kill Carey if they could find him. And they *will* kill him—I——'

Then she cried out again, frightfully, heaving her body up in bed, tearing at her night-rail. At that same moment the fattest, largest woman Katherine had ever seen—a woman with a little nose, three chins, and a great belly—came in.

'Well, what is this? A child to be born? That's no great matter. God-a-mercy, cry as you will, my pretty. The woman cries and then the child after her. No one minds your crying.'

She bustled to the bed, pulled the clothes down, laid her big red hand on Lucy's body.

'Aye, it is coming, it is just on the way. I can feel how it is heaving, the gallant little fellow—for 'tis a boy I'll be bound. Another wicked man in the world when there is a plenty of them already—and this very Christmas-time when Christ Himself was born, and He in a manger and you in a soft room with friends about you and fire burning . . .' She was out of breath and doing but little.

Katherine said impatiently: 'Is there no physician?'

'Physician! Why, for Christ the Lord's sake, on the night before Christmas! They will be as drunken as a dairymaid by this time. But what want we with physicians? With my own first I was walking on a summer day in the hay-field when my pains came on me, and I was delivered in a hay-cock. Mary! Mary! What are you standing there for by the door? Fetch the heated water and some warm clothes, tell Cook. An you've not seen a child born 'tis time you did, for you'll have many, I'll be bound, and that before a year or two. . . .'

Lucy was in her agony. The room shrank inwardly to a small hell-heated purgatory. The horrid nails of the wild beasts of the Apocalypse tore at her body and their steaming breath was in her eyes and nostrils.

She saw this vast woman like all cruel maternity bending, a vast fleshy cloud, above her.

She screamed for pity, throwing up her hands for mercy, and blackness descended upon her, plunging her into yet deeper tortures.

After sinking below waters that were fiery with pain she rose again and heard the thin, feeble wail of a child.

All was over. Everything that ought to be done had been done. Mrs. Mattison had been most excellently efficient and had returned downstairs to a good jug of ale. The inn was still in the dusk of the afternoon. Children's voices came up from the kitchen. Their shrill, selfless voices were singing a carol. Afterwards, Katherine looking from the window, saw the orange-coloured light of the lantern leading the little dark skipping figures across the snow.

Lucy lay in exhausted sleep. The baby was in a rough basket near to the leaping fire. And *what* a baby! Very small, with a protruding under-lip, a sharp arrogant toy nose, and his head covered with bright red hair. He had showed, from his first yell, strength, arrogance, and resistance to all the powers that be. 'Some,' said Mrs. Mattison, 'are from the very first kick with the feet daring the devil.—That is what this one is. . . .' She slapped his bottom and he cried again.

'His father,' said Mrs. Mattison. 'His father is out riding.'

There had been in all probability gossip enough downstairs. In any case Mrs. Mattison understood the whole situation. Lucy was sleeping.

'A father? What does a babe want with a father? If 'tis a girl the father spoils her, and if 'tis a boy father and son will never understand the one the other till they meet in Paradise, which, by the nature of the wickedness of this world, 'tis most unlike they'll ever do. A husband now—there is something to be said for a husband. But who wants a father? A husband can be useful and even agreeable, and at least 'tis his seed makes the child, but a father! This babbie will never cry for a father, but he'll fight for a packet of plenty, that I can tell him.' She went over to the bed and her large eyes that swam, like soup, with kindliness, drink, and a warm animal nature, in and out among the fleshy folds of her face, looked down at Lucy with tenderness and pity.

'She is a sweet thing and rid of a bad man. She has too much heart and cannot defend herself, so what can her end be?

'Ah, we women, from the Queen of Denmark's shoulders to the base feet of the cow-girl, there is peril and pain for all of us. Men want but one thing of us. We want their hearts and they want our maidenheads—there's the pox of it.'

'I must be responsible for the charges,' Katherine said, holding out her hand. 'And I cannot thank you sufficiently.'

Mrs. Mattison took Katherine's hand in hers. 'You're of another sort. The loveliest lady that ever came to this inn. But there—I have a confusion of duties and my man drinking himself to perdition if I don't stop him.'

Katherine came into the wide kitchen for some water. One more service to Lucy and she would be gone, late though it was. The kitchen was a roar of voices, hot as damnation. The wide stone door heaved open, a flurry of snow blew inwards, and a gentleman, cloaked and snow-scattered, stood there.

The landlord hurried over to him.

' 'Tis the other door, but come in, sir—come in.'

'My horse must be cared for. Have you a room for to-night and to-morrow?'

Inside the kitchen he seemed gigantic. He appeared the Christian Knight of the Miracle Plays. He took off his broad hat and shook the snow from it. Behind him was standing a broad-shouldered, wrinkled old man with a body as sturdy as though he was twenty.

'I am Mr. Nicholas Herries,' the tall white-haired gentleman said to the landlord. 'Is there a lady——?' He broke off. 'Have you a room where I may speak to you?'

He moved, as though he commanded the inn and everyone in it, out of the kitchen, through the little panelled passage, into the parlour.

Katherine followed him.

She held out her hand. 'You have forgotten me, Mr. Herries. I am for ever reminding members of your family that I know them.'

He looked at her with all the appreciation of an old man who has loved many beautiful women and sees now the most beautiful of them all.

He bowed. 'Your pardon——'

'No. It does not matter now—my name, I mean, or anything about me. You have come to find Lucy?'

'Yes. But why——?'

'She was delivered of a son early this afternoon. She is quite alone——'

Nicholas' face was red with fury.

'That villain! Where is he? I have come to settle with him. . . .'

'Nay. He is already gone.'

'He left her in childbirth? 'Fore God——'

'Lucy is asleep. But you may come if you step softly, and see her. Also the boy, who is as red as a coxcomb.'

(In her heart she thought: 'It is of no use. I am caught. This is stronger than I!')

Being wise enough to recognize Fate when she saw it, she surrendered and knew that this surrender was one of the most determining facts of her life.

END OF PART I

PART II

Dedication of the Heart

THIS MY MASTER

PETER GARLAND and Matt Turner were riding in the early afternoon of a December day in the year 1630 between Cambridge and Huntingdon.

This was to be one of the two most important days in Peter's life, but he was thinking of nothing save how pleasant in spite of the cold it was to be riding in agreeable conversation with his best friend, how magnificently hungry he was, and the supper and fire that the 'White Hart' would shortly be offering him.

On his horse he looked a heavy, stout man, very soberly clad. But his face, were it examined under a light, had the same child-like, almost boyish look in it, his clear eyes the same brightness, his mouth the same humorous lines, as in those long-ago days in Seascale when he had first kissed Katherine.

He was thinking of her as they rode along. He had seen her but three times since the meeting that festival day by the side of Derwentwater—once on the morning following, when he had visited her at the little Keswick lawyer's. On that day insanity had seized him, for he had fallen at her feet, told her that he loved her, sworn that if she were willing he would marry her within a week. What a Katherine he had seen then! She had abused him, scoffed at him, scorned him, had told him that she would rather cut herself into little pieces than marry a Puritan, and then in cold, hard terms explained very clearly the life she was leading, the gentlemen whose mistress she had been. She had added that if he dared ever speak to her anywhere again she would take a whip to his shoulders.

Upon that he had recovered his sanity, spoken to her very quietly and, he hoped, with dignity, and had left her. His last vision of her standing very still, and her face altered from passion to a strange, almost tender passivity, had afterwards been difficult to forget.

He had never spoken to her again, but had seen her on two occasions, both in London,—once in the Park, riding, and once looking from a window in Whitehall.

During the last two years he had heard of her many times. She had been taken up, it seemed, by the old Countess of Forres and was constantly at Court, being by all accounted the most beautiful woman there.

He had been spared the killing of Carey Courthope, the hand of God having fallen on that gentleman and drowned him, crossing the Channel on the way to Paris. Lucy had been living with her boy at Mallory, and the oddest thing was that she was a friend of Katherine's, saw her in London, and had even travelled with her on one occasion to France.

Although he was pleased with this particular moment he was, poor Peter, at this present time sadly disappointed in his life, the times, and the prospect of mankind's happiness. He was now at the great age of thirty-nine and had done, it seemed to him, nothing with his life at all. He fitted in, it seemed to him, nowhere. The imprisonment of Sir John Eliot had filled him with rage and despair. Eliot appeared to him the greatest man in the world. He had been present at the tumult in the House. He had watched while Holles and Valentine held down the Speaker while the doors were locked, and his heart had beat with fiery enthusiasm when, just as the King was approaching the doors with an armed force, Holles read Eliot's resolutions amidst shouts of exultation.

Ah, what a wonderful, what a great moment that had been! He had shouted with the rest, and how splendid the resolutions! Whoever brought innovations into religion, whoever advised the levy of tonnage and poundage without a grant from Parliament, whoever voluntarily paid those duties, was an enemy of the kingdom and a betrayer of its liberties.

It had seemed that the world turned over towards righteousness when the shouts of 'Aye, Aye!' rang out, the doors were flung open, and the members poured forth.

And then—nothing had happened at all. He did not know, of course, that from that moment England was to have no Parliament for more than eleven years, but he did see Eliot, refusing bail, enter upon that imprisonment that he would never again leave. He had seen Weston made Lord Treasurer, Laud Bishop of London, and Wentworth President of the North. In this very year Alexander Leighton, who had attacked the Bishops, had been flogged and mutilated by order of the Star Chamber. He saw Laud persecuting the Puritans. In every direction it appeared to him that his beloved country was submitting tamely to an absolute tyranny. He was apt to express himself about this so violently that it had become difficult for him to have any intercourse with his brother Rashleigh, whom he dearly loved, or to visit Mallory where old Nicholas was a tempestuous Royalist. He thought himself the loneliest man in England.

On the other side, he was on no close terms with the Presbyters, because of his deep conviction that life should be lovely and gay. He detested their hypocrisies and their violence. And yet when he was with the moderate middlemen he raged in his heart because of what seemed to him their lazy, humorous indifference. His chief friend was Matt Turner, and even here there was a breach, because Matt cared nothing for politics but only thought of writing poetry and squibs, and leading a hole-and-corner life with the riff-raff of London.

But most of all he was indignant and angry with himself. Here he was, hale, hearty, no fool, half-way through life and he had made nothing of it. There must be in him some central weakness that spoiled all his energy and usefulness. He recalled—how often he recalled—the cruel words that Katherine had hurled at him in Keswick.

'Your excuse,' she had said, 'is only that you have never grown. One forgives a child contemptuously.'

Yes, that was perhaps true. But Christ had encouraged the simple of heart and had promised them fine things in the Kingdom of Heaven. All the same, he did not consider himself quite so simple. Only the week before he had argued with a Papal priest against the Roman religion altogether to his own satisfaction. In London at Mr. Pym's table he had been no such fool. It was rather, he thought, that there was no centre to his life. His politics cut him off from his own people, the memory of Katherine from other women, his work was casual in that he served as occasional secretary to a number of different gentlemen—his only centre was God, and God did not appear to need him very deeply.

At last he burst out to Matt. Their path, now beginning to stand out in the dusk, lay through flat and orange-shadowed country. On the horizon a church steeple pinked the grey mat of the sky. Save for the clop-clop of their horses' hooves there was no sound at all. The last colours—saffron and red—lay like shining scarves on the sky-line. Then, as though a hand withdrew them, disappeared.

'Matt,' Peter said with a prodigious sigh, 'I am most unhappy.'

'So am I not,' answered Matt, 'for suddenly I have thought of a new poem to be called "Psyche: or Love's Mystery." Although why "Mystery" I cannot tell you, for all action in love is merely absurd, never mysterious.'

'Nay, but I mean it, Matt. I am unhappy, not merely selfishly. My country is in sad trouble and I can do nothing for her.'

'I have observed in history,' Matt answered, 'that prosperity, whether for man or country, is never for here or now, but always behind you, like a receding Bird of Paradise, or in front of you, like the end of the rainbow. And so I have learned never to trouble myself.'

Peter replied: 'I am thirty-nine years of age. More than half my life is gone. I have done nothing with it save watch the tyrannies grow and our liberties strangled. There have been three tragedies, Matt—first that I took a distaste to psalm-singing in my nursery, second that I have loved and still love a woman I have barely seen, third that I have no home, cannot speak with my brother, feel a shyness with my sister. But for yourself I have no friend—and you are not all to my mind.'

But Matt Turner had pricked up his ears at a sentence.

'What did you say—a woman?' Now Peter had never opened to any living soul his passion for Katherine. He was not in any case a man to bare his heart; he was always afraid of his own tenderness. Then, when you told it, it was a poor little story.

However, to-night in this dark open country, unable to see Matt's whimsical mocking face, feeling a longing for friendship, something that would rid him of his melancholy loneliness, he suddenly and to his own surprise poured it all out.

'It is not, Matt, much of a story and very little to my own glory. It began when we were children with our father and mother at Seascale.

There came a day when old Nicholas Herries arrived on a visit, only he was not so old then and was the grandest man I had ever seen. A travelling magician came with a boy, a donkey, and a little girl. I kissed the little girl and held her in my arms.

'Years later you yourself saw her, Matt. Do you remember at a feast that Nicholas gave in London for old James Courthope there was a conjurer, a magician?'

'I remember well,' Matt answered. 'There was a monkey, a stiff paper cone, flowers fell through the air. The magician had a white nose. I dreamed of my triumphs of poesy—and of your sister,' he added rather lamely.

'With the magician was a little girl—his daughter. Now she was older and beginning to be beautiful. Again I kissed her.

'Well, Matt, here is the sorry sequel. Once more you were present— that day of the Children's Festival by Derwentwater Lake. Out of sympathy with myself, I walked, sulking, into a wood. She was standing there, dressed in crimson, a whip in her hand. Matt, you are a poet, or at least by yourself so estimated. I tell you that there has never from long, long before Helen of Troy been such beauty as hers. The trees were on fire with it—it was an autumn day, you may remember. She recalled me and told me where she was living in Keswick. After a night without sleep, I went the next morning to find her. I fell on my knees and invited her to marry me. She scolded me like Juno discovering Ganymede in Jupiter's hairy arms.

'She said that if I ever spoke to her again she would whip my ears. After that I have seen her only twice and in London, where now she is much spoken of as the most beautiful woman at the Court. The strangest thing of it all is that she is a friend of Lucy's and of old Nicholas. She was present at Keswick when Lucy's child was born. And the unfairness of it is that I, who can never have her, whom she despises—if indeed she remembers—cannot rid my heart of her. She is seated there whether I wish it or no.'

'Maybe,' Matt said, 'she has not forgotten either. There is something strange about it to me. In the wood by Derwentwater she was kindly, was she not? And then, within the twenty-four hours, she rated you.

'But of course I know her well. Not that I have ever spoken to her, but since old Lady Forres sponsored her at Court she has been in everybody's mouth, and not always so handsomely either, for they say she has the tongue of the Devil and through her father, who was mixed in the Overbury business, she can cast spells and work magic——'

Peter broke in angrily. 'She is nothing but what is good!'

'I am all for goodness,' Matt answered, 'when it is not confused with too much chastity. And chastity is not, I understand, her quality.'

Peter pulled up his horse.

'Are we to go different ways, then?'

'Why, no,' Matt answered, laughing. 'She is no hypocrite by all I hear. Why should you be one?'

For a moment he drew his horse close to Peter's, and laid his arm about his neck. 'I am a topsy-turvy mountebank and I live with my heels in a spider-web and my nose in the placket of a seamstress, but I am yours, Peter, unto the last echo of the final trump. You are sad, let me tell you, not because of Mistress Christian or the state of our country, but of a certain emptiness in your soul which should be well filled with the rich aroma of saintliness. For you are not enough of a saint, nor of an artist, nor of a presbyter, nor of a courtier, nor of a soldier, nor of a lover, nor of a lecher, nor of a man of business to give your soul an impulse in any fiery direction. You need a fire-cracker to your tail. And it will be supplied. Have no doubt. There are fire-crackers in plenty, but not sufficient tails worthy of them. Now yours is an excellent tail worthy of any mare's rump. It is handsome, formed solidly, and of an admirable roundness. Any moment it will leap heavenwards and you will split your innocent forehead against a star. You are made for such a work—God's knight-errant—while I squat in the cinders.'

Words always poured from Matt and very often Peter did not listen. Even when so slightly seen, as now in this dusk, Matt had the look of some odd thing with his hat peaked and crooked, his spare body hunching up its shoulders so that they seemed those of a deformed man.

'And yet I have my prides,' Matt continued. 'I am myself and independent both of shame and glory.'

'And of God?' Peter asked.

'Of God? . . . That is the familiar question of all our family. There never was such a family as the Herries for following both God and

Mammon. There is yourself, Peter, questing after God like a puppy its mother, and there is Robert, Nicholas' son, with his nose for ever in a peck of barley and his sharp little eyes counting up the house-estimates in the steward's room.'

'I like Robert,' Peter said. 'He has a sharp nose but a kind heart.'

'Assuredly. Well enough if we were all like Robert. But there must be fellows like yourself and myself, Peter—and none of us in the first order. Robert will marry a cautious wife but he will never be a great man of business. You will be half saint and I half poet, but there has never been a master Herries and never will be. And I . . .' he cried with a sudden passion that startled Peter. 'What do I see for myself? A crazy half-poet in a time when brother fights brother, and one half of England destroys the other, and I caring for none of these things but only for created beauty, with my head cut in half by a drunken pikeman for no reason that I wot of'—and here he dropped his shrill voice so low that Peter could scarcely hear him—'loving your sister as I always did—Misericordia! Misericordia!'

'You care for her still—after all there has been? I did not know.'

'What has there been? She has a child by a man—a filthy coward of a dog—who did not marry her. And what is that, pray, to a man who loves?'

'It was a sin,' Peter said.

'Ah, there is your God again. A fig for your God that can give His servants an itch for fornication that He may have the satisfaction of punishing them for it! Why did He make it so easy, man, if He forbade it? That is your God—the trap-layer, the Star Chamber Tyrant—whom Laud serves through the thumbscrew.'

Peter answered: 'He is a Glory and a Begetting. He sent His Son to us that we might learn the meaning of sin and suffering. He shows us the profit of our pain and whispers to us that our sorrow is but for a little time. He is our father and our friend. He lays His hand on our shoulder and we are comforted. And it is our own sad misfortune if we turn away from Him. He gives us our wills that we may grow strong through the exercise of them, and He is with us in the first and the last and the beginning and the end.'

'Then I say,' Matt, back in his mocking voice, cried out, 'that you should not be lonely, brother Peter, as you say that you are. For if He is your friend He is at your side even now, even here.'

The sharpness of Matt's voice died away and they rode on in a great hush and silence.

Everything that happened to Peter on this most wonderful evening was to be remembered by him for the rest of his days. This ride, that was to appear to him as a fitting prologue in its silence and peace, came back afterwards again and again with the striking of his horse's hooves, the faint rustling of the trees as though, with peaceful happiness, they were settling down for the night, the twittering of a bird that was like the broken intermittent confidence of a note of music, this eloquent shadowy silence with the sharp air and the muffled indifferent sky—he would never forget any of it. It was part of his life for ever.

Afterwards he would sometimes fancy that he was already conscious of a great event impending. This must have been a later fitting of event to circumstance, for his mind was a confusion of desires, regrets, hunger, sore thighs (for they had ridden far that day), thoughts of Katherine, and, above all, a longing to love and be beloved. His heart ached with desire that he might give himself to his country, to a cause, to a woman, to a friend. He was young in that and always would be. Life would never take from him that young urgency to be of service. But the urgency was not enough. There must be something worthy to receive it. Not that he rated himself high. It was his modesty, perhaps, that had hindered him. It was not vanity that made him know that he had in his heart and soul things of real price and value. God had put them there.

They saw the lights of the inn twinkling through the trees. There, very dim in the dusk, was the sign of the 'White Hart.' There were horses tethered near the door. Voices of men singing. The hostler came running out to them.

From the moment of their setting foot in the house, Peter was to remember for always every thing done, every word spoken, every scent inhaled. In the passage the landlord, a little wizened man with bright-blue eyes and a red nose, came to them saying that he regretted it greatly, but that there was not a room vacant. Some gentlemen had ridden over from Huntingdon and even they were sleeping two in a bed. At that he remembered, for he pulled his big nose and added: 'There is an attic-room, gentlemen—I had forgot. It is but an attic and the bed is small for two gentlemen. . . .'

Peter laughed. ' 'Twill not be the first time we've slept in one bed, Matt. That will do handsomely. And for supper . . .'

'For supper I have some beef and a pigeon-pie, a damson tart . . .'

'Handsome! Handsome!' Peter cried joyfully, for he was ravenous. But beyond that some especial happiness seemed to have entered into him as he had crossed this threshold. He had been melancholy, now he was merry.

And Matt noticed, as he had often done before, how it was that Peter Garland was given things that another man would be refused. He seemed to win people—people of the most differing kind—by exercising no arts, putting forward no charm, being quite simply himself. And Matt, looking on that stout, untidy figure with the round boy's face and the honest smiling eyes, loved him.

The landlord was their servant and hustled the indoors man to hurry up with the saddle-bags, and went with a candle leaping up the crooked wheezing stairs like a flea. It was a charming room when they were in it, small though it was, and the roof sloping. It was charming because the moon made it so. The moonlight lit the room with gentleness. Peter, leaning on the window-sill and looking out, thought that he had never known such peace, and the moon, nearly full, rolled through the sky in imperial silver, forcing the thin mottled shadows to accept her splendour and the darker whorls and bales of clouds to fly before her, seeming to scatter and spread away as she released the stars. The long flat country, broken by the clumps of trees and a shining river and a white-boned road, was coloured with insubstantial light, unreal to earthly reality, a proper background for spirits, fairies, angels even. As he stayed there, smelling the night scents (and there was a dung-heap directly under his window), he heard a fire crackling and, turning back, saw that the landlord had lit one. The room was filled with the autumn smell of burning wood. The bed was hung with curtains of bright blue, and there was an old brown picture hanging on the wall of an Elizabethan gentleman whose dark-crimson robe stood out ruddily from the smoke-brown amber of the fading paint.

They washed, and changed their clothing. Matt was much the same at the end as at the beginning, for his pointed hay-coloured beard had something mocking about it and his hay-coloured hair stood up like an interrogation. His body was shambling and no limb of it seemed to act with the consent of any other limb. His mouth was crooked, his nose thin, his cheek-bones stuck out in his face like a skull's. He struck an attitude and in his piping voice affectedly chanted Skelton:

> 'My pen it is unable,
> My hand it is unstable,
> My reason rude and dull
> To praise her at the full,
> Goodly Mistress Jane,
> Sober, demure Diane,
> Jane this mistress hight,
> The lodestar of delight,
> Dame Venus of all pleasure,
> The well of worldly treasure.

'Oh,' he went on, sweeping the air with a mock courtly bow, 'that I might have Dame Venus in my arms to-night, rather than the fat, lubberly pudding of this Puritan here——'

'Nay,' Peter broke in, 'you will have no Puritan in your arms to-night, Cousin Matt. That bed is too small for us both. We shall toss for it and the one or the other shall sleep on the saddle-bags. But come—I am frantic for the beef.'

He did not know why he should be so happy. His happiness continued. They had their meal in the public room. Close against the wall a fanatical-faced fellow was sitting, in dingy black and dirty white bands, gazing at them with a stern ferocity as though he resented their amazing appetites. At another table two young men, who seemed to be servants, were sitting and one of them had a little lute. He sang softly:

> 'What thing is Love? For sure Love is a thing.
> It is a prick, it is a sting,
> It is a pretty, pretty thing.
> It is a fire, it is a coal,
> Whose flame creeps in at every hole;
> And as my wit doth best devise,
> Love's dwelling is in ladies' eyes.'

But at this point the fanatical-faced man could endure no more and strode over to their table.

'Have you nothing to do but ruin your soul with lascivious fancies when the Lord is at the very gate with His great armies and His hand of vengeance is terribly raised over this country?'

The singer, who was little more than a boy, smiled up into that lantern-jawed countenance and said:

'Mind your own grim business, old bottom-breeches, and leave us to ours. You can start up a psalm if you will, and try which of us will prevail.'

The man would have answered in a fury, but strode from the room, banging the door behind him.

'Why is it, Matt,' Peter asked, his mouth full of pigeon-pie, 'that I was melancholy on the road and now am so gay-spirited that I could sing myself—if I had any voice for singing, so to speak?'

'It is because,' Matt said solemnly, 'your belly is full of meat and your throat softened with good wine.'

'I think not,' Peter answered. 'The moon has bewitched me.'

A door at the far end of the room opened, and a stout, country-looking gentleman stood there and stared about him. At sight of him Peter sprang to his feet.

'Mr. Manly!' he cried joyfully. The gentleman appeared a trifle short-sighted, for he rubbed his forehead with the back of his hand as though that would help him to see the better. Then his broad face broke into smiles.

'Why, Peter Garland! Peter Garland! Peter Garland!' He came almost running forward, then caught Peter's hand and shook it up and down, in and out, as though it were a duster. It was a very pleasant sight indeed to see these two hearty gentlemen enjoying one another's company. Peter introduced Mr. Manly to Matt: 'This is my cousin, Matthew Turner. Matt, this is Mr. Manly, a friend of Mr. Boarder of Finchley, with whom, as you know, I have recently been working.'

Matt grinned his crooked grin, then set on to the food again.

'Now, Peter Garland, you are to continue your meal. After, myself and one or two gentlemen—Mr. Parley and Mr. Singer, Mr. Round and Mr. Cromwell of Huntingdon——'

'Mr. Cromwell!' Peter broke in.

'Yes. Indeed yes.'

'Oh, I will come!' Peter said. 'We will come with the very greatest pleasure.'

Mr. Manly smiled, clapped Peter once more on the back (and he had hands like a blacksmith's), and returned to the other room.

'Now that's good fortune,' Peter went on eagerly, 'for I have had an ache to meet Mr. Cromwell ever since they talked of him at Mr. Pym's house.'

'And who is Mr. Cromwell?' Matt asked.

'A Huntingdon gentleman. He sat in this last Parliament. They say he can roar at you like a bull but can kiss you on both cheeks the moment after. He is a most godly man, but is for songs and dances just as I am.'

'Very fortunate for this Mr. Cromwell that he should think as you do, Peter.'

'But you shall see. They say he is a man.'

When, the meal ended, they went into a private parlour, they found three gentlemen beside Mr. Manly, seated about a sea-coal fire. Peter and Matt were introduced. Mr. Parley was short and choleric-faced, with little sharp angry eyes. Mr. Round was his opposite, being a thin man with brown hair and a most amiable benevolence. Mr. Singer was very tall and loud-voiced and restless.

They were all gentlemen from Huntingdon and the neighbourhood. They were talking about Wentworth, whom Mr. Manly knew. Wentworth had in the preceding year entered the Privy Council.

'He is a man of mark,' Mr. Manly said, 'that is certain, and all England will have to reckon with him. First there is his devotion to the King, which is fanatical. The King is his master and his mistress, his child, his lover, his father. With him absolutely the King can do no wrong. With that he is not blind, I would say, to justice. In Parliament in '28 he was in the forefront against that accursed war which the vile Buckingham was so clumsily leading. But for Felton's hand, directed by God, he would, I am certain, have seen to it that Buckingham lost his head. Equally he is against Parliament if Parliament is against the King. He will always be against anyone or anything who is against the King. He is thorough and ruthless, but not with any personal vindictiveness. He has a noble spirit, without meanness, but he will prove, I don't doubt, the forefront of the attack on our liberties and our most dangerous enemy. And yet he is Pym's friend and, through Pym, may be worked to a greater righteousness.'

'And the Bishop of London?' Parley asked.

Manly's eyes clouded. 'A little grey-faced obstinate. He sees nothing but the letter and ceremony of the Prayer Book—never its spirit. He has no heart nor bowels. No human feeling. Pain is nothing to him nor the suffering of women nor the cry of the children. Ah, England! Poor England! A dreadful pass she is coming to and her children with her!'

Little Mr. Parley broke out in a fury. 'She can come to no pass if there are men enough to fight for her freedom.'

'And that is civil war,' Mr. Round said, shaking his head.

'War then let it be! Nay, *must* be! Better that ourselves, our children, our children's children, perish every one of them! Let us fight in every lane, in every street, on every hill, and with God at our back we may be certain of victory.'

The door at the room's farther end opened and a man came in. Peter, looking up at him, knew a revelation. It was instant and the power of it was so great that his hands trembled. There was no difference in it from an immediate falling in love. He knew at that great moment that his life was settled for him and that never again would he feel, as he had done on that very afternoon, that he was empty of purpose and had no centre of direction. It was as though a voice spoke in his ear: 'Here is your master. He is your destiny'—as when Christ Jesus spoke to the fishermen, saying, 'Follow me!'

And yet this man had not spoken, but stood there looking at them. He was then about thirty years of age. He was five foot ten in height, but what first caught your attention was the massiveness of his shoulders. They seemed to be made to carry, without flinching, all the burdens of the world. His head was nobly shaped. His hair, falling below his collar, was thick and brown. His nose was ugly, broad, and long, but seemed an index for the rest of him, so strong and purposeful it was. His mouth, too, thick-lipped, expressed absolute resolution. His colour was high and promised later to be ruddy. He was therefore not handsome, and it was already clear that in his resolution he could be cruel, and in his wisdom, when he saw a thing to be the right thing, ruthless. But now, as he looked at his friends, his full rugged countenance was kindly and even tender.

He was dressed in rough country clothes and looked what he was— a gentleman farmer. There was much of the animal about him in his physical strength, but much of the spirit too. Even in his great shoulders and thighs and the breadth of his chest there was a sort of simplicity and warmth of heart.

This was Oliver Cromwell as Peter Garland first saw him. He was to see him in many guises, as friend, as fighter, as mystic, as self-doubter, as tyrant, as wordy philosopher, but he would never lose this first picture of him.

Love, when it strikes like lightning, has no reasons. Peter knew no reasons as his eyes met Cromwell's, but in that exchanged glance he surrendered himself totally.

It happened that Cromwell himself looked more at Matt than at Peter and his eyes twinkled at Matt's oddity. But he shook them both by the hand. That was a remarkable grip, so strong, so firm, but the flesh of the palm friendly and almost confiding. 'I'm your friend,' the hand seemed to say. 'Be mine, and there will be no one more faithful: betray me and I'll crush you.'

He came and sat in the settle by the fire between Mr. Manly and Mr. Round. He stretched wide his strong thick legs, pinching his broad nose, yawning, fingering the wart on his face, spitting into the fire, raising his legs and lowering them again, staring into the fire as though he saw the future there, throwing up his head suddenly as a bull might in a field. Then he turned to Manly and said: 'I heard someone singing.'

Mr. Manly answered that it had been someone in the other room and he had gone to look.

'And it was then I saw my friend, Mr. Peter Garland. He is a friend of Pym's, Oliver, and is thought of highly and may be of use to you.'

Cromwell looked at Peter with almost stern penetration, but all he said was: 'Why did that man cease his singing?'

Matt broke in. 'There was a tiresome pedantic fellow who told him that he should be preparing himself for the Lord's vengeance rather than singing. I hoped the young man would give him a kick in the buttocks, but no such fantasy.'

Cromwell paid no attention to Matt. He was thinking of something else. He was humming and beating time on his knee. He turned abruptly to Peter. 'And how is Mr. John Pym?'

Peter, to his own surprise, stammered as he answered. He wondered afterwards if Cromwell had known how his heart was beating.

'I have not seen him, sir, for many months. I have been a temporary secretary for Mr. Boarder of Finchley.'

'Ah, Mr. Septimus Boarder. I know him. With a snuffle in his nose like this.' And at once, throwing back his head, he executed a wonderful imitation of Mr. Boarder's snuffle. Everyone laughed, and Mr. Singer, who could not keep still, jumped up and cried out: 'Oliver, I have that throw—the one you beat me with.'

To Peter's amazement Cromwell got up from the settle, threw his coat on to the floor, and, planting his legs, prepared himself for Mr. Singer. They were a strange contrast, for Mr. Singer was as thin as Cromwell was broad. Now without his coat, his back to Peter, you could see his shoulders and his thighs working. His head, set thick in those shoulders, went forward. He seemed a Hercules in homespun. They strained together, Cromwell's cheek against Mr. Singer's, his face bent sideways and his eyes watching the floor speculatively, but in two turns Mr. Singer had him and, as Cromwell fell, caught him to lessen the force of his fall. For a moment Cromwell lay flat there, his stomach heaving, then he staggered to his feet, kissed Mr. Singer gently on his cheek, and returned laughing to the company by the fire.

'It is a good fall,' he said complacently. 'Strategy. Strategy. With strategy and the help of the Lord we will drive God's enemies like the chaff before the wind.'

Peter felt then that they were waiting to talk their own business, so, with a glance at Matt, he rose, making his apologies.

To his surprise and delight Cromwell rose also, and at the door rested his hand on Peter's shoulder.

'I have already forgotten your name,' he said simply.

'Peter Garland.'

'You are an older man than I?'

'I am thirty-nine years of age.'

'We are intended to work together in the Lord's service.'

Peter, looking into Cromwell's eyes, said:

'I believe that we are.'

'You are to be found at Mr. Boarder's at Finchley?'

'Yes, Mr. Cromwell.'

The two men stood, their hands clasped, for a brief moment. Without another word Cromwell went back to the settle.

THE FLAMES ARE HIDDEN

But Peter was to see Katherine very much sooner than he had thought was possible.

That winter Nicholas had a Christmas family party at Mallory.

Although now he was between eighty-six and -seven years of age, the old man, save in one particular, ailed nothing. His back was as broad and straight and erect as ever it had been, his hearing as sound, his heart as strong. The only thing that worried him at all was his eyesight. That would play strange tricks on him and, because of the obstinacy of his nature, he would always explain those tricks away. But Rosamund and Gilbert Armstrong were anxious for him.

His son Robert, now over thirty years of age, was ruler of Mallory. He was short, sturdy, strong, and a perfect man of business.

Old Sir Michael was gentle, a little slipshod, but because he was loved, Mallory in his time was pleasant. Nicholas, in his turn, during his great youth, had been in the main a farmer and the cattle at Mallory had become famous. But Robert Herries was universal. Nothing escaped his attention from the cut on a farm-hand's knee to a new breed of cattle imported from the Low Countries. He had no use at all for any waste of time, and an idle man or woman was to him a horror only to be explained by disease. He also did not understand what he called 'the flimsy-flamsies'—that is, the Arts. He never read a book unless it had to do with agriculture, finance, or domestic economy. A picture was to him a thing of naught; to no kind of music did he ever listen.

He was greatly proud of his family because of its common sense. He would say: 'Save for a zany or two we are the most sensible family in England. We believe only in what we see and what we can touch —especially in what we can touch.' Of his cousins he liked best Mark Turner, Matt's brother, now transformed into a saving, cautious man interested in leather and acquiring a fortune. Mark had married a foolish wife, Celia, and had one idiotic brother, Matt, who wrote poetry; the other, Paul, was an exceedingly able lawyer.

But Robert was not all business. Rather to his own dismay he had a heart, and especially for anything that belonged to him he showed a warm and extenuating pride. His father and mother and old Gilbert Armstrong belonged to him, and so did every man, woman, and child at Mallory. He hated to show any feeling, and was gruff and monosyllabic when he felt most warmly—but his servants adored him.

He took no interest in politics. Religion seemed to him an absurdity, and when someone cursed or praised the Bishop of London he would stare contemptuously. What matter was it whether the Prayer Book was read thus or thus, whether the Communion Table were the one end of the church or the other? He approved of the King because under him, at the present, the country was prosperous. He thought it right that the King should have money if he wanted it. The country must have a navy and an army. He had always considered Buckingham a dangerous fellow, disapproving altogether of the Rochelle expedition, nor did he like it that there should be a French Catholic Queen—on the other hand he deprecated strongly the behaviour of Sir John Eliot, who, it seemed to him, had simply been there to make trouble. What he wanted was that everything should go smoothly on so that he might care for his cattle and see that his fields were properly ploughed. But he could not understand at all either the fantastic passion for Royalty that his old father showed, or the anger displayed by men like Peter Garland at the way that the Court behaved.

It seemed to him the most moral and virtuous Court that England had ever had. Why not leave it alone, then? He was, however, most tolerant about morals. He had had certain adventures of a carnal nature, being the most normal man possible, but they had been always sensible adventures, leading to no scandal, uncostly and decorous.

He welcomed Lucy and her boy (who was called by everybody Rupert Herries) to Mallory. It was supposed by the outside world that Lucy had been married for a brief while to a Herries cousin, who had died in France of a tertian fever. Some of the family who knew the true story were, of course, greatly shocked that Lucy should be thus received at Mallory. The old maids, Janet and Martha Herries, were two of the shocked ones, and Celia Turner, although she was very friendly to Lucy's face, was another. They said that Nicholas' infatuation for that girl had been always a madness. But Robert liked Lucy and her queer, hideous little boy.

In appearance Robert was a short little man and this had once distressed him, especially when he was standing beside his gigantic father. But by this time he looked upon his figure as he looked on everything else—with common sense. If he did not trouble he would have a little round belly—well, let him have a little round belly. He had clear, steady, far-seeing eyes. Never did he lose control of his temper. It was in fact when his adversary lost his temper that he, Robert, found his advantage. His cheeks were childish and plump and his hair sandy-coloured. He wore always the soberest, soundest clothing and had the clothes made from fine serviceable cloth by a tailor in the village.

Nothing frightened him and he quailed before no one.

Because he used few words, his words were attended to. He was in the whole district greatly respected, his advice constantly asked. He was a man of importance, relished that it should be so, but avoided pomposity, which would have been easy for a man of his figure, by never saying or doing a vainglorious or foolish thing.

He was exceedingly careful about money, but not at all a mean man. He trusted finally nobody but his father and mother and Gilbert Armstrong. Save for these three, human beings were, he thought, gullible and greedy, and lied when they could. But he did not dislike them because they were thus, they moved his sense of humour.

He liked Lucy and considered her almost as his sister, but he felt a little contempt for her as he did for most women. Silly things they were, always wanting to be loved! There was Lucy Garland (or Herries, as everyone called her) feeling crazy about a ne'er-do-well worthless like Carey Courthope, allowing him to give her a baby without making her his wife.

Nevertheless he was fond of Lucy: he liked her gaiety, merry spirits, recklessness, abandon—all qualities so very different from his own. He liked her because she was the very opposite from the kind of woman he would one day marry. She was the symbol of all that he would leave behind him on his marriage day. He even flirted with her a little in his silent, sandy-haired fashion.

For Lucy, alas for morality, had altogether recovered her spirits. Life was to be lived day by day. What was past was past! Poor Carey (she saw him all the more with a charitable tender eye in that he was dead)—what had he been but a weak, feckless boy? This is the eternal feminine excuse for all the bad men women adore. Carey had nothing to say for himself, as Katherine sometimes told her.

'But, Katherine, you despise all human beings.'

'Yes, Lucy, all—save myself.'

We are happy not because of outer circumstances, but from inner fires. Lucy had these inner fires, as Nicholas had noticed in her so many years before. She was the moth so fatally attracted by the candle. Her wings had been burnt but had grown again. Although she was now just over forty years of age, she looked fifteen years younger than that. Her colouring was fresh, her figure slim. There was something of the eternal child in her. Widows are appreciated by wise men because they have had experience. There were many wise men around Mallory and in London. Lucy felt safe because she had known the terrors: a little flirtation hurt no one. She was in fact a Herries scandal—one of those Herries scandals that are for ever appearing in the Herries records because a matter-of-fact Herries hates to be tied to a romantic Herries. Families have their spots like leopards. Nicholas adored her, as he had ever done, but more now in his mighty old age, for she was his daughter and granddaughter and she could supply for him all the qualities that dear Robert lacked.

After Lucy was her son, Rupert, a boy now seven years of age. And what a child! He was so ugly as to be interesting. Wherever he was people looked at him. He was very thin and very small of build. His hair was a carroty red and his colour pale and pasty. He had little sharp restless eyes, and his body was never still. He had a frenzied temper and would stamp with his feet and swear, using the most terrible words. He was for ever falling into trouble. His better qualities were his courage, his loyalties, and his generosities. He was afraid of nothing and nobody. Physically he took so many risks that it was a miracle that he was alive. The great game among his contemporaries was to dare him to do something. For dare him, however audaciously, and he would perform. He had already climbed on to the top of the Mallory tower and placed thereon Celia Turner's favourite spaniel. He rode already any horse near at hand, and he was quite an adept with a little gold-hilted rapier that Nicholas had given him. He enjoyed the company of low hands like stable-boys and dairymaids.

His loyalties were steel-wrought. First his mother, then Nicholas and Rosamund, then Robert, for whom he had an odd respect. Concerning these and others he was unshakable. Their enemies were his. He was immovable also towards those whom he disliked. Benson, the major-domo, a pompous and conceited very stout man, was one of them. Celia and Mark Turner were two more.

His generosities were universal. He loved to give anything away, even to his enemies. He was a flame of mischief and, with his red hair, long nose, excited, pale, volatile features, and restless little body, could not ever be overlooked wherever he was.

The human being he detested most in the world was Frederick Courthope.

Frederick Courthope, the son of Somerset, nephew of the late lamented Carey, was now eighteen years of age and was a member of this Christmas party at Mallory.

Frederick was a very wise young man. His whole person proclaimed his wisdom. He was handsome in a grave thin way, very neat, very punctilious, with manners always a little too good. He was most modest about himself—proclaiming to all and sundry that he was nobody and nothing, and most obliged when anyone took notice of him. In politics he was on everybody's side, always seeing the good points in anybody's argument and agreeing handsomely with the speaker. His voice was low and agreeable. He appeared to be always on the verge of advancing some confidence. He was most particular with all ladies, who, for the most part, admired him. He never quarrelled. He had no sense of humour and had never been seen to laugh. He was studying for the law and it was said of him that he would go far. He was an especial friend of Celia Turner.

Nicholas disliked him and was for ever begging him to speak up. He had a very sweet singing voice. He disliked all physical exercises and any sort of sport. He was a great man for secrets and knew so many things that no one else knew that some weak and timorous people feared him.

Robert admired him, which was why he was staying at Mallory. Robert thought him 'a wise, no-nonsense young man' and often asked his advice in business matters. He quite openly showed his dislike and even horror of young Rupert, but otherwise guarded all his feelings.

When Peter Garland accepted Robert Herries' invitation to spend those Christmas weeks at Mallory, he realized how fundamental a change had come to him since his meeting with Cromwell. He had not seen Cromwell again. When we meet someone who in a moment seems to transform our whole life, we expect, if we are wise, that as the weeks pass the effect of that transformation will change. The colour and fire of that great moment must yield to quieter, more reasoned emotions.

In a sense this had been true of Peter. The excitement that caused his hands to tremble passed. Nevertheless in the sober character of his later thoughts he realized that the alteration in him was fundamental. He had found for ever the one thing that his life had lacked—direction. He enquired from people who should know about Cromwell's character and personality. Strangely little was known about him. To his fellow Parliamentarians he appeared a country gentleman who had but little to say. He was happy, it seemed, in his wife and family and was more deeply interested in the small local affairs of Huntingdon than in anything else. Some said that he had lived loosely in his younger days, and suspected his present godliness. Nothing that he heard made any difference to Peter. This was one of those dedicated devotions that come to any man only once or twice in his life, but to most men never at all. Had Peter heard that Cromwell was a murderer, a fornicator, a beater of his children, it would have made little difference. Here was his leader.

Peter's nature was suited to such a devotion, for although in character he was strong and independent, he had a deep desire to serve. It was not that he needed to be led, but rather that he could not work only for his own advantage. He needed something larger than himself, something larger and more lasting.

Six months earlier he would have refused the invitation to Mallory, partly because he did not wish to be involved in political discussion with Nicholas whom he loved, partly because he thought that he despised the luxuries and comfort of Mallory. But now he welcomed Mallory. No discussion with the old man could affect him; he could live as soft as he pleased without shame. His soul knew that it was dedicated. He rode down on January 3rd of the new year and arrived late in the evening. When he had washed and changed his clothes and eaten something, he went down to the hall.

At the far end of the hall a great fire was roaring in the stone fireplace and its flames lit up the wainscoting, the carved oak, the hangings of rose and gold, the silver and cut glass. Everything was alive. Frederick Courthope was singing. Nicholas was seated in the corner of the oak settle by the fire, Lucy near to him. Celia Turner—whom Peter did not like—was embroidering at the fire end of the central table; her husband nearly asleep with his mouth open. Rosamund was giving some orders to Mr. Benson in a low voice at the far end of the hall.

Peter stayed at the bottom of the staircase until Frederick should end. His voice was a small but perfectly accurate and controlled tenor. The words floated into the air like little birds:

> *'Another shepherd you did see,*
>   *To whom your heart was soon enchained.*
> *Full soon your love was leapt from me;*
>   *Full soon my place he had obtained.*
> *Soon came a third your love to win,*
>   *And we were out, and he was in.*
>
> *Adieu, love, adieu, love, untrue love!*
> *Your mind is light, soon lost for new love.'*

Before he began the last verse Frederick looked round the room. His eyes at once alighted on Peter and he gave him a look of recognition.

'How he hates me!' Peter thought. 'Even as I do him.' A little stir of a warning caught at his brain: 'He will try to do you an evil one day.'

In any case there was something almost ludicrous in Frederick's modest self-satisfaction at his singing. It was as though he said: 'Good people all, I am nobody—nobody at all—but you must confess that my singing is beautiful.' And so it was. He ended:

> *'Since you have made me passing glad*
>   *That you your mind so soon removed,*
> *Before that I the leisure had*
>   *To choose you for my best beloved;*
> *For all my love was past and done,*
>   *Two days before it was begun.*
>
> *Adieu, love, adieu, love, untrue love!*
> *Your mind is light, soon lost for new love.'*

The applause was lost in the welcoming of Peter. 'That also he won't like,' Peter thought with amusement.

Lucy was the first to get to him, running forward, almost tumbling over the steps of the dais, throwing her arms around him and hugging him as though she were a woman of twenty rather than forty. Nicholas came after and kissed him on both cheeks. Mark Turner seemed truly pleased that Peter was here and Celia was affected and chattering. Almost best of all was Rosamund's quiet true welcome. They poured him out drink and he was seated between Nicholas and Lucy.

'Well, you rebel!' Nicholas roared at him. 'What plots have you been concocting now?'

'In any case,' Peter cried, raising his glass, 'here is a health to the King!' And they all gave it with shouts and cries.

On other occasions here Peter had at once been conscious of his close-cropped head, his plain unornamented clothes, against the luxuriant locks and crimson finery of Nicholas and the others. Not so to-night. His spirit was blissfully tranquil. But not for long. His hand was in Lucy's, he was enquiring about young Rupert, when he saw, slowly coming down the great staircase, as though it were a dream-splendour, Katherine Christian.

She paused on the stairs, looking across the hall at him. Being of all women the most unself-conscious, she did not stand there to be observed but because of her surprise at Peter.

She had arrived at Mallory only three hours before, and no one had told her that he was also to be a guest. He on his side saw her for the first time as a great lady. Her miraculous hair (for it seemed to him a miracle in its long ringlets) held under the candle-light depths of rich liquid dark, light upon light of ebony. Her dress of that crimson that she preferred, cut very low as was the fashion just now with the Court ladies, following the taste of the Queen rather than of the King, who was a moralist. Her neck and bosom, so exquisitely formed, were white in the candle-sheen. Her height and splendid carriage made her regal.

He quickly thought of her as the little daughter of the magician, crying to Lucy: 'Put me down! Put me down! My father needs me.'

He sat there like a fool, gaping. Then she came towards them all, a very mischievous look in her eyes. Her first words were to Celia:

'I fear that there is a puppy in your bed. I heard its wailing and went into your room to rescue it. Pray forgive me.'

Celia gave a scream. 'It is Rupert!' Turning to Lucy: '*Your* Rupert. He shall be whipped when I have him. . . . You, Lucy—you are to blame. You never correct him. You have no control over his wickedness. . . .'

'I think,' Katherine said slowly, 'your door was open and the puppy saw his opportunity. No harm was done. I have him now under my arm.' And, laughing, she produced a morsel of spaniel, all ears, eyes, and legs. 'If Mr. Herries will allow me I shall take him as a present. Your good servant who assisted me assures me that there are four others.'

Robert, who appreciated beauty in women as much as another man, bowed as though to a queen, quite an unusual courtliness for him.

'He is yours, Mistress Christian. And now we must name him!'

Everyone cried out delightedly. But Katherine said:

'I have already named him—on the staircase. He shall be called Mercutio after Shakespeare's play, for he has, I fear, a gay morality. He has been already in the bed of a married lady.'

After all this she held out her hand to Peter.

'I am glad to see you, Mr. Garland. It is some years since we talked last.'

And yet on the very next morning she sought him out. He was in the long library that ran above the garden. The father of Sir Michael, the grandfather of Nicholas, had made the library, being a lover of books; now in their gilt and leather and parchment they ran the whole length of the room with busts of Homer, Cicero, Plato, and others proudly guarding the tops of the shelves. Peter was hunched over the fire, for it was cold, a pile of books on the floor beside him.

Katherine was in a dress of dark satin lined with fur, her hands gauntleted, and a hat with fur shadowing her face. She threw the hat and gloves on the chair and drew a gilt embroidered stool close to the fire, holding out her hands to the blaze.

They were both silent for a little. Then she said, looking at him and smiling:

'Have you forgiven me?'

'Forgiven you for what?'

'The things I said—in Keswick.'

'I was never angry at them.'

'Oh, yes, but you were. I have kept a picture of you always, standing, before you left me, with rage, pity, contempt written on every part of you.'

'I thought you had forgotten.'

'Oh,' she said, laughing, 'I am not very good at forgetting.'

'I have seen you twice since then—both times in London. Now you are a very grand lady.'

'Oh, no. On the outside only.'

He said slowly (for he scarcely knew what to say):

'You have been very good to Lucy.'

'Well—that is as may be. I have done my best not to be. I detest your family.'

'Detest us?'

'I cannot be free of you. You—your sister—Rashleigh—are the only beings in the world I cannot rid myself of.'

'I?' His face slowly coloured.

'Yes. Why not?'

'You do not know me. You have nothing to do with me. When you last spoke to me it was to abuse me.'

'Ah, I see that you have not forgiven me. But I am a necromancer, you know. I can foretell the future. We are all bound together. Against my will. Against my will.'

She looked at him curiously.

'Do you know why I abused you in Keswick?'

'Because of my impertinence.'

'Not at all. I liked your impertinence. But you made a claim on me—or would have done had I allowed it!'

He said nothing.

'It was the same with your sister. It was Fate that brought me to the Keswick inn the day her baby was born. It was Fate that she should be deserted and so stir my pity. It was Fate that caused Nicholas to arrive that night. . . . Any lesser man but not Nicholas, than whom I had never seen a finer.'

'You need not,' Peter said, 'have kept with us after that.'

All she said, as though to herself, was: 'It is harder to be free than you know. . . .'

She studied him.

'Peter, there is a great change in you.'

'I am thirty-nine years of age.'

'Ah, no! Not years! They are nothing. You are a man. I am almost afraid of you.'

He felt a terrible desire to fall at her feet as years ago he had done at Keswick. So with a mighty effort he tried to make the conversation impersonal.

'Tell me about the Court. About the King. I live altogether outside the world.'

'The King? He has a very sweet nature. He is obstinate. He sees most clearly what is right for himself to do but less clearly what it is right for others to do. He is a pedant. He is fantastically shy. He is loyal to the death, but indeterminate at a crisis.'

'And the Queen?'

'The Queen is still a child. After her French rabble were sent back to France, she found that she had a husband. There is an utter devotion between them, but a blind one.'

'And the Court?'

'The Court is the best that England has ever had—decorous without stupidity; loving learning more than licence; religious without bigotry. But it is like the King. It sees only itself. Its world is an ideal one without reality. Reality is outside it and very threatening.' She spoke with sudden energy. 'If I had the power and the influence—but I have none—I would say to the King: "Sire, go out and seek in the streets and the hedges for men who know the people. Win them and keep them. Listen always to what they have to say. For the world has changed—the English world. You must share with others your power. Your power will grow stronger as you share it. Even Elizabeth could not act alone, and men are not passive any longer, nor ignorant any longer, nor slaves any longer. Be one with them and you will be all the more above them."'

Peter cried out: 'Yes. Yes. You are right. Those are noble words!' She shook her head.

'There, you see, Peter, how you affect me! For I care for none of these things. I do not even believe them. All men are base, pursuing their own ends always. Nothing can prevent their destruction again and again, because they are stupid and greedy and false. It does not matter whether it is John Pym or John Eliot or John Hampden. There is none good—no, not one. Not you, Peter, nor I neither.'

'There *is* one good,' Peter said. 'I have found a man.'

'And who may he be?'

'Mr. Oliver Cromwell.'

'Cromwell? I have not heard of him.'

'You will do. He is a Huntingdon man. He was in the last Parliament.'

'It may be. Until he has power. Then he will be like the rest.'

He looked at her almost beseechingly.

'You do not in reality believe that all men are base?'

'Indeed I do. Save only, of course,' she added mockingly, 'the Herries. There is a certain sweetness in your old Nicholas and in Rosamund and in Lucy. I would say, too, that Rashleigh is the noblest of you all. But cold. An icicle of virtue.' She rose and stood before him. 'And you think I am changed, Mr. Garland?'

'I do not know you yet. First I saw you as a little wandering child. Then I saw you as a beautiful woman alone in a wood. Now I see you as a Court lady, very certain of herself, contemptuous, kind against her will—not happy, I think.'

'Happy? Happiness? Do you put great charge by happiness, Peter?'

'It must depend—the right kind of happiness.'

'And what is that, pray?'

Her smile and the ring of her words made her seem to him as though she regarded him as a child. That fired him and he answered her almost fiercely.

'Happiness is living with God. There is none other. All else fails.'

'And so—are you happy?'

'From time to time. To live with God is not easy. It is not intended to be so. You must rid yourself of all the things that hinder you from hearing His voice, feeling His touch, realizing His word of command. Oh, I know that you are saying that you are hearing this so often, that any labouring man can stand at the street corner and spout the Bible as from a pump. But I rejoice in that very thing. This country is discovering two mighty things—the purveyance of God in everything and the necessity that every man shall be free—free to worship as he pleases, to think as he pleases. His living shall not be unjustly taken from him by any court, his body shall not be tortured that he may swear falsely, he shall not be forced to fight on the side of corruption. Englishmen are like this; they are slothful and tolerant until the last moment. When that has come and they see their peril, they rise and fight as the men of no other country in the world can fight—to the bitter last. So, I think, they are rising now.'

'Yes,' Katherine said. 'They will fight and they may, peradventure, win. They return to their sloth again. What virtue there?'

'Dr. Donne, the Dean of St. Paul's,' Peter said, 'in a sermon said that we think too meanly of Time, as though we were shut in a small room. That to see progress we must look back to the marsh and the great animals that crept and staggered there, and we must look forward to the stars who, in their order under God, count Time as a moment.'

'And there is progress even there?'

'Every fight righteousness wins is a step on the way.'

She did not answer him, but knelt down beside the fire, holding out her hands again to it.

He rose, almost stumbling over the pile of books. 'I have things that I must do,' he said, stammering. 'I—— Forgive me.'

She smiled across her shoulder at him.

'Pray to your God to convert me,' she said.

He turned upon her; he seemed in a rage.

'I pray every day for you. You did not know that, did you? I have done that ever since my seeing you at Keswick. I have loved you ever since you were a child in Nicholas' London house. It began then. For my misfortune, and yet—perhaps not. I love you without hope of any satisfaction. You will be always to me the most beautiful lady God ever made. I think you are not so cruel nor so contemptuous as you say, but I shall never have any joy of you. Not in any contact with you. Only in my thoughts, remembering you, considering your lovely beauty, praising God that He could make such a loveliness. You have kept me from evil because by the standard of your beauty all other women are faulty. I was born perhaps to love what I could not attain. Now, besides, I have found a man whom I can serve. I have seen him but once, yet I know that he is my master whom I must follow. I had seen you but once when I saw you again as a child, and yet I knew how it must be. . . .' He stammered again, blushing a little in the firelight. 'You think me a preacher, a Puritan. You despise me in your mind. Yet I am no hypocrite, and I think no one but is proud at another's love, even though there can be no return. You will not hear this again from me. . . .'

She answered him angrily. She was almost, he thought, as she had been at Keswick.

'Proud? And why should I be proud? Men love me because of my body. What have I to do with that? Men can have my body, but my own independence survives it. I have seen the world, its wickedness and base usage. I have seen in a Chelsea house things done and spoken so evil that your God must, I should suppose, have been sleeping. I have seen my father hang from a beam with soiled and twisting feet. I will give myself to no one. No one until I die shall touch me. I am beyond approach. Pray for me if you please and waste your breath.'

He looked at her with a sternness that made him seem to her a man quite new.

He bowed. 'Very well. I asked for nothing. I expected nothing. I, too, am independent. You cannot touch my love for you.'

She burst out laughing. Then she went forward and put her hand on his arm.

'My inviolability, Peter, allows me a friend—and your God, if He knows all as you say, knows how I need one. Need? No! I need no one! But I *like* a friend, Peter. Evil as the world is, a friend is a good thing. For with all this fine talk of my freedom I enclose myself with the rest. I, too, am unworthy of any sort of praise. On the steps of this universal low order you are in a higher place than I. If you will be my friend you will see my own scorn for myself—a scorn universal but particular, too. You *are* my friend?' she asked, holding out her hand. He took it.

'Yes,' he said. 'I will be always anything you ask.'

Snow began to fall lightly in the morning. By early afternoon the flakes were large and white, like feathery farthings. The snow lay on the cut figures of the box hedges, making ships and dogs and lions and peacocks of ivory.

Little Rupert stood beside his mother in the hall. Over and over again he ran to the great door and looked through the slit to the right of it. He was dressed in a jacket and pantaloons of brown leather, and he carried the small sword that Nicholas had given him proudly at his side. His red hair stood on end. His pale forehead had freckles on it and his long, fierce nose quested the air like an animal's. They were alone just then in the hall, except for Mr. Partis, the chaplain, a long, lean man very much of the Laudian persuasion.

Robert kept him because it was decorous to have a chaplain. Mr. Partis was reading a book by the fire, and now and then he would snap his long fingers as though he had made a discovery.

Rupert stood in the hall and practised with his rapier. Lucy, looking at him, realized that in the right use of his rapier he was as natural as breathing. His small, spare body moved as though it belonged to the best duellist in the kingdom. He was extraordinarily lissom, all his muscles moving as though to an absolute law. When his arm was stretched it was as taut as a bow; then, in a moment, it was as alive and flexible as a darting snake, the little rapier flashing and curving in the firelight. He stamped with his foot and cried 'Ha! Ha!'

Lucy, watching him, was quite unreasonably happy. This happened to her again and again; she was often ashamed of it, for her life had so far been nothing to be happy about, and she was the scandal of the Herries family. She should at least have been ashamed that she cared so little about *being* a scandal. She did not extenuate anything. It was all her own fault to have felt so foolishly about a worthless fellow like Carey. It was her own fault, but she did not care. She still loved Carey but she loved a number of other people as well—Rupert first of all, then Katherine, then Nicholas and Rosamund, then Sir Timothy Strickland, Colonel Rander, Fortescue Basset. No, that she *loved* these gentlemen was too strong a statement, but she enjoyed immensely to be with them and to know that they admired her.

She was known everywhere as Mistress Herries, and she did not care in the least whether people were aware that she had never been married. She enjoyed being a widow. She enjoyed everything. She simply could not help it. She was aware of her monstrous age, but if she did not feel it and did not look it, what matter?

She knew that the day must come, and perhaps shortly, when Rupert knew who his real father was. She did not think that he would mind very much. That nasty Frederick, who was Carey's nephew, would in all probability tell him. Frederick was always telling people unpleasant things in the pleasantest manner.

She was a little uncomfortable sometimes when she considered that the future of herself and her boy was so very uncertain. In the course of nature Nicholas must soon die. As it was, he must be one of the oldest men in England.

After his death she could not hope to continue living at Mallory. Robert was kind to her and would ask her to stay, but would not expect her to make her home there. She had no money and saw no prospect of any unless she married. Whoever she married must be told that Rupert was illegitimate. However, sufficient for the day was the evil. When the critical time came Katherine would advise her. Not only did she adore Katherine, but she considered her also the fountain of all wisdom. That strong and independent character had all the things that Lucy had not.

Rupert stopped his exercises and came over to his mother.

'Mother—of what like was my father?'

He had never asked her that question before. She came to the sudden resolve—all her resolves were sudden—that she would tell him. She put her arm round him and drew him close. His eyes, which were very much his best feature, regarded her seriously.

'Your father was not my husband. He was Carey Courthope, Frederick Courthope's uncle.'

She spoke low lest Mr. Partis, the chaplain, should overhear.

'Then, Mother, you and my father were not married to one another.'

'No— we were not.'

He thought reflectively.

'They were beating a woman in the village because she was not married.'

'Yes, dear.'

'Why is it wrong not to be married?'

'Because everyone must be married if they have children.'

'Why, Mother?'

'Because the Church says that it is wicked to have children if you are not married.'

'Then you are wicked.'

'Yes, dear.'

'I do not care how wicked you are. I do not care for the Church, neither. Mr. Partis is the Church, is he not?'

'Hush, dear. Mr. Partis is a very good man.'

He considered this.

'And you are very good. But I do not care whether a man is good or evil. I will kill anyone who is not good to you, though.'

She kissed him. Of course he did not like to be kissed, but his mother, whom he adored, could do no wrong.

'If they try to beat you, I will kill them.'

'They will not beat me.' She laughed.

'Is someone not your father if he has not been married?'

'No. He is your father.'

'Then what like *was* my father?' he repeated.

'He was handsome—and . . . I would rather not speak of him, because he is dead.'

'I am glad he is dead, if you were not married.'

Lucy sighed. 'Yes—it is better so.'

Half-way along the hall there was a small postern door that led into a private garden, in the summer fragrant with roses. Rupert ran to it and, after wrestling a little with the handle, pushed it open.

'Come back, Rupert. I told you no. You are letting cold into the house.' But he stood there, looking out at the snow, hopping on first one foot, then the other. A soft scurry of snow blew in, dancing around his red hair. He came back to his mother.

'I wish to go out into it.'

Frederick Courthope, who seemed to have come from nowhere, said with an agreeable, indulgent smile: 'The cold would kill you. But still, if you do not care . . .'

Rupert ran up to the dais, found Katherine Christian's puppy and began to play with it.

Frederick leaned his slender back against the table and looked appreciatively at Lucy.

'How beautiful you are, Mistress Herries!'

She half turned angrily.

'If you think to provoke me——'

'No. No.' He drew nearer to her. 'Tell me, Lucy—do you think your friend—your lovely friend—could bring me to Court?'

'Katherine? Why do you wish to be there?'

'Because it would suit me very well. Because there are great things brewing. Because she is a friend of the Queen's. Because she is a great friend of Lucy Carlisle, your namesake, who is the deepest intriguer in London. But finally because, when once I am inside, I can further myself. And because, yet more finally, your brother Rashleigh will detest to see me there!'

Lucy said quietly: 'How you do hate us, Frederick—Rashleigh, Peter, and me.'

'No,' he said, also quietly, 'I have no liking for Rashleigh because he does not see me when I am with him. There is no better reason for not liking. But I will tell you something, Lucy. I care for no one but myself, and I will take any step to advance myself. There! Is that not frank?

'And I have a curiosity insatiable. I am not a gossip, but I am a discoverer of secrets and so would go to Court and play at cards with George Goring, ride out with Mr. Jermyn, the Queen's friend, and talk in a corner with Lady Carlisle——'

'Yes,' Lucy said quickly, 'and out of all these games and talks make evil. I know in my heart, Frederick, that one day you will do us all hurt—Peter, Rashleigh, and me. We are one person. Peter may have different politics from Rashleigh; nevertheless we are one. If you hurt one of us you hurt the others. You said that if Rupert ran out into the snow it would be his death. Will *you* not try it?'

'That will not kill me,' he said calmly. 'But tell me of your lovely friend. They say so many things of her—that she is from the streets, the daughter of a necromancer who was in the Overbury affair, that she was anybody's mistress but now is more disdainful. That when old Lady Forres first brought her to Court on the first day she slapped the cheeks of Madame St. George, the Queen's French woman. And yet the Queen loves her. That Buckingham, before that last fatal expedition, implored her to be his mistress and she consented. Mr. John Felton frustrated that. That when Jeffery Hudson, the dwarf, was ill of a fever, she nursed him with her own hands when no other would come near to him. That she can discuss architecture with Inigo Jones, poetry with Davenant, and painting with the King. If I were an amorous man I would myself persuade her. . . .'

'If you were an amorous man,' Lucy said, laughing, 'you would have a heart—if but a momentary one.' She added scornfully: 'For a boy of eighteen, Frederick, you are too old. But do what you can with Katherine. She alone of all of us cannot be harmed by you, for she is as hard as yourself when she pleases.'

To Frederick's intense annoyance Rupert ran down to them. It was true, as Lucy said, that Frederick neither hated nor loved, for he knew already that emotions were bad for an intriguer. Moreover, he was not a very bad young man, but conceited of his gifts and anxious to keep them exercised. If, however, he did dislike any human being, it was this child. Mockingly he said to Rupert:

'Now run into the snow as I said. A boy of real spirit would go naked!'

'Frederick!' Lucy cried, but it was too late. Rupert, after first putting his tongue out to Frederick, ran to the postern door. Here, with a swift movement, he threw off his clothes, kicking his shoes into the air, turned to them for a moment as bare as he was born, pulled at the door, and was outside.

With cries Lucy ran after him, Frederick after her. She ran desperately into the garden, and ahead of her, the snow almost hiding him, ran Rupert. They followed and, to Lucy's extreme horror, saw him spring into the little river that ran on the farther side of the white lawn. For a moment only his red head was visible, then he was out again, danced fantastically on the snow, ran past them crowing with pleasure, and was into the house again.

When they returned he was kneeling in front of the fire, to the shocked exclamations of Mr. Partis. Then, a naked gnome, ran past them again, turned, crying: 'My sword! My sword!' bent down to pick it up from his clothes and, brandishing it, vanished up the great staircase.

Lucy, still exclaiming, picked up his little clothes, and hurried after him.

'That child,' Frederick said solemnly to Mr. Partis, 'will one day be hanged. I shall be in the audience. '

There was a small pool of water in front of the fireplace.

They were seated handsomely about the fire roaring in the high stone fireplace in the great hall. Supper was long over. Soon time for bed. Nicholas, Rosamund, Celia, Mark Turner, Lucy, Katherine, Frederick—Ladies, sweet ladies,—Gentlemen, gentlemen—very soon time for bed. Grave-faced Robert had all to do to keep awake. He blinked across the hall at the tapestry, the armour, the heads of animals, the old weapons. The gallery at the far end was well lit with a great piece of candelabra. Illumined by it Robert could see the bad family portraits, the dark, sombre-painted boards, with here a ruff and here a gold chain, there an eyebrow, a white hand, or a crimson cheek.

He had had a busy day. He had visited the deer in the park to see how they would be for hunting, and inspected his small pack. This hunting, whether of otter, badger, deer, or fox, was carried on within a gentleman's own boundaries, a family affair and private. But he was not like many of his gentlemen neighbours, simply a besotted squire who hunted all day and ended up at the ale-house. He enjoyed fowling with the hawk or net (the use of the shot-gun was still forbidden by an old law). He liked riding and hunting. But his days were really occupied with examining minutely every aspect of the estate. His ladies, Rosamund, Lucy, whoever lived with him, were occupied the day long with household duties. They were the doctors of the house as well as the housekeepers, and Rosamund had a wonderful knowledge of simples, charms, and white magic. All food and drink came off the estate, and Rosamund was a marvellous hand at cooking, fruit-preserving, and the rest. When you consider that she was the daughter of a gay, unpractical painter, this is to be wondered at. But she had lived her life long with Nicholas as her hero and she knew that he was a practical man. Moreover, she was a Herries—who, except for the divine few, are soaked in common sense.

To-day, since the snow began to fall, had been an indoor day for Robert. He had inspected the dairies, the stables, the outhouses, the farms as though he were an official inspector. So he was weary, pleasantly so. He had on his lap a sheaf of papers; he did not look at them but sat back and watched the flames leaping.

Frederick was in another part of the hall, trying over, with his viol, softly some song. Both Katherine and Lucy were working at tapestry, Katherine most deftly, Lucy with little murmurs of impatience and annoyance. Celia Turner and her husband played at chess. Peter was reading.

Old Gilbert Armstrong, with his snow-white hair and brown wrinkled face, stood not far from Nicholas, his fingers busy with some fishing-tackle.

Rosamund and Nicholas talked softly together.

'You know, wife,' he said, 'I all but fell at the fountain this morning. My eyes were misted. I must remember that I am an old man.'

She felt anxious—she had long been anxious about his sight—but she said nothing. She took his hand between hers.

'And I am an old woman. I wish sometimes that I had given you another child.'

'A daughter—a daughter would have been pleasant.'

'You have Lucy.'

He looked across at her with love.

'Yes. Dear Lucy.'

They had all been talking of the Rupert episode, and Rosamund had been doctoring him, very much against his will.

'Poor Lucy,' Rosamund said softly. 'And how strange a child. He said to me before I blew out the candle: "Madam, I am a bastard." '

Nicholas roused himself a little.

'He knows, then?'

'Yes. Lucy told him to-day. Then he said: "But I will fight anyone who calls me one!" '

'He has a fire-eating spirit which may be needed when he grows. I had one—and much good it did me!'

'I remember how proud I was when I heard of it. Even as a child I said, without hope: "That is the man for me!" '

'And so I have been. And you the woman for me!' He leant over and kissed her cheek. She was never to forget that caress.

'Of everything in my long life,' Nicholas went on, 'you have been the best. And for how long I was blind to it! I had another passion, a vision, a ghost. I was at this same place when Gilbert told me——' He broke off. 'I was never a man of much imagination and my perception of the true love came to me slowly. Strange, too, it is how all the past now is huddled together. Only moments remain. That day when Gilbert and I fought those men on the Moor,—the Queen riding at Chartley. Our wedding. The other Queen dying.' He leaned back over the settle and called out: 'Do you remember, old friend, the fight on the Moor?'

Gilbert Armstrong grinned.

'I remember everything.'

They looked at one another with love. On this same place Nicholas had struck him. They both remembered and loved one another the more.

But Nicholas was sleepy. He was always sleepy now of an evening.

His great head nodded: his hand slackened in Rosamund's hold.

He began to dream. He dreamed, as he had not for a long time now, of his old enemy, Philip Irvine. He dreamed of him and of Fawkes together. Irvine was struggling as Fawkes had done, his face terrible and wild. Nicholas endeavoured to hold him but, in spite of his great strength, Irvine slipped from him. He rose and shouted triumphantly: 'I have you now! I have you now!' With that cry in his ears Nicholas awoke.

He awoke and everything was dark. The leaping flames of the fire were not there.

He passed his hands in front of his eyes. He could not see them. He staggered to his feet, crying: 'The flames. . . . The flames!'

Everyone turned towards him. He stood there, gigantic, like Samson, his eyes staring, his face working terribly.

He called out in a loud voice: 'I cannot see! . . . Oh, my God, I cannot see!'

Rosamund put her arms around him, but he pushed her off as though he did not realize her. He took a step forward, then fell to his knees.

'Help me, God . . . I am blind.'

It was Gilbert Armstrong who ran to him and held his shoulders. 'There, master. Quiet—quiet. It is but for a moment. Patience, patience.'

Nicholas leant against him, his head against the old man's chest. The most terrible thing was that he began to cry, soundlessly, the tears running down his cheeks. Gilbert raised him, holding him in his arms.

'It is I, master. I am with you. No evil can come. In a moment all will be well.'

Nicholas turned his head.

He stared at Gilbert.

'Oh, Gilbert, I cannot see you. Oh, Gilbert, the light is gone and I cannot see!'

PORTRAIT OF A KING

Pages from the Journal of Rashleigh Garland

March 14, 1635.

Yesterday was my birthday.

I was forty-seven years of age and discovered a proper shame of myself. George Goring, who is never to be trusted and least of all by himself, said to me that I never aged a day and implied that the reason of it was that I kept myself apart from all men in a sort of icy chamber. He has a kind of respect for me but can understand no man who has not a constant traffic with women. There is matter here for consideration. How is it that I am not, ere now, an ancient married man with young men and maidens, sprung from my loins, active about me?

It is not that women mean nothing to me. Three times at least I have been on the narrow edge of matrimony. I have not been continent but incontinency has had little pleasure for me. My life has been and is a dedicated one—not to my God nor to my fellow-men, but to one man only.

Writing in the secrecy of my heart and putting down what I would say to no living soul I may ask myself—What is there in this man that has commanded and ever will command my absolute devotion?

Were I to encounter him in some tavern gathering, dressed in homespun and quaffing his ale, what would I see? A little undersized fellow with bandy legs, an awkward stammer, and a grave, obstinate countenance forbidding intimacy. I have watched him disrobe, retire into the cabinet to relieve nature, stand, yawning, in his night-dress and furred slippers, climb into his bed, turn over on his side with a final yawn.

I have known him with the colic so bad that for a day he could scarcely leave the stool. I have seen him crawl on all-fours with his children so that they may pull his beard.

I have heard him giggle with his Queen at some humour that would not amuse a ditcher. (He has, when in absolute privacy, an appreciation of fun. Never of humour.) I have heard him argue with a blind obstinacy that has altogether said good-bye to all intelligence. I have known him trust men whom a baby would discover, and fasten to that trust like a blind and deaf man. I have heard him make a man a promise and an hour later make another man a promise of the exact opposite. I have watched him love with a complete devotion as bad and muddling and scornful a rascal as God ever made—my Duke of Buckingham to wit.

Is this service of mine then only to an idea? It is true that, since I was a child, I have believed that the King is appointed by God, that it is his Divine Right to rule, and that all men owe him an absolute obedience. Truly I have seen ill things done by Kings, for they are mortal men, but I have seen no evidence to prove to me that by this or that man less evil would be done. Have Eliot and Pym and Hampden not been fallible men? And for what has my King been fighting? As a father for his children. He has said to them that if they will give him the money that a ruler of his people should rightly have he will guard them, protect them, watch over them. In what ten years of our history has England been more prosperous than in the last ten years of this present reign? What Court more virtuous, what people in general more cheerful and contented?

And what, beside this money, has he asked of them? That they shall observe the decencies of religion before God, that they shall not write against the worship of God, that they shall respect his Queen and himself. I have no great personal liking for little Laud, who is as a fussy terrier-dog, sniffing and nosing and spying out. But if we had not guardians such as he, into what disintegration would we not fall, nay, are not already falling? What would they have, this rabble of Parliament who are with every day more noisy and pestilent? They would have their own power and the country's servitude. They would have the common people their slaves, even as they declare they are themselves slaves of the King. They would worship in any way that pleases them, which is no way at all. They would take from the common man all his little pleasures, his songs and his dances. They would have us fight with all the world and yet will not pay for a navy to defend us.

Yes, but the Man, the Man!

I am writing now in my room, quiet, shaded, with the two candles guttering a little in the breeze that comes from between the curtains. My drawing of the Virgin and Child, attributed to Raphael, a gift from the King, hangs opposite me between the silver mirror and the window.

It seems to me—for I am almost half asleep and can write little more—that the King stands beside the window, very still, watching me with that grave and solemn look that I have seen so often. He challenges my devotion. But he need not. He knows my heart. Often I have seen him examine a painting or listen to music with just this same earnest enquiry. At such moments you may behold his truest self when he moves into another world in which he may be altogether reassured. In such a world there is no one to ask of him save his God, no one to betray him, no one to challenge him in the things that he knows to be right.

It is his misfortune, in this evil, false, and turning world that he sees so well what is right and, seeing it, no one may move him. Thus I love him, for he is the one integrious man I have ever known.

March 26.

This day I accompanied the King when he visited the Queen at St. James' Palace. He went to visit the children. I alone accompanied him. When we arrived first at the room where the Queen was, Gregorio Panzani, the Papal envoy, who arrived in England last December, was present. He is a very amiable, courteous gentleman whom I do not trust at all, who is, I am greatly convinced, of serious danger to this country. The King is himself a devoted adherent to the Anglican religion and nothing and no man nor woman shall ever turn him from it. But he is not sufficiently aware of the hatred in which Catholicism is held throughout the country. He loves the Queen with so great a passion that he is blinded to the effect of many things that she does. I understand that she has recently informed Panzani that she is resolved that she can win the King to the Catholic faith. She cannot be so persuaded in her heart as she pretends, but she is reckless and obstinate and is well aware of the devotion that the King has to her. She is not, however, all foolish. When a fragment of the true Cross was recently discovered in the Tower it was exposed to public gaze in one of the palaces. This offended her propriety as greatly as it offended the King and she has asked it for her new chapel at Somerset House.

Panzani, whose Jesuitical smoothness is all contrary to honesty, knows well that I do not care for him and is anxious to win me. He took me now aside and praised my wisdom. His fingers touched at times my arm. He has a belief, I fancy, in some kind of hypnotic power, for he stares into your eyes as though he would draw you into himself. But I am not so readily drawn. He had cut himself on the right side of his cheek and I fixed my eyes upon that, which discomforted him.

Panzani departed and we found the Queen with Lady Carlisle and the three children. Prince Charles is now five, Princess Mary four, and Prince James two. I have a liking for Prince Charles; he is a brown little boy with a roguish eye. He is for ever laughing and is as brave a child as I have ever seen, save Lucy's boy.

When the King called the two elder children to him, Princess Mary came with docility. She is grave and obedient but has, I think, underneath this the obstinacy of both her father and mother.

But Prince Charles would not at first come to his father. His remarkably fine eyes shone with mischief.

'Come, Charles,' his father said. 'You must obey me. I am the King.'

'I also will be King one of these days,' he said.

'I am also your father who loves you.'

The child came over and put his little brown hand into his father's.

They began then to play. Although the Queen is now twenty-six years of age, she can at a moment transform herself into a child. Little James began to crow with delight. The King was on his knees, Prince Charles riding his back. The King moved about the room, and Prince James, who had a little whip, solemnly cracked it. Then the King, exhausted, sat up, Prince Charles still clinging to his neck. The Queen clapped her hands with delight. Across the room they exchanged a glance of deep and devoted love.

It was strange to me, as I looked at him, to remember the ill-beginnings of this marriage; how the Queen, child as she then was, cried that she was not met at Dover on her first coming, the King being at Canterbury; how, when they began their journey to London, her beloved (but evil) Madame Saint-George was not permitted to sit beside her; how, on the nuptial night, she hated the stocking-throwing and the rest, and later had the Duchess of Chevreuse with her and not the King; how, when the King was determined to send her

French people back to France, and locked the door on her apart from her women, she shrieked and yelled and kicked, and that last picture of her dear Madame Saint-George being pushed into her coach in the Strand, gesticulating and screaming, and the mob throwing stones at her.

That was long over, but had Buckingham not been so fortunately slain it would, I am convinced, have lasted.

She was but a child then, she is but a child now. She is in stature so small that it is fortunate that the King is also of low stature. Her eyes are immensely fine and the whole shape of her small head exquisite. As she stood now, holding Prince James by the hand, in her rose-coloured gown, her eyes fastened with worship on the King, I understood well his slavery. . . .

April 2.

I have had so curious a talk with Katherine, at this present one of the Queen's Bedchamber Women, that I would wish to record it. To give, too, a sketch of her—something after John Earle's *Micro-cosmographie,* which is now everybody's favourite and is, anyone will allow, a brave effort for a Bishop. When he writes of his 'Self-Conceited Man': 'Men are merciful to him; and let him alone, for if he be once driven from his humour he is like two inward friends fallen out. His own bitter enemy and discontent presently makes a murther.

'In sum, he is a bladder blown up with wind, which the least straw crushes to nothing.'

Nay, but that last applies to neither Katherine nor myself. It is hard to know us, but it is harder still to blow us down. My self-conceit is founded in an obstinate, almost mystical service; hers, I would fancy, in a reaction from a cruel childhood that has made her despise all mankind.

She is, of course, the most beautiful woman in England, and is well aware of it although without conceit. I, too, have been flattered incessantly that I am handsome, and could wish that I had more joy of it. My bodily appearance has, however, never made me a target for men's (nor women's) hearts. I can say with a perfect honesty that no living person in all the world loves me. My brother and sister? Lucy loves all the world. She cannot, although she has been evilly treated, believe in the wickedness of man. Peter would love me had I other doctrines and faith. For the King I am a good and faithful servant—no more.

Katherine, against this, is much beloved. The Queen loves her. The Court loves her as it would a bird of paradise whom it would encage. Many a man loves her through the hope that he may one day share a bed with her. And I think that poor Peter loves her with a devotion exceeding all the rest.

She has herself told me that only our Herries family has any claim on her and she resents the claim. Not that *we* make it, but that something within herself ties her to us—old blind Nicholas, Rosamund, we three.

She has told me that our fate is bound one with the other's and that our history is one. There is some spell, she says, that we cast upon her and she hates us for it, and loves us too—or that myself she does not love, as no one can, but that she is bound to me nevertheless.

She is, as I see her, a woman of many virtues—kindly, generous, wise, and tolerant with an excellent charity and forbearance. Men say that she is libidinous and it is certain that she has been the mistress of one or two. It has been said that she had promised to be Buckingham's mistress before he went on his last journey to Portsmouth, but this I do not believe.

She is of great courage, speaks her mind when she will, is afraid of no man. To my thinking, behind the grandeur there is standing always the little girl with the necromantic father. She can never escape from this.

She understands with wonderful perception the Herries mixture in us—that there is always a striving towards the spirit shooting through our mediocre English clay, that we are restless and questing in spirit and so of the English English, who will for ever be making poets out of haberdashers and fighting the whole world for a Cause even while they count their pennies in the back-shop corner.

And now to another business. I have a new friend. It has not been and is not of my seeking. The Marquess of Newby is freshly come here in a minor office about the Court. He is a man over thirty years of age, fresh and vigorous and simple as a pippin apple. In appearance he is big and broad and fair-haired and blue-eyed, with no subtleties of expression. He has no sulky lip or beaten brow or menacing hand.

What he seems he is. He is of a most cheerful temperament and of a great pride. He will forgive all save an offence against his family.

He came here with my young cousin, Frederick Courthope, a young man of twenty-three summers, as his secretary. Frederick is the nephew of the wretched Carey who wronged poor Lucy, and so from the first I had no liking for him. He is, however, an able young man, keeping his counsel, watching all things, telling nothing. He is ambitious for himself and for no one else. He is of the Herries business variety, only his business is in men's souls.

He wishes for my regard and with frankness tells me so. He will never have it.

Meanwhile Charles Newby is in a passion for Katherine. From the first moment that he saw her he was flattened to the hard ground. He is dog-like, patient, determined in his devotion, and all the Court laughs at it.

April 3.

A strange piece of family history has been recalled to me this day and all the evening—I have been alone—I have been thinking of it.

Charles Newby has told me that he has a mansion ten miles only from Seddon! All our lives—Peter's, Lucy's, mine—Seddon has been a place of romantic and curious interest to us. The yet more curious thing is that but a month or two ago Robert told me that he was planning a visit to Seddon. So quickly then is Newby drawn within our orbit.

Our link with Seddon is strange and deserves a family note here. Michael Herries of Mallory, old Nicholas' gentle father, had a brother Francis, of a very different character. This fellow, who was in many ways a rapscallion but had some power with Elizabeth, was interested, as were several members of our family, in the mines for silver and other metals that the Queen encouraged the Almaynes to develop in Cumberland. He built himself a little house in the Borrowdale valley, near Keswick, and also purchased this house, Seddon, north of Carlisle. For some years he was a bachelor, married men not being favoured by our swarthy Queen, but late in life he married, and lived peacefully enough at Seddon, and became father of a daughter. His wife died in giving birth, and this drove Francis into despair; his original wildness overtook him and he retired to live, as I have heard, more like a beast than a man, in the Borrowdale house. Seddon he abandoned to his eldest brother, who, a bachelor, took guardianship of Francis' child. This girl married a man of Scottish family named Blaikie, and Seddon was their home. Their child, Margaret Blaikie, now fifteen years of age, lives at Seddon with her parents.

As children we heard nothing of Francis or his doings, and I believe that when Nicholas went North, as he often did, he never visited Seddon. Francis was the black sheep for all of us. Robin Herries, Nicholas' brother, afterwards lived in Borrowdale for a time, and it was there that he came to ruin over his Catholic practices.

Why has it been that the three of us have thought always so romantically of Seddon? It may be that Francis' abandoned character has drawn us. This child, Margaret Blaikie, is old wicked Francis' granddaughter. Of what like is she?

But now Newby has asked me to visit him at Thornhurst, and that being but ten miles from Seddon it may be that I shall see the child. It may be that Robert, who is a dry little man, will be at Seddon.

This conversation that I had many days back, but was too weary on that evening to write down here, comes back to me. A brief one but revealing.

They are preparing another of those eternal Masques in which the Queen delights so much. As ever, Katherine and myself are to play our part, she as Juno, I as a poet lost in the Classical Age.

There was the accustomed crowd and babel, and Lucy Carlisle, with her busy efficiency, Goring with his breezy laughter, Jermyn fluttering about the Queen.

And we, alone in some corner, reached a new intimacy, or so, when I glance back, it seems to have been. I recall some sentences.

She said: 'Rashleigh, this is the edge of the pit.'

She continued swiftly:

'Rashleigh, you have influence with the King. You must break through the wall that protects him, and tell him that there is no moment to be lost.'

'We are all very well here, it seems to me,' I answered foolishly.

'*We* are well! But what does it matter as to *our* well or ill! He sees nothing. He hears nothing. Go to him and say this to him: "Sire, I have been for many years your faithful servant. Discard all those about you and go out yourself into the streets and ask of this man and that. When you have heard, act as though you were alone. Summon your Parliament, place yourself at its service, abrogate your power that you may retain it. Forbid Laud and his Church offices. Call quite other men into your counsel——" '

I interrupted her.

'*That* would be ruin—they will spare him nothing. If they have him in a little way, then they will have him in a great one.'

'I have had a dream,' she answered, 'and I have seen a vision. This room here—do you see the silver hangings, and Jermyn there, standing on one leg, the brocaded chairs, the painted Christ with the wounded side, the carpet with the Chinese patterns?—the curtains will be torn down, the wounded Christ trodden upon, the carpet dark with blood —I know it, and I would give my soul to save him. But also I know it and I would not stir a finger, for out of the destruction I would accrue my advantage. I have no pity, for we are all fools and life is too contemptible for any action.—And yet—why? Not because he is a King, not because of his Queen whom I serve. Is it his eyes, that are as lonely and unhappy as a lost dog's? Is it because when he is kind he is so very gentle? Is it because he is so wilful that he can see with no man's eyes but his own? Is it because he has no friend since Buckingham and will, I think, never have one any more?'

She laid her hand on my arm, looking me very closely in the eyes.

'We are solitary, Rashleigh, you and I, and so it may be that we can save him who is also solitary. It is not too late. For the sake of Christ Jesu in whom I do not believe, for the wrongs of this world are too many, but who may nevertheless wish that power may be given him, speak to him. . . .'

And it was here, I think, that Goring joined us.

I have never seen her so deeply moved. I did not think that she could be. At night in my bed I have felt a chill wind as though the windows were blown apart.

May 3.

The King is greatly disturbed. We are all, even the most careless of us, aware that there is much trouble abroad.

I have had a curious and intimate conversation with the King this evening that I must record.

Certain public affairs are going badly.

One. The Archbishop, Laud, is about his metropolitan visitation and the King is altogether in his hands. Myself, I believe the King to be very far at heart from accepting Laud's rigid and pedantic cere- monial, but nevertheless he *has* accepted it and is under the Arch- bishop's rule in this. The result of what is happening under Laud is that very many devout Protestants are being driven into the arms of the Puritans.

Two. He has for some while had a nightmare concerning the French Navy which, in combination with the Dutch, could reduce the English to a nothing. They say that the King talks of the Navy in his sleep. The writs that he has issued to the port towns, ordering them to send ships to sea, seem to him the veriest patriotism. Just now the ship-money writs are being extended to the inland counties, and I, and many others, fear that there may be much trouble therefrom, but the King will not see it.

I believe it to be the greatest peril at this time to this nation that the King has no imagination. He has taste to admire, but cannot create. He can judge a picture rightly but cannot paint one. So it is that, for lack of this imagination, he can see no one right but himself. The Church must be in order. Right indeed. But it must be *his* order (or rather, when all is said, the Archbishop's order). So also the country must be defended and her only safety is the sea. Therefore there must be a strong Navy. But there is *not* a strong Navy.

Why not? Because there is not money to make a strong Navy. Sum- mon Parliament, then, and provide the money.

Yes, but Parliament has said that it will not provide the money unless certain wrongs are redressed. The wrongs are *not* wrongs, therefore cannot be redressed. *Therefore* dismiss the Parliament. How get the money then? Order that it shall be given. But if the citizen will not give it unless ordered by Parliament? Imprison the citizen! Yes, but with all the citizens imprisoned, how are we better? We have no Parliament, but also we have no money and no Navy. At this point the King shuts tight his eyes (as I so often have seen him) and says: 'I must have the money. I must have the Navy. I am the King.'

Meanwhile from the imprisoned citizens the cry grows louder and louder. Prynne loses his ears and his ears sprout again in every cabbage-patch. Sir John Eliot dies in the Tower. When he was ill of consumption he implored the King that he might allow him liberty to die in. The King refused, nor would he deliver Eliot's body to his son for burial.

I can see him now standing, with his eyes shut (one of them squints a trifle), and repeating in a slight stammer: 'No. N-no. I am the King. Eliot was a traitor. I am just in my refusal.'

Just, perhaps, but not wise. How cleverly did Elizabeth always observe the moods of her people and trim her sails to them—even James, until the intricacies of Villiers' brilliant body beguiled him. But this King who is so virtuous, whose cheeks blush at an obscene word, who has been ever faithful to his wife, who believes devotedly in his God, he has no imagination to read the mind, thought, purpose of any other man. I have served him now for ten years, been in his constant presence, knelt and rubbed his bare back when he had the rheum in his loins, eaten with him, drunk with him, slept in his chamber, read to him for many an hour, played chess with him by the night, bathed with him, laughed with him (but not very much), sworn with him, even governed with him (for he has permitted me to know many secrets as in this present underground advance to Spain)—so I have served with him—and yet in all this time his imagination has never once played upon me. He has never said to himself: What is in this man's heart? With whom does he go to bed withal? How addresses he his God? Whom does he love and whom hate? From what people has he sprung? Why is he serving me with so devoted a will? Why is he not married? Does he prefer men to women? Or has he boys concealed between the sheets? Is he to be trusted by me? How beats his heart and where are the secret places of his imagination?

He has never asked himself a single question concerning me!

Am I disloyal to my service in writing all this? (It will never be seen by any other eye.) I think not, for my devotion is not lessened by my setting down all the sides of the case. The King is mortal like the rest of us. Had he been given the power of imagination and insight into the minds of others he would be the greatest king England has ever known—for he is honourable, chaste, courageous, of a fine taste and erudition and, behind his shyness, of a warm heart. But the ill fairy at his christening gave him a blind eye to the world outside. I love him perhaps the more for this, because it gives me a great tenderness.

This evening I was in attendance. No one was present but the Archbishop. The little man used the King almost as his scholar to whom he is tutor. One of the King's spaniels misbehaved himself in the fireplace. The page clearing the mess with a shovel, neither the King nor the Archbishop paused in their conversation—only the King regarded the disaster with melancholy eyes but was not aware of it. I was amused by the spaniel who, ashamed at his crime, crawled to his master begging for mercy, with large amber eyes; but when it perceived that the King had not even been aware of the affair, it was deeply offended in its pride, and went and sulked in a corner.

The Archbishop has no let nor give in his countenance. His little body might be made of old documents and ancient ceremonies beneath his clothes. It is impossible to imagine him engaged in bawdry or, indeed, any of the natural functions of the body. This evening he sneezed and so suddenly that it was altogether to his own surprise. He was reminded for a moment that he *had* a body! His knowledge is immense, his ruthlessness as great. He is not cruel, but he also is not human. To my mind he is the worst possible adviser for religious matters to the King.

Afterwards we were alone. The King was greatly depressed. I read to him from a manuscript copy of Mr. John Milton's *Comus*. He was quite enchanted with it, it being altogether to his taste. He has already seen it performed. Mr. Milton is beyond question a poet of promise, although his political opinions are by no means what they should be, as I hear.

After a time the King asked me to put down the book and, almost as though he were speaking to himself, talked to me of his childhood. This he has never done before.

He said that his father did not care for children. When he himself was over three years old he could not speak nor stand. They wished to slit the string under his tongue, and to place his leg in irons, but fortunately both cruelties were prevented. He told me that he was as lonely a child as ever lived. His elder brother was precocious, a fine horseman, an admirable player at tennis. He, the King, because of his bodily weakness, was feeble at all sport until he came to ride a horse well. He was frightened of women, so they neglected him. He was therefore very studious in default of better, but his brother Henry, whom he nevertheless loved, ridiculed him and tormented him.

'And this,' said the King sadly, 'is the original of my nervous temper, so before I am aware of it I am angry.' He longed to be as other boys, and envied them. He practised vaulting, archery, the game of tennis. He was often so weary that he could have shed tears. 'But I was ever of a determined nature,' said the King, 'and if a thing is to be done, it is to be done.'

I could see as he spoke the mingling of the romantic, the idealist, and the stubborn conformist in his eyes and mouth.

He rose and I was dismissed. I perceived that he had been scarcely conscious of me. He said something about the Prayer Book that the Archbishop is preparing, and the enforcement of ship-money.

'Our Navy is a disgrace. I *will* not have it so. I *will* not have it so!'

His face and body then were rigid, like a figure painted on wood. I went from the room, but he was not aware that I was gone.

I have in my heart a deep tenderness for him, almost as though he were my vexing, obstinate, blind-eyed, suffering, lonely, lovable child. And I fear that there is much trouble in store for us all.

KATHERINE AT SEDDON

KATHERINE STOOD looking out of her bedroom window on a most perfect summer morning in the ancient Newby family seat of Thornhurst.

It was one of those English mornings of early summer that belong only to England, and because, in spite of the promised heat, there was an almost harsh sea-sharpness in the air, this morning could belong only to Northern England.

Below Katherine's window and stretching far away was the park. Beyond the park could be seen faintly the silken shadows of the Firth waters, now inflowing. The great trees held in their leaves colours of metallic darkness and already their shadows fell heavily on the grass —the grass newly green with the first summer stillness. The deer moved as though they cropped an insubstantial food between sky and earth. That sky was of a faint white-blue radiance hold. heat by the thinnest bonds, that light and heat so quiv passion to break through and flood the world that it c held captive much longer.

The stillness was the stillness of ancient days—of cent with human living. No new country could have the character of this stillness. Battles with their screams, murderous weapons, disasters, and victories had to be before the soil could know what it was to be still. Both behind and in front of this hushed silence were songs and dances and musical instruments. Also all the monotony of human lives—generation upon generation of births, marriages, deaths, feasts and funerals, love-makings, separations, hopes and apprehensions.

The great park with its deer, the thick, strong, grey tower set up against the Scots, all solitary by itself on a little hill, the flood of brilliant green running to the very edge of the faint, pale water, the deer bathed in the early light, the dark thick hardness of the massed metal of the giant oaks, all these gave Katherine a sense of settled loveliness that woke in her breast a sharp nostalgia:

'I have never had any of this. I do not belong to it. I am here under a false pretence. If I marry Charles Newby and pretend to be mistress of this place, it is still a pretence and I am a humbug. Charles belongs to this, Rashleigh belongs to it, even wild flitting Lucy belongs to it, but I do not.'

In the early morning, when she had just woken from sleep, her determination, the force of her character, was less strong.

She knew that another great crisis was upon her, might be settled that very day. Something in her longed for the peace and the security that this place would bring. Charles Newby might, nay, probably would, ask her to marry him that very day. If he did, she would be honest with him, but by this time she knew so many things about men that she could recognize very well that wild and passionate desire in his heart. When a man felt that for a woman, no caution, no reason would prevent him. Yet afterwards, as also she well knew, the caution and reason would return. They were part of his character. Also his deep, deep family pride.

He would marry her now in spite of all the reasons against it, but afterwards all the reasons would return. She did not belong to any of this. It was not that she would be weary of it, but rather that she could not stay still in it. She was, and would be to the end, a wanderer, a vagabond, the magician's daughter.

It would not be, of course, that Charles would be always here. He had his corner at Court—he was ambitious for his family's sake. But she knew well enough that trouble was coming to that same Court, was even now there. For that reason, too, she should not marry Newby. She wished, when the crisis did come, to be, as she always wished in everything, a free woman.

She had many friends at Court, she owed a loyalty to the King and Queen, who had been good to her. She owed an especial duty to the King, who must have heard many of the scandals connected with her, and yet, with all his proprieties and conventions, he had overlooked them.

Nevertheless, with all her duties to him, she kept her freedom of judgment. She had a sympathy with and an understanding of both political parties. Here she thought of Peter Garland. She was not in love with Peter, she saw him very seldom, but he was caught, held at the back of her mind. Her admiration for him was stronger than her admiration for any other human being. And it was more than admiration. There was a tenderness too—a tenderness because of his boyish integrity, because of his love for her, because—because—she did not know. He was, like Lucy, part of her life.

She liked Charles Newby, but he was not part of her life nor ever would be. He had something of Peter's boyishness—but after all, were not all men children? He, too, had integrity, courage, loyalty. But he had no fire. He had that English lack of imagination. His very faithfulness to duty was easy for him because he could see none other.

And his mother? His ancient, incredible mother?

She would never forget that moment of her arrival when, in the dark hall, hung with the heads of animals and barbaric armour, she had first seen waiting for her, as a queen waits for her subjects, that little white-haired woman in black with the icy-chill countenance, the beautiful hands, the erectness that seemed inhuman, the clear small voice like a ringing bell.

The old lady was *very* old, but nevertheless Katherine realized at once that she would have to fight her if she married her son. The big, stout, clear-eyed man stood beside her and her little delicate hand rested on his broad arm. Her pride in him and her pride in his family

—these were the two things that Katherine realized immediately. She saw other things in that moment. First the old lady's start (she so marvellously controlled) at the first sight of her beauty. Katherine was accustomed to that, but she grasped at once that the old lady disliked her all the more for it. Then just behind the old lady was Charles' secretary, Frederick Courthope, now twenty-three years of age and a very sleek young man.

Katherine guessed that he was in the old Marchioness' good graces. Katherine, Rashleigh, and Lady Carlisle had travelled together. Outside in the courtyard there was a great bustle of servants and baggage. The warm summer evening pressed into the stone hall which even now was still.

The other thing that Katherine noticed was the passionate love that sprang into Newby's eyes. The old lady noticed it too.

They were all offered drinks and then they moved up the stone staircase to the drawing-room. The house was all very grand and very untidy. This untidiness, it appeared, was Charles' fault, for when he lived in his Northern kingdom he delivered himself altogether over to sport. He had many sport-hounds that could hunt fox and otter, hare and badger. There were hawks' perches in most unexpected places, guns, huntsmen's poles everywhere. In the long drawing-room hung with faded and tattered tapestry there was a great stone fireplace and all over this were lying, on their first entry, dogs of all kinds, hounds, terriers, spaniels.

At sight of Charles Newby they all ran, yelling, yelping, shrieking towards him; only one little black terrier, lame of one leg, could not get to him and stepped delicately, limping with a look of almost desperate anxiety on her countenance.

In the wide stone windows were arrows, old cross-bows, dog-whips, pistols, fishing tackle. The whole house was built of stone. There was a small and decorous chapel which was bitter cold. The food was excellent and well cooked. One night in the gallery there was a chorus of men who sang hunting songs, and to these Charles listened with exceeding pleasure.

Charles barely left Katherine's side during the week that they were there. Lucy Carlisle, who was exceedingly good-natured, laughed and occupied herself with winning Rashleigh's heart. She could never be with any handsome man without attempting this. She had known

Rashleigh for years at Court, but there she had her own lovers. She was piqued because everyone had told her for so long that Rashleigh was impregnable. She was to discover during this week that that was true.

But although Charles was always at Katherine's side, he did not speak to her of love. She liked him better, far better, here in his own place than she had ever done at Court. Here he wore his country clothes and strode out attended by men as ruddy as himself, by crowds of dogs. Or he rode with her (she was a beautiful rider) and they went down to the Solway or to the town of Carlisle or over the Border into Scotland.

In his own village and county he was worshipped. None of the trouble now spoiling, in the South, so many of the relations between master and man seemed to exist here.

At the country church all attended and there were no heresies. Charles sympathized with complainers, was tolerant of immoralities, was cheerful and fair with everyone.

'You must understand,' he explained to Katherine, 'I am too stupid a fellow to be aught but complaisant. Then both my dear father and my mother were little tyrants in their time, so it has been made easy for me. Then I was born and bred here, so they have all known me from the moment I was pushed from my mother's womb.' He looked at himself a little ruefully. 'The size I am, the size my mother is— was it not something of a miracle?' He laughed heartily and smacked his thigh.

'Your mother worships you,' Katherine said.

'She adores me and scolds me.'

'She is jealous for you.'

'Are not all mothers for their sons?'

'Ah, but she is punctilious. You must marry a saint sprung from an Immaculate Conception.'

She was hinting to him, but he was lost, sunk deep. He conveyed with every word, every look, every movement that he worshipped her.

She saw very soon how sadly terrified was the old lady. This, although she was seventy, was the most terrible happening of all her life. Katherine did not doubt but that Mr. Frederick Courthope had informed the old woman of every possible and impossible scandal in her life, including the rumoured transaction with Buckingham.

She would have liked to bend down to the old lady's tiny ear and whisper: 'Have no fear, I will never marry your son.'

The trouble was that she was not at all sure that that was true. She liked Charles, she sometimes wanted (or thought that she wanted) peace and security against the coming storm, she could act the grand lady, the lovely Marchioness of Newby, exceedingly well, she was in love with no other man—why should she not then? The fact that the old lady hated her and was terrified of her tempted her rather than otherwise.

This wonderful summer day when Katherine looked out of her bedroom window had been chosen for the visit to Seddon. This was the day, Katherine was certain, when Charles would make his proposal. She dressed with great care. Her dress had the low-necked, tight-waisted bodice of convention, but the narrow waist-girdle usually tied with a rosette or bow in front was in this case fastened by a strong gold band and her skirt was straight and severe. Except for the low neck, this was almost a man's dress of deep-green velvet studded with gold buttons, the arms ornamented with gold tissue. She wore a large hat with a high feather. As she came down the stone staircase to join the others in the courtyard, they saw her through the great door, the rich green of her dress, the dark hair, but above all the superb unconscious carriage. Newby looked and saw in a kind of dream her rightful descent of that staircase, his worship of her, her tenderness to him, their children . . .

What if her life *had* been careless? What if her father had been a scamp of no origin? She was fit to be Queen of England—better suited than the little French Catholic mischief-maker they had.

Newby, Frederick close beside him, Rashleigh, Lady Carlisle were all waiting, the sky above their heads a blazing blue, the horses striking the stones with their hooves, the park shifting in the heat of the sun-haze, a lark singing somewhere above them like the sun's voice, the heavy, broad, grim stone house behind them.

As Katherine came through the great door, she thought: 'Before I come back here—what will it be—what way will I have gone?'

'You must forgive me,' she said, smiling, to Newby. 'Your mother had a message for Mrs. Blaikie.'

They stood about, not moving because the heat made them lazy. Katherine put her hand on the neck of her horse Diogenes. He nipped at her glove. The dogs were in a cloud, laughing and jumping.

Frederick Courthope, very neat and plain in his dress, his face more mature now, sharp, smooth, a polished skin, eyes like a clever priest's, came to her.

'Katherine——' he said and paused. He had never called her that before.

'Why?' she asked him.

His upper lip trembled, almost as a child's does. This was a phenomenon that she was to notice again, at a later time.

'Because'—he had a beautiful voice: some notes in it were like music —'we are almost related.'

'How is that?'

'You almost with your own hands delivered Lucy's child—the child of my uncle. And, if I may be permitted, *what* a child!'

'Does that then constitute a relationship?'

'I wish that it might.'

'Listen, Mr. Courthope,' she said very quickly. 'It does not. We have a relationship of acquaintance—nothing more.'

He looked her full in the eyes. She realized with a sudden shock that he was physically desirous of her. She had never credited Frederick with animal feelings. Moreover, there was something quite ludicrous about it. She was old enough, very nearly, to be his mother. She was thirty-five. He was twenty-three. Nevertheless, his eyes were fixed greedily on her neck and the line between her breasts. This offended her.

'No—no, Mr. Courthope,' she said lightly. 'We keep as we are.'

This made his eyes darken. Strange that effect, as though the lids fell over them, a hooded bird's. He bowed, a little mock bow.

'Your orders are the only orders.'

'And, Mr. Courthope,' she said, 'remember, I have a revengeful nature—even for a lightly spoken word.'

That, she thought, as she watched his back, was a foolish thing. Why had she let him know that she thought him of the slightest importance? For once she had been impetuous against her better judgment. In a moment she was to be more impetuous yet!

It was time to be off. Newby helped Lucy Carlisle on to her horse, then came to Katherine.

'We must be by ourselves for an half-hour at Seddon,' he said.

'Only half an hour?' She stood close to him, striking gently her long thigh with her gold-headed whip. He touched her gloved hand.

'Thank you,' he said.

Many of the dogs followed him to his horse, but the little lame terrier bitch that Katherine had noticed on the day of her arrival stayed near Katherine. Frederick Courthope, moving towards his horse, found her in the way and, being perhaps in an already poor temper, kicked her. She limped, yelping, and Katherine struck his cheek with her glove.

She was a blazing fury. She seemed to tower to heaven. He thought that she would strike again and he stood his ground.

'To kick a lame dog, Mr. Courthope,' Katherine shouted—(Yes, she shouted. She might have been heard at the park end. She was at the Thames bank bawling for a wherry. She was seated in the boat. The Puritans were reading their psalms. She was holding a black dog in her arms. Later she was giving it to a little round-faced Puritan by the river)—'To kick a lame dog, Mr. Courthope, before ladies is bad manners. You are yet young enough to learn.'

She mounted her horse, feeling a confusion of satisfaction and regret. 'That young man,' she thought, 'is now my enemy for life.'

They rode away and she kept close beside Rashleigh. The farther she went the more uncomfortable she was! A breach surely of good manners! To slap the cheek of the private secretary of her host! She showed at times bad manners when her instincts were too strong for her, but she had not wished to show them to Charles Newby.

What *must* he have thought of her! Maybe he would be warned by it and so not wish to be married to a termagant. There would be some merit in that! But would there be? She felt a chagrin, almost a dismay, at the thought of losing Charles Newby for ever.

Yes, and Lucy Carlisle! What a story for her to tell at Court, and would she not take advantage of it! Not that she did not like Katherine, but a good story was a good story wherever it might be.

Should she apologize to Frederick? No, indeed she would not—and she would slap his face just so another time if she caught him kicking a limping dog. But here her necromancy came in—she felt a cold chill about her heart. She knew well that sensation and how it came from an apprehension of the true character of a man or woman.

All life was a battle from the first moment to the last, and every encounter we made was with, in lesser or greater degree, a friend or an enemy. She was often treading the shadow of the coming event. So it was now.

Almost shamefacedly she drew her horse close to Rashleigh's.

'There's a thing I should not have done,' she said.

'What thing?' he said, turning to her.

'Struck Frederick.'

'Yes—I saw you.'

'You saw me. Charles Newby saw me. Lucy Carlisle saw me. The maids from the bedroom windows saw me . . .'

'What roused you?'

'He kicked a limping dog.'

Rashleigh laughed. 'I like him no more than you do, but . . .'

'Yes. But . . . ?'

'He is a young man who remembers. And he is Charles' secretary.'

'I know.'

'If you marry Charles——'

'I shall *not* marry Charles.'

'I think you will.'

'Why do you say that?'

'Because *you* do not care very much either way, and Charles cares so very much.'

'I wish *you* cared a little!'

'I!' Rashleigh looked at her with surprise. 'Why, pray? What I do, feel, or say means nothing at all to you.'

'I have told you,' she said almost impatiently, 'that everything that you and Lucy and Peter do means something to me. . . . Besides, it would be interesting to see you feel something. You are so beautiful on your horse—but the shadow of the King's shadow . . .'

'Shall I tell you something?'

'Yes, if you wish.'

'About our family—the Herries family. We are very ordinary but we are the microcosm of England. If you love England but do not know why, study us. If equally you hate England and do not know why, study us. If you care for money, we have it—in moderation. If for poetry, we have that too. If for achievement, we have *that*—in moderation. If for desire, that will never be fulfilled—here, too, you can study it in us. If you are outside normality we can give you for companion any kind of perversity. But for normality—perfect English normality—there is no family like us.

'Our secret is that we are composed of opposites,—we are the male and female person in one body. We are like Everyman—the normal man, the perfect citizen. The building built upon English rock—yes, but in the attics live the wild goose, the rat with two heads, the eunuch, the pretty boys, the knight in his armour, the saint in his sacred fire, the searcher after the Grail on his bare knees, praying . . .' Rashleigh broke off, waving his whip.

'Dear Katherine, you must have all of us if you would have one of us—Frederick as well as the rest.'

'To my doom,' she murmured. 'I am doomed if I am not free of you.'

'And lost if you are,' Rashleigh answered. 'Lost and lonely. But Charles will be for slapping *my* cheek if I monopolize you. Join him. He is longing for you.'

She did so. Charles turned to her a face so radiant with joy and happiness that she was frightened. Her impulse was to drive her horse like the wind and ride madly over the Border and never see any single one of them again.

'Are you angry with me?' she asked.

'Angry!' He laughed. 'Angry. . . . No. But why?'

'Because I struck Frederick in the face for kicking a dog.'

'Ah—that is what he did. . . . I wondered. I'm afraid that I have kicked a dog before now.'

'This was a bitch. A lame one.'

'Well'—he turned his head, looking at her in the eyes—'why should I be angry at anything you would do?'

'He is your secretary.'

'Yes. He is able. But he will take your attention as an honour.'

'No, I am afraid not.'

'Then what does it matter?' His voice sank lower.

She thought: 'Now it is coming. What am I to do? What am I to say?'

But it did not. He pulled back. He withdrew his horse a little and they rode on in silence.

The day would be very hot. They rode slowly along, keeping to the shadows.

Here was the land of perfect peace. Under the summer haze cottage and manor smiled at them as they passed. They were in the Border country, a place of stone and bare ground; nevertheless the ten miles of their journey seemed rich indeed. Some buildings were of plaster and oak-beam, others of stone with soft colours of blue and grey and pink; some were of red brick that faded very pleasantly under wind and weather. But all the buildings had individual life. Each little cottage appeared as though none other had ever been made like it before. The country itself was living through a period of change from open landscape to enclosed field, but here in the North that change was not very greatly felt, and for the most of their ride they were on broad open common with rough tracks running into woods. From the heart of woodland a crooked chimney would grin, purple smoke rising straight into the blue-misted sky. For there was not a breath of wind.

As Katherine rode she was half asleep. The smell of the sea, mingled with the rough hot carnation-scent of the summer morning, made time for her stop still.

So many strange and different things were occurring at the same moment. She was in a large dark hall and against her childish gaze was a suit of gold armour and an old torn flag hanging from the wall. The place was crowded with people, and her father, wearing a peaked cap of silver paper, suspended his hand and from it fell lazily through the air roses.

Anne Turner bent over from behind her and pinched her breast. 'You will shortly be a woman,' she said.

There was a Masque at the Court. It was Montague's 'The Shepherd's Paradise.' It lasted for eight solid hours. Dressed as a shepherdess with a crook and a woolly lamb, she stood in the rear of the shepherdesses. The Queen was advancing down an artificial hill while Cupids (decently covered, for the King was particular) strewed the ground with roses. She felt her hand touched; it was Simon Conder, who was madly in love with her. A candle scattered and a piece of scenery flamed. There were cries from the shepherdesses.

Now Peter Garland was walking towards the wood near Derwent-water and at the same time she was in the mean little room in Keswick and she abused him. She thought of all the things she could say to wound him, and he hung his head a little, like a boy. He suddenly looked up at her and his eyes were filled with tears; she had all to do, in the middle of the abuse, not to kiss him.

Had not that been for a swift moment love?

Then it was the Court again, and the Queen presenting the King with a little picture by Andrea del Sarto—a lovely picture of a young man with a dark beard and an orange dress. They all knew—the King knew—that this was part of the plot to win him to Rome, but the two things unmistakable were, first the love the King and Queen had for one another, as her little face with its fringe of dark curls on the forehead, the beautifully formed beseeching mouth, bent towards him; the other the love that the King had for the picture as he put out his white, long-fingered hands and took the picture in its dark gold frame so tenderly, with such adoring care.

Again she was at the inn of 'The Peacock' near Keswick and battling with her desire to be free of Lucy. She had lost that battle. It was because she had lost it that she was riding now to Seddon. How did one thing lead to another? What now would she do? To what degree are we masters of our own fate? If this had not happened, if that . . .

She turned her head back and saw the pale young face of Frederick Courthope.

He took her glance backwards for a sign, and rode forward to her side. He spoke like a grave man of the world.

'Mistress Christian, I have to come to beg your forgiveness. I did impetuously a churlish thing.'

As ever, for her heart was always warm, she held out her hand and he took it. Their horses paced soberly side by side.

'I am a fanatic about nothing save animals,' she said. 'I cannot bear to see them in pain and especially when they are crippled. But I, too, acted impetuously and wrongly. If it were my own father I should have acted the same.' And could not but smile in her heart for thinking of what would have occurred had she struck the cheek of her revered father.

When he spoke she was held once again with the beauty of his voice:

'I was rebuked rightly. I am not cruel by nature.'

'No, I believe you are not.'

'And,' he went on eagerly, 'there is nothing I would not do in your service. I am young and unformed, but I have my ideals—and one is to serve you. That comes from my heart.'

'That comes,' she thought, 'from your own assurance that shortly I shall marry your master.'

'Tell me,' she said, 'have you heard anything from our friends at Mallory?'

'No. But we shall have news in a moment, for Robert and Lucy are at Seddon.'

'How does Nicholas endure his blindness?'

'Very patiently, I believe, but it has altered him. He is greatly aged, but the sweetness of his character is increased.'

'It would have been better for him to have died, I think.'

They were approaching Seddon. They could see the chimneys over the trees. When they came to it, it was all Katherine could do not to clap her hands.

Looking clear over a miniature park with some miniature deer there stood this compact, sturdy little house of plaster and oak-beam with a garden of clipped hedge, silver-tossing fountain, roses, carnations round a bowling-green, while behind the house was a dark protective wood. A statue of a goddess with a cornucopia and high, stiff-pointing breasts stood in the middle of the little park.

As the cavalcade rode up, the doors at the top of the stone steps opened and a group gathered. Rashleigh recognized Robert, Lucy and her child Rupert, a short lady in a high cap who must be Mrs. Blaikie, and an elderly gentleman, his head covered with a wide straw shepherd's hat. He held by the hand a little girl in a long grey dress who must, Rashleigh thought, be Margaret Blaikie.

The short lady came down the steps, and Newby, jumping lightly from his horse, ran up them and saluted her on the cheek. He then presented to her Lady Carlisle and Katherine. There was a great deal of talking, and they all moved into the hall together. This was a charming place. It had an Italian look, for the floor was of black-and-white squares and in the middle of these a little fountain playing, Cupid shooting his dart. The walls were of a very white stone interset with gilt squares.

It was all very cool, and a stout and beaming manservant handed them all drinks. From the hall ran a very beautiful staircase, called 'dog-legged' because it had two flights. The balustrade, made of a pierced and most beautifully carved acanthus scroll, was exquisite. Rashleigh gazed at this with luxurious appreciation, for he was an authority on such things.

'Here am I,' he thought, 'at last in Seddon. Lucy too. Only Peter isn't here. How often we have thought of it, wondered what it was like, and whether we should ever see it.'

He looked across at the short and homely little lady who was Mrs. Blaikie. 'And you are actually the daughter of the wicked, sensuous, romantic, mysterious Francis who shut himself up in the wilds of Borrowdale valley and went melancholy-mad because you cost your mother her life. And now look at you! After all that romantic origin, there you are so domestic-housewifely commonplace. But perhaps you are not that in reality. It is like the Herries family to which you belong. One chronicler might draw them, selecting such figures as yourself and Robert and Frederick, as the complete stay-at-home, tidy, un-coloured variety. "How real and true!" the readers of the chronicle might say! While another chronicler would care only for figures like old Nicholas' brother Robin and the girl he loved and maybe myself, Rashleigh—and we would turn out in that chronicle as though from the *Faerie Queene* or Mr. Milton's *Comus*. But the true chronicler takes all of us, higgledy-piggle together, and makes what he can of us!'

The short lady, he thought, could not be much more than fifty, for the little girl was not a day more than fifteen. She, demurely and not moving, stood quietly at her father's side. There was another older girl, and a pale boy with something of a hunch-back. These, Rashleigh later discovered, were called Elizabeth and John.

The children indeed had their eyes fixed on Lucy's boy, Rupert. He had been in the house now several days and, it was plain, had thoroughly made his mark.

Rashleigh had tried to care for him for Lucy's sake. He was, however, too queer for Rashleigh's sober and autocratic taste. For the one thing, he was never for a moment still and, with his red hair on end, dashed ever from place to place, enquiring into this, testing that, thinking always of some new daring thing that he must be doing, and constantly calling out at some discovery that he had made, in his strange shrill little peacock cry. Odd indeed that he should have sprung from the weak loins of worthless Carey! Odder still that the beautiful and light-hearted Lucy should be his mother! He was human only in the way that he ran backwards and forwards to that same mother, showing her this, asking her that, laughing and crying out and threatening and beseeching.

Another mother would have found him a handful, but Lucy found nothing a handful, taking everything as it came, seeing the best in everything and everyone, never stopping to think, saying what was in her mind, ready to flirt, for kindness' sake, with anyone who wished it.

Rashleigh saw, too, that Katherine, as she always did, astonished the Blaikie family with her magnificence. As she sat in the tall chair with the gilded arms, drinking her wine, she shone with beauty. Lucy was so happy to see her again that she sat beside her, pouring out a stream of talk, and all that Katherine had to do was to listen. Lady Carlisle on her side was charming Mr. Blaikie, not because there was any reason for her to do that, but because she always sought to charm anyone she was in company with, simply because you never knew but that one day it would be useful.

Now the time had come for them all to see the house. They trooped up the fine staircase laughing and chatting and asking questions.

There is a word here necessary about Robert Herries, for he is now, as Nicholas' blindness had made him helpless, the head of the Herries family. This Chronicle, in all its parts, is not a neatly devised story, nor a history of England, nor a philosophy of life, nor a series of period paintings. It may be, and often is, all of these things, but its theme, purpose, driving intention, is always one thing—the history of an English family seen from a personal angle.

(The narrator must of course be allowed his angle whether it be flamboyant, garish, sober, realistic, prayerful, allegorical, discordant, smug, vigorous, lazy, tuneful, merry, lugubrious, patriotic, or whatever. He must have his angle, poor happy industrious narrator! Pray allow it to him!)

This, in short, is a history of the Herries family through four hundred years—it is not more and it is not less. If Kings, Queens, Fools, murderers, business gentlemen, domestic wives, and ladies of the easiest virtue come into it, that is not the narrator's fault. Every family has had such or thinks that it has.

So here is Mr. Robert Herries head, in this year 1635, of the Herries family, combing his hair in front of the looking-glass, preparatory to the family meal. He is dressed in a tunic of brown velvet (warm for this weather) with large lace-edged collar and cuffs. He would like his somewhat sparse locks to fall in rich profusion on to the collar, but they are dry and thin. He is pulling anxiously at one of them now, and in the glass is framed his serious face with the steady grey eyes, the broad puckered forehead, the strong mouth. Then with a sigh (for he is very conscious of wishing to be fine before two such grand ladies as Lucy Carlisle and Katherine Christian) he turns round and surveys his short, thick-set person with a certain satisfaction. He has a grave and steady appearance; he looks a man of substance and acumen. He is, but this he does not think of, a good little man with a warm heart—that is when preoccupations with business allow him to be mindful of anything else.

His preoccupation at this moment as he walks up and down the floor before descending the staircase is with the question, the very grave question, of matrimony.

Shortly, as in the way of nature, his father, who is in any case now but a wreck of a man, must die. Then he will be in very truth the family head. He takes the Herries blood with exceeding seriousness. From his babyhood his father has taught him so. Nicholas has said to him: 'Robert, in this our family there are the wild and the home-keeping. The wild are good enough—I, alas, in my time have been one of them—but the family is stayed in health and prosperity by the home-keeping. You will be the chief of these in the Herries tribe during your own time. All things will depend on you.'

And so they did. Not on Rashleigh or Peter or a crazy poet like Matt Turner, but on a sober, God-fearing citizen like himself. And indeed he had so greatly improved Mallory that it was one of the show places in the South of England.

To continue the noble work he must, however, marry and marry wisely. He must have children to carry on the noble work after him. Yes,—but marry whom?

It was well enough to jump into bed with a pretty woman—that was a momentary act and had no consequences were you a wise man.

But he had never yet, in all his life, felt the passion of love. He had never lain awake tossing on his lonely bed, or ridden miles only for a glance of the beloved, or stammered or blushed or been cast into any confusion by any woman. He was thirty-five years of age and it seemed to him unlikely now that this emotion would come to him.

He must marry, then, not for love but for wisdom. Aye, for wisdom! But where shall wisdom be found? He saw no wise women anywhere. Either they were flirtatious and gay like poor Lucy, or impossibly grand Court ladies like Katherine or Lady Carlisle, or impossibly low like the pretty dairymaid he had noticed a week or two ago working at Mallory. He had money enough; he had position enough. What he wanted was a woman of wisdom and common sense who would give him children.

There was a knock upon his door and, after his call, the door opened and there stood the little girl, Margaret Blaikie.

'They have sent me to bid you to dinner,' she said.

He regarded her. He had not been slow to notice that from the first moment of his entering Seddon he had been the object of her attention. She was a grave little girl who spoke but seldom, and stayed beside her father and mother. Nevertheless when he had picked up her horn-book and asked her to repeat the Lord's Prayer, she had done so with the greatest alacrity, speaking in a clear bright musical voice that reminded him of a sunlit brook running gaily over cool stones.

She was not pretty, but not ugly either. Her body was sturdy and strong, her nose straight, her eyes of a pleasant honest brown. She was exceedingly clean and neat. She was now but a child. He was twenty years her elder. But in another three years or so he would not be too old and she would be capable of child-bearing for many a day. Moreover, she had what he liked—good-humour. Her laugh was very pleasing. He had talked to her about his famous herd of cattle and her interest had not been only feigned. Also he had, in these few days, discovered to his own surprise a great liking for Seddon. It was the prettiest house he had ever been in. It might be that his father's great love for the North Country was in his blood also. He saw himself, in a moment of vision, living very comfortably in this house with Margaret Blaikie.

He was surprised, too, to find that his heart, a very well-controlled instrument, was beating thickly.

He held out his hand.

'Come,' he said, 'we will go down together.'

That night they were all in the garden, and from the garden into the little park that was still warm with the sun of the day, alive in the moonlight where the shadows clung to the pointed breasts of the classic goddess.

Beside the goddess, on this sea-stung honey-warm summer night Charles Newby poured out his love to Katherine Christian.

'I am no child, nor would I say that I have never loved before, but I *would* declare to you that I have never known before that love is like this. I was told by my old nurse when I was a child that I was born of a woman and would die of a woman. If you refuse me now, Katherine, I will die of you. Truly I will. I shall have missed my best, and whatever else my life will be it will have failed. Not the failure of it—that is not the important thing save to myself—but it is rather what we might make of it together, you and I. I am so ordinary a man that I have no claim to you. You should have married a Sidney, a Raleigh, or even an Essex, Elizabeth's Essex. You might have saved him that wildness—saved him for better and greater things. But as it is at least I am honest and what I seem. There is dullness there, but I feel that, if you were my wife, I could do something with a fire at its heart and a drum to beat for it. I love you so much that I—that I—words come like a bees' swarm—I have seen you these last days in a mist. At a touch of your wrist or hand I am subdued. I have never been thus before. If you refuse me now, I am only a second man hereafter and all that I do will have the flavour of your denial upon it. Oh, Katherine, love me—love me—love me—marry me—be my wife, the mother of my children——'

She had said nothing. She had been looking a little upwards, across at the stars that were little fires in a net of yellow mist. But she stopped him now.

'Charles! Dear Charles! It is all so useless. I do not love you. Not at all. And that should not hurt you, for I love nobody. No one in all the world. But I will not marry you without loving you. You are too good for that falseness to be used on you. And beside . . . I would not make you happy, nor indeed any man—you are deceived, just as this moonlight deceives——'

'I am not deceived,' he answered quickly. 'I know this well—that if you refuse me I am only half a man henceforth. I have much pride in myself: in my family, in my house. I have said over and over: "Nothing can touch me. I am not afraid. I am not hesitant. What is right, that I will do." Well, I know now how silly a boast that has been. For I will do anything that you say—anything. . . .' He knelt on the dry grass, bowed his head. His hand very lightly touched her dress.

She was deeply moved, for she knew his hand-fasted pride and how strong a man he was.

She raised him, drew his cheek to hers, kissed his forehead, and then, with her hand lightly against his cheek, went on:

'Now, Charles, listen to me. I will tell you the truth. I do not marry you because I am quite worthless and you are too good a man to spoil. There is no good thing in me whatsoever save an occasional softness of heart that small cats and little dogs and babies crying in a cradle rouse in me.

'Listen, dear Charles. I have been the mistress of a number of men, and shall be mistress of more—and this for the worst, shabbiest of motives. I have never loved a man, but have given him my body because of what I might get from it—money, clothes, a warm room. I can only say that I have never deceived anyone—but I have seen men, and found men as worthless as myself.

'Listen, dear Charles. I was the child of a proverbial rogue who handsomely knew the Devil. As an infant I have seen things that I, callous as I am, would shame to tell you. Even as a little child my body was fair and so I learned early the vile things that men can do and say. My father hanged himself. I resolved from that day that I would care for no man, respect no man, expect nothing from any man, depend on no man, request nothing, fear nothing, give thanks for nothing.

'Against my will my heart has been caught a little—not love, not love, but a sort of kindliness, a generous heart; I have found it, to my chagrin—in a sister and two brothers. There may also be other excellent characters in the world. I would not say that there are not. But for the most, and in the mass, men are mean, base, cruel. And I am like them. I have the qualities that I am honest and I am not afraid of anything that man or God can do to me. But you, Charles, you!—whom at least I must except from the tiger-worm variety, yourself, good, honest, family-proud, to marry such a vagrant, to bring her into your good house, daughter to your mother—and why? Because my nose is straight, my breasts are firm, I have strong legs, and my hair is black.

'I have no good in me, Charles, anywhere! If I bore you children they would be spotted. My blood is a bad blood, and it must not be continued. Put me out of your mind. Put me behind you, as you would Satan.'

He took her hand and kissed it.

'More simple, Katherine. We must the both of us be more simple. You are not as you say. I knew all that you have told me. When I first came to Court they told me all these things and worse. Some may be true. You say that they are. But they have not touched you. You are obsessed by a terrible history that has happened to a woman. But you are outside it, beyond it. For a long, long time I have been coming to this. I have watched you a thousand times. I know that you have closed yourself up and despise men as you say. But even as we rode to-day I have said to myself: "I will show her what one man is. I will love her and protect her and live with her so she will learn to trust herself to me." ' He was continuing, but she stopped him.

'And your mother?'

'My mother loves me and will learn to love you.'

'No. She would always hate me and despise me for as long as she lived. You know it. You have faced it and to yourself you have acknowledged it.'

'You do not know my mother.'

'I know her very well. That first sight of her as she stood in the hall waiting for us told me everything.' She added more gently: 'And our children——?'

'What of our children?'

'With your pride of family—afterwards, when my body is no novelty—when they are in my charge, when I am forming their characters, you will remember what I have been, what I am. You will see things in our children that you think have come from me. You will watch me with children. Oh, no, no, Charles. You must see the hopelessness, the impossibility——'

'You will love our children and so shield them from harm.'

'Yet another thing. If I were unfaithful to you after marriage——'

He said, almost in a whisper: 'That would not be.'

'But it might be. I would make no vows of chastity! If I loved a man, yes; I would serve him, I would follow him through the world. I would be utterly his. But I do not love you, Charles. I love no man and my freedom is more to me than any man who ever was born. I think I shall never love a man—but if it happened, were I your wife a thousand times over, I would leave you and follow him.' She rested her hand for a moment on his head.

'I say, as all women say at such a time, that I am your friend and proud to be your friend. These are not mere words. They come from my heart. But I will not marry you or any man unless he is worthless and I care nothing if he suffers, or if I love him. You are one of the best men I have ever known, and so I will not marry you. I do not love you, and so I will not marry you. Now let me go in by myself, and let me be your friend always.'

She walked away towards the house.

Later they all rode home through the summer night. Katherine was so happy that she could scarcely prevent herself singing.

'I have escaped the danger! I am free! I am free! . . . I so nearly fell. Poor Charles! But he will recover and marry a beautiful lady who will stroke his mother's wrinkled hand and bear him twenty children. I am half-way through life and still I am free. I owe no man anything, nor any woman either. I have told no man a lie, nor myself. I am myself. No one owns me. I belong to no one. What was it that made me at one moment almost yield to him? That was terrible. That would be ruin for both of us. Oh, golden night, noble world, if it were without men, as at this moment for me it is! I am free! I am as happy a woman as there is in the whole of England.'

She bent and stroked her horse's neck and he bounded forward. She was caught into the stars and sailed radiantly on the amber moon. And when she was clear of the others and the moor opened about her, she began to sing.

PETER AND HIS CONFESSION

PETER GARLAND one fine evening in the summer of 1637 rode into the town of Ely and sought for Oliver Cromwell's house. This was his third occasion of staying with Cromwell and his family but he had never stayed with him in Ely before. The first visit had been to the Huntingdon farm, the second to the St. Ives house. Then in 1636, Sir Thomas Steward, Cromwell's uncle, had died, and Cromwell had succeeded him as farmer of the Cathedral tithes at Ely. So now the Cromwell family lived in Ely, close by St. Mary's Church. It would be a big family now with the children. Also Cromwell's mother had joined them.

When Peter received the letter from Cromwell asking him to spend some weeks with him at Ely, he was greatly excited. He was always in any case excited before he was to see Cromwell.

There are some relationships of love in this world that are independent of all questions of sex, that seem in their nature to pass altogether beyond the bounds of the physical into the spiritual. A relationship of this kind is perhaps more durable than any other possible to man, even that of husband and wife, for it cannot be arrested by sudden sensual change or affected by a flaring passion for another human being: it is outside the passions, outside sensuality and jealousy, physical satiety and ingratitude. Yet it can itself be passionate, for it contains in it all the finer elements of love—self-sacrifice, nobility of purpose, unselfishness, the highest idealism.

Peter thought of Cromwell with passion, but with the passion of soul rather than of body. It is true that this passion affected his body. He enjoyed to be near to Cromwell, to look at him, to mark his great strong nose, his fiery commanding eyes, his encompassing shoulders and breadth of chest, his back like a wall set against corruption and tyranny. Peter loved to hear his rich flooded voice with its touch of Huntingdonshire accent, its roaring oratory, its humorous chuckle, and often its soft tenderness.

For Cromwell was all compounded of opposites. He had a desperate need of affection and in this was like a woman. He would dig his hand into Peter's shoulder, draw him for a moment and hold him close against his heart, kiss him on meeting or at the close of the day as though he was most truly his brother. When his daughter Elizabeth was born in 1629 he loved her from the first moment with an intensity that was almost frightening. He had cared for all his other children—up to that time they were Robert, Oliver, Bridget, Richard, and Henry. At St. Ives Mary was born. Later at Ely there was to be his last child, Frances—but to none of them did he give that fiery love that he bestowed on Elizabeth.

His love for others shook him with its intensity. His hatred also. Early in 1631 Peter had stayed with him (his first visit) at Huntingdon, and had witnessed Cromwell's anger with a man called Barnard.

Barnard was the new Mayor. Cromwell was a justice of the peace and defended the rights of the burgesses to the common land against Barnard. Barnard complained to the Privy Council and Cromwell was summoned before it. It was at the time of the summons that Peter was staying with the Cromwells. Oliver's rage was a fearful thing and made the more fearful in that he often wore a piece of red flannel around his neck because his throat was weak. The way in which the muscles of his throat swelled when he was angry, and the red flannel stretched until it was about to rend itself, was an alarming sight.

His contradictions were further extended in his manner of speech. He was a very practical, experienced farmer, and had a great love of sport. When he was supervising the farm or out with his hawks, his speech was short, direct, and sharp. He knew what he wanted and said so. But when in his own house or riding with a friend, or in the town place, he talked of politics, religion, or general philosophy, he would become often as wordy and confused as one of the worst of the fanatical Puritan preachers. Words poured out like water from a pump, and often you would swear that he himself did not understand himself.

It was the same with his morality. During these years he was often deeply unhappy, 'wrestling,' he would say, 'with the Angel.' He was repenting of his past sins or bewailing the persistence of his present ones. He would often allude to his past years at Cambridge and in London as spent 'in lewdness and vice.' Peter, for his part, did not believe much in the 'lewdness' and often noticed the very touching innocence on Cromwell's part of what the real practices of lewdness truly involved. Peter was certain that Cromwell had never known any other woman but his wife, and looking at the kindly, comfortable, good-natured features of Mrs. Cromwell you could be assured that all conjugal relationships had been of a most proper and gentle sort. Yet Cromwell was a man of the most violent animal passions, he could use expressions of the coarsest and even most indecent character, and Peter was well assured that in the silence of his own chamber, with his door bolted and barred, Cromwell did indeed wrestle with Satan and fight ferociously to hack and hew his path to the Lord.

Two men in one also were there in his public nature—the one the sturdy, strong, thick-set man of the country, loving his wife and children, sharp on his business, practical, and finding nothing too small for his interest. Behind this sturdy farmer Peter seemed to see a great shadowy figure with his eyes staring fiercely to heaven, his hands gauntleted, his voice raised in a thunderous roar of command. For it was clear enough to anyone who was intimate with him, as Peter was, that already his ambitions were ranging far beyond his farm and his gaze was taking in the whole of England.

There were times in the Cromwell house when, a few friends gathered around the fire, a hush would fall upon all of them because of the potentialities that seemed suddenly to hang about Cromwell like smoke and fire. They all recognized this. By the time that he got to Ely Cromwell was a man apart.

Peter found quite easily the house by St. Mary's Church. He was weary, for he had ridden a long way that day, but he paused to embrace the beautiful evening. The Cathedral towers rose against a sky that was alive with rosy-feathered clouds: these were driven gently by a breeze that was filled with the scents of summer. The towers were black against the rose and delicate blue, while birds sang from the trees. The town was still and seemed to be smiling at the awareness of the warm days and flowers. The Cathedral bells began to ring, and a small boy ran shouting down the street with his hoop.

Peter pulled the stout bell and its jangle brought a broad-shouldered young man, who grinned at sight of him and took his horse round to the stable. Peter walked in unannounced and came at once upon a family scene. Some of the children were playing a game with counters and a chequered board; Bridget was demurely sewing. Richard was reading and Mrs. Cromwell was busy with a housekeeping book. Cromwell was seated in a settle by the fire and was telling Elizabeth, who was now eight years old, a story.

Of all the children, Peter liked Richard the best; he was a quiet, gentle, studious lad. He was shy of visitors but had at once been captivated by Peter's kindliness and warmth of heart.

Peter stood quietly in the doorway. Cromwell's deep voice continued:

'And Abraham took Isaac, as the Lord had bidden him, on to a hill and bound the boy and laid him on a stone. This was very grievous for Abraham, for he loved the boy as a father must love his son.'

'That was most evil of Abraham,' Elizabeth said.

'Nay, the Lord had commanded it, and whatever the Lord commands, that must be done.'

'If the Lord had commanded would you bind me on a stone and cut me with a knife?'

Elizabeth's eyes sparkled, for she thought that she had a poser there; her father would never bind her on a stone.

Her father, with the impetuous gesture that Peter had by now come to know so well, caught her closer to him.

'Yes, if it was the Lord's Will. But the Lord God is of great goodness. He knows how I love you.'

'More than Abraham loved Isaac?'

'Nay, but it was not the Lord's Will that Abraham should slay Isaac, for when he had all prepared——'

Cromwell looked up and saw Peter. He jumped to his feet and strode towards him. He caught him in his arms and embraced him on both cheeks.

'Peter! Peter! Welcome in the Lord's Name. See, children,—here is Peter.'

They all gathered around him, and there was a great deal of noise. Richard took Peter to his room.

'Well, Richard,' Peter asked him, 'how has it all been?'

'Father is disturbed in his mind at what is happening in London.'

'Yes—so are we all.'

'He says it must come to a civil war. Do you think so, Peter?'

'Things must be worse, I fear, before they are better.'

Richard's eyes were frightened.

'I hate war. And war among ourselves. . . . What good can come of it? And Father will fight. He is always thinking of it. He says men are not prepared enough, and to put down tyranny we must have arms and soldiers. He says they talk and talk in London, but they do nothing.'

Peter sighed. 'He is right. I see no end to this. The King and his party grow more resolved——'

'I hate the King and his French wife and his Archbishop and all that crew! . . . But I would not fight them. I would reason and show them the peril the country is in.'

'But you would fight to defend your house and your mother and your sisters——'

'I would do what I could. But I am no fighter. Henry is all for fighting. He would have them storm the palace and execute the King. And I say to him: "And after that, what would you do?"—I think,' he added, laughing, 'that he would make Father king.'

After supper, when most of the children had gone to bed, they talked together. There was staying with the Cromwells a little fat man named Mr. Abbott. Mr. Abbott was as round as a dumpling, with a short stumpy nose and very mild, gentle eyes. Peter had met him once before and knew him to be a saint before God. He had, however, none of the characteristics of the accepted saint, loving his food and laughing a great deal. But he was the first man Peter had ever met who lived entirely with God.

They were greatly disturbed that night, the Cromwells and a friend, Mr. Paul Handley, but Mr. Abbott gave you the impression of absolute peace and serenity. He was no fool neither, as these saints are sometimes, about worldly matters. In the grave discussions that filled that evening he had wise things to say.

For, only a month earlier, on June 30th, 1637, in Old Palace Yard, three gentlemen of good quality—a physician, a London clergyman, and a barrister—had been set in three pillories. Their ears had been cut off—as a chronicler says, 'bare knives, hot branding-irons.' Their cheeks, poor men, had been stamped with the letters 'S. L.'—Seditious Libeller. This had been done 'in the sight of a great crowd, silent mainly and looking pale'—to quote the chronicler again.

The gentlemen thus punished were William Prynne (he for the second time; his ears had been sewed on again after the first time), Dr. John Bastwick, and the Rev. Henry Burton, minister of Friday Street Church. And what was this punishment for? Their crime was against Archbishop Laud, no other person and no other thing. Laud had ordered surplices at All Hallows-tide. Prynne would not have it, nor the Rev. Henry Burton, in his church. Surplices! A small thing, you may say—but behind it the right for every man to worship his God in his own way—*not* a small thing! So Prynne defied Lambeth and Rome at the back of Lambeth. He cried to the people: 'If I fail to prove it let them hang my body at the door of the Prison there'— the Gate-House Prison—'Whereat the people gave a great shout,' to quote the chronicler.

Observers had told Cromwell how Bastwick's wife, on the scaffold, received his ears in her lap, and kissed his poor bleeding scalded face. He heard, too, how Prynne's ears had been sawed, rather than cut. And Prynne had cried: 'Cut me, tear me,—I fear thee not. I fear the fire of Hell, not thee!' Also that when the summer sun shone hot on their faces, Burton, when they carried him, nearly fainting, into a house in King Street, cried: 'It is too hot to last.'

There was more than this Prynne business, for on this very day there had come news to Cromwell of what had happened only a week before, on Sunday, July 23rd, in Edinburgh.

Laud had managed at last to get his Scotch Liturgy fairly landed in Scotland, and on this Sunday, when the Dean of Edinburgh opened his book: 'A number of the meaner sort, with clapping of their hands and outcries, made a great uproar, and one of them, named Jenny Geddes (she kept a cabbage-stall at the Tron Kirk), hurled the stool on which she had been sitting at the Bishop's head.' 'Let us read the Collect of the Day,' said the Bishop (no true Bishop to the Scottish thinking. A *Laud* Bishop). 'De'il colic the wame of thee,' answered Jenny, and hurled her stool. 'Thou foul thief, wilt thou say mass at my lug? I thought we had done with the mass. And here it is back again.' And all the people shouted: 'A Pope! A Pope!'

Well, there it was. The ears of three men and a wooden stool thrown by a cabbage-stall keeper.

The evening was so warm that they stood by the open window. It was not a large house, filled with twists and corners and little crooked stairs. The scents of the roses and carnations came in through the windows. The sky now was a pure pale stainless blue.

'The dark of the soul is upon us,' Mr. Handley said.

'Nay,' Mr. Abbott answered him, 'it is never dark for long. It seems so to us who sojourn for so brief a while in a strange country. Any pilgrimage must have many dark passages, for how is a pilgrim to prove his fortitude else? How are we to be proved, that we love God, unless He tries us?'

Cromwell was very quiet. He knew, perhaps, that night, as he had never known before, that the hour had come, and the certainty may have been a glory and a happiness to him. He had told Peter on his last visit that his uncertainty as to his proper course was his worst and hardest trial. He prayed and prayed to God for guidance as to how best he could help his country. His one experience of Parliament had seemed so futile; many of the men he had encountered in London had appeared to him weak and effortless. Indeed his despair (he being deep down always of a foreboding and dark-seeing temperament) had been so complete that he had at that time thought of leaving England altogether and departing with some friends for Massachusetts. Now his eyes burned with a great fire. His hand was on his wife's shoulder.

'We must be of good heart,' he said. 'I have no gifts of prophecy but I know to-day that the matter is determined for us. There is only one way now—and praise be to God that He has shown it to us.'

They were all silent, looking out to the quiet street and the towers of St. Mary's Church.

Peter was never to forget the solemnity of that moment and, as always when he arrived at some crisis, he saw Lucy and Rashleigh concerned in it also. They seemed to move there as one person, Lucy with her smile, her bright adventurous eyes, caring nothing what the adventure might be if it were an adventure, her whole body in movement; and Rashleigh so still, governed by one purpose only, a knight in armour although serving in the wrong army. Cromwell's mother, an old lady with a placid disposition and a very determined character, was seated on a stiff-backed chair, her little wrinkled hands folded in her lap, She nodded her head from time to time and made unexpected remarks addressed to no one in particular.

Now she suddenly said: 'The Queen's a French Madame—she's a worshipper of idols.'

While she loved her son, she kept her own independence. She did not like Mrs. Cromwell very much, kind though that lady was to her. She worshipped the children, and tried to spoil them whenever their mother was away. She was very greedy about certain foods, especially anything sweet. It annoyed her that she could not now, through old age, be useful in the house. But she had good spirits, more sense of wit than her son—who had very little. She had the long nose and troubled eyes of her son. She was proud of her family, for she came of the ancient Norfolk house of Styward and a kinsman of hers had been the last Prior of Ely. She had borne ten children; six daughters had grown to maturity, but only this one son, Oliver.

He came across to her now.

'Time for bed, Mother.'

'I think I will remain a little. The evening is so fine.'

'Time for bed, Mother.'

His heavy face bent over her. He was smiling.

She drew back from him into her chair, looking up at him, with her eyes rather mischievous and rebellious.

'Pah, Oliver. I have but a little time to live. Why should I spend it in bed?'

He suddenly bent down and picked her up in his arms, his great back and shoulders straining, for she was no light weight. She kicked a little with her shoes, then, with a sigh, partly of content, partly of rebellion, she put up her hand and touched his flushed cheek.

'To think that once I bore you, and now you carry me. . . .'

He was back again almost before they were aware, and they all turned to him almost as though they expected a message. He already had that power of making men who were present with him listen before he spoke.

'Nay, nay.' It was as though he were arguing with himself. 'It is the Cause. Not the man. Not the King. Nor Laud nor Wentworth nor any other. Neither dancing nor idolatry nor branding in the Palace Yard. But that men in England must be free. Freedom has been a light word until men were threatened with the loss of it. And we are so threatened. . . .' His face was convulsed. Great quiverings ran through the cheeks and mouth. 'I tell you, Mother' (speaking to his wife), 'that you must bear with me in the days that are coming, every wife with her husband, every mother with her son. And here——' The convulsion had suddenly gone from his face. Like a hasty boy he tore off his coat so that he almost split it. 'These buttons here. Two of them. And you let me put on that coat this morning. . . .' He took her chin in his hand, lifted her face, kissed her on the forehead. 'And now for some music,' he said. 'Mr. Handley has his viol.'

But it was not to be. There was a knock on the door, and there entered a small simpering man, rather grandly dressed, with a little sword and long shining curls. They all stared, and Peter saw that Cromwell's face at once clouded over. How swift, he thought, that face was to change.

The little man bowed, especially to Mrs. Cromwell.

'Mr. Hampton . . .' Cromwell, looking massive without his coat, began.

"I know . . . I know,' the little man interrupted with an odd mixture of nervousness and pertness. 'But it was not sufficient, what you said this forenoon. Sir Thomas Holcroft says it was not sufficient——'

'I am in private with my family,' Cromwell said.

'Yes, Mr. Cromwell. But it is as to whether you will be present to-morrow. The syndicate——'

'I will not be present to-morrow.'

'But, Mr. Cromwell, the syndicate——'

Mrs. Cromwell looked troubled. This syndicate was a company of adventurers, headed by the Earl of Bedford, who had secured the right to drain the fens around Ely. There was much anxiety about this among the smaller common-holders in the district lest their rights should be taken from them. Mrs. Cromwell feared that this was to be yet another example of Oliver rushing in to defend small men's rights and receiving afterwards more kicks than halfpennies.

'The syndicate wishes to have your views.'

'The syndicate already has my views.'

'But they fear that they may be strongly controversial.'

Cromwell took two steps nearer to the little man.

'Mr. Hampton, I shall not be present to-morrow. So tell the syndicate. Good evening.'

Mr. Hampton summoned his authority. He stiffened his little body and thrust forward his head.

'I warn you, Mr. Cromwell, that the syndicate——'

Cromwell took another step: '*You* warn me! *You* warn me——!' And at once his anger filled the room. It came with a suddenness that seemed to shake the whole house. His heavy body shook as though with the palsy. His face was again convulsed, but not as it had been just now. The heavy forehead lowered, the eyes seemed to stare with a light almost of frenzy. There was cruelty in the sharp line of the mouth and the thrusting-out of the lips.

His hands were raised.

'By the Lord God, leave this room or else—— It is not your place, Mr. Hampton. It is not your place. We have a right to our peace and it shall not be invaded . . .'

His shoulders were working. He took another step forward. His voice when it was angered had a deep roll in it and a commoner accent. He seemed to flash anger like a message to some approaching army.

Mr. Hampton opened his mouth to speak, thought better, and, with an absurd twinkle of his legs, vanished from the room.

Later Mr. Handley was gone, and little Mr. Abbott was in bed. Cromwell and Peter had the lower room to themselves. They sat on the settle side by side. Through the open window they could see the summer stars. A horse kicked in the stable. A falling star shot through the sky. The night air was mild and fragrant.

'Peter,' Cromwell said, 'to-night may be the last night we are like this, heart to heart, brother to brother, with nothing between us. The last night of tranquillity.' He held out his hand, took Peter's, closed it between both of his.

'I have felt to-day as though the Lord has given me a sign. These many years I have been struggling with Him for one, struggling as Jacob did with the Angel. I did not know whither we were going. But to-night I know.'

'And that is——?' asked Peter.

'To win freedom for the men and women of this country. To work God's Will in the land although we enforce it with the sword.'

Peter said: 'You know, Oliver, where you go I follow—wherever it is.'

Cromwell looked at him.

'Why is that, Peter?'

'Because I have loved you since the first moment I saw you.'

'But that is not enough—human love.'

Peter hesitated, then he said:

'I have been, all my life, coming to this point. Like you I hovered for many years in my direction. I wished to do God's Will but I could not see it clearly. I have a brother whom I dearly love. He worships the King. My sister, whom also I love, also follows the King when she thinks of it. And—there is another.'

Cromwell said: 'You are of a very soft heart, Peter, and that is your danger. We must put softness now behind us. Serve God and our country—even if it must be against our brothers, sisters, wives, lovers——' He moved right round on the settle, his body squared to Peter's. 'Peter—what do you think of me? What kind of man am I to you? I know you love me, but behind that you are clear-sighted and cold-brained. What kind of man am I?'

Peter looked at Cromwell—at the big, red, coarse-skinned face, with

the heavy brow and brilliant, disturbed, staring eyes, the large prominent nose, the thick lips.

'You know yourself, Oliver. I have never been friend of a man
who considered himself, his soul's welfare, his standing with God,
so often and so seriously. You must know yourself.'

'I do so consider myself, Peter—for if I am not right with God I
am right with nothing. If I am doomed to hell-fire, what matters it
what I am? On which side am I? "Wilt thou join with the Dragons?"
Have I not fire in my veins, Peter, like another man? My flesh
strengthens and turns and hardens, my breath comes in hot pants as
I lust after the meat and drink of the Devil. It was so from my earliest
youth. I remember at Cambridge how I stripped myself naked and
whipped myself with cords until the lust of the body was over. And
in London likewise. Now it is other. The lust of the flesh is behind
me, but how am I with God? Around and about this world there
is a circle, and beyond the circle a circle, and beyond the circle a circle.
Through these the angels pass bearing messages to God. I have seen
them in visions, Peter, with their faces shining through the feathers
of their wings. They pass me with grave countenances bearing their
witness of me to the Throne. And when they have borne their witness
how is it with me? Has the Lord turned His face away from me?'

He cried this out in a voice of agony. He caught Peter so fiercely
by the arms that the pain was sharp; his eyes stared into Peter's eyes
as though he saw beyond him into eternity. He held Peter so close
to him that his breath was hot on Peter's cheek.

He cried out:

'Oh, Lord God, Lord God, am I saved for Thee, am I saved for
Thee?'

Quite suddenly he seemed to collapse, letting Peter go, dropping
his head in his hands, his body shaken and shuddering.

Then it was Peter's turn to comfort him. It was not the first of
these fits he had seen. He put his arm around him.

'Oliver . . . Oliver . . . think of the deed, the Cause, the Cause,
as you yourself said this evening. I believe, and others also believe,
that you have been called by God to save this country. From Pym
and Hampden to little Mr. Abbott here, they all believe it. I have seen
and known many men but never a man like yourself. At the first sight
of you I surrendered. So it will be with the armies that you will create

from these English fields and fens. You will raise them everywhere
and teach them to fear God as you fear Him. And with those hosts
of the Lord you will set up God's reign on earth.'

He drew him close to him until Cromwell's head was on his breast.
He was older than Cromwell and at this moment felt as though
Cromwell were his lost, tormented child. It was the last time for ever
that he would so feel it, the last time for ever that he would hold
Cromwell in his arms.

And now it was not for more than a moment. The fit had passed.
Cromwell sat up, his face calm, resolved, strong. With that calm he
became at once again the superior of the two. He sat, thick, square,
his head up, his eyes staring into the flashing sparkle of stars.

Peter began awkwardly:

'Oliver, I am troubled.'

Cromwell nodded. 'Aye. . . . Tell me. But no trouble can separate us.'

'Separation? Oh, no—it is not that. But since I arrived here to-day
I have been feeling—in my heart I know—that from now I should
give myself only to the country, serving God with you as my
leader——'

'God as the leader——'

'Yes, but with no personal love nor attachment. You would sacrifice, if it had to be, your wife and family—even Elizabeth?'

Cromwell hesitated. Then he nodded.

'Well, I cannot. I have a love who is more to me than you, my
country—God. Now turn me from this house and say that you will
never see me again.'

Cromwell laughed and put his hand gently on Peter's arm.

'Nay—why should I? We are friends. And do you think that I do
not know the lusts of the body? I can pray God for you, but I would
not leave you.' He went on: 'It may be that I am too light to the sins
of the body. Some men think so. But Christ was tender toward such.
The body is a small thing. It is when lust clouds the soul and pre-
vents it from seeing God that the soul may be lost. . . . Is she your
mistress?'

'No. I have seen her barely half a dozen times in all my life. First
as a little child, when I kissed her. Then as an older child. Then in

the North, beside a lake. Then in my cousin's house at Mallory. Twice
or thrice I have seen her at Court but have not spoken to her.'

'She is at Court?'

'Yes. She is by common consent the most beautiful woman in
England.'

'Is she married?'

'No. Not at present. Any day it might be.'

'Is she virtuous?'

'No. She has been the mistress of several.'

'She is evil, then?'

'No. She is not evil. Her childhood was terrible and bred in her a
kind of defiance. She cares nothing for any man—and for no woman,
I think, but my sister Lucy.'

'She does not return your love, then?'

Peter laughed. 'No. She despises it and me.'

'You have had no traffic with her—not embraced her body or, for
a night, lain with her?'

'Since she was a child I have scarce touched her.'

Cromwell nodded. 'Ah, that is why. . . . The fever might have
departed easily.'

'It is more than a fever,' Peter said. 'It is a possession and it will be
with me till I die. I thought I should tell you it, for you are my
greatest friend, to-day that is a kind of dedicated day. I cannot go
with you to fight except I tell you that, were she to ask me, I would
leave you and the Cause and England and God.'

He looked down, but Cromwell cried: 'Look up, man! Look up!
God is not so easily left. I understand it well. She is beautiful. She
scorns you. You do not see her. If she loved you and you were with
her every day, God would shine brightly again and she would be blot-
ted out.'

Peter shook his head. 'I think not. But it will never be tested so. But
I do not ask you to advise me, Oliver. There is no advice can be given.
I make a confession to you but I do not ask for any absolution. There
is a love, I fancy, outside the accustomed rules. Oh, many men may
know it, but I fancy that it does not come to the same man many
times. I love God. I love you, Oliver. I love my brother and my sister
as though they were myself. I have had experience of physical love, its
expectation, its ecstasy of the moment, its satiety. None of those loves

is like this love. She is part of my body, my heart, my soul—although she would not wish to be. She is with me although she does not know it. She is at the Court and it may be will make a great marriage. That does not separate her from me. I can say in this, before God, that I wish nothing for myself. Ah, but of course I wish that I might have her in my arms, that she might surrender to me, love me even for a night. I wish it more than anything in this life. But if it is not to be—and it cannot be—my love is not affected. I wish nothing but her happiness, more, far more, than my own happiness. I am not a child. A man of middle age. I am not telling you, Oliver, because it is a fight with God. I do not fight God for her or pray Him that I might be released. I do not wish to be released. I am not penitent. I am not asking you to strengthen me in any fight. There is no fight. The thought of her is my greatest happiness. She is about me and within me all the day long. But I had to confess it to you, Oliver, because I think of no man in the world as I do of you. I love you to the utmost as one man may love another. I will follow you to the end of the world.'

'And so you shall,' Oliver answered him. 'And farther than you now know. You shall fight for her and your country together and I will be your leader if God wills it. And I am glad that you have told me. Now this is a dedicated day and we will say a prayer.'

They knelt down together, facing the stars, their bodies close so that they touched.

Cromwell said a prayer:

'O Lord God of Battle that knowest Thine own hour and the servants Thou wilt have to bring Thy purposes to victory, take now Thy servants into Thy true regiment that they humbly obeying Thy command may destroy Thy enemies and save this fair land for Thy conquering. And make them mightier in Thy Cause than they can ever be in their own, their hearts never failing them because they know well that it is Thy armour that they are wearing and Thy regiments in which they serve. And so they pledge their mortal lives and their immortal souls to fight for Thy victory. So help them, Lord God. Amen.'

Peter said 'Amen.'

And so these two pledged themselves to God's service in the battle that was soon to come.

LUCY IN CUMBERLAND

LUCY HERRIES, as she was now known by the outside world (and quite wrongfully known), happened to be sleeping peacefully in the very same bedroom at 'The Peacock Has Flown' where she had borne young Rupert. And she was sleeping, her pretty head in her hand, dreaming of her brother Peter at the very moment that Peter was on his knees with Cromwell, staring into the star galaxy, and praying to God.

Lucy, smiling sweetly, saw Peter as a little furry dog chasing a cat in the garden at Mallory. She called 'Peter! Peter!' and woke up.

She, her boy, and Matt Turner had been staying at Seddon. Lucy adored, worshipped, was ecstasized by Seddon. All their lives she and Peter and Rashleigh had wondered about it and longed for it, and now for Lucy at least it was more, much more, than she had expected. She was gay, merry, eager for company, more than middle-aged though she was, and there was not much company at Seddon, only demure little Margaret and her parents, yet Lucy loved it. If there were not grand gentlemen to flirt with, there were local gentry and even gardeners and hostlers. For she was no respecter of persons, especially when they were male. Never was anyone less of a snob. She did not forget herself, of course, in commoner company. She simply wished to laugh, flash her eyes, be kind. They all loved her, even respected her.

'Poor lady,' they would say. 'Married for so short a time in a foreign country, and then left alone with such a demon of a boy.'

Wonderfully she kept her figure and her looks. She would tell no one her age, although it was easily guessed. Women became matronly at thirty. But not Lucy, now much older than that. People said of her that she looked little older than the Queen, whom she was thought to resemble.

Lucy herself did not know how she had kept her figure so slender, her cheeks so fresh-coloured, nor why she felt none of the oncomings of age. These years from thirty-five to fifty were a difficult time for women, but she had as yet known little inconvenience. She could walk and ride and dance without breathlessness. She lived for life. Every tiny incident was excitement to her. She was all heart. She could not bear to be ill thought of. She must win everyone she encountered.

Many women in the Herries family had this same gaiety and abandon, and many Herries women were quiet and dour. The types were as sharply distinguished as the spiritual and material, and always, through Herries history, this battle would continue. But it had happened with Lucy that she had been fortunate, for the only *quiet* Herries woman she had lived with had been Rosamund, who loved and indulged her.

That had been fortunate and unfortunate, too, for there had never been anyone to check Lucy. The unhappy affair with Carey, the unquestioned truth that she was a scandal among the sedater Herries, none of this affected Lucy at all.

Matt Turner, who loved her and had always loved her, saw with clear attention, and he saw, sorrowfully, that no woman, however slender her figure and bright her eyes, could, in the forties, behave as though she were in the twenties. Ludicrousness would begin to creep here and there about. Men would say things behind their hand, women make malicious glances; there would be a wrinkle in the pretty neck, a faint hollow in the cheek, a gentle sagging of the bosom. Age was stronger than any beauty.

But it was not that Lucy was in love with her own beauty. It was rather that she was in love with life.

It pleased her to be told that she was like the Queen, her hair as soft and dark, her eyes as black, her laugh as bright, but she forgot the compliment as soon as it was made. She did not think of her beauty, but she did not think of her age either. She thought of nothing but the goodness of life, the goodness of every minute of it.

It had been, however, something of a relief to escape from Mallory to Seddon. Mallory was not as it had been. Nicholas' blindness, Robert's absorption in business, Rosamund's care for Nicholas, all this had changed it. The house was now quiet and still save for herself and Rupert. The gentlemen in the neighbourhood enjoyed her company, but it was not so easy to get about as it had been and few visitors came now to Mallory. Like all people who enjoy life intensely, Lucy did not care to be reminded that there was a more sombre side to it.

Nicholas blind was a constant reproach to her. He fought his misfortune with a wonderful courage, but his hatred of being dependent on others was always there. He was an old, old man now and at last he appeared one, his shoulders bent, his mighty body forced to refuse its own impulses because it had not the old strength.

There was also the problem of Rupert, now growing into the queerest boy the Herries family had ever fathered. Every family has its own problem, and the problem of the Herries stock was, and always would be, that, composed for the most part of steady, sensible, level-headed, normal persons, the oddity, the poet, the saint, the rogue, the immoralist was for ever being born into its midst. The family resembled England in this, for England has never known what to do with odd genius, has always tried to reject it, until, too late, it has been forced to be proud of it.

Rupert, in himself, was simple enough. He was of the type out of which the Elizabethan adventurers had been made. Give him an adventure, place him against impossible odds, and he was as tractable as an angel. His restlessness was his spirit refusing to be bound. His apparent callousness was his absorption in the action of the moment. He had a leader's mind and so fiery a spirit that already his oaths were a scandal in any company. He wanted nothing of anybody. He loved his mother but no other. He scorned all softness. He lived laborious days.

To most people he was, it is to be feared, a nuisance. Had he been a beautiful boy, tall, slim, and romantic, he would have been found to be fascinating—'something over-bold but a coming hero.' As it was, his short stature, red hair, pale face, and impertinent nose made him the darling of nobody. He never asked a favour nor paid a compliment. He was too deeply intent on the matter in hand to pay much attention to the bystander. His sense of the comic was loud, shrill, and often wounding. Those who loved him—his mother, Matt Turner, Rosamund, and certain more disreputable persons—remarked his eager kindness to Nicholas, always on the look-out to lead him from room to room, to entertain him with stories, to fetch him anything that he might need. They said that he was always kindly to any suffering man or animal, and that he was generous to a folly, wishing to give anything that he had to anyone who wanted it.

They admitted that he was noisy and thoughtless, and that his physical restlessness was a severe trial. In this last he was almost inhuman, for his red head would be seen in one spot at a moment and then directly after in some place incredibly distant. He could climb trees like a monkey, use a rapier with genius, could ride any horse, swim like a fish, and run like the wind.

With all these gifts he should have been the admired hero of any boys he encountered. But he was not. They did not like him. For he must always lead and expressed contempt, in shrill tones, of any stupidity or failure.

He was considered vainglorious and arrogant. Those things Matt, who was his friend, declared he was not. 'He has no vanity in the world. He has no time for it.'

It has been said that a man who talks much is modest, for, if he is vain, he guards his tongue that he may not appear a fool. Then was Rupert Herries modest indeed, for he never ceased to talk.

After the visit to Seddon, Matt Turner was the guardian of Lucy and her boy back to London again. They would ride by slow stages, and for the first stage Matt stopped outside Keswick, at 'The Peacock Has Flown.'

This was a strange experience for Lucy. She had not seen the place since her desertion by Carey and the birth of Rupert. That had been then mid-winter. This was high summer. For those who love Cumberland late July and August is the worst period of the year, for all is green and the rain falls with a sort of satiety; the country shrivels in size. The hills are diminished and the sky without luminancy. But on the day of their ride from Seddon to the inn the air was golden and scented, and Skiddaw, above their heads, seemed to swing like a gigantic censer in a bee-dust haze. The streams were not dry, for there had been rains and they fell languidly, laughing above the stones.

There was a lawn with deep thick trees behind the inn and, after changing and washing her face and hands, Lucy came out here to enjoy the golden evening. Beneath one of the trees, a little table in front of him, a glass of ale in his hand, sat Mr. Humphrey Caroline.

Because he was a man Lucy looked at him, and because she was a lady Mr. Caroline rose and saluted her, for he was very fond of ladies. Especially did he like them mature. He was impatient of a girl's inexperience. This lady was mature, but her figure was divine, her dark hair and eyes bewitching, and her manner promising.

It was promising indeed, for Lucy, after a whole day's riding with poor Matt Turner, longed for an adventure. All her adventures were decorous—up-to-the-last-moment decorous at least. Her sensual passions were never very deep—if indeed they could be called deep at all —and her heart too good and true towards those she loved to be betrayed into sensuality—but she *did* like a man.

She liked Mr. Caroline. He was of middle age, a fine broad figure, his face round and merry if a trifle flushed, his clothes rich and gentlemanly, his curls that fell luxuriantly on to his lace collar of a rich brown. He carried on his ample lap a small spaniel dog.

She advanced. She gave a little cry of dismay.

'Oh, excuse me, sir! I thought for an instant——'

Mr. Caroline knew well this opening gambit. He rose, dropping the spaniel, and bowed.

'You thought, Madame——?'

'I thought it was a friend. I thought that I recognized the dog. '

'It is more than likely. If I am not impertinent, I fancy that I have seen you in London.'

'Oh, it is not impertinent at all. It may be. I am often there.'

'If Madame would accept my seat——'

'Oh, no, I am returning into the house. I came but for a moment. The last time I was here was in the winter. There was much snow.'

'The evening is delightfully warm. . . . You are staying at the inn?'

Mr. Caroline said this in a manner peculiarly his own, a manner very successful with ladies, almost tender but not quite, almost intimate but not quite, almost admiring but not quite. . . .

'Yes, sir—with my little boy.'

Ah, a widow! Mr. Caroline preferred that.

'We shall meet then possibly again.' Lucy did not answer that, but gave him a radiant smile which implied that she would be very happy to do so—and that was no lie.

She walked back to the inn, knowing that her dress of lilac and silver was worthy of any man's attention.

Poor Matt was very unhappy that night. He sat in the inn parlour, grizzling and groaning. The night was hot. His shirt was open and showed his thin spindling breast. His hair was as ever on end and untidy. His long fingers were restless. He kicked his thin legs backwards and forwards. For he was a failure. His age was over fifty and he had done nothing with his life save love Lucy and write plays, poems, pasquinades, political squibs that very few had wanted. His brothers were respectable and settled. He was neither respectable nor settled. The fact that Robert Herries had paid for his holiday to Seddon was not very consoling. There was something coldly disapproving in Robert's eye when he had asked Matt to go with Lucy and Rupert and look after them.

'You will enjoy your holiday, Matthew,' he had said—implying, Matt thought: 'You never work. You are a vagabond. To talk of holiday to such as you is absurd!'

To take a holiday with Lucy whom he loved and young Rupert was at first to Matthew the miraculous peak of happiness. He lived a most unhealthy life. He had had a lodging for years in the Minories by the Tower, and all about him drinking, robbery, the most indecent and open lewdness, gaming and murder were constant. Noise was incessant, night and day, with men issuing from the brothels or tipstaffs attempting to arrest the brothel customers, or the press-gang carrying men off to the Navy, or merry gentlemen from the Court killing a beadle or two.

From all this, and much more than this, escape into the country was for Matt a new paradise. But this paradise was, like all paradises, invaded by serpents. The serpents were, first, that he loved Lucy more than ever and that Lucy loved him even less.

They were not very grand at Seddon, and the Blaikies had a decent reverence for anyone so clever as Matt was, but they could not but think him an oddity, thin to a caricature, stammering, snapping his fingers, books everywhere, his fingers ink-stained, his eyes red-rimmed and bewildered.

They saw that he had a good heart and loved Lucy—both of these were obvious to anyone—but Mr. Blaikie would feel almost terrified when those fingers were snapped and a voice shouted in his ear: 'A Woman Is a Weathercock!' 'A Woman Is a Weathercock!' and found it to be some comedy that Matt had just been reading; or Mrs. Blaikie when she felt her arm grasped and the shrill voice crying in her ear: 'Here is Fidessa; more chaste than kind—Sonnets, dear lady, by Bartholomew Griffin. Here I have a copy bought for a penny in the Temple, and you may have it. It is good reading, I can tell you'; or to hear that shrill cracked voice reciting like a crowing cock:

'Her garment neither was of silk nor say,
But painted plumes, in goodly order dight,
Like as the sunburnt Indians do array
Their tawny bodies, in their proudest plight:
As those same plumes, so seemed he vain and light,
That by his gait might easily appear;
For still he fared as dancing in delight,
And in his hand a windy fan did bear,
That in the idle air he moved still here and there. . . .'

Yes—here and there on the beautiful broad Seddon staircase Matt
Turner would be dancing, moving his arms in imitation of the 'windy
fan.' He seemed to poor Mrs. Blaikie like a spirit or a goblin and
of endless height.

It was the two children, Margaret Blaikie and Rupert Herries, who
best understood him. They were both so different, but alike in this
that, as with all children, the absurd things were the natural things,
and the natural things were absurd. Matt Turner could do the things
that they required grown people to do—stand on his head and clap
his heels together, crow like a cock, draw pictures with his quill, race
Rupert in the park, make monstrous faces, tell stories of King Arthur
and his Round Table. Margaret felt for him a tender motherliness,
Rupert a sort of brotherhood.

But none of this helped him with his dear Lucy. She had known
him from babyhood, and always recognized and accepted his oddities.
She was fond of him as one is fond of a dog who looks ridiculously
and behaves madly but loves one. It would have been a loss to Lucy
had Matt Turner not loved her. But she had never before this been
away with him in a foreign house. The Blaikies were kind and good
to her, but she did not know them so well that she need not be shy
of them. Matt, at Seddon, followed her about like a gambolling clown.
She spoke to him sharply.

'They laugh at you, Matt—and myself with you.'

'Alas—I know that they do. But kindly—they laugh k-kindly. I am
a laughable c-creature altogether, but none the worse for it. And now
there is my comedy *The Sparagus Garden*—is not that a pretty title?'

'You should not show them all that you love me.'

'Ah, there—it is so old a story. It was hidden once but has worn its way through to the very thread of the tunic. Its head is out, and shortly its s-shoulders will follow.'

All, however, was not so bad until they arrived at 'The Peacock.' Over their evening supper in the parlour there was trouble because a stout elderly gentleman joined them. Lucy was acquainted with him, it seemed. His name was Mr. Caroline.

How Lucy could be already acquainted with him poor Matt could not imagine. The swiftness with which she picked up her gentlemen! So, although he knew well that he was a fool, he sulked, and then was directly rude to Mr. Caroline. But it was never Mr. Caroline's rôle to be offended, and he talked then with Lucy as though Matt did not exist. So then Matt went out and sulked under a moon the colour of a pat of butter, and his heart ached, until he thought of a new line for his comedy, when he went skipping indoors to write it.

On the following morning, about the middle of the day, they rode into Keswick. It was sultry warm weather. Matthew was in a sulk, so Lucy proceeded to charm him because she could never bear that anyone should be out of temper. Moreover, the thought of Mr. Caroline, although she did not suppose she would ever see him again after to-day, was pleasant to her heart.

'The hills are crawling with thunder,' she said. She liked a poetical phrase and was proud of this one.

Matt made no answer.

'I know another who is crawling with thunder.'

'A very ill phrase,' Matt said. 'Hills do not crawl. At least these hills do not.'

Rupert was on a small sturdy horse that would carry him grandly to London. He was a better rider than either Lucy or Matthew. He was as good a rider as you would find, for he was always part of his horse and could do anything with him. He wore no hat. They could see his red head disappearing round the corner.

'Please, Matt—we are the oldest friends in the world. Why must you quarrel with me?'

'Because . . . b-because . . . Why, Lucy, must you always have a man about you—a man you know nothing of, who may be and indeed looks a most worthless f-fellow?'

Lucy laughed.

'Mr. Caroline.'

'I care n-nothing for his n-name.' Then he added most unfortunately: 'You and I—we are not children. We——'

Lucy nodded her head.

'I see. You are jealous.'

'And if I am? I have loved you all my l-life. You know that I would marry you to-morrow.'

'And live on what—porridge?'

'There are worse things. Had I you and Rupert to care for, I would write something finer than *Comus,* than Shakespeare's *Julius Caesar.'*

She looked at him with pity.

'Meanwhile it is *The Sparagus Garden.* I know. You have read me a scene from it. And so, through all these years, you have been reading me scenes and poems and satires and romances—all after Spenser or Shakespeare or Sidney—and nothing comes of them, nothing at all. . . .' Then looking at him, his woeful countenance moved her so that she did not know whether to laugh or to cry. 'Nay, Matt, I did not intend any disloyalty. I believe you to be a genius like Sidney or Shakespeare, but—but—why in all these years has nothing come of it all? The world is waiting. It has not so many poets or playwriters. And I am bad at waiting. This may be our last moment, Matt —this heavy lowering day. And in a second of time it is all over. There is only darkness. All the love, the dancing, the music is over. We cannot share in it any longer. I know that evil days are coming. It can be foreseen by everyone and I want—I want'—she stretched out her gloved hand—'I want, while the light lasts, to be happy and to see others happy. . . . Marriage? Would there not be something sad for us in that? We two—I in some garret watching the fire that won't burn, you at the bare table, scribbling an Epic. . . . Oh, no! no! no! I love you almost as a sister. . . . Let us be free and happy on this one day, taking it hour for hour, gathering what we can. . . .

'I have known very much unhappiness. I will not be unhappy again till I die.'

They rode on into Keswick, and at once were aware of some unrest there. It may have been in the first place the day itself, for when the clouds are low in summer and there is thunder, the hills crowd about the little town, drawing in closely, the Lake seems to shrivel in size, and that threatening power that always is in the heart of the hills here—not malevolent but rather suggesting a force that it may not always be willing to control—comes down into every house and fills every room and lies at wait outside every door.

The inn was one of the finest in the North of England. Lucy, as she sat there, drinking ale, did not know that, nearly a century back, Nicholas and Robin, young men with their lives before them, met joyfully here, after something done by Nicholas that would change their lives for ever.

The three of them sat quietly at their table; even Rupert was quiet, for he was absorbing the room and everything in it.

They saw a man with his back to them standing at the window. He was a little man with rather bandy legs, but even in the shape of his back there was an important officialdom. Another man entered and came over to him.

The first man turned.

'Well?' he said sharply.

There was a dull roll of thunder.

'There are some men in the Square,' the second man said. 'This news from Scotland has excited them, and the suspicion that there may be an army in Carlisle.'

'I care nothing for their excitement,' the little man answered—he had a sharp furrowed face with a scar above one eye. 'I must have those lists. The tax has to be paid whether they wish it or no. By God, they have had time and over . . .'

'It would be better,' the other muttered, 'nevertheless to stay here until the morning——'

The first man sharply interrupted him.

'Rather I will go into the Square myself and speak to them. Do they suppose that this is Scotland? In York Wentworth was paid his ship-money. Does *this* beggarly place deny the King? Do they suppose that because in Edinburgh an old woman throws a stool at the Bishop, therefore they can avoid their just charges?'

'It is not that,' the other man explained. 'They are willing enough, most of them. But it seems that there is some injustice. A Mr. Hendrick, by Skiddaw——'

'A Mr. Hendrick!' The little man tossed his head contemptuously. 'Richard Hendrick, of Bonthill. I know him. A John Hampdenite, if ever there was one.'

'And a John Niemoller. . . . His father was an Almayn—came over forty years ago to help in the mines here. His son refuses . . .'

The little man stamped with his foot—a funny effect. ' "Refuses," does he? We'll see about his refusing. . . . Tell Bostocks, Williams . . .'

But the other was imperturbable.

'There is also a preacher in the Square, haranguing about the altar being moved somewhere or other. There was some trouble, I understand, last Sunday in Crosthwaite Church——'

The little man's face now was as red as a cardinal's gown, and he stamped out, muttering and puffing.

'Oh, we must see!' Lucy cried excitedly. 'Oh, Matthew, never mind the ale—we can pay later.'

But Rupert was already ahead of them, flying to the door and his head straight into the stomach of Mr. Caroline.

'Oh! Pouf! Pah! . . . What's that! See to your step!'

'Oh, sir,' Rupert cried as shrill as the wind through the keyhole, 'you must come with us. There is to be fighting in the street because they refuse the taxes and there is a clergyman preaching against the Archbishop . . .'

But Mr. Caroline never cared at any time for fighting and thought this would be an admirable opportunity for being alone with Lucy.

But he did not yet know his Lucy.

'Ah, Madame! How happily we are met, and there will be presently a terrible storm of rain. Moreover, they are quarrelling in the street, and I fear it is a King's matter.'

But Lucy pushed him aside, crying, 'I must see to my boy!' while Matt Turner passed him without a word. So Mr. Caroline, seeing this rapid exodus, stood surprised, his mouth a little open, scratching his plump thigh. But he had dreamed of Lucy during the night preceding and, having ridden to Keswick in search of her, did not wish to lose her out of his sight.

So he hurried after her.

The scene that met their eyes when they came to the Square was sufficiently remarkable.

Keswick had been raised, during Elizabeth's reign, from its humble status by the development under Elizabeth's direction of the silver and lead mines. These mines had been worked by German miners who, after some quarrelling with the Keswick natives, had settled down and intermarried.

Owing, however, to the non-discovery of silver and gold and the difficult markets for lead and the inattention of the Crown, the mining had by this time lapsed almost into discontinuance. Nevertheless the blood of the Germans mingling with the already stubborn and obstinate blood of the Cumbrians had led to a stiffening of the younger generation, who at this time were in Keswick as stalwart and determined a body of young men and maidens as was to be found in any town in England.

The North was not as yet by any means as sharply roused against possible tyrannies as the South, the reason perhaps why Wentworth was able so peacefully to extract his full ship-money out of Yorkshire; nevertheless Keswick was rather more than the North. It was almost Border country. Carlisle was only thirty miles distant and Scotland itself little more. Keswick and its neighbourhood had for hundreds of years known the proper meaning of Border raids. Anything that happened in Scotland might very quickly affect Cumberland. And now Edinburgh was in an uproar, and an old woman—whether Jenny Geddes or another—had thrown a stool at the Bishop.

Keswick had always been tolerant about religion, but the Guy Fawkes adventure, the Spanish Marriage scare, the discomfort of having a French Catholic Queen, these things all worked in men's mind and souls. And here was Archbishop Laud, urged by the King, taking the first steps towards Romanism with his altar-moving and his prayer-books, and here was the same King cutting men's ears off in the pillory for speaking their minds, and forcing men to pay taxes when he hadn't summoned a Parliament for a succession of years.

When therefore Lucy, Rupert, and Matt, followed by Mr. Caroline, arrived in the Square, they saw under a sky wrinkled like a snake's skin and threatening with thunder a greatly disturbed scene.

The Square was filled with people. About them the pleasant oak and plaster houses, their gardens brilliant with roses, the black hills behind them leaning forward as though they were listening, seemed to smile and bless. But the people themselves were angry. A tall thin preacher with a rather ludicrous wart at the end of his nose shouted on a turned-over ale-cask in a shrill wailing accent. He flourished a Bible and waved a skinny arm. He was very angry, and phrases like

'Yea, and the rivers shall be filled with blood . . .' or 'Woe, woe, I say unto you, for the Lord has revealed unto me . . .' came floating over the murmurous buzz of the general conversation.

A fine stout gentleman in a plain dark-purple suit, wearing a handsome grey beard, stood engaged in conversation with the King's man who had been at the inn. Behind this gentleman was a crowd of boys and men with quiet but angry faces. Behind the King's man was a little posse of some six or seven attendants, their noses lifted contemptuously in the air, their hands on their swords.

With every moment the Square was filling, voices were rising, sheep were bleating, cattle lowing, and the thunder, from time to time, growling beyond the hills.

The Square grew ever fuller and fuller, and as people pushed from the rear, so was the pressure upon the central figures more alarming.

Cries were heard: 'Taxes! Taxes! 'Tis nothing but taxes.' 'What of his Romish wife? 'Tisn't right to have t' Pope back. . . . Mr. Hendrick is a good man. He'll listen to common sense if ever . . .'

Lucy, who was in the back of the crowd leaning on Matt's arm, was frightened. That was unusual. It was perhaps the thunder and the sudden rumble behind the houses as though bricks were falling.

Then she saw that Rupert was missing.

'Oh,' she cried, 'Matt, Rupert's not here!'

'Wait! I will find him!' Matt said.

It did not seem very far into the middle of the crowd, and quickly Matt was behind the King's men looking anxiously for Rupert. There was no sign of him.

Matt heard the King's man say:

'Now, Mr. Hendrick, sir, you must come with us for examination.'

'What if I refuse?' came the quiet answer.

'It is in the King's name. You refuse on your peril.'

Mr. Hendrick's voice was lifted.

'Good folks, we are not here to incite any disorder. We intend no defiance to the King. Were the King here in person I would kneel on those stones and ask him of his justice whether it is right that, having already paid my tax, I should pay it over again for no reason given and for no just cause. He would, I am truly convinced, disperse this injustice of his own charity. Therefore, before I pay my money, I demand to set my case before the King. And if he were here I would ask him to call a Parliament of his subjects again that all his loyal people might put such questions as these truly before him——'

He was interrupted, plainly not to his own pleasure, by the preacher, who came pushing through the people and waved his fist in the very face of the King's man. 'The Lord, the Lord,' he cried, 'is upon you and with His mighty word will dry the flesh upon your powerful limbs. For He hath punished us all for our iniquities and especially for our iniquities of the lighted candle upon the altar and the wearing of vestments and the forcing of the people to recite prayers that are not truly in their mouths. I tell you that fire and the plague will descend from heaven upon his head——'

But all this was quite sufficient for the King's man, whose patience was by now not unnaturally exhausted. He gave the preacher a blow with his fist that sent him reeling, and cried to his men, pointing furiously at Hendrick:

'Arrest that man in the King's name!'

Everything after that seemed to happen at once. Matt saw two officers move towards Hendrick, one of them struck with a piece of wood, which felled him, his fellow catch Hendrick by the arms and the two of them begin to wrestle rather ludicrously together.

Meanwhile the little King's man was having his clothes torn off his back and, with a bare chest and his cheek bleeding, was fighting to save himself from falling.

He had his friends not far away, for two men on horseback began to ride in upon the crowd. Here there was real danger, for with the pressure of bodies, women screaming, swords and sticks flourishing in the air, tempers rose and faces turned into masks of a strange unreasoning anger. There were enemies who saw a chance to pay off old debts, and women protecting their children. Matt's one thought was for Lucy. He was sure that Rupert would see to himself. Matt turned back and came at once against the enormously stout body of a countryman who stood, stolid, where he was, and repeated over and over again: 'Nay, lad. Tak' thy time, lad—tak' thy time!'

There was something nightmarish in the opposition of this mountain of flesh. Bodies fell up against it and rolled off again. His thighs were clutched as though to pull him off the ground. Men tugged at his shoulders. Matt, in a frenzy, beat at his chest, tearing at his shirt, crying: 'Let me by. Let me by. There is a lady——'

But only, the sweat making channels in his huge cheeks, he repeated: 'Tak' thy time. . . . Tak' thy time, lad——'

Suddenly the heavens opened and the rain came down in torrents.

Lucy was in evil case. When the crowd began its dangerous earthquake swaying she had to escape from it. She could look back and see, to her astonishment, Mr. Caroline standing well away from it all and politely interested. She could not, however, reach to him, for a new inrush of men and women drove her forward, almost carried her off her feet. She struck out with her hands, caught a man's coat to save herself from falling. After that stones began to fly and quite suddenly she felt one rush past her, the wind of it was in her ears, and it hit the forehead of the man whose coat she was holding. He was an elderly man, laughing and shouting, and very strange it was to see his face suddenly carved into seriousness and the blood, as though it had spontaneous life of its own, pouring down his face, blinding his eyes, and trickling over his beard. He would have fallen had Lucy not caught him.

Then, for the first time in her life, she felt the crowd-panic. She thought nothing of Rupert or Matt, but only of her own preservation; for everything was unstable. The earth did not hold. There was no place for her feet. She was hot as in hell, she was bruised, her curls were about her face. But at the heart of the crowd-panic is the certainty of coming death. Soon your flesh will be torn from you, your heart will be hammered, your legs and arms broken. The old man whom she was holding fell from her as though into space. A fearful pressure began. Closer and closer. Thousands and thousands of bodies began, of their own intention, to crowd in upon her. The rain was thundering down, but it seemed to her very distant, like the hissing of a kettle. The sky, like the lid of a black box, began to slide, slantways, down upon her. Hands caught at all parts of her body, and screaming, although she did not know that she uttered a sound, she plucked at them.

Then the earth opened and swallowed her.

She opened her eyes, lifted her face, and the rain fell upon it like a thousand kisses. She saw Matt, ragged, with a bleeding nose. She began to laugh: 'Oh, Matt! Oh, Matt! Oh, Matt!'

Although it seemed that her neck was broken, she could move her head. The Square seemed quite empty, full of puddles into which the rain was spitting. Some dark figure passed leading another. The rain revived her. She suddenly knew that all was well. Her body was not destroyed. She could feel her heart beat steadily.

'The h-horsemen,' Matt stammered. 'The men on h-horseback. They cleared it.'

His arm was behind her. She leant against his breast. Her eyes met his and she loved him—Matt, who would always be watching over her, would be always there when danger threatened.

'Dear Matt . . . sweet Matt . . . I would have died but for you.'

It was the sweetest moment of his life. He dared to kiss her.

Then she remembered her son.

She started to her feet.

'Rupert. . . . Oh, God! Where is Rupert?'

They saw him, like a small gargoyle, perched on the ledge of a roof above the door. He was shouting and waving his arms, the rain deluging him.

THE MOON IS DARKENED

Pages from the Journal of Rashleigh Garland

Dec. 4, 1639.

This morning I received two letters from Mallory—one was from Rosamund begging me to pay a visit when it was possible for me, as she was resolved that Nicholas must soon go. He had said to her: 'I would like to rest my hand on Rashleigh's shoulder. He is the nearest to my Robin of them all.' She also told me that three days back my dear sister Lucy was married in London to Matt Turner.

The second letter is from Lucy herself—a letter written from Mallory before her marriage in London. A criss-cross confused letter. She gives no reason for this save that 'once he saved my life'—an ill-foreboding for a happy marriage if ever there was one. And it *cannot* be a happy marriage, for Matt is a poet without means—the most desperate of all God's creatures. I have visited his room in the Minories which stank of civet and damp straw, had a mask of Caesar hanging with a spider-web on the nose of it, a dried plate with mutton-bones, a tumbled bed, and a cat kittening in the clothes cupboard. Nor is Lucy the one to straighten disorder, for she has neither time, patience, nor the means for it.

That Matthew loves her I doubt not; he has always loved her. But he sees her as an Epic, a Pastoral, or a Satire, and Lucy is all flesh and blood. Then there is the Wild Boy who blazes heaven with his head and will be fighting every rascal in the Minories before he is a month older. . . . No, no—this cannot work.

And yet I, who am charged with no feeling, have at this instant a heart more tender and suffering than philosophy allows. For now truly am I alone. Lucy is married, Peter my enemy. This last word is too strong. Enemies we cannot be, now or ever, or only as man is enemy of himself. We are one. We are even, as I see it, engaged side by side in the same cause.

Had I the leisure and the patience and the final ability I would write an epic of an English family from, say, Norman William to our present time and the grand theme of it should be—the Lust for Possession and the Fight for Freedom. For, as I see it, these two are never-ceasing in the life of man. I would demonstrate it, finding examples plentiful enough in our family who are for ever fighting to retain and possess, like Robert at Mallory, or his great-uncle Henry, or Humphrey before him; on the other side the finer spirits, whether for wickedness like Nicholas' other uncle Francis or for goodness like his own brother Robin.

This longing to be free, clear of all bonds whether of vices or possessions, or loves or hates, I take to be the great motive of the saints urging towards heaven—and it must lead surely to this conclusion, that to attain happiness in this creation man must love something or someone other than, greater than, himself. So some throw themselves at the feet of Christ Jesus, others yearn for a Paradise, others wash the malodorous limbs of the poor, yet others content themselves with the ills of this immediate world and would better the herdsman who, poor clown, wishes for no bettering; others will love a body—the breasts, the loins, the feet—but that is a perilous, easy-changing worship. For others it is a Cause—and for a few, merely the love of goodness and the hope to be with God at the end.

For both Peter and me there is the Cause and in that we are together. My Cause is Divine Right, and his the people's freedom. This last I also desire, but it must come, as I see it, within the command of the King's Right. This cry, growing now louder and coarser with every minute, of the people's freedom stinks in my nostrils. To be free for what? To have the intelligence or education or sense of taste to be free for what? The people. . . . The people? But they know nothing save how to blow on their porridge, to tumble one another's bodies, to scratch lice from their heads. And men such as my brother would have them rule the country and tell the King what he must do and how much money he should have, and whether he must pray and *when* he must pray, and how he should lie with his wife. Faugh! Peter will now neither see me nor write to me because on the last time, a month ago at Mallory, I mocked at his Cromwell, a Huntingdon farmer whom Peter worships to idolatry. But I am sorry. For if I worship the Divine Right I also love my brother, I had never realized how dearly until now. I saw, at the last meeting, that he had grown most truly into a man.

I might mock at this Cromwell of his, but he has stiffened Peter, turned the light in his eyes into a steel colour. But I love him and he will not see me. It is my destiny to be alone. I do not think that I complain, but in loneliness you hear Time's baffled moves like a squirrel in a cage.

A dream that I had three nights ago has remained with me. It is not my habit to dream, nor do I remember when I wake. But every detail of this is clear to me.

I was in a dark rocky country, a black sky and a barren waste. I came upon a lake of steel and edged by sharp, towering rocks. There was a great white horse swimming desperately in the lake. Soon if he did not escape he must drown. He was in the greatest terror, his nostrils distended, his eyeballs starting. A superb horse he was, with a flowing white mane and a noble carriage of his head. He struggled against the slippery rock-edge but could obtain no hold.

There was a moment when it seemed certain to me that he must drown and I longed to help him, but, as so often in dreams, I could not move. I saw despair in his eyes, and then, with a great magnificent heave of his body, he caught with his hooves a ledge, hauled himself up, gave the rocks a clanging scornful kick, and was off gallantly across the plain. I woke, still feeling the agony of his effort and sharing his fear of a terrible death.

December 19.

I must write down while they are clear in my memory the events of this afternoon and evening.

It is late. I am fearfully tired with more than a natural weariness. I am not a man of superstitious kind but to-night I have looked into Death's eyes.

Wentworth (there are rumours that he will shortly have an Earldom) is here. The King and his full Court are here.

Two days ago I had a conversation with Mr. Endymion Porter. He has been very close to the King since those early days when he had much to do with the Spanish Marriage. Being moreover a close friend of the Queen, he is strongly suspected of Popish leanings and he does not disavow them. But as events are now marching, he knows well that he is marked out by many enemies and has no hesitation in saying that his early death is certain.

He is a gentleman of much courage and a pleasant humour, but in his talk with me he made it very clear that he foresees a grim future for our country.

He told me that the King's march towards Scotland was most disastrous. The Scots were stiffened with many thousands of old soldiers who had served in Germany in the Thirty Years' War. The reports ever since last June current here that the Scottish army was a rabble, Porter strongly denies. The Scots had their heart in their cause, the English had no cause to have a heart in.

The King in his tent was almost shot by one of his own soldiers. There was great disorder and poor food. When on June 24th an agreement was signed, and it was arranged that all affairs, civil and ecclesiastical, should be settled in agreement with an Assembly and a Parliament, the Scots, Porter considers, pulled their noses at the King, and it is certainly to be acknowledged that the actions of both Assembly and Parliament have been, since then, very little to the King's liking.

What then will he do? Attack the Scots a second time?

Endymion Porter thinks this would be a matter here of great risk, the Town being in its present uneasy state.

So he has sent for Wentworth.

I had myself never spoken to him before this time. At one while he was supposed to be thick with the Parliament, Pym, and the others. But now Pym is his dearest enemy and would have Parliament impeach him had he the power.

None, however, may deny that in Ireland he has wrought a miracle. There are tales of cruelties and privilege as there always must be concerning any man who has ruled Ireland. But I would say that Wentworth's integrity is as clear as his hanging forehead and frowning lip.

They say, too, that he is the lover of Lucy Carlisle, who has others for certain but one more is little to her. I would say, too, that he has only one love and that is the King. It is because of this, perhaps, that in the conversation I had with him four days back, we were instant friends. I felt none of the fear that men allege they have with him. His face is deep-lined with resolve and iron will. Also it may be with physical pain, for there can have been few men who have suffered to his duress. When the King called for him from the North he was, he told me, in such an agony with the gout that he longed to die,—but not, he added, until he had done the King his service. While I talked to him the gout twisted his leg as though demons were about it. But his will is so strong that he can never be defeated by man or event. Only I think he would be defeated if the King were ever to betray him. All his trust, his faith, his love are there.

When we spoke of principles I saw that we were on common ground. He wishes for nothing so much as the happiness of this country—its prosperity and the comfort of every man or woman under it. But as the Archbishop in matters ecclesiastical, so Wentworth in things civil would have thorough order and discipline under the benevolent fatherhood of the King.

He knows how his enemies—John Pym, Sir Henry Vane, and many more—pursue him. He is afraid of none of them, but I believe, beneath his steel armour, a warm heart beats and there is a devotion to loyalty here that I have never seen approached.

And so to my story.

I have known this old Whitehall Palace now for so long that I am well accustomed to all its moods—but it is a place as in my final judgment I must acknowledge it, dark and spirit-haunted. It is not unnatural that it should be so, for many dark things have been done in it. I have heard Buchanan say of it that 'it forgets nothing.' The ghosts that haunt it are in number so many that there must be a tiresome jostling when the morning cock crows for departure. Myself, although I am not given to such imaginations and on the whole see things as they truly are, have, on a night of long and weary watching, seen, heard, and felt more than I could sensibly name or would dare to before wise judges.

The Queen has told me that she hates the place for this very reason, has always had a detestation of it since her first entering it.

The King has done what he could to lighten it since his being king, and there are rooms that are brilliant and light-hearted. There are many excellent pictures and some fine statuary, but there are by a long way, to my thinking, too many dark passages and sombre corners for comfort. I know that old men who served in it in James I's time have stories of perverse debaucheries that are fit only for dogs and monkeys. It is an obscene chuckle as of a man sensually moved by some filthiness that I have heard in my ears when I have been on guard outside the King's bedchamber at the very thick of night. There has been a touch on my cheek of a sweating hand and a smell in my nose of hot candle-wax—but what may one not imagine at the dead time when the candles blow and the blood runs slowly? All this is but a prelude to the event of this evening.

At late afternoon it was my duty to be in the ante-chamber outside the King's room. He was in consultation over some papers from Scotland. There were with me young Vane, Sir Henry's son, a boy for whom I have no liking, and Charles Newby. The room was hung with dark russet. The two long thin windows looked out on to Palace Yard. Snow was lazily falling. Newby was busy reading a book of falconry, his stout, good-natured person all drawn up into the absorption in the affair as is customary with anyone to whom reading is not an accustomed habit.

I walked across to the window and I remember that I nearly tripped over young Vane's rapier, its scabbard stretching in front of me. This angered me, for, I know not why, I was in a condition highly nervous and ill-strung.

Dusk was falling.

'It is a new moon to-night,' young Vane said. I fancied that he was watching me with some malice. I have attained at Court, through these many years, a reputation for strong personal control. They say that no one has ever seen me angry—or indeed merry either for that matter. 'A dull dog,' they must have said many a time. 'He does not play at cards nor any game; he lies rarely if ever with women; he is never drunken, he is never in a fury. He has never even a malady like the pox or any scandalous fever. A very dull dog indeed!'

If I were to answer them that it is within myself that all my humours play they would mock at my inhumanity—yet it may be that I am more lively human than the most of them.

I answered young Vane with courtesy and he, maybe feeling that there was no sport to be had from me, went from the room.

Charles Newby came and stood by me at the window. We could see a faint shadow of yellow light over the darkening buildings against whose sombre mass the snow was now falling more thickly. Charles laid his hand on my shoulder.

'Rashleigh,' he said, 'I love you. I know not the reason, and that, I fancy, is the best way of loving.'

'There are few who do,' I said, laughing.

'You are a dedicated man,' he said. 'I have known in these last years what it is to be dedicated. You to the King. I to Katherine.'

'And she will not have you?'

'No. She will not have me—yet.'

He went on: 'I am a dull fellow, only seeing what is before my eyes —not given to phantoms. And yet I have felt in these last months that this place is full of forewarning. Every hanging seems to me to conceal dark figures—and I hear voices.'

'What voices?' I asked, laughing again, for it was a comedy that Charles Newby, of all men, should have a superstition.

'I cannot tell you. But it is an evil place. There were bad things done here in the late King's reign—aye, and before him too. The other night I was late on duty and walked through the western passage. It was dark and I felt my way against the wall. Then a door opened with candle-light behind it, and I saw Buckingham.'

'Buckingham?'

'Aye, as he was—laughing, insolent, fearless.'

'It was a trick of light.'

'Most certainly it was, for as I approached, some servant carrying two candles came from the room. But how clearly I saw him, with his lip curled as it used to be in pride, and his audacious eyes. Once I should not have imagined it. Now I can imagine anything.' He added in a low voice: 'I fear that the Scots have been too many for the King.'

'Wentworth will have things to rights.'

He sighed—a deep, heavy sigh.

'He is a sick man, and they will have his head, Pym and Vane and the others—if they can get it.'

The dusk seemed to me to have something sombre and moving in it—'the restless fur of the yellow cat,' old Skelton nearly says somewhere.

Dark fell almost as I watched and a moon like a snitch off a yellow penny looked of a sudden penitent, lonely, on a chimney-edge. Two pages came in bearing candles and to draw across the curtains, maroon scattered with the Royal crest. All these minutiae had importance to-night. It was as though someone had whispered in my ear: 'Watch, Rashleigh, to-night. Watch. . . . Nothing is of too slender an importance.'

The pages set down the candles on the card-table in the corner under a drawing of the Holy Family, by Giovanni Barbieri, known as Guercino.

It is one of three drawings sent the other day to the King by Guercino. I saw it as it was unpacked and fell in love with it. The Holy Child is leaning forward from his mother's lap washing his hands in a bowl that St. Joseph on his knees is holding for him. It is in sepia. The Baby is an Italian peasant baby, plump, healthy, strong. I hung the drawing on this wall with my own hands. I know well also the two gold candlesticks that the pages have just brought in and placed under the drawing. They belonged to Anne of Denmark and were, I believe, always in her bedchamber. They are carved with leaves and grapes and Cupids.

Placed there in the corner near the window, they left the remainder of the room in a dusky-golden darkness.

The door opposite the King's room opened and a man came in. He stood outside the King's room thinking. I knew at once who it was, as did also Newby. He laid his hand lightly on my arm.

It was Wentworth.

He looked in the candle-shadows a double man. It seemed that he must see us, for he was staring directly at us. Van Dyck has but recently painted him. The picture hangs in the King's room. But that picture shows him in armour. Now he was in plain black velvet with a lace collar and a gold rose at his neck, otherwise no ornament. He leaned slightly on an ebony stick with a white ivory top.

His face seen by me in the candle-light was one of resolve, pain, sadness, irony, but no cowardice. He is not a beauty—his countenance is too rough-hewn for that—but his eyes are so deep, so strong, so far-searching, and his mouth so resolute, the *bones* of his face so manly, there is something so fiercely high-minded here that you say: 'This is a Man!'

Now as, unseen, I looked at him I wondered to myself how differently the fortunes of England might not now be going were Wentworth only a man of physical fitness. I could see well the pain that he was now in; the eyes were pouched with weariness. His right leg lifted for a moment and waggled in the air as though of its own volition. He bit his lower lip above the short beard. His beautiful long fingers tightened above his small-sword. He was hesitating whether to enter the King's room or no, and I was about to step forward to show him that I was on duty when the door opened and someone came out. Wentworth stepped back into the shadow. It was Sir Henry Vane, his great enemy. The two gentlemen stood very close to one another, but Vane did not see Wentworth. He appeared impatient, for he tossed his head and went away.

Then I stepped forward to tell Wentworth that I was on duty and ask whether I could be of service to him.

He seemed to be pleased that it was I.

'Ah, Mr. Garland. . . . Yes, you can do me some service. Do you know—can you tell me—is Lady Carlisle with the King?'

I said that I would discover.

'If she is there and would for a moment only speak with me . . .' We exchanged a deep, long glance for which there was no reason. I am bound to him since that exchange, for I realized then that Wentworth and I are engaged on the same task—I very humbly—to serve and guard the King.

I entered the King's room. It is a long, draughty place hung with sombre green tapestry. The King and Queen were there, the Queen's confessor, George Goring, and a number of others—Katherine, Lucy Carlisle.

Three men were playing on stringed instruments. I whispered to Lucy Carlisle. She came out with me immediately. Wentworth spoke

to her and they went away together. Newby called to me softly:
'Who is in there at present?'

I told him.

'I wish Katherine would come out to us.'

He caught my arm.

'Although the window is closed I hear something.'

I pulled aside the heavy curtain and looked out. The little moon
had left the roofs and risen into heaven. Piles of white cloud lay like
witches' necromancy in bales over the houses. There was a faint sickly
light. But what drew my attention was that crowds were forming in
Palace Yard. Because the windows were closed those moving figures
were like actors in a silent Masque, coming from all sides but without
any sound. They seemed to have no purpose but to assemble there
and were as immaterial as the buildings behind them in the thin,
sallow moonlight. Such crowds had not been uncommon during these
last months; ever since the day of Prynne and Bastwick in the pillory
they had from time to time assembled, but there was something
to-night of a dark foreboding that shook my heart.

'In God's name, Charles,' I said, 'what is to be the end of this?'

'Aye,' he answered, 'truly. In God's name.'

I dropped the curtain. The door opened again and it was Katherine
who came out. She was dressed in dark velvet with a thin necklace of
diamonds around her throat. She stood staring into the uncertain
candle-light. Charles Newby went eagerly forward to her.

'Was Wentworth here?'

'Yes.'

'Ah,—that was the message for Lucy.'

She came towards me.

'There is a great crowd in the Square,' I said.

'The Queen has been urging'—she dropped her voice—'has been
trying to persuade him to take action. Wentworth is here for that
also.' She caught my arm. 'Rashleigh—tell no one—but watch!'

'Watch?' I asked.

'Yes. Lucy. Lucy Carlisle. I do not trust her——'

'But she and Wentworth——'

'Oh, I know. . . . But also she and Pym——'

'Pym!'

'Hush. . . . I know what I say. I have sure information.'

'But Pym is Wentworth's deadliest foe. He will have his head——'

'He must not have it. Rather it must be Pym's head. And quickly.'

'That means civil war.'

'In any and every case now it means civil war. And the King let the Scots go. Have you heard of our army, riotous, disordinate, without proper food. . . .'

'Yes, but now there is Wentworth.'

'He is sick and has so many enemies.' She dropped her hand. She turned so that the candle-light was full upon her face. I had never seen her so beautiful nor so strange. There are times when she is like a prophetess, a seer of visions. At such times I have the feeling that part of her is not mortal. She looked at me and smiled.

'Rashleigh, I hate those candlesticks. I had a plan once for concealing them behind the musicians' gallery in the dining-hall. And then I considered that some wretched servant would be accused of stealing them. They are of bad omen. . . .' The gaiety left her voice. She seemed for a moment old. 'There are times, Rashleigh, when I could creep into a corner and weep like a baby—or would ask some kind gentleman to take me and care for me and protect me——'

'Ah, if you would!' broke in Charles, who was standing near.

'You think to wear me down, Charles. Maybe you will. But no mood lasts, Charles. After I have wept and you have comforted me, I run away.'

'At least,' he said, 'I will have comforted you.'

'And later I should hate you for that—and despise myself. I have noticed that there are so many obstinacies and piques and jealousies between men and women that only true love can soften and forgive them. And, alas, I love no one in this world. Neither does Rashleigh here—not at least with his body as well as his soul.'

'There are many kinds of love,' I said sententiously. The candles blew in a little breeze. I seemed to see the three of us—Newby, Katherine, myself—held in a kind of trance together as though we were waiting for news. A great pity for us all and for all men and women under God caught me.

Something of the same must have troubled Katherine, for she shivered.

'This room—these candles. That crowd outside. From to-night the first act of the tragedy——'

But she was interrupted because the door opened. Everyone came in, the brilliance lighting them from behind,—the King, the Queen, Mr. Jermyn, Goring, Endymion Porter, a number more.

The King stood a little away from them as though he were uncertain as to what he would do. He was dressed at his most royal, with his orders glittering upon his breast.

I thought how noble he looked. Whenever I think of him I consider that nobility. Short of stature though he is, he can command the greatest dignity of any man I have ever known. It was to-night a lonely dignity. He was lost altogether, I think, in his own thoughts, which must have been dark enough, but there came to him, I don't doubt, that reassurance, always so strong in him, that nothing and no one could touch him, that in his blood was divinity, that always what he did was best. I would not say that he was proud of himself; there was rather in him *for* himself a deep humility. But not for his position, the seat whereon God had placed him. There he was as proud as the dark angel Lucifer. If, as I have known him do, he will break his word or go back upon a friend he will always feel that he has been shown by God a better way and must follow it. He believes, too, that he is a great wielder of men and more able than the rest in following a tortuous path. The end justifies the means because it is God's end. All this may at any time override his heart, which is tender. But his heart and all will go before God's purpose that he should stay where he is. And so he stays—with his feet planted.

His face wore now that look of mingled pride and obstinacy. He looked like a half-blind man. He saw Charles and myself and moved forward to speak to us. As he came I saw his most splendid order, a glittering wheel of diamonds, rising and falling to the beat of his heart. As always when he was close to me I was eager to anticipate his least desire.

My heart beat for his heart.

'Sire,' Charles said, 'there is a crowd again in the Square.'

The King seemed but little interested.

'Charles, when I go North again I must visit Thornhurst and see the family portraits.'

'They are not very good, sire. We were always a beef-eating lot.'

The King did not laugh. I have very rarely on any occasion seen him laugh. But when anything amused him his upper lip trembled and his pointed beard quivered a little—and always his eyes looked out with sombre patience into a world that was behaving with great stupidity.

He moved across to the candlesticks.

'These are ugly,' he said almost petulantly. 'Too heavy by far and the workmanship coarse.' He held one in his beautiful thin fingers. The flame flew upwards like a savage tongue.

At the same moment a stone crashed through the window. It would have struck me had I not by a chance stepped back. I felt it close to my ear. It fell almost at the Queen's feet. By an odd fate it had found the thin space between the curtains left by me after I had looked out.

Everyone cried out. But the King was furious. Before anyone could stop him he dragged fiercely the curtains back and threw open the window. A blast of cold air and flurried snow blew into the room.

He stood there, drawn up like a soldier. We heard the murmur of the crowd but no raised voices. For a brief time we were all, as it were, paralysed. We lost perhaps the personal, physical sense of the King as a man in the consciousness of him as a symbol.

George Goring sprang forward, caught the King and pushed him quite roughly back, interposing his body between the King and the window.

'Pardon me, sire. . . . You must pardon me.'

He closed the window and drew over the curtains.

I had meanwhile taken a steady look. The little moon was obscured by the curd-coloured clouds that yet held some of its light.

The great crowd was dark. I could just see the bodies of three men raised on some stones or hoarding above the rest. Whether they spoke or not I could not tell.

Then the moon was more completely darkened and a black shadow like the approach of death fell over the scene.

NICHOLAS SEES THE SUN

ROSAMUND HAD WRITTEN to Katherine and Peter, as well as to Rashleigh, asking them to pay old Nicholas a visit before it was too late.

Early in the January of 1640 Katherine had a month's release from her duties with the Queen. She at once rode down to Mallory, vile though the roads were.

In the back of her mind had been the thought that Peter Garland might be there, but when in fact she saw him it was as though she saw a ghost, a symbol, a phantom—until he touched her, and then she knew, beyond any question, that at last and for the first time she loved a human being.

It was in the gallery at Mallory—a place, as it seemed, of especial meaning for these two.

She had arrived, dirty, weary-backed, and in a very vile temper, early in that cold, blowing, bitter January afternoon. She had washed, and changed her clothes. She was wearing a dress of very dark purple, shadowed-mulberry colour with a white lace collar. In her hair was a half-moon of diamonds. She entered the gallery, which was dark save for two high candles in chased silver candlesticks at the far end. There standing in the candle-light was Peter Garland. He stood rigid, his hands at his sides. She had not been sure that he would be at Mallory: she was not sure now that he was alive. She stayed as he stayed. She herself was carrying a small lighted candle; the flame lit her face, which seemed to Peter so exquisitely beautiful as to be beyond all earthly quality. So one ghost stared at the other ghost.

But Peter Garland was a very substantial ghost. He stood there, a symbol of iron determination. His body, clothed in black with only the plain white collar to relieve it, was solid and set as in earlier days it had never been.

His round friendly face had still something very honest, simple, even naïf about it, but the mouth was tight and the eyes bright with honour. His hair was not cropped as it had been, but fell to his collar. This was Cromwell's habit and Peter had taken it from him. His chest, arms, and legs were thick with strength. He gave a certain impression of heaviness. His forehead, eyes, mouth had a nobility they had not known before.

They moved towards one another, she holding her candle high. When he was quite close to her his face broke into a charming smile so that he was like the old Peter that had been more boy than man.

His hand touched hers and at once she let the candle that she was holding fall to the ground—for his arms were round her, their lips were fastened, her hand had moved up and the back of it rested, warm and soft, against his neck.

They moved to the blazing fire where once they had talked before.

They were hidden here by a crimson curtain from the far door and could themselves see the others. He knelt on the floor: she lay back on his knees, her face straining up into his. At last she said:

'Do you know, Peter, what age I am?'

'Age? . . . Age——?' He hardly heard her words. He bent down to her raised face and his cheek pressed hers. The softness of her cheek that he had so long desired was, in reality, a clutch on his heart that caught his breath. He could not have believed that anything could be both so soft and so strong.

When he put down his hand and cupped her breast she breathed very deeply as though through all the current of his own body.

'No. . . . At this moment you would not care. But it is a remarkable testimony. I am aged—well, no matter . . . and until this moment, ten minutes from four of the afternoon of the sixth of January, this year of grace 1640, I have never loved man nor woman——' She suddenly, with a little cry, raised herself, threw her arms around his neck, brought his head down to hers, covered his face with kisses.

'My dear . . . my dear . . . my lovely dear . . . my dear.'

Then she was out of his arms, on her feet, away from him, looking at him with a glance so deep and penetrating that it seemed to try to tell him something that he should know.

'That now,' she said, as though to herself, '—so late—that I should understand so late.'

He also had risen, and almost as he did so the door opened and Nicholas Herries entered. By the door there was the light of the two candles. The fire blaze was hidden by the curtain.

Peter and Katherine came towards him together.

Nicholas Herries was ninety-five years of age. His hair was snow-white, his face coloured a ruddy tan. His great height was lessened because his shoulders were bent, but his body was huge, not awkward nor cumbersome. He had the appearance of extreme cleanliness, as though his body had been washed and scrubbed by time. Stripped, his flesh had the purity of the new-born. His sightless eyes were brilliant and clear.

His attitude and behaviour now were very gentle; he was never angry, always of a quiet courtesy. Often when someone was talking his mind would wander. He was for ever thinking of the past, and especially of his dead brother Robin.

He would sigh at times as though he were deeply weary of life. Indeed his blindness must have been a never-ending burden to one who had been so greatly active, but he never complained, never appeared distressed by anything awkward that happened to him, like a stumble or the spilling of food.

If Rosamund had ever asked for any reward (which, being the woman she was, she had not) for a lifetime devotion she had it now. Upon her and Gilbert Armstrong, now an old, ruddy, wrinkled man, still strong and of absolute health, Nicholas altogether depended.

It was more than physical dependence. Perhaps the finest luck that can happen to a man in this world is to have a woman who loves him and a man who is his friend. The circle of love, in all its kinds, is then complete. It may be, too, that in old age, when all the powers and the glories, the lusts and ambitions are worn by corroding time away, a man realizes that love is the greatest power in all experience, and that with this enclothing him, he can march to the grave with high courage and a fearless step.

Nicholas had always loved both Rosamund and Armstrong, but he had been an active, fighting, hurrying kind of man and to every day there had been action. Now, when action was over, although he was not a deeply thinking man he might perceive that the true meaning of life, 'Brethren, see that ye love one another,' was clear and clean before his heart. So when he joined his dead brother—who was not dead to him—to his living wife and friend he was happily content.

During this last year or two everyone around him felt that he had entered into a new happiness. And when neither Rosamund nor Armstrong was close at hand he became restless.

'Are you there?—Are you there?' he would ask, and when the one voice or the other answered him his eyes would lighten and his mouth break into a contented smile.

He liked to be out of doors whenever possible. He loved to feel the sun, the wind, the rain upon his face. He would hold up his head and stare into the sky. He would look up and up until you would feel that he was gazing into immeasurable distances and could see far more than normal-sighted men.

He liked to go with Robert about the farm and fields, but even then he wanted Armstrong in attendance. Robert was very good with him, quiet, attentive, and patient, but Robert had much business; his life was increasingly full of it and especially since he had begun to be greatly interested in Seddon, was breeding northern cattle, and riding north a couple of times every year.

Robert and his father loved one another but never with intimacy. Robert was not a fighting man; he was for the King but wanted above all things peace in the country so that business might prosper. He had friends of both parties.

But Nicholas had a very simplified view of the whole matter. Simply the King could do no wrong. He listened to disputes and arguments but never joined in them because for him the whole affair was completely settled. He was like a man who had seen God and therefore argument was needless.

Had he been thirty or forty years younger he would have become, as events moved, the perfect example of the grand old Cavalier— single of heart, courteous to all, fearless, gay, unquestioning. England would have many of those before a few years had passed. But he did not join in any battle; he was outside it. When Peter talked to him of Cromwell and Hampden and Pym he did not curse them for rebels against the King but, in his heart, pitied them for lost men.

He had still a love of beautiful women. He could not any longer tell whether they were beautiful but he liked to kiss gently a young girl's cheek or hold her hand, and he would talk to them of how it had been in earlier days, and of the most beautiful woman he had ever known, and of a Lake that she had stood beside while the sun set over the hills.

But he was now wrapped right inside Rosamund's heart. His blindness seemed to give him a deep insight into her nature. He had always known that nature to be beautiful, kind and true, and altogether unselfish, but now he found riches there that before, perhaps, he had never suspected.

He would sit close beside her while she was working at something and would hum to himself (he loved now in his old age to hear singing and often wished that Frederick could be there). He liked, too, to hear men sing a catch or a round and would join lustily himself, always a little out of tune.

He liked Rosamund to tell him everything that had happened to her during the day. Very often his mind would wander while she talked, but he remembered surprisingly what she told him. He would sleep a good deal during the day, and when he slept he seemed to dream, for there was often a happy smile on his face.

When he made a false step or blundered against someone he would make a most gentle apology, explaining that he wished to put no one to any inconvenience. His consciousness of his brother Robin grew ever more clear to him and it was perhaps the only matter in which he was a little wild. He would talk to Robin, welcoming him as though he had just come into the room. Their great enemy, Philip Irvine, was also sometimes there and he would warn Robin of Irvine, telling him not to trust him in anything.

This was the only instance in which his face would grow stern, his bright eyes darken, his mouth grow hard. He would speak of Irvine as though he had struggled with him on the Guy Fawkes night, only then he had not slain him as he should have done but had allowed him to escape.

Peter Garland, after his meeting with Katherine in the gallery, stayed in that state of bliss that is shot with rays of light so blinding that there is no vision, while music from heaven entrances the spirit.

Recovering a little from this state he discovered Nicholas blind, Frederick Courthope arrived on a visit, a letter from Cromwell, and Katherine herself in a mist of heat and beauty.

The letter from Cromwell was as follows:

Let me hear from you as you can. Instead of pitying you I can a little bewail myself; have I not one friend in our society to whom I can unbowel myself! You are absent, Darby is gone, Hampden is in London. I am left alone, almost so, but not forsaken. Lend me one shoulder. Pray for me. The Lord restore you. My hearty love to you. If I had more you should have it.

What would Cromwell say to his marriage with Katherine? She was a lady of the Court, a close friend of the Queen. He consoled himself by remembering how many persons belonged to both parties. It was said everywhere that Lucy Carlisle was a friend of Pym as well as of Wentworth. George Goring was thought to be a comrade of both camps, and so with many more.

Katherine had never shown any compelling interest in politics.

Nevertheless he could not see her with Cromwell, Hampden, and the others. But then he could not see her anywhere but in his arms. When you stand in a room with the mirrors so arranged you may look and find the same scene repeated back and back and so into infinity. It was so with him now, seeing her lie against his knees, pull his head down to her, cover his face with kisses. Her half-whispered confession that at last she loved came into his heart with a burning delight and spread through all his body, so that his limbs were in a fever, his throat was dry, his eyes were hot.

And, as to every lover since time began, it seemed to him that no one had ever loved like this before nor ever would again.

For three days they scarcely spoke together. She would not allow herself to be alone with him; after Frederick's arrival she appeared nervous, over-excited, quite unlike her amused, collected, scornful self. Then he caught her—in the little ante-chamber to the chapel. This was a room approached by stairs hung with a deep gold-and-green tapestry of the Journey of St. Ursula, the heavy door gilded. It was a room used for the most part for musicians to practise in. He came out from the chapel and saw her about to leave. He slammed the door, set the bolt in it, stood with his back to it. A moment later they were in one another's arms.

She thrust her lovely hand down inside his vest and laid it, with a coolness like heaven's peace, against his thumping heart. Once again he knelt on the floor and she lay strained against him, her mouth on his.

After a while and they murmuring one another's names in a lovers' litany, she sat on one of the small stools that the musicians used, he knelt against her looking up into her face, his hand closed on her breast.

She spoke very low and at first he did not listen very much, for he was in such a delirium of ecstasy that he spun like a gilded top in an airy maze, hot, filled with her scent, and whirring. But her voice came through the maze at last.

'And so, Peter, I wish you to understand this. At last I know what love is. I am of middle age. I have had all experience but this——'

'I think we have loved one another always but did not know it until now—or you did not.'

'Perhaps I did.' Her voice was thin and sweet like the low string o a viol. 'Perhaps that was why I said things to hurt you years ago in Keswick.'

She put up her long, delicate hands and cupped his face. Then she kissed his cheeks, slowly, with long-drawn kisses.

'I think I have clung to my independence like a hermit to his virtue —because I have known how sweet it would be to lose it.'

He took her hands from his face.

'Now that I have you at last after these days we must be serious. When do we marry?'

She looked at him, staring into his eyes.

'Do you wish to marry me?'

'But of course—of course.'

'You know, Peter, how it will be? What will your friends, Cromwell, John Hampden, say to me?'

'They will accept you triumphantly.'

'Ah, but they cannot accept me—I belong to the King.'

'You belong now to me.'

'Nay, but, Peter—would you desert Cromwell for me?'

'No. Not Cromwell. Not the people. Not God.'

'Well, then——'

'Ah, but you have no politics. You are free. I am the first person to bind you. You have said so.'

'Yes, to bind me. But in what sort? I love you, Peter. You are the first I have ever loved. I will love you until I die. I love you and will love you through all circumstance. But I will not move *against* circumstance. For your sake I will not.'

She looked into his eyes as before, but she had moved away from him. She was not touching him. The note in her voice was changed and, as all lovers know, he feared with a sudden ghastly dismay what her next words might be.

'Against circumstance? What circumstance could there be?'

She leaned over from the stool and kissed him again with a long, clinging passion. Then she got up and moved to the door:

'The one irremovable circumstance—I married Charles Newby in secret six days ago.'

In the morning Peter heard that Katherine was gone. Rosamund said that she had suddenly resolved that the Queen needed her. Rosamund was sorry.

That day Peter walked in the cold rain along a road that had no ending. He had spent a night of wild agony.

The lover rejected after happiness recalls the minutiae of past passion, forcing them into gigantic figures, sounds, colours.

The two occasions of their intimacy tortured him by their insistent presence. Every word, every movement was actual and bitterly ironic. The warmth of her body as she lay against his knees, the scent of her hair as it brushed his lips, the whiteness of her neck, her eyes gazing into his expressing her own wonder that at last love had come to her, her voice, deep, beating with her amazement, above all the moment when her hand had found his heart—all these and many more were such gibing torment that he stood in his bed-chamber straight, taut, his arms stretched as though he were being crucified.

At one moment in the early morning hours, when the rain was beating on the windows, he cried aloud. A new demon possessed him. He would have her and throw all else away—the Cause, his soul, his God. He would go to her and tell her that he was hers to use as she would. He knew that half an hour alone together and they would be lovers. Even through that thick madness he realized that, in doing this, he would certainly lose his soul, as he understood the meaning of life, and that, for such as he, all miseries would follow.

But he sat on the bed-edge and like a cunning devil invented what he would do, going to her in the morning, surrendering to her, following her to London, going with her into some dark hidden place, holding her naked in his arms, having his moment of savage glory. . . . His brain spun, his eyes were small and bitter, his mouth a little loose and wet, his hands clenched, his legs apart as though now he held her. He whispered: 'Katherine! Katherine!'

But in the morning she was gone, and for that minute at least he was saved.

He strode out into the rain and walked that unending road. He saw Katherine as she cupped his face with her hands and he saw Christ crucified.

In the thin spidery rain it seemed to him that someone walked at his side. His vision of Christ Jesus had been always an intensely personal one. He had, since his childhood, known Christ as his friend rather than as God. That was why all ceremonies had seemed otiose. If you had a friend you touched his hand and all was well. The Roman Mass had appeared to him as worship belonging to someone with whom you could never have friendly talk. And so with gold vestments, lights, incense. Christ Jesus was more actual to him than his own body. When Christ walked on the waters it was he, Peter Garland, who was in the boat. When the children gathered around Him it was Peter Garland who guided their steps. In the Garden of Gethsemane he slept.

For the first time in his living experience another figure interposed. There were three of them walking that road. Her sweetness was so profoundly in his heart. Even when she had abused him in the Keswick room there had been that last look before he left her; he now saw it as a sign that she had loved him even then, although she did not know it.

He now saw with a dreadful vision that, whatever he did, she would be always between him and his friend Christ Jesus. She would be between himself and Cromwell and the cause of the liberty of the people of his country and all the good, simple, determined things that had been in his heart. She would be always with him and *against* his true life. He could not escape that.

He cried out: 'God save me! God save me!'—and even as he cried he felt the cool, strong back of her hand against his neck.

But the figure still kept company with him—a dull, persistent figure. He was fearfully weary. It was a weariness of his whole body which ached as though it had been chastised. His clothes sodden with rain hung heavily about him. The rain stung his face as though it were a bee-swarm.

Still the figure stayed beside him.

'Christ's sufferings were harder than these.'

But Christ may walk beside you and yet the lust of the flesh is more real. One does not challenge the other unless you wish it. Why had she done this to him, allowed it when she knew her own secret? But he could not condemn her. He had never condemned her.

He was so weary with unhappiness that he sank down by the side of the road, pressing his hands to his head. Then it was that his Companion stayed beside him, his hand resting on his shoulder, absolute comprehension in that touch.

'Are you there? Are you there?'

Nicholas' hand reached out and found Rosamund's. He could feel the heat of the fire on his eyes, and when he put his arm around her and drew her close to him he sighed happily.

But she noticed at once that he was changed since yesterday.

'Ah, Catherine. . . . Ah, Catherine! You contrive that puzzle wisely, for once in my arms. . . . Has Gilbert had you? Are you treacherous then? No, no . . . never. . . . I will never hold it——' He pressed Rosamund's hand and said quite sensibly: 'What's for dinner, wife?'

'A veal pie—an apple pudding——'

'It is like the day we were wedded.'

'Nay, snow is falling. Then the sun was shining.'

He sighed and caught her hand, and held it against his cheek.

'Aye, to see the sun again! To see the sun!' He kissed her. 'We have never been so close as now. Know you, wife, that I have never been so happy as now? Fighting and kissing young maids are all well enough, but to sit down, fighting done, quietly with those you love is the true reward. Have I been an ill husband to you?'

He spoke with real anxiety, his old face wrinkled up, his eyes brightly staring.

'No. No. . . . A better husband has never been.' She laughed. 'You know, Nicholas, if you had been a tyrant, I would have forgiven you everything. As it is I have nothing to forgive.'

They sat silent together, wrapped in perfect content.

That same night they lay together in the high poster, fast asleep. Rosamund woke to find that he was struggling to rise from the bed. In the stone fireplace a fire was still blazing. She put out a hand to stay him because she knew that his heart was very weak.

'Stay. Stay. . . . What is it?'

He was wearing a thin lawn shirt drawn to his waist and over it a fur robe.

He stood up with the firelight on him. He had his head forward as though he were watching. She could not tell whether he were still asleep but there was something so urgent in his fierce appearance that she did not move. She would be sworn that his eyes could see. The fur robe fell off him and his great neck and legs and arms were bare.

He said in a soft, low voice: 'Why must you kill her? She never did you any harm.' Then he added to himself: 'Had she been there or not been we must have met.' He nodded his head.

It was then as though someone had thrown himself on Nicholas, for he started back, swerving, then pushed the white hair from his eyes, stamped his foot, and stretched his arm as though in sword movement.

His breath came fiercely. He cried sharply: 'Ha! Ha! Ha!' Once he cried: 'The wind! The wind!' He moved about the room fighting, it seemed, a duel. He drew himself to his full height, his shift rising above his navel. His forehead grew dark and gloomy. He moved forward, he retreated. He bent back his great throat as though a dagger were stabbing at it.

Then it seemed he had someone in his arms. He swayed on his feet. He raised himself to tiptoe as if he were lifting a body.

'Ugh!' he cried. 'Ugh!' Then, his white head thrown back, the cords in his neck strained, his knees bent and then straightening, his whole giant height extended, the vast muscles of his back standing thick and distended beneath his shift, he cried 'Hulloa! Hulloa! Hulloa!' and again 'Hulloa! Hulloa! Hulloa!' then moved as though throwing something from him. . . .

He sighed, his chest heaved. He staggered towards the bed.

He looked at Rosamund and beyond her.

She caught him in her arms as he fell forward.

His face against hers he murmured: 'The sun! The sun! I see the sun!'

And died in her arms.

END OF PART II

PART III

Kinsmen at War

THE BETRAYAL

Pages from the Journal of Rashleigh Garland

AT LAST the Palace is quiet. The confused roar of this last terrible Saturday, the dismal horror of that foulest of all Sundays—both have died away. My bed-chamber window is open, but there is no sound from the Square save just now the linkman crying ironically the quiet of the night. It is May and there is a smell of blossom—possibly from the King's room—out of his window and into mine.

I am cold and feel encased in horn. It has not been for nothing that all my life long I have been growing that covering. It was to meet that moment when the King, yielding to the Queen who heard that her mother was threatened by the mob, bowed his head. As I saw that and watched the King's eyes lidded, I knew, for ever and for ever, that man is of no worth, is false and traitorous and a coward. I will not call the King these things. The King is divine, but as the Pope, being God's representative, may curse because soup is hot in his mouth, so does this man, inside his royalty, betray his fidelity.

I serve him none the less. Nay—the more rather. For he must have men about him to guard his Kingship.

I must go back and put everything down.

I had been on duty the preceding night and was for sleeping late, but on that Saturday morning I woke abruptly to a knocking on the door and another noise which at first to my waking ears sounded like water slapping on a rock. This was mingled with my dreams until, erect in bed, I realized that the sound of water was men's voices and that the knocking on the door had panic in it.

251

What is this panic? How easily our security can be broken and dispersed! I had in fact been dreaming of Wentworth—or Strafford as he now is. If there is one thing in this ill-adjusted world that I admire, it is fidelity. That rock-bound man has an infinite courage, but more than his courage is his fidelity.

I had had one last conversation with him before they took him to the Tower. He knew that Pym and Vane and the rest would have his head if they could. But he was sure that he would beat them.

When Pym on November 6th had proposed and carried a motion for a committee to enquire into the complaints of the King's subjects in Ireland all knew what that meant for Strafford, and his friends implored him to return to Ireland or at any rate not to appear in Parliament. Instead he instantly took post to London. This he reached on November 10th and it was on the morning of the fatal 11th that I saw him and spoke with him. He had been to see the King and was then on his way to the House of Lords.

He came out from the King and stopped when he saw me.

'Ah, Mr. Garland,' he said. I had not thought that he would know me. He was wearing a suit of dark purple. I could see that he was very far from well. His brown, dark, furrowed face, the eyes set in it like sombre-blazing lights, could yet have much sweetness when he saw a friend.

As his hand touched mine I knew well his faults—his imperiousness, arrogance, stubbornness, narrowness. But I knew also his strength, his fearlessness, his great loyalty. I saw his breast rise and fall. I could see that he suffered under an immense excitement, as well he might, seeing that he was at the very crisis of his fortune and was going at that very moment into the stronghold of his enemies.

'The King is very gracious, Mr. Garland,' he said. His face melted into sweetness. He had been married three times, Lucy Carlisle and others had been said to be his mistresses, and yet he was not at all, I think, a sexual man. He loved the King, his children, his country, and more than any of these, save the King, his own way, but in none of these was there anything of the flesh. You might think that his limbs were made of granite, save for the aches and pains that were for ever prostrating them.

'Your friends, my lord,' I answered, 'have wished that you might be in Ireland until this danger is past.'

'Danger! Danger? Why, man—so long as the King is behind me what can they do?' His strong, stern mouth twisted ironically. He rested his lean hand on my shoulder. I fancy that pains attacked him.

'I have my enemies, but so must any man who sees his way clear. And for myself, what do I care?' His hand dug deeper into my shoulder.

'Mr. Garland, had you suffered in physical torture what I during these last years have suffered, death must seem to you a kindly resting-place. Only my children—I would have them provided for. . . .' He stood looking out over my shoulder.

'Ah, well. . . .' He grinned at me and his face was monkey-like. 'We must see what they have to say. . . .' And he marched away.

All know by now what happened after that. Some say that he had not taken his seat on that afternoon when Pym presented himself at the Bar of the House and prayed their Lordships to commit him immediately to prison. Strafford, however, moved towards his place. There rose then a great clamour, voices calling out that he must 'void the House.'

He was nevertheless allowed his place and from there pleaded for his liberty. He was forced to withdraw, however, and in his absence the Lords committed him to the custody of the Black Rod. On his return he stood erect but was ordered to kneel, and knelt. Some who saw him say that he never looked more splendid and commanding than in that last moment before he knelt. 'Like a rebel angel,' some have said. The order of the Lords was then read to him by the Lord Keeper from the Woolsack. He left the House in the Usher's charge. He passed the night at the house of his guard and soon after that he was taken to the Tower.

After that there is the story that all the world knows and that history will finger again and again. Sometimes in world or national crises events outrun Time. They snap their thin, active fingers at the slow old man. So it has been now.

On December 10th Laud was arrested and lodged in the Tower, but it was not till three months after this that the accusation against Strafford was complete. In that time the charges against him grew to ninety-eight!

On January 30th he came by water from the Tower to Westminster and was cursed and abused by the crowd all the way. Because of his gout he was permitted an extra fortnight to prepare his defence.

At seven o'clock on the morning of March 22nd he was at last conveyed again by water to the Tower. A hundred soldiers guarded him. He presented himself then at their Lordships' Bar and remained standing while the charges were read out to him. Everything they could summon to mind, even to frivolity, was brought against him. The Committee management of the Commons against him (I have as yet written nothing in my Journal of this trial) were Pym, Hampden, Whitelocke, Stroude, Lord Digby, Oliver St. John, Sir Walter Earle, Sir John Clotworthy, Geoffrey Palmer, Serjeant Maynard, and Glyn, Recorder of London. Pym, who hated Strafford, was of course the leading spirit (and Lucy Carlisle the mistress of them both! What confidences she must cherish!) Pym from the first called Strafford 'the wicked Earl.'

There was unfairness from the outset, for Strafford, a gravely sick man, was kept on his defence from early morning until late afternoon, and on one day (March 26th) was forced to declare that he was ready to drop down in respect of his much sickness and weakness. I, aware of the man's character as I am, know full well what the torture must have been before he would come to such a plea!

On April 9th he failed to make an appearance and peers visited the Tower to see how severe his sickness might be! As though Strafford were a man for malingering!

Things appeared to be well for him when on April 10th, the door of the House having been locked, Pym, rising, produced a paper containing Sir Henry Vane's rough notes of the proceedings at the Committee of Council. It was here that Strafford was accused of speaking treason.

Young Vane (for whom I have always had a great detestation) stood up and confessed that he had illicitly stolen these notes from his father's cabinet. Strafford's reputed words were as to the using of Irish troops for the service of the King against rebels in England.

After that, on April 13th, Strafford offered a superb defence: I would estimate it one of the great speeches of all time. He ended with these noble words which I now copy into my Journal:

You will be pleased to pardon my infirmity; something I should have said, but I see I shall not be able—and therefore I will leave it. And now my Lords, for myself, I thank God I have been, by His good blessing to wards me, taught that the afflictions of this present life are not to be compared with that eternal weight of glory that shall be revealed hereafter. And so, my Lords, even so, with all humility and with all tranquillity of mind, I do submit myself clearly and freely to your judgments, and whether that righteous judgment shall be to life or death, *Te Deum laudamus, te Dominum confitemur.*

Well,—'stone dead hath no fellow.' The Bill of Attainder was read for the second time on April 14th, and on the third reading Lord Digby rose and said he could not vote for the Bill. He said that the charge that Strafford could be proved to have advised the King to bring over the Irish Army for the reducing of England—the only charge worthy of death—had *not* been proved. Digby said: 'I do with a clear conscience wash my hands of this man's blood.'

Afterwards printer and publisher of this speech were declared delinquent and the speech ordered to be publicly burnt by the common hangman, and the King *requested* to confer no honour nor employment on Lord Digby! To such a pass has my poor country come!

On April 30th the King (myself among others in attendance) went down in person to the House of Lords, summoned the Commons, and informed Parliament that he could not consider Lord Strafford to have been guilty of high treason but that 'he could not say he could clear him of misdemeanour.' He desired therefore that he should be found guilty on the minor charge.

It was thought by all of us at the time that these were the tactics advised to the King by Lord Strafford himself. Whether they were so or not, the results were the terrors of these last two days that I am now to describe. As I have said, it had been on this Friday night that I had been dreaming of Strafford.

In my dream I encountered him in the garden at Mallory. It was the quiet silver twilight of a summer evening and he came out suddenly from behind the dark box-hedges and confronted me. How real and actual dreams are—so real that day life fades often into unreality beside them! I could hear the water of the fountain falling, and a voice singing. I could see a thin dew veiling the bright grass; Strafford's face stern and anxious. He greeted me like an old confidential friend, and I had no doubt in my dream but that we had known one another for years with intimacy.

'I have been telling them,' he said, 'it is of England that we should all be thinking. But we are not. Only of our own fears and greeds.'

'You at least are not afraid,' I said, for he seemed to stand in that garden towering against the pale night sky, dark and lowering.

'No, I am not afraid. But we must not do things by halves. Once I thought to save England in that way, but the people are not ripe for it. They are not ripe for it, my friend. They do not know enough, they are not wise enough, to rule themselves. Not yet. One day perhaps. Not yet—not yet. And so it must be the other way. Their ruling must be done for them. Their King must rule and he must be thorough. I with him. I for him. Always for everything—for him.'

In my dream he did not seem to be agitated but calm and grave, as though he knew that a very important hour had come.

But as we stood talking it seemed to me that it grew dark about us, and the hedges closed in on us.

I felt my own apprehension and I knew that he felt some also, for he drew nearer to me and his breath came a little hurriedly. Then he smiled with great sweetness.

'At least I am the King's friend and he is mine. I do all for him and our country. He knows that. I will be faithful to him and he will be faithful to me.'

A little wind that had gone creeping among the thick, trim hedges seemed to repeat:

'I will be faithful to him and he will be faithful to me——'

I woke myself murmuring those words, and I was at once aware of the noise beyond my window and the knocking on my door.

I pulled my bed-gown about me and went to open the door. Frederick Courthope stood there. Frederick is now, I should imagine, near thirty years of age. I do not care for him and yet I have nothing whatever against him except that he is ambitious, and why should I hold that against any man because I am not ambitious myself?

Soon after the marriage of Katherine to Charles Newby he left Newby's service. The new Marchioness of Newby had never a deep affection for him, I should fancy. But he moved, not only out of personal chagrin but, as he always moves, to better himself. He entered George Goring's service and is an intimate with Lucy Carlisle and an intermediary with King Pym and the others, I should not wonder. He has in any case no God but Frederick Courthope.

But I repeat—why should I dislike him? He is slim and sleek, with a beautiful voice both for speaking and singing. He is able and active, malicious, I am sure, and not one to forget an injury but with no great evil in his heart. A Rosencrantz or Guildenstern from the play *Hamlet*. Abler than either.

This divagation is because I have long wished to make a note of him in my Journal—a family note. He is of importance in our family.

He pushed past me into my room. I could see that for once he was too deeply agitated to remember his manners. Without a word he went to the windows, pulled back the curtains. The May morning sun flooded the room. He stood there looking out. I saw by the clock that it was later than I had supposed.

Then he turned and made his apologies.

'Cousin Rashleigh . . . it is unpardonable. . . . My excitement . . .'

He *was* excited, but not as a true man ought to be. There was a chill, calculating colour to his eye.

I went to my window. The Palace Yard was packed with an angry crowd.

'It is said,' Frederick began, 'that Bristol has been killed—torn from his coach—and that they say they will do the same by Digby.'

I watched a man, on an upturned barrel, yelling. Women, like mad-women, shrieked, running hither and thither like distraught hens. A deep disgust of my fellow-men seized me, of the mob, of the people —the people that are, and for ever will be, blown any way, for any mad end, without reason, because a man abuses them, or flatters, or promises.

I thought of Shakespeare's *Julius Caesar*.

Frederick was watching me.

'They say that there is an army plot for Strafford's rescue.'

'They say—who say?' I asked contemptuously.

'I said—it is a rumour.'

Against the wall was the flat bath, three ewers of water beside it, that I daily used, much to the humorous scorn of certain of my fellow-courtiers.

'And now I will dress, Frederick.' He still lingered. 'Well—if you have a fancy to see me bathe . . .'

I threw off my bed-gown and filled the bath.

He watched me.

' 'Fore God, Rashleigh, any woman——'

'I am fifty-three years of age, Frederick. I might be your father but am not——'

I could see that he was intrigued by me.

'You have no vices, Rashleigh. Women mean nothing to you. You have no ambition—no friend although you might have the world—only the King——'

'Where is the King?' I asked sharply.

'With the Queen.'

I thought of Strafford who still seemed at my side.

'The King will never forsake Strafford——'

Frederick said nothing. He watched me as the water poured down my back.

'The King will refuse the Bill.'

Still he said nothing.

Moved by a sudden intolerable, ungovernable rage, I leaped from the bath and, the water showering from my body, seized Frederick's thin shoulders and, with my soaking hands, shook him. My lank hair fell into my eyes but I was also blinded with anger.

'Speak—you dolt—you fool.'

But Frederick, who cared for his appearance and must have hated my soaking bare body so close to him, did not retreat. He did not move. He stared straight into my eyes.

'Your only faith, Rashleigh . . .' he said. 'But you do wrong to believe in a weak man. It is too dangerous——' And he left me.

I felt an exceeding grime about my body. The dirty people! The dirty people—who would run here or there as you called them—and Strafford in my dream saying: 'I will be faithful to him and he will be faithful to me. . . .'

As night fell I felt a great horror and dread in Whitehall. I do not wish at all to exaggerate my words. I wish to set down only what is true. Many others beside myself felt as I, and will never so long as they live forget that night.

Although it was May the night was cold. In the outer hall a great fire burned in the brazier and, as I saw the guard clustered about it, I thought of Peter and his denial. But we were all of us there in that building thinking of the same thing and of the same person. Strafford was not in the Tower; he was there, with all of us, in the Palace. Would the King sign the Bill or would he not? I knew that he would not, but behind my certainty was a dark unpenetrated dimness. Frederick's last words haunted me all that day. Rumour was flying everywhere. It had not been true that they had murdered Bristol, but Pym had seen to it that the London crowd that day and night was excited to madness. They would have Strafford's blood. They would murder every man and woman in Whitehall if they could not have it.

But that would not frighten the King. I had never seen the King frightened.

And for every reason worthy to God and to His angels the King must now stand by his man. Right or wrong, all that Strafford had done, in the North of England, in Ireland, in every place, had been for the King and with the King's knowledge. If the people judged Strafford worthy of death, then they must judge the King worthy of death also—and that night, as I stared into the hall fire, death seemed a little thing beside dishonour. But then I have never valued life over-much. Neither had the King. I saw his whole life to be judged by this moment and I did not doubt but that he would so see it.

However that king of the people, Pym, might stir the mob and frighten the women, he could not frighten the King, by divine right, of England. So I saw it, so Strafford saw it, so the King must see it.

But as the night advanced, rumour crept everywhere. The Palace was filled with strange sounds and stirrings. No one slept. The Palace Yard was still. I was on duty for part of the night outside the King's bedroom. How strange and foreboding seemed that long, dark passage, quivering at the far end of it with a covered flare that blew in the wind. I could not rid my mind of the absurd fancy that Strafford stood beside me. He slept in the Tower, and yet he was at my side asking me gravely whether he might see the King. He must not, I told this shadow, disturb the King's rest.

But the King was not resting. Once, about two of the morning, he sent his bed-chamber man out for me.

I entered and saw that he was sitting, dressed, at a candle-lit table, writing. His bed had not been slept in. Two spaniels stretched by the fire stirred at my entrance and slapped the floor with their tails. The King raised his head and looked at me for a moment bewildered, as though he did not remember me—he who saw me every day of his life. Then, still staring at me, he nodded his head.

'Ah, Mr. Garland!'

He was very pale, but he never had a bright colour. His eyes expressed an infinite weariness. He looked at me as though I could answer some question for him. Then he asked me to find ᴗoring and send him to him.

I bowed and went out.

I found Goring with several other officers pacing the hall.

I liked Goring although I did not trust him. I told him that the King wished to see him. His stout, florid cheeks drew in a little.

As we walked away he said eagerly:

'Well—what is the news?'

'There is none that I know of.' We had lowered our voices as though there were a sick man somewhere.

Goring said: 'It is rumoured that he has consulted the Bishops— the King, I mean.' Then he added: 'How narrow a majority for the Bill—twenty-six for, nineteen against.'

I said: 'The King most certainly will not sign.'

He looked at me anxiously.

'You think so?' He went on: 'If he wishes for my advice now—what am I to say?'

'Say!' My voice was louder and indignant. 'Why, that he must refuse the Bill, come what may.'

Goring rubbed his cheeks. 'Come what may—the death of all of us . . .'

'Strafford must not be left! Never, never, never!'

I was shaking—for I knew that my life was concerned—a small thing beside Strafford's—but mine was spiritual, my very faith in life itself.

I know that often, in later times, when I look back on these events I shall wonder what Goring really felt that night. He is a mystery, so bluff and hearty as he seems. Is he against the King or for him?

He pulled me up abruptly with a hand on my arm.

'Hi! Who goes there?'

We were at the beginning of the long, dark passage that led to the King's room. Under the shifting light of the covered flare it seemed to both of us that we saw a figure. I could feel Goring's heart beating against my side. I knew that he thought it was Strafford. When we approached the place there was no one there.

I had one other visitor during that night—not an intentional one.

About six of the morning Katherine passed me. I stopped her.

'Katherine!' I cried softly.

Since she had become the Marchioness of Newby we had had no intimate talks. She seemed to be twice as proud and reserved as she had been. I could tell from her behaviour to Charles Newby that she was perfectly aware that, in marrying him, she had committed an irrevocable fault. I could tell this from her solicitude for him, her tender kindness to him. He appeared to be in a state of blissful happiness. She knew that I knew, so she avoided me.

Now she stopped. There was a veil on her hair. Her face was pale and anxious.

'Rashleigh—I am going to the Queen. She is afraid for her mother's safety.'

'The town is very quiet,' I said.

'For the moment.' She looked into my face and smiled, a sad friendly smile, making her seem, at the moment, almost an old woman.

'Is there anything I can tell the Queen?'

'Nothing that I know.'

She shuddered. 'It has been a horrible night.' She drew closer to me, lowering her voice.

'You know that Strafford has written to the King entreating him to assent to the Bill. There he is his noble self. Like you, Rashleigh—always the King, the King . . . ! In the letter he appealed for his children——'

I nodded my head. I had heard of the letter.

'And the Bishops have said to the King that his public conscience as a King might oblige him to do what was against his conscience as a man.'

She caught my arm.

'Oh, he will not think so! He will not think so, Rashleigh!'

My body was shivering but I caught her hand and held it firmly.

'He will not desert his servant. He is not of that colour.'

She looked at me, her eyes speculating in mine. 'Oh, we are caught, Rashleigh! So suddenly! The Devil catches us. . . . He may be caught. Because of his children, because of the Queen, because of his people.'

'Anything rather than such a betrayal—such a dishonour!'

'Ah,' she said lightly, 'that, Rashleigh, is because you have never yet betrayed a man!'

And she passed like a ghost, without footfall, on her way.

I come now, with all the speed that I may, to the scene that, although I am recording it only some twelve hours after its occurrence, will, I know, mark the turning-point of my life's experience. I have, because of it, to dedicate myself to an obedience that would seem perhaps to any other man a hollow one—but an obedience that I already perceive to be as necessary as it was when I believed in the object of it. I dedicate myself henceforth to an idea and not to a man.

Whatever I may think afterwards of last night and the day that has followed it, it must stand to me as an allegory of my own spirit, set down before me in a figure—and that figure is the figure of the King.

After my short conversation with Katherine I was released from my duty. I sought my room, undressed, and slept in a deep, dreamless abandonment.

When I woke it was full day and I was struck immediately by the stillness everywhere. I was in attendance on the King at midday. I dressed, read for a half-hour in *The Faerie Queene,* and then went to the King.

I found him pacing his room while Goring, Bishop Juxon, and one or two others stayed silently in the background.

On seeing me, but regarding me blindly as he had done on the preceding day, he broke out:

'This is a falsity—a false reckoning. . . . You advise me to a life-long regret.'

He was addressing, it seemed, Bishop Juxon. In his voice there was a desperate weariness. After he had spoken he turned his head towards first one and then another—to everyone in the room. He rested finally on myself:

'They are persuading me, Mr. Garland. . . . I must not do it. I must not do it.'

Goring spoke then:

'Lord Strafford, sire, in his own letter to you . . .'

But the King interrupted him hysterically. 'I know it, man—I know it. Do you think I cannot estimate after this time and these doings what a nature he has? But were he to bid me a thousand times over

. . .' He broke off and then, pitifully, his voice broken, speaking as no king should: 'Oh, God, that I must decide this! There is the Queen, my children, this kingdom. And will they listen if I refuse to sign—Pym, Vane, and the others? What will it be but the same?'

Here I spoke: 'One lead from you, sire, and the country is behind you and Strafford himself——'

'Behind me? Behind me? Why, no, Mr. Garland—in front of me rather. The country would lead me, tell me where I should go, what I should do, what moneys I should have, how I should be with my wife and my children. . . . And Strafford—whether I sign or no they will kill him. They have sworn it.'

I knew then that this was the crisis not only of his life, of mine, but of all of ours, and I saw with great clarity in an instant of vision that what he decided now would settle the fate of England. Had I been but his equal, his close friend, I believe even then I might have turned him, taken his arm, held him close to me, shown him the vision that I saw.

But he was my King.

Even then, though, it had been almost settled, for his body straightened, his head was lifted. He said with a new sternness: 'Gentlemen, I cannot betray my honour. . . . I will not . . .'

And at that moment, that exact moment (for so men's fates are hardened, the Devil waiting for the moment to strike again where his former blow has been planted), there was a scurry of voices outside the room, the door was thrown open, and the Queen entered. Only Lucy Carlisle was with her.

She was a child in a desperate panic. She threw herself at the King's feet. Her cheeks streamed with tears; she clasped his knees, drew him, standing as he was, towards her, and cried out. She had been all for saving Strafford and on a preceding night had worked on a letter to both Houses that the Prince of Wales had taken. But now she could think only of her mother, Marie de Médicis. The people were crying that the Queen's mother was responsible, that but for her Strafford's death was certain. They were moving to tear her to pieces. In broken French and English the Queen cried to the King to spare her, to save her, to surrender Strafford.

She seemed to all of us truly a child as she knelt there on the floor, calling him endearing names, appealing to his love for her, beseeching him. . . .

The King looked over her head into my eyes. I am sure that he did not see me. And yet he seemed to say to me:

'We are lost.'

Then his eyelids fell. He bent his head. He raised the Queen. I knew that it was true—we were lost.

THE BETRAYED

Pages from the Journal of Rashleigh Garland

AT ELEVEN OF THE CLOCK on this night, May 11, 1641, the King called for me and gave me a letter which I was to deliver to Lord Strafford in the Tower. The King's face was white and drawn but he was perfectly composed. His hand did not tremble.

As I rode with my man, Hendricks (a Dutchman recommended to me by Charles Newby—a perfect servant), I could see that the town was preparing as though for a great festival. A mob was already pushing towards Tower Hill. The town was doubly filled with visitors, every house and tavern being overcrowded. As we rode, I with my cloak about my face and wishing that, after all, I had gone by boat, people pressed about me crying:

> '*After Black Tom Tyrant's gone*
> *Then you'll see what shall be done!*'

It seemed to me as a dream rather than reality. The King's action had committed him, as I saw it and now still see it, to certain lines. I am shamed indeed to write these words in my Journal, but, after this, how can any man ever trust him, and if men do not trust him, how can he abide as King? My own self, on this night, was quite dead within me. It was exactly as though I had died and these wild faces, lit with torch and lantern flares, belonged to creatures of another world. Hendricks, a fat, phlegmatic Dutchman, rode at my side wondering, I am sure, that Englishmen who could be so orderly and obedient could also be so wild and rebellious.

For the rough joy on every side of us was no joy at all. It was a raging portent of the future, a prophetic savagery. A long, thin ragged man danced beside us for some of the way. 'There's a good time coming for England!' he cried.

> *'When Black Tom Tyrant has lost his head,*
> *Then the others will soon be dead.'*

There was drinking everywhere and I saw a woman thrown down on her back in the gutter and two men leap upon her.

But Hendricks felt as surely as I did that this was revolution in England and that civil war had indeed begun.

The dark crowd, humming like a top, was pushing towards Tower Hill. As a matter of history, by half-past one in the morning the crowds were thick on Tower Hill, and by dawn, as Newport afterwards told me, there was nought to be seen there but one great sea of heads choking all of it; every side street, alley, lane that could command the remotest cater-corner vision of the scaffold on the top of the hill was by daylight crammed. Goring told me, half an hour ago, it is estimated two hundred thousand people were there.

I entered the Tower, because of my passes, with no difficulty at all, but I will confess it that my cheek paled and my heart stopped its beat to see how even then the mob pressed against the Tower gates. For it was a new mob. I had seen it assembling through these last years—first a man or two, then a trickle, then a flood, now a sea. The people of England growling, snarling, demanding vengeance for wrongs they had not felt. King Pym—may he be cursed for ever—has done his proud work well!

I sent my message to Lord Newport. I was bidden to wait.

At one moment Wentworth's brother George came in. I had known George well for some years. Seeing me, he joyfully drew me aside. It seemed that Wentworth had charged him with a last letter to his son, Will—a lad not yet fifteen. George had fears that this letter might be taken from him before he reached safety from the crowd. Under the eye of the guard, who did not prevent us, he requested me that I would copy it so that if he could not get it to the family I might do so.

I have the copy with me and insert some part of it here, for it appears to me a most sincere and beautiful letter, from a man a few hours before death and most deeply betrayed.

He wrote to his son:

My dearest Will—These are the last lines that you are to receive from a father that tenderly loves you. I wish there were a greater leisure to impart my mind unto you, but our merciful God will supply all things by His grace, and guide and protect you in all your ways; to whose infinite goodness I bequeath you. . . .

Be sure you give all respect to my wife, that hath ever had a great love unto you. Never be awanting in your love and care to your sisters, but let them ever be most dear unto you; and the like regard must you have to your youngest sister; for indeed you owe it her also, both for her father's and mother's sake. . . .

The King I trust will deal graciously with you, restore you those honours and that fortune which a distempered time hath deprived you of together with the life of your father. . . .

Be sure to avoid as much as you can to enquire after those that have been sharp in their judgments towards me, and I charge you never to suffer thought of revenge to enter your heart. . . .

And God Almighty of His infinite goodness bless you and your children's children; and His same goodness bless your sisters in like manner, perfect you in every good work, and give you right understandings in all things. Amen.

You must not fail to behave yourself towards my Lady Clare your grandmother with all duty and observance; for most tenderly doth she love you and hath been passing kind unto me. God reward her charity for it. And once more do I, from my very soul, beseech our gracious God to bless and govern you in all to the saving you in the day of His visitation, and join us again in the Communion of His blessed saints where is fullness of joy and bliss for evermore. Amen. Amen.—Your loving Father.

It was a strange scene while I sat writing this at a rough table to a lantern's light on parchment that George had provided.

A stout, heavy-armoured guard stood above me as I wrote. I noticed him, for he had a resemblance to Goring save that his chest and thighs were more massive. But he had a round baby face as Goring has—a good, simple country face, which indeed Goring has not.

But it happened that after a time George began to weep. He turned his head aside; he put up his gloved hand to his eyes, but he could not prevent it and he sobbed. Then this soldier also began to weep. His face did not alter save that his eyes opened a little wider. He stood stiffly at attention and allowed the tears to trickle on to his cheek. There would have been in the ordinary way something infinitely ludicrous in this, but to-night it was not so and these weeping men seemed to myself to be crying for more than their brother and their prisoner, but rather for their country that was, from this night, in such infinite peril.

I could not but remember also the faces of the people pressed against the Tower gates, and the cloud of witnesses packing, all through the night, on to Tower Hill to see one man die.

My writing task ended, I waited for my summons. It seemed to me strange that, bearing the King's letter, I should wait at all. I at length sent the soldier to demand the reason.

He returned to say that James Ussher, Archbishop of Armagh, was holding prayers privately with Strafford. This Ussher was an old friend of Strafford's from Irish days—a rough, rude, abusive man, I had always heard of him. But, when they would not allow Strafford to see his fellow-prisoner Laud, his mind turned to Ussher, and Ussher, from that time, scarcely left his side. He reported to his friends that he had 'never known a whiter soul.' He was a fierce fanatic who spared telling no man his sins so that the verdict is something from his mouth. He had been even to Whitehall and told the King to his face of the mortal hurt to his soul that betrayal of Strafford would be. He went to him again after the King had signed the Bill, and the King besought Ussher to tell 'my lord of Strafford' that had it not been for danger to his wife and children he would never have signed the Bill, that he (Strafford) was indeed innocent, and that the King would remember his children.

Alas, alas—a confession indeed for a King to make, but Ussher told Strafford of this and it comforted him.

Ussher also told Newport that nothing in his experience of men had astonished him more than Strafford's humility and self-abnegation. For here was the proudest of mortals, one who had made himself hated because of his pride. Myself I think that, after he was deserted by the King, he discarded all his earthly duties. While the King was at his side he fought for the King to the last order, the last word, the last breath. But when the King was with him no longer all this fell away from him and he surrendered himself humbly to God.

But I was myself immediately to hear and see something of this at first hand. All that I record here is true.

A man-at-arms arrived to say that I was to follow him. I saw the stout, giant-like soldier search me with his eyes. There was a dog-like simplicity about him. I was suddenly aware that he would die, if need be, for Strafford.

Strafford was alone in his little room when I entered it. He was seated at the table, pen and ink-horn in front of him. One leg was propped up on a stool. His black jerkin was open at his brown neck. He was staring in front of him, lost in some vision. There was something terrible in his face. Van Dyck's portrait of him, his head bent towards you, his frowning forehead, his beautiful anxious eyes, his long lively sensitive fingers, the lights and darks of his handsome armour—this portrait, fine though it is, omitted one very important element in him—namely, the prophetic. No man that I have ever seen showed in his forehead, eyes, mouth so clearly a foreboding of his future. His smile was enchanting, but even as he smiled his eyes seemed to portend some catastrophe. Much of this was no doubt due to his physical suffering.

He did not now rise but held out his hand.

'My friend,' he said, 'welcome, and forgive me that I kept you.'

His hair curled on his high forehead; his neck was strong and wiry and brown like a Spaniard's; his beautiful hand lay in mine; his smile was gentle and winning. With all this I knew that the iron had entered into his soul and that that iron was not death.

I gave him the letter from the King. He broke the seal and read it. Then he looked up at me with a cheerful smile. 'You will thank His Majesty, please, Mr. Garland, and tell him that all was well with me. In this he begs that you may be with me to the end, keeping close to me his warm care and feeling for me. I welcome that.' He took my hand again and held it tightly, but I shall never know, I shall never, never know, whether there was any irony in this.

The story is already current and will doubtless pass into history, that Dudley Carleton, one of the royal secretaries, told Strafford of the King's fatal decision. I have known Carleton in a considerable intimacy and he is a man of strict integrity. It is said that after this tragic interview with Strafford he visited Laud and told him that Strafford had accepted the King's decision with resignation. But that may have been to comfort the broken old man, for Mr. Whitelocke asserts that Carleton told him another story. Carleton, as he told Whitelocke, must repeat the King's decision twice before Strafford could understand it, and then Strafford broke out, with great bitterness: 'Put not your trust in princes nor in the sons of men, for in them there is no salvation.'

Whether this was so, whether Strafford spoke in a momentary bitterness, whether Carleton altogether invented the story, no man can say. He was now very gentle and kind and invited me to draw up a stool to the table. I told him that I had read his letter to his boy Will, for I would not have him ignorant of that. I gave him the reason.

'My brother George,' he said, smiling, 'was always more of a considerer than myself. He is for meeting the event half-way. I am for letting the event meet me.'

He asked me what was my family, whether I had brothers or sisters. I answered that I had one brother whom I greatly loved, but that he was a strong Puritan and worshipped Mr. Oliver Cromwell, a relation of Mr. John Hampden.

'Mr. Oliver Cromwell,' Strafford said. 'I have heard of him. He was from Huntingdon, in the last Parliament. From what I have heard of his character I could imagine that we might have worked together had things gone otherwise. We would both serve our country.'

He asked me whether this difference in politics severed my brother and myself, and I answered with a sigh that alas, it did, for now we could never meet although we still loved one another. I told him also that I had a sister married to a poet.

'A successful poet?' Strafford asked.

'No,' I answered. 'An unsuccessful one.'

He spoke then a little of himself.

'It is a strange thing, Mr. Garland, but I have always thought that to know the moment of one's death before it comes must be of all things the most unfortunate. In the heat of battle, yes, or to be struck down with an unexpected thunderbolt. But for your soul to say to you, as mine now says to me: "To-morrow at midday as the bell strikes your head will be severed from your body. At two minutes past the hour the bird will fly into the tree, the wind will blow the petals of the rose, your horse will kick with its hoof, but you will not be aware"—that has seemed to me, for I have condemned men to such a death often enough, a searing trial. But it is not so, I assure you it is not so. In these days any man may come to it and it is nothing to fear, for there are greater things than an overhanging bodily death.

'Mind you, Mr. Garland,' he said, suddenly laughing, 'this leg of mine may have much to do with it.'

Even as he spoke there was a twinge from it, and his face puckered. He bent forward and touched the ankle. 'Very hot, Mr. Garland— very hot for an angry man like me. When the pain has been bad I have taken one salve or another and said: "Why, now—in an hour it will have cooled"—or I have thought: "By this time next year this torture will seem as nothing." ' He laughed, throwing back his head. 'And so indeed this time it will. Aye, by this same hour to-morrow night that leg of mine will be out of pain. So the man with the axe is but my kind doctor.'

He was speaking as though to himself. His brow darkened and I saw the fire of anger in his eyes of which I had so often heard.

His hand was clenched. Through his body he drew a deep angry sigh:

'For myself—yes. For myself—nothing. But the country . . . the King. Let no man say after that I did not try to serve my country as well as my King. Once I was for it even *against* the King. Pym was my friend then. But the people—how can the country be placed in their hands? They are not yet ripe for such command. One wise man and three drunkards—will not the three drunkards rule? Two lechers and a saint—what can the saint do? And so I was for the King, to establish him strongly, and then, through him, for wise men to govern. Maybe I drove too hard. I have ever wanted my own way, seeing so clearly how men should go. Maybe when I had power I did not yield God thought enough.'

I could tell that he had been over these arguments in his mind, and others like them, again and again. He sighed and realized my presence.

'Shall I be right with God, Mr. Garland? My friend of Armagh tells me that my soul is cleansed. Can that be—in so brief a moment? For I can charge myself that I have up to this very last moment stained it with lasciviousness and high-mindedness. Cruel thoughts of dishonour . . .' He stayed staring into space. I wondered whether he were thinking of Lucy Carlisle—or of the King. Yes, surely, of the King.

At last I said—for he seemed to wait for an answer:

'I trust God's wisdom—yes, more than His charity and forgiveness. He need not forgive, for He knows our exceeding weakness—not of our own fault. Dishonour comes from fear as God well knows—and when we are afraid God must pity us as we would our own children.'

We were both, I knew, thinking of the King.

At last Strafford said:

'That is a wise answer. God forgiveth us—why, then, Mr. Garland, we must not wonder at any human weakness—our own or our friends'.'

I felt then that beneath his courage he was infinitely sad. And I knew that my sadness and his were on the same ground. Oddly then I envied him, for, by this time to-morrow, either he would understand the King's betrayal of him and so joyfully forgive him, or he would be in blankness, non-existing. . . .

While I must, until I also found death, serve the King knowing that there was only a man there, a weak fallible man, by Divine Right, but not by character, a King.

Yes, I almost envied Strafford and I laid my hand on his, and he drew my head towards him and kissed me on the forehead. I retired then to a little room that was shown me and lay down on a pallet and fell into a deep sleep. I dreamed, but not of Strafford. Rather of Peter, whom I met riding over a lonely darkling plain. We got off our horses and embraced. We were so happy to be together again that we laughed like children and walked holding hands while our horses nibbled at the stiff spiky grass, and the sky grew ever blacker about us. Then there broke, quite suddenly, a thunderstorm of exceeding fierceness and we ran for our horses but they were not there. We were also hidden from one another. I awoke crying his name.

At a quarter to eleven I was called to Strafford's room. He was standing there, quite ready, dressed in his ordinary black, the two chaplains behind him.

Poor Sir William Balfour, who had come to fetch the prisoner—I was sorry for him!

He had, I doubt not, slept very ill. He was in any case of a nervous and hypochondriacal temperament. He made now a most unfortunate scene. He appealed to me as having come from the King. What was he to do? The mob at the Tower gates was quite desperate. At any moment they might break the gates down. The civil war might begin this very moment, this very morning, here in the Tower. They were roaring like wild beasts. Go into the passage and you must hear them. When he brought his prisoner out they would assuredly break the gates and tear him limb from limb.

I felt that this was shameful, for he had lost all control and had forgotten what this must be to his waiting prisoner.

But I looked at Strafford and was reassured. Never, in all his long, adventurous life, can he have been as fine as he was then.

'It is not your fault, Sir William,' he said, 'if there is any mishap. I would as lief die one way as another.' He added almost in a whisper: 'It is I now. To-morrow——'

But Balfour was not calmed.

'I beg of you, my lord, to send for your coach. That we can protect, but you may not walk up Tower Hill in safety.'

Strafford grinned, wrinkling his face until he had that monkey-look of which I had often heard.

'Why, Sir William, that word "safety" has an odd sound. There is none in this world—our trust in God is our only armour.'

He said that scornfully as though, with due respect to God's deity, it was his trust in himself that he valued the most.

Among the group there at the door of his room he was a lion among sheep.

Then he shook his head, laughing outright. 'No. I dare look death in the face,' he said. 'And I hope the people too. I care not how I die, whether by the hand of the executioner or by the madness and fury of the people; if that may give them better content it is all one to me.'

By now we were all gathered: Strafford's two brothers, William and George (George nodded to me, intimating that the letter was now in safe hands), his cousin Cleveland, Ussher, Archbishop of Armagh (what a fierce, eye-darting man!), his two chaplains, Lord Newport.

I noticed, too, a mean knave whom I had seen about the Court in talk, at a time, with Goring and Lady Carlisle. He was a furtive, bowing, obsequious fellow, one John Rushworth. He had now with

him a pencil and paper and from time to time he wrote. He was
Clerk to the Parliament, and was there as spy from them.

I must confess that my heart beat thickly when we set out, one
of his own gentlemen leading the way, Strafford himself between
Archbishop Ussher and Cleveland, his brothers and friends clustered
close about him, myself a little ahead of Newport and his soldiers,
Strafford's servants, some of them weeping, bringing up the rear. At
the last, as we went into the open, I saw the massive soldier with the
blue eyes and baby face following us.

I heard a soldier say as I passed: 'This will not end it—to kill this
man. The cause lies deeper.'

I was at the first frightened as we passed on. I had expected a great
roar of hatred and execration, for now we went narrowly through a
lane of the people. But no man nor woman murmured; no one pressed
forward. There was a silence as though we were already with the
dead. It was like a miracle. Then I saw the cause of it. It was in himself. They did not love him any more than they had done. Their
hatred was as keen, but he appeared so noble and such a soldier that
in his presence they were still. I could see only his back, but it seemed
to me as though he were in armour, as in Van Dyck's picture—the
black-and-silver armour with the sun upon it.

His hat was in his hand and now and then, when someone saluted
him, he made a slight gesture. Those that saw his face have said
afterwards that it was like a general marching to certain victory.

He stood alone on the scaffold; I was not far distant and found
the stout soldier close to me.

There was a lovely May sunshine lighting his face; he spoke quietly
but very clearly.

Among other things I remember these words very nearly:

'I speak in the presence of Almighty God, before whom I stand, that
there is not a displeasing thought that ariseth in me against any man.
I thank God, I say truly, my conscience bears me witness, that in all
the honour I had to serve his Majesty, I had not any intention in my
heart but what did aim at the joint and individual prosperity of the
King and his people. I am not the first man that has suffered in this
kind, it is a common portion that befalls men in this life; righteous
judgment shall be hereafter; here we are subject to error and mis-
judging one another.'

After speaking of the Church and Parliament, he ended:

'I wish that every man would lay his hand on his heart and consider seriously whether the beginnings of the people's happiness should be written in letters of blood. I desire Almighty God that no one drop of my blood rise up in judgment against them. I desire heartily to be forgiven of every man, and so, my Lords, farewell, and farewell all things of this world. God bless this kingdom and Jesus have mercy on my soul.'

The big soldier next to me cried out in a loud voice:

'Amen, my lord. Amen to that.'

Strafford heard him and turned towards him, smiling at him, and then, recognizing me, he waved his hand.

Impulsively on the moment I turned to the soldier and said:

'Friend, would you care for a new service?'

He said he would, if it were mine. I asked him his name. It was Richard Clarke. I told him to come with me when all was done.

Strafford then took his brother, his nephew, his friends by the hand, and asked them to join in prayer with him.

The chaplain read the Twenty-fifth Psalm. These words, so significant, so ominous, will remain in my ears for ever:

'O my God, I trust in thee: let me not be ashamed, let not mine enemies triumph over me. . . .

'Turn thee unto me, and have mercy upon me; for I am desolate and afflicted. . . .

'Consider mine enemies; for they are many; and they hate me with cruel hatred. . . .

'Let integrity and uprightness preserve me; for I wait on thee.

'Redeem Israel, O God, out of all his troubles.'

Strafford talked apart with his brother George. Late that same day George told me that he had said (George spoke as it were in Strafford's voice there in my darkening room—as though it were Strafford himself. But this was only the first of our hauntings that same night. Even now, as I write these words, he seems standing beside me in that gleaming armour):

'Carry my blessing to my daughters Anne and Arabella, charge them to fear and serve God and He will bless them; not forgetting my little infant that knows neither good nor evil and cannot speak for itself: God speak for it and bless it. I have nigh done, one stroke will make my wife husbandless, my dear children fatherless, and my poor servants masterless, and separate me from my dear brother and all my friends, but let God be to you and them all in all.'

Before he knelt down he said with that monkey-grin to Ussher: 'I do as cheerfully put off my doublet at this time as ever I did when I went to bed.'

Ugly and harsh as his features were, his face appeared beautiful at that moment.

When the executioner offered to bind a handkerchief over his eyes, he put it away, saying: 'Nay, for I will see it done.'

He knelt before the block and prayed with Ussher. Then the chaplain came and lifted Strafford's hands, praying with them. Then he laid his head on the block. I drew in my breath and the whole scene spun about my eyes as a whirling ball with the sun in it.

But I saw the executioner hold up the bleeding head.

It must have been very still, for I heard the soldier, Richard Clarke, say:

'It is ended. I am ready to go with you, sir.'

On the night of this day, last night as it was, there were rejoicings through the country. Men rode everywhere, crying: 'It is done. It is done! His head is off! His head is off!'

There were bonfires on the hills and in every window lighted candles. It was like the news of a great victory.

On the same evening the King showed me, with much quiet pleasure, a drawing of a soldier by Raphael that had been given him.

On the next morning, on this day, May 13th, Richard Clarke came to be my servant.

THE ROCKS

THE ROCKS! The rocks!

Lucy Turner, wife of Matthew Turner, poet and dramatist, was on her knees at the low window of the upper room in the farm-house at Watendlath.

Watendlath! The rocks! The rocks! Watendlath!

Now, as she looked down the space to the Tarn, the rough tumultuous beck flashing with sun and turmoil on the left and the slabs of rock gleaming with glittering mica against the fell-side on the right, she felt she was in some bewitched country.

This was not real, *could* not be real, this little valley high up in the hills with the sleeping Tarn, the remoteness, the sounds of singing wind and chattering stream, and now, in May, the lambs crying and the birds calling. Why, you could remain here, here in this very farm, and stay here for the rest of your days, and no one know where you were. The sudden thought excited Lucy so much that she felt her heart stop, and put her hand to her breast. Her throat tightened, she pressed her body forward against the stone window-ledge.

She, Lucy Garland—to this she had come! She who her life long had loved people, company, lights, song, the making of love—and now this strange place at which they had arrived so unexpectedly had bewitched her so that she was crying out to be alone in it for ever more!

May is late in Cumberland and is more like a richer April. Even now on the sloping fells there were patches and streaks of snow that seemed to move, so glistening were they under the sunshine. The Tarn was black, but the sun lit up the reeds on its borders so that they were like brilliant green swords. The sheep with their lambs moved about the pasture beyond the Tarn, and they, too, were caught by the sun so that there was a shining about their fleece.

For a moment, as Lucy watched, the scene was unbearable in its brilliance, the rocks, the snow-patches, the reeds, the sheep unearthly with sun-sharpness. Then like smoke blown from a funnel clouds rushed across the sun and even the chatter of the beck seemed to be dimmed.

Lucy sat back on her haunches and pressed her hands against her forehead. What was she to do—oh, *what* was she to do?

She and Matt and Rupert, the last the strangest young man in the world—yes, young man, for he was eighteen years of age—had been to Seddon for Robert Herries' marriage to Margaret Blaikie.

Oh, but Lucy had been joyful to go! She had had enough—oh, most certainly she had had enough—of the artistic life with Matt in London. How, she now asked herself, rocking herself on her heels, had she ever imagined that she was in love with poor Matt? A certain tenderness for him, oh, that she had. But as in her childhood, so still, she had a certain tenderness for every man, woman, child, and animal in the universe, including herself! But the fool she had been to translate her gratitude to him for saving her that day in Keswick into love. Had she ever loved anyone in her life save Carey Courthope? And her brothers, her mother and father, Rupert and Katherine . . . But love of a man, *real* love with the beating of the heart, the aching of the body, the touch, the wonderment, the loss of self—had she ever known that save with Carey? Certainly not with Matt Turner. Poor Matt, whose embraces had been always apologetic, in whose arms she had lain in the truckle-bed with the books falling from the rickety table, the mice gnawing at the chair-legs, the dust festooned in the firelight, and the bed so narrow that when she turned to ease her aching back, Matt had fallen, asleep as he was, hard to the floor.

Ah, but she had hated that London life. For the one thing it had been so bad for Rupert, who was wild enough in any case, who revelled in the dirt and debauchery and looseness of Alsatia or White-friars or whatever you called it—that world of ribaldry and loose singing and murder and poetry, the only one for which Matt cared.

Not that Rupert was debauched. Lucy sighed here and rocked herself a little on her heels. She almost wished that he were. In a fight or a quarrel he was as reckless as you please, as dare-devil as any boy in England. He liked nothing better than to quarrel. His red hair seemed to stand up on his scalp, and he would have his sword out and be stamping with his foot before his opponent could tell what crime he had committed. He was as cool as a snow-drift at the making of a quarrel. He felt no animosity; he must fight, that was all, and he made every possible excuse, here, there, and everywhere, for doing so.

During these last years there had been constant opportunity, for London had been in a turmoil of fighting opinions; the trouble was that you could never be sure on which side young Rupert Herries truly was. If you called King Pym a word he would be at your throat, but he wounded two men a year back for exulting over the death of Tom Tyrant—yes, on the very day of Strafford's execution.

With all this he could be most generous-hearted and, in fact, never kept anything for himself. He could kiss a woman from a very early age—that is, when they allowed him, for he was an oddity, with his little stature, his red hair, his pale long nose, his small fiery eyes.

He disdained to show affection and despised those who did, but he *had* a heart—for his mother, for Matt (mixed with contempt). He was in his younger day followed by a rabble of boys who all called him 'Captain.' Like all small men he was inordinately vain and was given to strutting. He could not bear to be still, never opened a book, but had a liking for music and would sing a song in a queer cracked voice.

Whether he was now for King or Parliament no one could say—the only thing that was certain was that he would soon be fighting somewhere. He had wished, to everyone's surprise, to go with his mother and Matt Turner to Robert's wedding to Margaret Blaikie. This was because Robert was the head of the family, and he, Rupert, was proud to be a Herries even though an illegitimate one. So they all—Robert's mother, Lucy, Matt, Rupert—travelled north in the Herries family coach together, taking weeks in the doing of it.

Robert chose to be married at Seddon because he had business just then about his northern cattle.

It was no very good time for travelling. They had many adventures; you could make a book out of them. Lucy had insisted on staying two nights in Keswick. Rosamund, Nicholas' widow, an old lady now of seventy-six years with snowy hair and bright, bright eyes, had been only too pleased. They all visited 'The Peacock' and Lucy thought of Mr. Caroline, and they rode out to Rosthwaite and visited the house where Nicholas' uncle—the wicked Francis—had hidden himself.

During these two days Lucy, who had been provoking and uncertain of temper for a long time past, was sweet and charming to everybody. She loved this country. It was hers, it was hers! Had not the happiest time of her life been spent in it? And she thought of Seascale, her father and mother, Peter and Rashleigh, and she cried a little.

Rupert was interested in 'The Peacock,' and his mother showed him the room where he was born. 'I would not have lived, I think, but for Katherine.' The Marchioness of Newby! How strange and how sad! She saw Katherine bending over her and stroking her damp forehead. Dear Katherine! Was she happy? Happier than Lucy was, Lucy hoped.

Lucy sat in that little bedroom at 'The Peacock' and looked out of window at the shelving hills beyond the Lake, and shivered. A chill caught her body. She thought with passion of Katherine, Peter, Rashleigh. She was separated from them all and soon there would be civil war—Peter against Rashleigh, Katherine following the King but belonging to no party.

And herself? A dreadful grey spirit of foreboding for all of them, herself and the others, caught her. She burst out crying. How unhappy she was! She could not return to that horrible London life, such dirt, such poverty! Against the gleaming colours and purity of this Lake scene she saw the dark and filthy streets, smelt the odours, saw one man knife another at a corner, heard the mob yelling in Palace Yard, saw Matt describing to her, waving his long thin arms in his excitement, the scene when the King had gone to Parliament to arrest the Five Members, the indignation of the City that the King had used armed force, and how on January 10th the King had left Whitehall.

That January 10th seemed to be written on Lucy's heart. She did not know much about the King, but she was for him with all her soul. What had he done, poor man, but ask his people for his rights? And he with his lovely sad eyes and his baby wife and his children whom he loved. Why should he be driven from his palace?

She hated the drinking, smelling, cursing friends of Matt who treated the country's troubles as a kind of play or masque, making poems and bawdy jokes, not caring for their country although they could write clever poems as though they cared. But they would all, Lucy was sure, be out of the way when danger came along.

Not Matt. Lucy with all her disillusionment was sure of his courage, his integrity. Poor Matt! He loved her but was so wild-headed, so inconsistent, so absent-minded that he could give her nothing that she wanted.

She sat there on the bed at 'The Peacock' crying. Rupert came in and found her. He hated to be disturbed by pity for another. He could *do* things bravely, but sentiment he abhorred. So he was rough with her, although his heart ached for her, and she was the more miserable and hated her son.

Nevertheless, such was her unalterable temperament that at Seddon she was cheerful again and as gay and happy as a bird.

It was a very quiet wedding and Robert looked like a sturdy farmer and Margaret his little pony. They were both very matter-of-fact in the affair. They would not, if they could help it, have a child for the first year or two. And yet, Margaret confided to Lucy, she had decided on the names of the children when they *did* come.

'The first girl shall be Maria, the first boy Matthew.'

'And why?' asked Lucy, who thought them ugly names, although she herself was married to a Matthew.

'They are good steady names.'

They looked steady enough in the little quiet church where they were married. Margaret might have been Robert's daughter and yet she had already a maternal air over him. Robert would be paunchy later. He carried himself with much dignity. He was not only head of the family but now a man of some national importance. He had, it was well known, lent the King money.

The two mothers cried at the ceremony, but in the evening there was fine gaiety and Lucy danced madly with the house steward, a handsome young man, and Matt got drunk and Rupert helped in the kitchen and kissed the cook.

Oh, but there was something of heaven about Seddon, poor Lucy thought. Its compact, restful beauty, with the statue in the park, the flowers blowing, the black-and-white-squared floor of the hall, the lovely staircase.

She liked it, she must confess, better than Mallory.

She was an old woman now and look what she had come to! Look at Matt with his canary beard and his drunken voice, and Rupert, elfin, crazy, always fighting. What a husband and son for a decent woman to have! And she might have been a decent woman—so easily with her beauty and gaiety and sense of life.

She remembered the great party so long ago that Nicholas gave at his London house for the old Courthope, and how Nicholas had taken her aside on the stairs and prophesied such things for her. How happy she had been that night! She remembered old Janet's monkey and the flowers falling through the air, and Katherine as a beautiful child.

To this it had all come—to be married to an inconsequent, crazy, poor poet, and to have for illegitimate child the ugliest boy in all England.

She did not feel old. She danced that night with a frenzy, and the young man, who might have been her son, had pleasure in it. She did not appear old to *him*.

Then they rode away. Rosamund was to stay at Seddon and so would the family coach. So Lucy and Matt and Rupert went their ways. Once more Lucy insisted that they should stay in Keswick and, after a night or two, they rode up the hill from the Lake and on through a winding valley until, without knowing it, they found themselves in Watendlath.

There were rooms in the farm and they stayed.

Lucy, who was ever in extremes, found Watendlath the place for which she had always been searching. They had come at the right time when the cuckoo cries as though down the empty echoing halls of Olympus, and the larches burn against the firs, startling you into the belief that your eyes are opened for the first time. The lambs, so soon to be the ugliest and most faithful sheep in the world, stared at the waters of the Tarn and then with a hop and a skip ran, alive with optimism, to tug at their reluctant mothers. The clouds shadowed the fells in passing gestures of ebony and purple and elephant-grey. Sometimes the May wind roared up into a spume of tossing cloud, and the sunlight, where it shone, had the freshness of dancing water.

But Matt did not share Lucy's ecstasies. He was weary and empty away from London. Moreover, he had a plan now of a play, suggested to him by John Marston's *History of Antonio and Mellida,* but could not write it unless he had the roar, rattle, and stench of London about his senses.

All creators know that there is nothing in the world more desperate than to have a masterpiece pressing to be delivered but time and circumstance preventing it. Matt cared nothing about politics: the names of Hampden and Eliot and Pym, of Strafford and Laud and the King's Majesty itself, came to him but dimly through the clouds of bewitching imaginations that hung about his eyes and ears and nose.

He was a true Bohemian too. He would rather not know whence the next meal was coming than know it, he would rather there were a stench somewhere about than there not be one. He was not himself a lusty drinker, for his stomach could not endure it, but he loved his friends to be drunken. The tiny aesthetic gossip and chatter of the moment delighted him. Authors were then, as now, seldom contented with their lot, and no one enjoyed listening to a literary woe, triumph, catastrophe more than Matt Turner.

He knew, however, as well as anyone the mistake that he had made by bringing Lucy into this environment. He loved her more than ever. He was never weary of looking at her and marvelling that she, over fifty as she was, looked on her best days not a week more than thirty. For she had, and would always have, did she live to be two hundred, that child look of pleasure, anger, surprise. There were lines about her mouth, and neck, but her forehead was as serene and clear as it had been at twenty, her figure as slim, her energy as astounding.

He had done everything he could to make her comfortable; yes, and more than he should—for, because of her and her boy, he had run into heavy debt and saw little likelihood of quickly running out again.

She, on her side, had done what *she* could, pretending to like what she did not, making the most of his dirty and drunken friends, declaring that she believed in his genius.

She paid visits at times to Mallory and it was lucky for him in a way that Nicholas was dead, for now there was no one at Mallory who could amuse Lucy. Rosamund an old woman and Robert always busy with affairs. Lucky, too, in the later years that Katherine became the Marchioness of Newby and was swallowed into a world where Lucy lost sight of her.

So Lucy must fall back on her husband and her son. A strange couple for a lady to fall back on to, that Matt must confess. Rupert they seldom saw; how he lived they did not know. But, surprisingly, a strong friendship developed between Matt and Rupert. You could not have expected anything less, for Rupert despised the arts and contemned any loose, shambling body such as Matt possessed.

Nevertheless there was something in Matt Turner that young Rupert appreciated; he sniffed Matt's humour, good-nature, courage, optimism. Matt, in spite of his oddities, was a man. Rupert could never endure someone who was for ever complaining, and this it was that he had chiefly against his mother, for what Lucy had in her mind she must say, never pausing to consider whether it were wise or no. Not that Lucy complained monotonously. It was the more painful for those who loved her to watch her as she made her resolution again and again *not* to murmur! But the murmurs were there. They were all the more evident in that they were not expressed.

Poor Lucy! As now she knelt by the window, her long ringlets falling about her cheeks, her eyes wide and distraught with trouble, she was repeating: 'What shall I do? What shall I do? What shall I do?'

To-morrow they were to return to London—to the filth, the stench, the ordure pouring down the gutters, the gorging and guzzling at the ordinary; the madman, naked and bleeding, hooted up and down the street by tiny children, the crowding of their little room with the passion for tobacco, the horse-play, the stealing, the crazy ranters, and now, in these last years, the preaching Puritans in the street below, the pulling-down of the hobby-horse, the crying-out of young men after you because you wore a bright-coloured gown, the psalm-singing in those discordant nasal voices . . .

Her thoughts stopped abruptly, for directly under her window even such a psalm was beginning.

She leaned out cautiously and saw to her surprise the piece of ground in front of the farm-house crowded with men. Very sturdy men, too, wearing the oddest assortment of armour, a helmet here, a breastplate there, and carrying every variety of arms, from the crudest farming fork to an up-to-date musket. There were several pikes, there was a drum, and one magnificent Amalek carried on his shoulder an axe.

Lucy soon passed from the instruments of war to the men themselves. Young and old, they were grave and severe—for the present occasion at least. By an odd freak of memory she remembered one of them. Her memory flew back to that fatal day of the riot at Keswick when Matt had rescued her. She heard the King's man in the inn speaking to his assistant; she saw in the market-square the King's man's victim as he faced the tax-collectors. He was there below her now, sturdy, stern, resolved. Someone addressed him—'Mr. Hendrick.'

'Yes, Mr. Bastable.'

'I suggest that the Psalm . . .'

'Yes, Mr. Bastable. The second verse, my lads, and not too lusty. We wish the Lord to hear but not Sir John Bankes. . . .'

A very sweet singing arose, tuneful, gentle, melodious, filled to the brim with feeling. A farm-hand and two small children, some geese, a dog or two were the audience. The slabs of rock on the fells flashed to the sun and the dark of the Tarn changed to faintest blue. A swan rode on the Tarn, arching her neck. The men—there were perhaps some sixty of them—did not move as they sang. After the singing they stayed as though welded into the white wall of the farm, the dun grey of the fell-side.

Then, from Mr. Hendrick, there was a short, sharp command. Instantly they were formed in order, then at another command they marched off, like ghosts, into the hills.

'They are against the King,' Lucy thought. 'They are rebels.'

She knew at once the confusion that was in a month or two to be universal, save for some fanatics, through England. She loved the King, but also these men whom she had just seen were her own countrymen, fine and God-fearing: for patriotism Peter, her own dear brother, was with them. For what, then, was this fighting? Who could hate the King, but who could hate the men either who fought him? Brothers and husbands and fathers would all be fighting one another and for what purpose? To have another King? Was not this one good enough? To fight because men would not pay taxes? When, after battle, there would only be more taxes to pay?

She rose to her feet and, as she did so, a surging disgust at all men, men universal, man as man, rose in her heart and soul. She *hated* men, the oafs, the idiots, the lazy, quarrelling good-for-nothings. What a misery and confusion these men had made of this life on earth, and yet would not allow women to make of it a better. They gave women no freedom, despised women, and yet had so little to boast of themselves.

As she stood there she thought of Matt Turner and her own Rupert with absolute loathing. What had they ever done for the world? Rupert was young but even now thought of nothing but fighting. She hated them both. She would never see either of them again. They were in Rosthwaite on some pleasure of their own. Well, she would be gone before their return. She would run. She would run—she . . .

She looked through the window and saw a gentleman leading his horse over the little bridge. In life there are many coincidences. In this portion of the Herries Family Chronicles there are but two—this is one.

The gentleman leading his horse over the little bridge was Mr. Caroline. Lucy had not set her beautiful eyes on him since that day of the trouble in Keswick. At first in London she had looked for him. Then she had forgot him, remembered him, forgot him again. Now, as in a flash of the sun from the mica-shining rocks, he returned to her. She had not an instant's doubt of him. He was dressed very grandly in a large hat with a feather and a deep-purple suit. He was stouter than he had been but, as he looked with care to lead his horse safely, he had the same silly, kindly, pursy, elegant face—the same face, the same man! Dear Mr. Caroline!

Queerly enough the first observation that struck deeply into Lucy's consciousness was that he was so very clean!

He had crossed the bridge and now stood, with his hand on his horse's mane, considering the scene. Once again, within the last five minutes, the colours had changed. Heavy clouds had rolled up and lay in dark bastions and towers high in air. But beneath them a white intense light broke above the hills that now in the shadow of the dark cloud were smoking mulberry. The Tarn was black again and the reeds dun, and against their ebony the swan, majestically hovering, was of a white so pure that it drew all the scene to itself like a magnet.

Lucy was always to remember this swan, for, staring at it, she made instantly her resolution. Poor Lucy! She was of those whose imagination, strengthened by desire, swings into the future beyond reason. All that she saw was that she must escape from Matt and the return to the dirty Strand. Mr. Caroline was there by a miracle.

She ran down the staircase that was too wide and too beautiful for so small a farm-house; she paused for a moment at the door. It seemed to her that Mr. Caroline was intending to mount his horse. She ran to him. He turned at the sound of her steps and instantly recognized her. She was the lady of the 'Peacock' inn who had almost gone to bed with him. He was himself lonely, feeling his age, wondering whether he would ever have an adventure again. He had money but no lady; the danger of the times made him apprehensive. In an inn at Carlisle the maid-of-all-work had returned his kiss with a slap on the cheek. He was in general of an amorous nature, but of the sort that is amorous because he wishes to be cherished, wishes to see in a woman's eyes that she intends to mother him. He had never needed comfort more piteously than now. Lucy, as she ran towards him, with her curls flying about her face and her bright-blue gown, seemed not to have changed in these last years.

'Mr. Caroline! Mr. Caroline! Do you remember me?'

He kissed her hand. His eyes sparkled. He was pleased that he was wearing his best clothes. He did not remember her name, but her eagerness, vitality, childlike pleasure at seeing him—these things he remembered.

'I am here with my husband. . . .' Ah! so she was married! That heightened his sense of adventure.

'This is most marvellous!' He looked around him. There were no observers but the horse and the swan. 'I am on my way to Kendal' —wondering suddenly whether he might not after all stay the night in Watendlath.

'You can help me. . . .' Her only thought now was to get away. 'You can take me with you to Kendal. I can find my friends from there.'

They discussed it. She told him that to-morrow her husband, who was for the day in the Borrowdale valley, was taking her back to London. She could not, she would not, return to London. She would be no burden to him beyond Kendal. She must show her husband how abhorrent to her was her London life.

'You do not know . . . you cannot.' She looked up into his face, her eyes swimming with tears. As her bosom heaved and her hands were clasped she looked, he thought, most beautiful. His passions, strong through abstinence, began to rise. He thought of the husband. He did not wish to be involved in a family affair, but after a night (two, three nights?) at Kendal, the affair would be ended. Meanwhile . . .

He held her hand. He nodded his head.

She did not care! She did not care! Something told her as, alas, it had so often in vain told her before, that she was a fool. She liked to be a fool. Consequences with her were always a world away.

She ran back into the farm-house to gather a few things. Then with a trembling hand she wrote the letter time-honoured in convention and laid it against the time-honoured cracked bedroom mirror.

In the evening Matt Turner and young Rupert walked up from Rosthwaite. On the floor of the bedroom clothes were scattered and against the mirror was the letter.

DEAR MATT—I love you but not London. I will not return to it. When you have found another way of life I will return to you.

Matt cried a little and then sat down with Rupert to the food that they had brought up with them. The food choked him, but he was hungry.

He thought of Lucy whom he loved, and of his drama which he loved also.

Dear Lucy! Dear, dear Lucy! Then he smiled through his tears, pushed the plate to one side.

'We will find her. She will soon repent. We will live in the country for a while.'

He pulled his beloved paper towards him and wrote, in his sprawling, illegible hand:

SCENE II. *The Palace of Hieronymus. A roll of drums. Enter Hieronymus, Queen Thalisba, the Captain of the Guard, Rosalinda* . . .

CROMWELL: FLAME AND CLOUD

PETER GARLAND, on a certain afternoon late in February of the year 1643, stood on guard outside a little farm-house off the road from Cambridge about three miles. He was waiting for Cromwell, who was to sleep there that night. He was wearing the 'iron pot' on his head and 'back and breast' armour. He carried a sword and a pistol. He had become massive in figure but from under the helmet there looked out the same rather simple blue eyes; his countenance was ruddy and round and he was as English in his solid and rocky quality as was to be found in the world anywhere. He was not only English but Herries, which meant that he was middle-class and neatly balanced between soul and body.

At this particular moment the balancing was very neat indeed, for he was desperately hungry and could smell coming from the passage of the farm-house the rich deep odours of a stew. His spirit was active, too, and not very happily so, for he was wondering how long it would be before the God in whom he believed would turn His eye towards His true servants and lend them a little aid.

To be truthful, the war until now had not been going any too well for the Parliament.

Since that day, August 22, 1642, when the King had unfurled the Royal Standard at Nottingham, almost everything had gone the

King's way. For one thing Parliament had appointed the Earl of Essex as its Commander-in-Chief, and a greater fool, Peter thought, angrily kicking the pebbles of the road with his foot, had never been seen. Why, if he had a victory there in his hands he did not know what to do with it!

Edgehill had had no decisive result, but had revealed in Prince Rupert, the son of the Elector Palatine and King Charles' nephew, a leader of immense dash and spirit.

Yes, curse him, thought Peter, with his red cloak and white dog! May the Lord God give me the chance of getting at his throat before I am very much older!

Then the King moved on towards London, which was in imminent danger. On November 13th it had been a toss in the air as to what would happen. But the City forces had a stout defender in old Ship-pon, and the King had ordered, thanks be to God, a retreat.

It was after this that Cromwell had seen that things were wrong with their side and, in Peter's presence, he had said to John Hampden: 'Your troops, John, are most of them old decayed serving-men, and tapsters and such kind of fellows. But *their* troops are gentlemen's sons, younger sons and persons of quality; do you think that the spirits of such base and mean fellows will ever be able to encounter gentlemen that have honour and courage and resolution in them? You must get men of a spirit and, take it not ill what I say—I know you will not—of a spirit that is likely to go as far as gentlemen will go; or else you will be beaten still.'

To simple and direct-hearted John Hampden this seemed almost a treachery. But of course Cromwell was right. Peter had seen at once that he was.

Cromwell, as was his way, had worked quickly. In October 1642 he had a troop of sixty men and three officers. In December he commanded eighty men. Then at Cambridge the single troop was increased to a regiment, and on January 26, 1643, he was made a colonel.

Peter, watching the cold grey February sky shot with thin bars of watery saffron, struggled with a mood of deep melancholy. God seemed very far from him and far from England too. In such a mood, he was puzzled, as were perhaps at that moment most Englishmen, save the fanatics of both sides, as to how this had all come about. Brother was fighting against brother, friend against friend. The Civil

War had already lasted long enough for him to be witness of sights of savagery and cruelty that chilled his blood. That same morning he had discovered, on the road a mile from there, a woman with her throat cut and a dead child against her breast. He had seen houses burned, cattle destroyed, fields laid waste. He had himself as yet taken part only in skirmishes and had discovered in himself, in the act of fighting, a wildness and exaltation that he had not expected. Why? Why?

It occurred to him, in such a mood as the present, that a little arrangement, a meeting or two between the King and Pym and Vane and the rest, might have found some solution. He knew in his heart that this was not so; he believed profoundly that he was in arms for the freedom of his country and the glory of God, but there was something more horrible in civil war than he had suspected. He did not want to kill other Englishmen. Nor could he assure himself that, in the qualities of character, the one side was much better than the other. Cromwell had never cared for differences in men's religious opinions, and now in the men that he was gathering under him there were Independents (the majority), Anabaptists, Separatists, Antinomians, and other yet wilder sects. Cromwell said again and again that he was for all who refused to let layman or priest come between them and their Maker. It was then that this new force that Cromwell was forging knew no class division. All Cromwell asked was that their belief in God should steel their arm and make them God's soldiers. So indeed the most of them were, stern, determined men with a fire at the heart that Peter often envied. But there were, as Peter well knew, hypocrites, traitors, self-seekers.

Perhaps the strongest element in his distress was his ever-present loneliness. He had now no relation that belonged to him. Mallory, of course, was altogether shut off from him, the more that, three months before the Royal Standard had been raised at Nottingham, Robert Herries had for his financial services been knighted by the King. Of his sister Lucy he had heard nothing for a long while; she had left Matt Turner, he knew, and he often thought of her with almost crying tenderness—of her impetuosity and foolishness and good heart and kindliness and irresponsibility. Where was she? In whose hands? How faring?

Rashleigh was with the King at Oxford, and it was one of Peter's deepest dreads that the day might come when he would suddenly find himself face to face with him in battle. And yet they loved one another, as he well knew, deeply and truly as they had always done. It was because of Rashleigh perhaps that he chiefly felt the irony and pathos of this war.

How often he thought of their childhood in Seascale, of their father and mother, of the Isle of Man lying on the sea horizon, of the line of hills so cool and calm and beneficent, of the great friendly sprawl of Black Combe stretching out lazily to the blue or white-flecked water.

All that love and security, and now it had come to this! But deepest and most persistent was the agony of his longing for Katherine. Time, absence, had not diminished it. It was the Devil, he knew, that would not leave him alone, but the awfulness of it was that he who was God's soldier welcomed in this the Devil. He would not lose a moment of it, the constantly recurring actuality of that moment when she had told him that she loved him, of every movement, word, touch —the passionate kiss, the pressure of her cheek against his, the look in her face, the soft radiance of her eyes.

It was a horror to him that it made no difference to him that she was Newby's wife. Here was a sin that he clutched to his heart and deliberately and defiantly cherished.

He thought of Cromwell. His devotion was the same, his companionship was not. How could it be other? Cromwell was climbing to the place where he belonged. Peter had, from the moment when his eyes first beheld him, known that he was the greatest man in England. But Cromwell had now a huge burden on his shoulders; it was a miracle the fashion in which he was welding those strange men under him into a new force such as the world had never seen. But the doing of it demanded constant preoccupation, a wisdom and knowledge of men that appeared almost superhuman. And was Cromwell himself changing? Of course he was—or rather the qualities that Peter had always seen in him were enlarging as fortune developed them. Was he sometimes hard and cruel? There had always been that strain in him. Was there an element of hypocrisy in the loud, confused, religious outpourings? Who could say, in this strange world where men used the Bible as their daily language, what was hypocrisy and what was not? The tenderness was still there, the curious feminine longing for affection, the passionate love for his wife and children, but what would this war make of him when he rose to great power?

Then Peter heard horses and, turning, saw men riding. Here *was* Cromwell! And at that knowledge his unhappiness seemed to drop from him and it was all that he could do not to run up the road to meet them.

Now Peter was older than Cromwell, but all the same he was like a boy who sees his father again, for so Cromwell was to him and all his officers.

As the little group of horsemen came closer, Peter recognized Captain Ayres, James Berry, Captain Jocelyn Tonks (whom Peter disliked and mistrusted), Jeremiah Battle (a gallant fellow), and a gentleman from Keswick in Cumberland, Mr. Richard Hendrick. The last was something of a rarity, for the North was at that time chiefly for the King. But Mr. Hendrick had joined Cromwell, bringing a number of Cumbrian men with him.

He was a fine zealous gentleman with no nonsense, but hot for the Lord, and there were the beginnings of a firm friendship between himself and Peter. Also there was riding behind Cromwell a stout, richly-dressed gentleman in the Royalist fashion. This did not astonish Peter, for at this time, when the Civil War was not yet as heated between the parties as it later became, gentlemen, and ladies, too, often rode over from the one camp to the other, to bring a letter or see a friend.

Cromwell grinned at sight of Peter. After he had jumped off his horse he went to the side of the road to make water. Then, fastening his breeches, he clumped in his huge, heavy boots towards Peter, caught him in his arms, and kissed him on both cheeks, for he had not seen him for several weeks.

Cromwell, his arm through Peter's, went off with him to examine the horses before it was too late. In any case Cromwell loved horses but he realized (and, strangely, more thoroughly than did the Royalists) the importance that cavalry was going to have in this war. Save for Prince Rupert, no one on the other side was to grasp the importance of this as did Cromwell. Further than that, horseflesh was costly. To mount a regiment was said to cost ten pounds a trooper, a horse anything from five pounds upward. The Parliament was hard up for money, but Cromwell had the Devil's cunning and his old farmer's experience for getting a good horse cheap. It might almost be said that these horses of his won Cromwell the war. He bought horses at markets and fairs, requisitioned them when he could, but most often stole them. For this he had a genius and he taught his officers and men to do likewise. More than this, he was a marvellous horse-master, and instructed his men so well how to care for horses that there were no horses after a while like these of Cromwell's anywhere in England.

He stood now at the back of the farm-house, his arm thrown over the neck of a heavy white mare which, although stolen only the day before, seemed to recognize him already for lord and master. He stood looking out over the flat country, his brow knotted. His complexion was rough and coarse, he had mud on his breastplate and his immense boots were caked in it. He was under six foot in height, shorter than Peter, and yet he seemed to tower over him. This was because the whole of his body, his rough hair (he had taken off his helmet to feel the breeze on his forehead), his coarse features, his thick neck, his heavy arms and thighs, were for ever alive. It was not that he was physically restless—he would sit or stand for a long time without moving—but he was mentally and spiritually so. Always it seemed that some convulsion was breeding inside him. You would watch him, wondering what was to come out of it all. The boils and carbuncles to which he was prone seemed to speak to the constant heat of his blood. He was for ever controlling some emotion that wished to be out, and Peter noticed that with every day that control seemed to grow greater. Peter knew that he had the privilege of watching a great man in the making. With all his tempers and excitements, flames and fires and angers and affections, he was becoming a most marvellous cool judge of men. He knew the characters around him better than he knew his own. Desborough, strong and formidable. Ayres, weak, sentimental, suddenly giving birth to a brilliant notion. James Berry, trustworthy, devout, simple. Tonks, a potential traitor. Jeremiah Battle, loyal, courageous, stupid.

Now, as he stood there, his head a little forward, his lip thrust out, it was as though his heavy body was poised to hurl itself across that even plain towards Oxford and get at the throat of the enemy. Peter knew that things were not very well.

Cromwell suddenly spoke. He had been fortifying Cambridge and, to do this the better, he had been pulling down houses, ruining the walks and new gates at King's College, and the bridges at Trinity and St. John's.

'They don't like it, the gentlemen of Cambridge,' he said. 'They don't like it but they must have it. I have kicked many an educated arse in these last days.'

'Who was the richly-dressed gentleman riding with you?'

'A Mr. Molyneux—a banker from Oxford. He has a letter for you.'

'For me?' Peter's heart began tumultuously to beat. From Rashleigh . . . ? From Katherine . . . ?

The grey level scene swung before his eyes. For a moment Cromwell faded from his sight. It was all that he could do not to turn and run back into the farm and find this Mr. Molyneux. But Cromwell said:

'It is well that we trust in the Lord. We have need of it.'

'Are things seriously against us?'

Cromwell turned round to him, smiling grimly. He scratched his right side under the fastening of the breastplate.

'I have an itch. In their rascally college where they put me there were fleas.' His heavy eyes were suddenly moody. 'Nay, not so serious as when the King marched on London. We should have been in evil case then had he continued. And why did he not continue? Because the Lord, to give us at the last His victory, has ordained it that this man Charles shall never continue in anything. He is for ever in two minds and obstinate in both. He lies without knowing that he lies and is proud of his integrity. He is faithful to nobody but holds that he is faithful to all. In the end we have him—we *must* have him.' He closed his great gauntleted fist. 'But for the time—and at present——'

'Well?' Peter asked. 'At present?'

'They have a plan. I have it in every detail. It may be that it is Rupert's or his white dog's—who is, they say, the Devil!' Cromwell suddenly laughed one of his rough farmer's laughs, throwing back his head and laughing so that the muscles of his neck stood out.

He had his hand on Peter's arm and pressing now so stoutly that it hurt.

'Nay, see you, Peter. It is an excellent scheme. Hopton moves east through the southern counties into Kent. Newcastle, south to the Thames. Then they join on the river below London and cut off from us all commerce with the sea. The King himself moves from Oxford and accounts for Essex.'

Peter took it in immediately, for he was an acute soldier.

'Yes, but that must be marvellously timed to be effective. If one of them is thoroughly defeated the whole plan fails.'

'Exactly. Exactly.' Cromwell beamed like a child. 'Were I in their place and had I the army that I will have six months from now, I could do it. I could do it, Peter, my boy! But can they? Can they?

'Mark you, Hopton must sweep Waller and Stamford from his path. Newcastle must break through our men in the Midlands. They must have Plymouth, Bristol, Hull. Will they? Can they? No, for their counsels are divided, half their time and money they waste in chambering and wantonness. Rupert is their only man of vision, and he can be crack-brained. . . . But here is our hour. If we fail . . .'

He walked away among the horses, examining first one then another. He spoke to them softly with loving terms. He found it difficult to leave them, but the February afternoon was closing down. He stood, with Peter close to him, staring at the last thread of gold that seemed to throb with life before it died.

'Ah, Peter, but I have been sick at heart these last two days. They are all at daggers among themselves, but it is not that. I can deal with men. Can I deal with myself?

'I feel that God is working in me for His own great purpose, but the Devil having at me for my own destruction. When, in these last weeks, I have seen what I can do with men, how I can lead them and direct them, make them have always God before their eyes until these men will be the delivery of this England, I feel such a pride in my heart that I am swelled until my belly would almost burst. This pride. This ambition. . . . There is a cloud no bigger than a man's hand, but one day it may hide God from my own eyes.' His voice dropped almost to muttering. 'I had not felt this in me once. I was a happier man, maybe, with my cattle at Huntingdon.'

Then he raised his voice and planked his hand on to Peter's shoulder.

'And yet not so. We are called, every one of us, to perform the Lord's work in the way that He shall command. He directs us. We follow. . . .' It seemed that he was waiting for some word from Peter. But Peter was thinking only of the letter. The letter! The letter! He must get back into the farm as quickly as might be. This Mr. Molyneux might depart, carrying by some error the letter back with him to Oxford. At the thought of this beads of sweat moistened his forehead.

But he was afterwards to remember this little scene and to wonder whether, in those few moments, he had not failed Cromwell at one of the crises of his life.

It seemed to him later that, after this evening, Cromwell went on his way with more determination, and from this day his course was set. This may have been no more than Peter's sensitive imagination, for this day was to be for himself the beginning of a course that had, perhaps, always been certain, but that had the opening of its last chapter at this time and place.

For both Cromwell and himself the real battle—that of character—was now to be fought. And maybe Peter might have done something for Cromwell that he did not do.

They went into the farm-house together.

Cromwell, his arm through Peter's, clumped into the big farm room. Something was happening. There was the light only of the big roasting fire, and in this flame and smoke the tall Desborough, James Berry, small and dark and merry, Tonks, fat, double-faced, Ayres, with the fiery eyes of a fanatic, the laced and ribboned plump Mr. Molyneux the banker—they were all wild and uncouth figures. Peter knew them all save Mr. Molyneux.

'He's still here,' he thought. 'He must have the letter on him. Thank God!' And yet he felt as though he had never seen anyone before. They made a half-circle, and in the middle was a boy, a very young boy with yellow dishevelled hair like the down of a gosling, terrified blue eyes, he doing everything in his power to prevent his body from trembling. At a sudden moment his knees would give a wobble. His thin arms were pinioned behind his back. Once and again he wetted his lips with his tongue.

'What's this?' asked Cromwell.

Every one of them moved. The duckling-like prisoner turned his eyes from Desborough to Cromwell.

'He has been asleep upon his watch. He was found this morning fast sleeping under a tree in Cambury Wood.'

Cromwell looked at the boy. There began to stir within him one of those convulsive rages that were so terrible. Ever since he had had any command he had been fighting against slackness, lazy indifference, wandering stupidities. . . . Already his regiment was beginning to be known for its iron, almost voluntary discipline. Unlike the men in any other part of the Parliament army, the men under Cromwell were forging their own discipline and forging it of steel. Cromwell was perhaps prouder of this than of anything. That banker from Oxford should see an example. Also it must have been the day and the time. He had come from Cambridge weary, vexed, self-doubting. More than self-doubting—wondering whether after all this war could be won. The King's resources seemed vast. Already the religious quarrels that afterwards were to broaden into the gulf between Presbyterians and Independents and at the fatal last produced the Levellers were developing. He was for the moment uncertain of himself, his party, his cause, even—who can tell?—his God. And here was something helpless and young. The temptation was to hurt, to justify himself before the banker from Oxford, to squeeze that boy's throat. . . .

His face flushed coarsely. His nose quivered, muscles in his back moved below his armour.

He came nearer to the boy.

'What have you to say?'

The boy could not speak. There was something very awful in this thick, coarse-faced man with the terrible eyes and the ugly relentless voice. He could only stare and the Adam's apple danced in his throat. It may be true to say that there was not a man in that room who did not feel something of the boy's fear. The fat-jowled face of Tonks was sallow but the eyes glistened with a sort of butter-shine.

Cromwell waited for the boy to speak and then, with a motion of his head, said:

'String him up!'

A soldier was taking him away. Peter himself was for crying: 'But you've heard no evidence.'

Then the boy himself, unexpectedly wrenching himself free, turned and words came to him. He poured out his defence. He was but seventeen, his mother was a widow and lived in Cambridge, he had joined the army only a week ago, all yesterday from early dawn he had been helping with the horses, he did not know very much about horses, in the evening someone had given him ale to drink, he did not know much about ale, it had gone to his head, he had had no sleep for two days and three nights, he could not hang, he could not hang, he was only seventeen, he was his mother's only child. What good to hang him when he was young and strong, and could work, he would work, he would work . . . but he could not hang . . . he could not . . .

His eyes looked round hungrily upon them all. His body was shaking as though someone jerked it. His shrill baby cry ended in a series of little gasps as though he were a bird dying.

Cromwell was not moved. He said at last:

'And is that all?'

But the boy could say no more. A tear of self-pity and terror trickled down one cheek.

Only one of the men there was thinking of the boy. The others were thinking only of Cromwell and the power that came from him like blast from a furnace.

Cromwell felt his power and liked it. His eyes moved round the room. He saw Mr. Molyneux with his mouth open. He was about to repeat his order when he observed Captain Tonks. The eagerness in those eyes revolted him. Tonks wanted to see the life squeezed from this boy's throat. Well, he should not.

'Who found this man asleep?'

A soldier answered.

'Is it true that he slept?'

The soldier affirmed it.

'He has been in the army but a week?'

That was attested.

'His age is seventeen?'

That was so.

'Let him go, then.'

They led the boy away. There was a silence. They waited for Cromwell to speak. But he said nothing. Only his eyes found those of Captain Tonks. They held them, pierced into them. It was as though he said: 'I know you, Tonks. You are a traitor before the Lord. The rats shall devour your guts before many months.'

Without a word to any one of them he stamped from the room.

Peter went over to Mr. Molyneux.

'Sir,' he said, 'I am Captain Garland. Colonel Cromwell tells me that you have a letter for me.'

Mr. Molyneux blinked his eyes and scratched his ear. It seemed that he was still under the influence of Colonel Cromwell.

'Dear me.' He had a high little voice, like a fluting parrot. 'Excuse me, sir . . . a remarkable man. A most remarkable man. Riding from Cambridge he discoursed to me on the right feeding of pigs. . . . As though there were no war. And indeed in Oxford . . .' But here he pulled himself up as though he might say something dangerous. He also blinked at the large and muscular Peter with some apprehension.

Peter's hands were trembling with impatience.

'Excuse me, sir. The letter may be urgent——'

'Ah, the letter. You are truly Captain Garland?'

Peter turned swiftly to James Berry who was standing close by. 'James—tell him. Tell him I am Captain Garland.'

'Well, then . . .' Mr. Molyneux felt elaborately in his breast-pocket, produced a vast pocket-book and from it a letter. 'I think——' he said, looking at it doubtfully.

Peter took it courteously.

'I thank you, sir. You are very kind.' He saw that above the seal it was a woman's hand. He went up to his little room which that night he was to share with James Berry. He lit a candle and sat on the window-sill.

Then he read the letter.

DEAR PETER—I have long intended to write to you and have composed many a letter for you in my mind. When we have tried all ways to happiness—which indeed I cannot yet admit to—we yet wonder whether there may not be a new way. You are my friend and I am yours. It comforts me to write those words, for I suppose that we shall never meet again in this world, and when that came to me with the sudden vision that these things have I was resolved that wherever you might be, at the least you should know that I build some of my defences on that same knowledge of your friendliness. I will say nothing to you about the situation here, neither personal nor political, so that you may show this letter to your friend Mr. Cromwell or anyone other you please.

I have always believed that melancholy does me a hurt and I have resolved never to yield to it—nor is it melancholy that I feel now when I think of you but rather I see you as in a glass but more honest than glasses can make the most of us. I feel indeed that only to you of all men and women I have known have I been truly honest, and so you must not wrong what is perhaps the only friendship I can claim.

I am writing perhaps for the only reason that I would hear from you how you are, and as it is this writing is a bird thrown from a window into the dark, for you may not be there to receive it.

And yet you are so real to me, and always so real that I cannot believe your non-existence. Only a word from you in your own hand will gladden me and make me happy.

Mr. Molyneux returns to Oxford and will bring me anything you give to him. 'Tis no more in my will than in my power to recall anything that there has been between us. Did you know that I have still your silver button?

KATHERINE.

He put down the letter and sat staring into the candle. His heart beat so that he could not hear his sleeve scratch the surface of the table as he pulled the ink-horn towards him.

He began to write his answer.

BRAVE BANNERS AT MALLORY

IT MUST BE ACKNOWLEDGED, as a piece of honest family history, that Robert Herries developed a certain pomposity after he received his knighthood from the King. He had always had a tendency that way, being a short man and a pursy. Moreover, there is in any case a strain of pomposity in the Herries character. Their sense of humour has always been rare.

Then Robert was an only child and his father was old at his birth. Also he discovered as he grew up that the Herries were an exceptional family and he an exceptional Herries. How many Herries have made that discovery! And it is, of course, an English characteristic to be kind, patronizing, self-assured, muddled, and lazy all at the same time. Robert was neither muddled nor lazy. He discovered very early that the majority of his fellow-men neither knew where they were going nor cared to know. Men like Buckingham, Strafford, Laud, Pym, Hampden, Cromwell, were not, he noticed, such remarkable men in themselves. They commanded because they were one-idea'd men who would not turn aside for anything or anyone.

So he also held on his own way, developing Mallory, then his own especial fortune, until he was one of the most famous of all men in England for his cattle-breeding. After his father's death his sense of his dignity increased, for he was now the acknowledged head of his family.

He took great trouble to invite the collateral branches, the Court-hopes, the Walpoles, the Grants, the Pickets. It is true that these were only Herries by marriage but he liked to consider the Herries Tree as now a huge oak sheltering under its branches all the most sober and sensible and long-living of the English family. Longevity has always been a passion with many of the Herries family, although why any family should be proud of having among its members ancient, physically-ailing, grumbling and complaining octogenarians, no one can ever explain.

But there it was. Robert's own father had lived to an immense age. Family tradition went all the way back to old 'Polyphemus' Herries, who lived eight hundred years ago in Fife and died at the age of one hundred and sixty-one. There was Mary Herries who, in the Wars of the Roses, defended Lancaster Castle (what she was doing there no one had the slightest idea) by pouring boiling pitch on to the heads of the invaders. She had fifty-eight grandchildren and lived to be one hundred and thirty-nine.

There was also the extraordinary case of one Ronald Herries who, at the Court of James I of Scotland, lived to be one hundred and twenty years of age and was then discovered, for the first time, to be a woman.

These stories sound fantastic enough, but after all some of the best fairy-stories and most of the best poetry in the world come from the matter-of-fact business English.

Robert, although he looked so set and stolid, never apparently saw a joke and certainly never a joke against himself, disliked even the hint of an abnormality or extravagance, was himself never in a heat about anything, never did anything in a hurry, and, although he thought the Herries the finest family on earth, instantly regarded with suspicion any Herries who rose to a high place or became publicly conspicuous—this solid, reserved, cautious, impassionate little man had nevertheless his poetry and romance. He was head of the Herries family, and everything that belonged to him, his house, his farms, his cattle, his servants, his mother, and his wife, was magnificent. He had not, of course, the very least notion that the Courthopes and the Walpoles and the Pickets who came to stay with him at Mallory laughed at him for his solemn pompousities. They laughed at him but respected him and even liked him, for he had integrity, courage, and a warm heart, *and* he knew his job.

After his marriage he was as pompous about his wife as he was about himself. He thought her perfection. Margaret Blaikie had had a wise father and mother, and the mirror had long told her that she was plain. In fact she was *not* plain, for she was as fresh and sweet and healthy as a ruddy-brown apple, and when she went around the place with old Gilbert Armstrong, as she often did, you might have thought her his granddaughter.

She had much more humour than Robert, although she was as quiet as he. She had learned as a very little girl that the great secret of this life is to keep your mouth shut—so that she never gave her husband the least idea as to the desperate fashion in which she missed the North Country, its dark folding hills, its ice-cold streams, its skies with the rushing winds. She never cared for Mallory, but she could sit for hours in the garden or by the fire with her mother-in-law, who was now, albeit a sweet old lady, stone deaf, and never show a sign of boredom.

She was a very remarkable woman, Margaret Blaikie.

When the Civil War came Robert shut his eyes to it. Like all normal Herries he disliked anything that threw life out of its ordinary stride, and like too many Herries after him he pretended that if he stayed quiet enough, making no noise in his corner, the wind would blow down.

He disliked politics as being bad for business, and did not see why he need take any sides in this quarrel simply because the King had knighted him.

He did not realize that if oneself does not take sides other interested parties are sure to take sides for one.

He realized, in fact, but little of the true situation. He felt friendly to the King because he believed in kings, because he had lent the King money, because he was for law and for order. On the other hand, if men like Pym and Hampden felt that there was injustice and intolerance it was fine and courageous of them to protest. All *he* wanted was to be allowed to continue his daily affairs without interruption.

When war broke out he was bewildered, shrugged his shoulders, decided that it would be over in a month or two, and refused either to discuss it or argue about it. For a long while the war came nowhere near Mallory. Robert was unaware, however, that slowly, in all the neighbourhoods near him, it was believed that he was supplying the King's army with money and produce. His own servants were devoted to him. He paid them well and had that honest man-to-man relation with them that they preferred. He would stand no nonsense from them, but on the other hand he would sit down with them and gossip about the fields and the cattle. He had a very simple way of talking and was the same with everyone. He sometimes thought that what he would really enjoy would be to go with Margaret and live in a small house with only a horse, a dog, and two servants. 'For a period, you know. For a period.' He suggested that one day they should go and live at the little house in Borrowdale valley where Francis, her wicked grandfather and his wicked great-uncle, had once visited.

He would talk endlessly in his steady, unemotional, monotonous voice to old Gilbert Armstrong, and old Armstrong, who was fond of Robert because of Robert's father, would pretend to listen while his mind was in truth entirely buried in the past.

But Robert's pride in Mallory was, oddly enough, more than his love for it. Those visits to Seddon had given him a taste for the North that he could not overcome, and after all he had found his wife there. This was in the Herries' blood. Let any one of them, man, woman, or child, taste the North and their fate was upon them.

Robert had none of the passion for Mallory that his father Nicholas had had. His mother had it. Rosamund was now seventy-seven years of age and a very sweet and healthy old lady; her deafness was her only affliction and really she did not mind this. What she liked now to do was to think of the past, and especially of her dear Nicholas. All the more because present sounds were shut away from her did he, Nicholas, seem close to her. She was not so deaf but that she could hear *his* voice! Because of this and her lovely life with him she adored Mallory, the pleached walks, the smooth lawns, the flowers with their colours and scents, the house with its black and white, the hall, the bedroom where Nicholas had died—through all this she moved in a dream—for the present *was* a dream to her. Only the past was real.

When Edgehill was fought and the path to London was open to the King, Robert thought that at once he would take it. It seemed to him then that the war would be over in another fortnight, and he allowed himself some very pleasant reflections on the good business that he would shortly be doing.

When, however, the King did *not* take London he began to wonder for the first time whether all was well with the Royalist party.

Not moving from Mallory and news coming slowly that way, he could never be certain of what was happening. He realized that the King held his Court in Oxford. He heard men speak of a certain Cromwell.

'That is the man,' he said to Margaret, 'concerning whom Peter used to speak to us.'

He learned that in certain parts of England there was much fighting, destruction of property, and so on. Then a friend and neighbour of his, a Mr. Manning, asked him whether he would not put Mallory in a state of defence.

'A state of defence? Certainly not! Why should I?' He was indignant.

'The Parliament thinks that you supply the King with money!'

'I! . . . With money? The King has had nothing of me for years.'

'They think that in your opinions you are on the King's side.'

'Opinions? I have no opinions! I am on no side. I wait only for this abominable fratricide to be over.'

'We must, I fear, all of us have a side. Hopton or one of the others may be coming this way.'

'If they do I shall offer them to rest their horses.'

'They may insist on more than that.'

After Mr. Manning had departed, Robert was for a while uncomfortable. He talked about it to Margaret that night in the splendid bed with the green-and-gold hangings. In the dark he stretched out his hand and felt the rough stuff of the hangings. They were his and Mallory was his, and no one could take anything from him. In fact both he and Margaret went comfortably to sleep in one another's arms, having never seen war nor felt its hot breath on the cheek. *They* were safe; no one would ever touch them!

Then one March afternoon in this year of grace 1643 Robert, returning across the field by the stream, saw a very odd figure advancing towards him.

He saw at once that it was Rupert Herries. That stride of the little body, the swinging of the arms, that defiant cock of the head, those things could belong only to Rupert. His red head was bare; he wore long riding-boots and a breastplate and huge riding-gloves. There was a big sword at his side. When he came near it was difficult for Robert not to smile, but it was always dangerous to smile either with or at Rupert. If you smiled with him he didn't see your joke, and if you smiled at him—well, his temper was as sudden and fierce as a snake's strike. There was, however, nothing of the snake about Rupert; what he was feeling you knew; he took care that you did.

What he was feeling just now was that he was very important, and delighted to see Robert. What he told him in his shrill excited voice was that he was on his way to join the King's forces and had come to stay a night or two at Mallory first.

His egotism was most inoffensive; he felt it was altogether natural that you should be interested in anything that concerned him.

'I have no notion where my mother is. Matt and I have looked everywhere for her, and never heard a word of her. She cannot be in London, that's quite certain. And then when no one liked Matt's play and we had only our shoeleather left for breakfast, he went as secretary to a usurer, and I——' Rupert broke off and, as was a way he had, threw his head back and laughed quite uncontrollably. When he laughed his whole body shared in it and his ill-fitting breastplate rattled and his sword shivered against his side and every hair on his head seemed to be flaming. So he laughed now, his long nose seeming to shake quite independently of the rest of him. 'I have been run-about boy to a lady who is afflicted with a passion for red hair. She saw me in the Strand one day and insisted that I go home with her.

'She was mistress to an elderly gentleman in Chelsea village. We would go there on a visit, and I made the acquaintance there of a Frenchman who had been at the Court in Paris, and he taught me some fighting that I am aching to practise in the war. For quite suddenly one morning, on my knees and tying the lady's garter, I looked up into her bare bosom and told her that that very morning I was going to offer the King my sword. She kissed me and gave me some gold pieces. But I thought that first I would come and see you, for my mother, if she is in trouble, will come either to you or Katherine. But Katherine is now a fine lady, a Marchioness, and you are a Knight, but I am plain Mr. Herries with only his sword and little horse—but I am not even truly Mr. Herries but nobody, nothing, a shadow, a snip, a nail's paring, a cutting off the moon. . . . That is the way Matt will talk by the hour. I have learned it from him. . . . Shoo! Shah! I have you! Thus! Thus . . . !' For a large white-and-black cow had been staring at him and suddenly he had drawn his sword and advanced upon her, whirling, twirling, swirling his sword until it seemed like a hundred, moving with his feet on the ground like a dancer.

'I swear,' Nicholas had once said, 'that child will be one day the best swordsman in England.'

Robert, watching him, seeing the perfect natural rhythm, the movements of the body that must be born in that perfection and can never be taught, marvelled and envied. He could herd cattle, but he could never use a sword like that.

The cow, almost mesmerized for a while, suddenly stamped with her feet, turned, and ran off.

When Rupert came back to Robert's side he was perfectly in breath. 'I shall join myself to Rashleigh at Oxford.'

'Rashleigh may not want you. He is very important now in the King's service.'

'All the better for me. I am very difficult to be rid of.' He added: 'There is also Frederick. He is Goring's right-hand man, they say.'

'He is a time-server,' Robert said. When he disliked anybody he spoke rather as a prim old maid.

Rupert laughed. 'What do I care what he is? I shall take service with Prince Rupert. There are only two men in England now, Prince Rupert and Cromwell. One or the other. It is the same to me.'

'What! Have you no principles?' Robert remarked—shocked, although that was precisely his own position.

'Not a fig! I'll fight on either side, only fight I must. I would have gone to Peter at Cambridge, for I think Cromwell is my man, but at Oxford there is also Katherine who has been a better friend to my mother than any and, beside that, is more beautiful than Venus ever was. I would tell my lady at Chelsea about her, describing every part of her as though I had seen her naked, which I have never done. Also in general there are beautiful women at Oxford and I enjoy playing with beautiful women.'

Robert laughed.

'Ah, you laugh! But although I am no beauty, because of my hair and my nose and my small stature, yet I have a way with women—a very successful way indeed. You have not seen me in my sentimental vein, Robert, and I doubt if, being a man, you ever will—not in its sincerity, I mean—but I can give you an imitation of it. . . .'

'No, no,' Robert interrupted hastily, for they were nearing the house and he did not know what devilish folly Rupert might commit. 'I can well understand that you are fascinating to ladies.'

But Rupert, pushing his funny ugly face up towards Robert's grave and compact one, began in a voice even more shrill than his customary:

'Yes, but, Madame, you cannot deny me. I am no fool. My eyes can see through a wainscot. I know I am not handsome, but I can love. But try me and you will be astonished. If it is fidelity you are wanting . . .'

He broke off, laughing, skipped in front of Robert, turned round in front of him, and so walked face to face with him, bowing:

'This way, Sir Knight. This way. All is prepared. The cushions are arranged, the posset heated, the bed quite ready. This way, Sir Knight. Take care of your step!'

But he did not take care of his own, for walking backwards he tripped over the grass mound by the fountain and went head over heels.

Robert was compelled to laugh over that; he picked Rupert up and they walked along, Rupert's arm around Robert's thick waist.

Rosamund had always been devoted to Rupert and he suited Margaret perfectly. Although she never showed it, she had something of his grotesquerie. Then she admired courage above everything and she had never seen courage like Rupert's. She saw also that with all his wildness and fierce temper and readiness to quarrel with another man on the slightest occasion, he was courteous to ladies and faithful to his friends. His attention to Rosamund was the best of all. He had been good with Nicholas' blindness, but Rosamund was a woman, and to himself who loved singing and running streams and the cries and murmurs of birds it seemed a dreadful penalty to be shut away from them. So he could not do enough for her.

Then, on the third evening, he came back from some ride abroad and said to Robert:

'Have you heard, Robert, of a Colonel Jeremiah Tofthouse?'

'Jeremiah Tofthouse! No, indeed not. I would not believe in such a name.'

'Jeremiah Tofthouse,' Rupert repeated. 'He is here with a force of Parliament men.'

'Here!' cried Robert. 'What do you mean—here?'

'At Nancehurst—five and a half mile. And this afternoon I was informed that they are coming here.'

'Well, if they do?' Robert continued with his pigeon-pie, making grave sucking noises over the bones as he greased his hands with them.

'If they do . . .' Rupert laughed. 'If they do! Why, Sir Robert Herries, you are a man of wealth and weight in the neighbourhood. Your house of Mallory is the best in the whole south. Jeremiah Tofthouse, I am told, is on a little expedition of his own and is a greedy fellow.'

But Robert was not at all alarmed. His dignity, too, was always a trifle offended when Rupert mocked his knighthood. So he replied calmly:

'Let them come. They shall have food and drink. I have not meddled in politics on the one side or the other.'

'Not meddled! You have been supplying the King with money.'

'Nay, nay—five years back. And for his private affairs, not for his army.'

'Well, Jeremiah would like some too.'

Margaret, who was, in many things, more acutely minded than her husband, was frightened, and before the evening ended she and Rupert and Gilbert Armstrong consulted together.

Rupert said that he was quite sure that the Parliament men were coming to Mallory on a raid, and that soon. Old Nicholas had been one of the most notorious Royalists in England and never minded to say so. Here was his son, knighted by the King. Yes, Rupert was afraid there was going to be trouble.

'What can they do?' Margaret asked.

'Do? Anything that pleases them. We have no defences. I hear this Tofthouse models himself on Cromwell, is anxious to be his rival. We can only pray that they have manners. Some of them are not without them.'

It was clear, though, that Rupert was spoiling for a fight. He marched up and down the hall twirling his sword. He leaped up on the dais and encountered six enemies at once. Old Gilbert Armstrong also smelt powder. This had been his master Nicholas' home, and no one should have it for an as-you-please. He furbished up some old armour and stood at the Mallory gates looking down the long winding road. Then he would go up to the little tower and look over the countryside. Save that it was a wild, chilly, and rain-scattered March the country was quiet enough.

The servants in the house were apprehensive, though. Many a story was passed round of the dreadful things that the soldiers of both sides were doing. Things had not been bad at the beginning, but now tempers were rising and men were more savage. All the women expected to be raped and some of the older ones thought it an experience they wouldn't mind trying just once.

Only Robert, so far as anyone could see, thought nothing of it. They wouldn't trouble him. He never troubled anyone—why should anyone trouble him? A fallacy that, all through the history of this world, has brought disaster on many innocent human beings.

One effect the scare did have on him, though. He discovered that he cared for Mallory with a love far deeper than he had suspected. He found himself coming down the long staircase at night, wrapped in his furred robe, his feet in fur slippers, and standing with his candle, staring about him. He moved softly on his slippers from the hall into the long withdrawing-room. Margaret, who had more taste than you would suppose, had hung this room with the fine printed cotton Pintado, and Robert, raising his candle, took a childish pleasure in the figures of the scene—the Indians with their trades and habits, plenty of the bright colours that Robert liked, orange and crimson and emerald.

He would raise his candle again and again, and stop and gaze at silver figures—'Venus and Adonis'—or an ebony casket, or a crucifix with turquoises, or the set of chairs with the legs carved like gryphons; or he would stand in the deserted kitchen (with only the cricket making music) and marvel at his own great possessions in the shining pots and pans, the huge carving-knife, and the beautiful drinking glasses.

All these were his and for his son (when he came) after him. Robert sighed and trotted up the wide staircase again.

Old Gilbert Armstrong, between eighty and ninety now, stood as straight as a soldier on guard by the high gates at Mallory, for he saw the enemy.

Down the road, sprayed with a light flicking rain, came a small company of Parliament soldiers. They wore their helmets, back- and breast-plates, steel gloves. They were pikemen. There were also a few musketeers with their matchlocks, bandoliers, and heavy pouch of bullets.

They drew up at the gates and Armstrong, looking at them, saw a new kind of soldier. These men had rough grim faces and sat their horses like statues. They were not like men—mere automata. They were very frightening. But Armstrong, although at the end of his days, was not to be frightened by man nor devil.

Their leader was a stout man with a broad heavy face, scowling brows, and a large wart on his cheek, which was perhaps why he considered himself another Cromwell.

He leaned forward and asked Armstrong: 'This is the manor of Mallory?'

'It is,' Armstrong answered.

'Forward, my men,' said Colonel Jeremiah Tofthouse.

On the steps of the house Robert awaited them. So they had come at last! Although he had said little to anybody, he had long been rehearsing in his mind how he should behave on this occasion. He was a born temporizer, a middle man. He was never in a passion. He believed it the resort of fools. Moreover, in this present case he did not feel passionately. He had nothing against the Parliament men. It was not *his* quarrel. There, however, was his mistake.

When he heard that they were coming he was relieved. In spite of his show of indifference this promised visit had been an anxiety. Now it was in his hand to deal with it.

But his diplomacy was at once hampered because, as they rode up the drive, one of the soldiers, seeing Robert's old spaniel bitch barking at his horse, leaned laughing down and pinked the spaniel in the side with his sword. The spaniel, blood dripping from its flank, limped off howling. The sight and sound of this sent Robert into such a fury that he had to dig his nails into the palms of his hands to control himself. To wound one of his favourite dogs before a word had been spoken! To drive a sword into old Calypso, whose fidelity and loving-kindness scattered the past years with happiness!

So when Tofthouse climbed off his horse and started up the steps, Robert's sturdy, short, stubborn body was already trembling with anger.

'Sir Robert Herries?'

'I am he, sir.'

'Colonel Jeremiah Tofthouse.'

Robert made no reply but waited. They stood now very close to one another.

'I have come now by order of Parliament to make certain enquiries.'

'Enquiries?'

'It is understood, Sir Robert Herries, that you have been supplying the Royalist forces with certain sustenance—in money and in goods.'

It was already going very differently from what Robert had intended. He had purposed to invite them in, to offer drinks, to show courtesies. Now he would be damned. . . .

Then, with all the strength that he had, he controlled himself. He remembered that Mallory had no defences and that his wife and mother were within.

He spoke stiffly, pushing out his little round tight stomach.

'I am a private gentleman. I have no dealings with either side in these present troubles.' Then as he saw an impatient movement on the part of the Colonel and thought that a brawl on the steps would be undignified, he turned on his heel.

'Pray enter,' he said over his shoulder.

It was not a dignified entry, for the soldiers, suddenly active and lively, threw themselves off their horses and tumbled up the steps in a body and pressed pell-mell into the hall.

It was plain that they were for the most part country fellows and little used, as yet, to grandeur.

Immediately the tragedy developed.

Rosamund, Margaret, and Rupert were together on the dais in

front of the great stone fireplace. Margaret, in spite of her natural self-control, gave a little cry, for she had not expected them to come in like this, tumbling over one another and one of them already calling out for drinks.

But Tofthouse on the lowest step of the dais said quietly:

'In the Lord's name if there is disorder here I will hang the first man from that gallery.'

For a while there was quiet. Robert and Tofthouse stood facing one another.

'I must examine your papers, Sir Robert. My men must search your house.'

'On whose commission?'

'On my own commission. I am a recognized officer in the Parliament forces.'

'I would see your papers—Colonel Jeremiah Tofthouse.'

Robert made a mistake there. There was scorn as he repeated the name. But he was thinking of his spaniel bitch. Unfortunately, too, Rupert laughed.

That laugh, it is to be feared, settled the affair and another page in Herries history was written (not the last that Rupert Herries would write).

Tofthouse sunk his chin into his heavy neck as though thinking. Then he barked out:

'Cornet Joyson, this house is to be searched!'

But before any soldier could move, Robert cried: 'Stop! I had not intended to be uncivil. All must be done in order. I am a private gentleman who has no official dealings with either party in this sad quarrel. If you will come with me, Colonel, to my library, I shall most willingly show you any papers that I have.'

But Tofthouse now had an evil look in his yellow eyes.

'So you realize, Sir Robert . . . A little slow, maybe.' He turned on his heel to the figures by the fireplace. 'And who are these?'

'My mother. . . . My wife, Lady Herries. . . .'

'And this?'

'Mr. Rupert Herries.'

But all was direfully resolved from that moment that Rupert had laughed. Now they stared at one another like dogs longing for a fight. Rupert had his hand on his sword.

It was on that tragic day that Robert first noticed something that would be afterwards so familiar to him—Rupert just before a quarrel, his body hanging forward as though, in a second, he would be off the ground, his head alert, all its seeing and hearing faculties doubly alive, and the hands especially vital. They seemed to quiver in the air. So he stood now, poised, all quivering to be at the throat of the heavy Colonel.

That decided Tofthouse.

'Search the house,' he said.

That was enough for the soldiers, who at once moved in every direction.

Robert started forward to protest. A soldier pushed him on to his knees. Instantly old Armstrong, who had entered during the questions, had flung himself on the soldier and had him by the neck. The soldier raised his sword and plunged it through Armstrong's body.

The old man fell, dragged himself a little towards the dais. His hand was on his breast where the stain spread and spread.

'Master—oh, master . . .' he cried brokenly, and fell over on his face.

Rupert was down the dais, his sword drawn, but before he could move forward he was caught, his arms pinioned behind his back. A young soldier with a rosy face told Robert that he should go and stand on the dais with the women.

'Remain there,' he said not unkindly. 'You can do no good.'

Rupert was by this time tied to a chair and sat there kicking. Armstrong lay on his face, the pool of blood spreading all about him. The others stood where they were.

There followed then a dreadful scene of destruction. In both armies there were good and bad. These, led by Tofthouse, were a poor lot.

They found liquor in the buttery, they kicked the old domo around his buttery, they kissed and pinched the women, they drank what they discovered.

These passions mount with the feeding. The noise now was terrible Glass, china were broken, curtains and bed-hangings torn, the silver figures of Venus and Adonis stamped under foot, clothes, stools books, utensils tumbled down the stairs in riotous profusion, and a last the poor spaniel bitch, its throat cut, flung from the gallery to the hall floor.

That turned poor Robert into a lunatic. He tumbled headlong down the dais, slipped, recovered himself, and rushed, shouting oaths, at Tofthouse. He tugged at his sword as he stumbled. The soldiers laughed at him. Three of them caught him, held him in air by his breeches, swinging him.

Then there was real madness. One of the musketeers lifted his match, lighted it, and set the torn purple curtains that were hanging from the stair-head ablaze.

The flames stirred, licking the woodwork, then a breeze caught them. The tongues flew with a loud laughing crackle up the staircase.

'Out! . . . Out! . . . Out! Fire! Fire!'

The soldiers were suddenly sobered, and Tofthouse too.

He even bowed to Margaret.

'Ladies—while there is time——'

But Robert, left by the soldiers, turned screaming to Tofthouse.

'You cannot! . . . You cannot! 'Tis Mallory . . .'

The whole of the hall-end was blazing. They carried Rupert out and in the garden tore him from the chair and flung him against the fountain. He was after all only a boy and he knelt there, his face in his torn hands, weeping his heart out.

On the high ground above the house they stood, four of them, the women of the house behind them, watching the great force of orange flame and surging smoke crackle and thunder to the sky.

Old Gilbert Armstrong was the sacrifice.

BRACKENBURN, *May* 24, 1941